KU-735-695

FREEWAY KILLING!

Just as he thought it was over, and that they'd survived, he felt something spraying through the car, sparkling and bright, and realised that it was thousands of tiny fragments of shattered glass. He pushed Vicki down towards the floor, and he was reaching for his father when the back of his father's grey hair flapped upward like a toupee, and in front of his eyes, his father's cheek and nose seemed to swell, as if a terrible black boil was growing on his face, and then burst open in a geyser of mucous membrane and blood. His father's hands were rising towards his face in surprise, but then he pitched forward and collapsed on the floor of the car.

The Sweetman Curve

by

GRAHAM MASTERTON

This first hardcover edition published in Great Britain 1990 by
SEVERN HOUSE PUBLISHERS LTD of
35 Manor Road, Wallington, Surrey SM6 0BW
This first hardcover edition published in the U.S.A. 1990 by
SEVERN HOUSE PUBLISHERS INC, New York

British Library Cataloguing in Publication Data
Masterton, Graham *1946–*
   The Sweetman curve.
   I. Title
   823.914 [F]

   ISBN 0–7278–4097–5

Distributed in the U.S.A. by
Mercedes Distribution Center, Inc.
62 Imlay Street, Brooklyn, New York 11231

Printed and bound in Great Britain by
Bookcraft [Bath] Ltd.

BOOK ONE

THE MIGHTY

ONE

He was the kind of man who could make a crowded room fall silent when he entered. He looked sullen, moody and unpredictably vicious.

He was sitting alone at a table on the narrow sidewalk terrace of the Old World Restaurant on Sunset Boulevard, forking up scrambled eggs with determined distaste.

He was unnervingly tall, you could tell that even though he was sitting, with black slicked-back hair, and reflector sunglasses. He wore black cord jeans, a grey utility shirt, and three heavy gold bracelets on his left wrist. By his sharp nose and his high cheekbones, you might have guessed that he was Armenian or Czech.

It was Friday. The morning was still hazy, and out over Los Angeles only the dim fretwork of skyscrapers and the twin towers of Century City rose from the smog. Across the street, next to a giant grinning billboard of John Denver, an illuminated sign told the man that the time was 9:27 and the temperature was 77°F. The traffic cruised ceaselessly past along the curving concrete spine of the street, but he only raised his eyes, and then almost imperceptibly, if a car drew alongside the kerb.

The young freckle-faced waiter came out to the terrace with a fresh jug of coffee.

'You want a refill, sir?'

The man held out his cup without a word.

'You want anything else, sir? We have waffles, blueberry muffins, ice cream with hot chocolate sauce?'

The man shook his head.

The waiter began to collect up his dirty plates. 'Did you see that Woody Allen movie on TV last night?' he chatted. 'I've been meaning to see that goddamned movie for five years. I broke my ass laughing. I really broke my ass.'

The tall man lifted his head. In the twin mirrors of his sunglasses, two young waiters, both apprehensive, peered out of two fishbowl worlds.

'The cheque,' whispered the man.

The waiter gave a twitchy little smile, then shrugged. 'Okay. I was just trying to be pleasant.'

'There's no need,' whispered the man.

The waiter hesitated, picked up the man's knife and fork, and then disappeared inside, glancing back uncertainly over his shoulder. The man ignored him, swallowed a hot mouthful of coffee, and then reached into the pocket of his shirt for his cigarettes. He lit one carefully from a box of matches with 'Benihana's of Tokyo' printed on it, and then sat back in his chair and blew out smoke. The sign across the street said it was 9: 30.

The man didn't appear to be thinking about anything. He looked at the world from behind those mirrored sunglasses with an expression that could have been interest, or pain, or boredom, or anger.

He didn't know what it was himself.

He waited four more minutes. Then he got up from his table, and went inside to the cashier. It was bustling in there, with waiters balancing trays of pineapple and alfalfa salads and bacon-and-eggs, and Sunset Boulevard's floating population all smoking and chattering and laughing. The man laid a ten-dollar bill on the counter along with the cheque, turned around and walked out.

Behind the cash register, the girl with the long tawny blonde hair punched out $6.25, and then looked around for someone to give the change to. She called to the young waiter, 'Hey, Myron! Table nine left his change.'

The waiter said, 'Okay – he only just left,' and hurried out into the sunlight after him. He glanced to his right, and saw that the sidewalk was almost deserted, except for a Mexican woman with hips as wide as a wheelbarrow; so he trotted around the corner into Holloway Drive.

He couldn't see the man at first. He squinted up towards the sloping parking lot at the back of the restaurant, but there was nobody there. Then he looked along the street, and about fifty yards away, under the shadow of overhanging trees, he saw the tall man standing by the open trunk of a silver Grand Prix.

He called: 'Hey! Sir!' but the man didn't seem to hear him. Myron began to pad along the concrete sidewalk in his worn-down sneakers, until he was only five or six yards away. It was then that he glimpsed something in the open trunk of the car, and stopped short.

The tall man turned towards him.

'Yes?' he whispered. His mirrored eyes gave nothing away.

The waiter held out a handful of crumpled bills and sweaty coins. 'You – well, you forgot your change. The cheque was only six twenty-five.'

The tall man didn't move for a moment, didn't answer. But then he slammed the trunk shut, and came towards the waiter with a slow, easy stride.

'Thanks,' he said with cold softness, and took the money out of the boy's hand.

The waiter wiped his beaded forehead with the back of his wrist. It certainly didn't seem like he was going to get a tip, and considering what he'd seen in the back of the car, he didn't much care. He said, cautiously, 'Have a good day, sir,' and retreated back up the sidewalk towards the restaurant.

On the angled corner of Holloway and Sunset, he paused and looked back. The tall man was still standing by the car, watching him. The sun flashed like a heliographic warning from his sunglasses.

'Did you catch up with him?' asked the girl with the long tawny hair as Myron came back into the restaurant.

The young waiter looked at her, and nodded. 'Yes. He said thanks.'

She glanced up at him. 'What's the matter, Myron? You look like you're sick.'

He blinked, as if he hadn't heard her. 'What? Oh, no, I'm not sick. I just think I had myself a lucky escape.'

'Escape? What from? Was he a faggot or something?'

The boy shook his head. 'That guy had more guns in the trunk of his car than a goddamned armoury. You

9

should have seen it. The whole trunk was full of guns.'

'So what are you going to do? Call the police?'

He mopped at his face with a paper napkin. 'Are you kidding? He's probably a homicidal maniac. Anybody with that many guns is going to use 'em, and I'd just as soon he didn't use 'em on me.'

'So you're going to let him drive around free? What kind of responsible attitude is that?'

Two glittery-eyed black girls in T-shirts came in, and the waiter picked up his order book. 'It's a responsible attitude towards my head,' he said emphatically. 'I want it to stay on my shoulders.'

The blonde shrugged and helped herself to a mint from the little basket beside the cash register.

TWO

The previous evening, the L.A. Strangler's eleventh victim had been found in the bushes at Griffith Park, and Mrs Benduzzi wasn't very happy about Ricardo going out for a walk. She sat on the plumped-up cushions of her pink velvet settee, a fat and florid commercial for what a daily diet of fresh cream cakes and pepperoni pizzas could do to stretch a pair of violet-coloured ski pants to bursting point. Her ash-blonde wig wasn't on straight, and she was clutching Ricardo so tight to her floral-printed bosom that the poor animal's eyes were bulging.

'Mrs Benduzzi,' John told her, 'I'm sure the Strangler doesn't go for poodles. It seems to me that he's more interested in humans.'

'Well, you can *say* that,' Mrs Benduzzi retorted. 'But Ricardo's almost human, aren't you, darling? He talks to me, you know. When we're alone at home here, he talks. You'd be surprised at the things he says.'

John patiently rubbed at the back of his neck. He was pretty sure that Mrs Benduzzi's cocktail hour had started a little early this morning. After all, what else was there for a middle-aged Beverly Hills lady to do, except wander around her expensive house all day, eating too much, and drinking too many tequila sunrises? She was too fat to take a lover, and too lonesome to diet. Apart from her husband, a casting director for CBS with a droopy moustache, droopy eyes, and about as much personality as a plate of stone-cold *tagliatelle*, Ricardo was all that Mrs Benduzzi had.

'You want me to skip the walkies, then?' asked John.

'Well, I'm not sure,' said Mrs Benduzzi. 'I mean, it looks kind of hot today, too. Didn't they say we were having a heatwave? I haven't been out yet. What with this maniac around, I'm not sure that I'm going to.'

'Mrs Benduzzi, I can promise you that Ricardo will be quite safe with me,' John assured her. 'I'll protect him with my life if I have to.'

'Oh, don't *talk* that way,' said Mrs Benduzzi, faintly. 'Listen – why don't you wax the car instead? Take Ricardo out tomorrow. Maybe they will have caught him by then. It's disgraceful, letting a man like that prowl around loose, terrorizing defenceless dogs.'

'Mrs Benduzzi, I don't think he's –'

But Mrs Benduzzi wasn't listening. She was too busy smothering Ricardo with kisses. It used to turn John's stomach, all this sentimental slobbering over animals, but since he'd been walking dogs around Hollywood and Beverly Hills, he'd grown to understand, despite his distaste, that dogs and cats were often the only devoted friends these women knew. Apart from that, if he was going to supplement his income at a reasonable rate, he was going to have to get along with his customers, and he couldn't command ten bucks an hour if he openly barfed every time a lady went into a romantic clinch with her Schnauzer.

'Okay, Mrs Benduzzi,' he said resignedly, 'if that's the way you feel about it.'

Mrs Benduzzi gave him an indulgent smile, and held out her pink and porky hand. 'You're so understanding, Mr Cullen. If I was five years younger, and fancy-free ...'

He squeezed her hand hard enough to press her diamond and sapphire rings into her flesh, and hurt her a little bit.

'Mrs Benduzzi, I'd better go wax the car,' he said, in a voice so deliberately husky that for one puzzled moment she thought he'd made some outrageously erotic suggestion. It wasn't altogether surprising. Even to himself, he had to admit that he'd never looked better in his whole life. He was tall and quite muscular, and his irregular employment had given him the chance to work up a deep, dark suntan. There was still something about him that told you he wasn't a native Californian – a kind of inner defensiveness, a constant tension, that characterizes men and women brought up in the cities of the East – but to women like Mrs Benduzzi, who were aroused by anxious young men, that was all the more attractive. He was thin-faced, with a long straight nose, and brown eyes that could be coaxingly soft with people he liked and disturbingly vacant with people he didn't. His hair was cut very short, and you could have mistaken him for a slightly macho telephone linesman or a would-be middleweight boxer.

He gave her his winningest smile, the smile he usually reserved for ladies in theatre box offices who were trying to tell him there were no more seats for *A Chorus Line*; and then crossed the soft-carpeted, brocade-draped room to the double french doors. They were the sort of doors he felt like flinging open and intoning: 'Dinner is served.' He turned around once, gave Mrs Benduzzi a last fading smirk, and then closed the doors behind him. He walked along the corridor, feeling more like smoking a cigarette than he had in days. It was a week now since he'd given them up.

He didn't quite know how or why his life had taken this particular turn. Walking dogs and waxing cars weren't the kinds of jobs you'd logically expect from a boy who had solemnly assured his parents at the age of eighteen that he was going to be the second Frank Lloyd Wright. But during his first tedious years as a junior draughtsman in Trenton, New Jersey, he had come to understand with increasing frustration that architecture had little to do with building ideal cities, or even reasonably pleasant homes for people to live in. His design chief had only congratulated him once, when he worked out a way of tiling a roof with a hundred fewer shingles than it usually took, and on the cheeseparing budgets that his first few projects had been allocated, he hadn't been able to allow himself the decorative luxuries of Charles Sale's privy-builder, let alone Frank Lloyd Wright. At the age of twenty-six, he had quit architecture, leaving two small supermarkets and a row of garages in Ewing, New Jersey, as his only contributions to America's heritage.

He had come to Los Angeles to look for his identity, or maybe to run away from it, he couldn't be sure which. He also wanted to discover why beauty and humanity were such expensive commodities; and for that quest, at least, he had come to the right place. He worked for five years as a salesman for Euclid Schwarz, the leading west coast builders of condominiums and retirement homes. John's leftish politics grated on Mr Schwarz's nerves, and he was eventually passed up for promotion so many times that he quit. He had a savagely bitter love affair with a British girl who worked in the ticket office at Mann's Chinese Theatre, all scratched backs and smashed crockery, and that had left him emotionally and morally exhausted and ready for anything so long as it was calm.

Now, thirty-two years old, nothing like wealthy, but healthier, and pretty much at peace with the world, John Cullen devoted his time to writing for the *Los Angeles Liberal Journal*, a mildly radical paper with bees in its bonnet about open government and legalized pornography, although not usually in that order. He also spent some of his time designing villages of the future for stylish architectural magazines; restoring his old green weatherboard house up in Topanga Canyon, where he lived with his new lady friend, Vicki; and drying leaf cups on his back porch in an attempt to find a substitute for grass, which he unaccountably disliked.

Today, though, he was out earning money. It was ten bucks an hour for walking pedigrees, seven-fifty for mutts. It was ten bucks for a custom wax job. He walked into the kitchen to collect his rags and polish.

The kitchen was a cathedral, all blue-and-white Italian tiles. John had privately dubbed it the Chocka-Fulla-Nutsa. In the sunlight that fell through the tall leaded windows, the black maid Yolande, in her white cap and white apron, was wiping up the butcher block centre island and singing, 'The Woman Behind Every Man.'

'How are the kids?' asked John, opening the cleaning cupboard and taking down the Turtle Wax.

'Oh, they're fine,' said Yolande. 'They're black and they're proud.'

'Still into racial politics?'

She looked up at him. 'Aren't we all, Mr Cullen? That's what politics is about – race.'

He shook up the car-wax bottle and loosened the cap. 'Race is only a part of it. Race is only a *fraction* of it. If the blacks were a little more laid-back about race, we might all get our stuff together a damned sight sooner.'

Yolande shrugged. 'You're white, Mr Cullen. When you're white, you can afford to be laid-back.'

He leaned on the kitchen counter. 'You can call me John if you like.'

'Mr Cullen will do.' She paused, then, 'You taking that powder-puff out for a walk?' she asked.

He shook his head. 'Mrs Benduzzi is scared of the Strangler. She reckons he might attempt dogicide, just to keep his hand in.'

'You talk like murder amuses you.'

He opened the back door. 'It's funnier than taking dogs for a walk.'

She smiled. She was irresistibly pretty when she smiled. 'You just get along there and lay a shine on Mrs Benduzzi's bumpers,' she chided him.

'How about a date?' he responded. 'Or just a quick rape?'

She laughed. 'If I didn't know you were living with someone, I'd still say no, honkie.'

'Please yourself. You'll regret it when you're old and grey.'

He closed the kitchen door and walked across the covered way to the garage. It was unseasonably hot for November, way up in the mid nineties, and he took his sunglasses out of his shirt pocket and put them on. The tall yuccas in Mrs Benduzzi's scrupulously landscaped gardens were scarcely rustling in the breathless breeze, and up towards the mountains he could hear a police helicopter flick-flackering on traffic patrol. He coughed.

In the cool of the air-conditioned garage, Mrs Benduzzi's Georgian Silver Eldorado was waiting, still glossy from the last time he had waxed it. The only time Mrs Benduzzi ever drove it anywhere was when she visited her hair stylist on Beverly Boulevard and it had probably covered fewer than a hundred miles from new. He wasn't covetous though. He preferred the automobiles of the 1950s, vast extravaganzas of fins and lights and gas-guzzling power. His own 1959 Chrysler Imperial Crown was awkwardly parked in the Benduzzis' love-knot-shaped driveway. He opened the double garage doors and drove the Eldorado out under the shade of the palms.

It was 11:02. If John had walked to the front gates of Mrs Benduzzi's house right then, he would have been just in time to see the silver Grand Prix slowly driving past on its way west. The tall man in the black cords and the grey utility shirt was driving casually, his fingers dangling on top of the wheel, and he was smoking a cigarette. He was thinking about a young blonde hooker he had picked up outside of the English Fish-and-Chip Shop on Hollywood Boulevard last night, and how she had sat wide-eyed in his room while he showed her his Colt automatic. He had taken it apart for her in forty-five seconds flat, and then put it together again and loaded it; and then, in the sweaty crumples of his divan bed, he had humped her, and while he was humping her he had forced the greasy steel muzzle up her back-side, until she was penetrated by both man and gun, and the mad danger of it had excited them both so much that they gasped and shook with sheer erotic terror.

THREE

John took off his checkered shirt and hung it on the garden standpipe.

He hosed the car down in rainbows of water and reflected light, then dried it with a soft cloth. It was kind of soothing, cleaning cars. It gave you a half-hour to yourself, to think whatever you wanted to. It was certainly an improvement on walking dogs. Cars didn't get themselves all lathered up when another car passed by, or try to sniff up each other's exhaust pipes. He polished the windshield. It was pleasantly cool underneath the trees, and the crimson leaves of Mrs Benduzzi's poinsettia danced ecstatically all around him.

After a half hour of strenuous buffing, he looked up and saw Yolande coming towards him with a cold beer on a tray. He stood straight, stretched his back, and refolded his polishing cloth.

'Mrs Benduzzi thought you might be dry,' said Yolande, with a hint of amusement in her voice.

John glanced over the black girl's shoulder towards the house. He saw Mrs Benduzzi at the window, fatly imprisoned in her air-conditioned palazzo, and he waved to her. Pleased, embarrassed, Mrs Benduzzi waved back.

'Play your cards right, honkie, and you could do well for yourself with her,' Yolande said.

John took a freezing mouthful of Coors. 'Me and Mrs Benduzzi?' he choked.

'Why not? She's wealthy. She likes you. She just spent the whole morning standing by the window, ogling your ass through her opera-glasses.'

'What does she expect it to do, sing *I Puritani*?'

Yolande smiled. 'I'm just telling you. The lady likes you, and she's rich.'

'Listen,' protested John, 'I like my marshmallow

chopped up into cubes and toasted, not on the hoof.'

The black maid shrugged. 'It doesn't look like you're going to have the opportunity anyway. Here comes trouble.'

The late morning air was cut by the high buzzsaw pitch of a motorcycle. Around the curves of the driveway, sitting well back on the saddle of a tiny Puch, rode a tall girl in a scarlet-metallic crash helmet, a white T-shirt, and tight white shorts.

'I'd better get myself back to the house,' said Yolande, with a wry smile. 'When Mrs Benduzzi sees her, there's going to be sulks and tantrums for the rest of the day.'

'I'll catch you later,' said John. 'And thanks for the beer.'

'I only brought it,' said Yolande, walking away with a sassy swing of her hips.

John folded his sunglasses and tucked them back in his pocket. The motorcyclist pulled up beside him, under the shade of the trees, and dismounted. She unfastened her helmet, shook loose her long brunette hair, and came across to where he was standing. They kissed.

'You look like Bill Holden in *Picnic*,' she told him.

'I never saw it,' he replied, kissing her again.

She was a striking, dark-complexioned girl with extraordinary squarish bone structure, and dramatic sky-blue eyes. She had a pouting mouth that always reminded him of Brigitte Bardot when she was young, or hitch-hiking jailbait on the dirt tracks of Alabama. She wasn't particularly pretty, but she was brown and sensual, and she had once appeared in a small pictorial in *Playboy*. She was very big-breasted, with wide dark nipples that showed through her T-shirt, and a pert, provocative butt which he knew from tiresome experience was an open invitation to any passing American male to slap.

'I thought you were finishing those Indian beads for Mrs Tadema,' he said.

'Well, sure,' she told him. 'I would have been.'

'Except what?'

'Except I had a telephone call.'

He bent over the Eldorado's hood and continued

17

polishing, but he watched her distorted reflection in the glossy silver enamel.

'Anyone I know?' he asked her guardedly. They'd been fighting a lot lately, arguing about which records to play, what TV channel to watch, what food to eat, and he was beginning to wonder if she was trying to bring herself around to leaving him. She was an impulsive, emotional girl. One minute she could believe that she loved him to distraction; and the next he couldn't work out why she even bothered to stick around.

She pressed herself against the side of the car. He polished away a triangular area of dull wax, and saw a reflection of white shorts that were impossibly and revealingly tight.

'Someone *you* know,' she told him. He detected an effervescence in her voice, and he stood up straight again.

'Someone *I* know? And it's so urgent you have to drop Mrs Tadema's beads and come straight down?'

She came around the car, put her arms around his waist, and kissed his sweaty cheek. 'It's your father. He's arriving this afternoon, four o'clock, LAX. Surprise visit. Isn't that fantastic?'

John could hardly believe it. He had always loved his father, always considered him special. He was a dotty, left-wing, absent-minded school principal from Trenton, New Jersey, and during all the years that John had struggled to be a politically creative architect, his father had stood beside him, cajoling him, counselling him, helping him to understand the frustrations and disappointments of being a committed liberal in a less-than-liberal society.

'What time did he call? Did he sound okay?'

'He said he was fine. He called just after you left, but I didn't come down straight away because I figured you'd be walking the pooch.'

John couldn't help himself from grinning. 'That's beautiful. That's really made my day. Hey – supposing we have lunch, and then drive out to the airport. I can stow your cyke in the trunk.'

He energetically finished polishing the already-glittering Eldorado, while Vicki looked around the garden and picked sprigs of poinsettia to wind in her hair.

'Okay,' he said, giving the mirrors a last breath, and shining them up. 'That's it. Give me a couple of minutes to get my money from Mrs Benduzzi, and then we're away.'

He backed the Cadillac into the garage, closed the doors, and then went into the house. Yolande gave him a raised-eyebrows look as he walked through the kitchen. That meant Mrs Benduzzi was slightly less than delighted.

He opened the 'dinner-is-served' doors, and there was Mrs Benduzzi, sitting alone on the pink settee, her head thrown back in a pose that could only mean 'you've thrown me aside like a used pair of shoes, but I don't care.'

'Mrs Benduzzi,' he said.

A reproduction Italianate gilt clock began, laboriously, to chime the hour of twelve, and for almost a minute conversation was impossible while angels with trumpets came in and out of little doors, and bells struck, and mechanisms whirred.

Then Mrs Benduzzi said, 'Your money is on the table. You needn't come tomorrow. Ricardo has told me that he feels like a change of walker.'

'Mrs Benduzzi –'

She glanced up at him. She looked fat, and pathetic. She gave him a small smile, a barely-noticed ripple on a plate of cream of wheat, and said, 'It's all right. Give me a week or two, and then I'm sure we'll be back to normal.'

John said, 'I'm sorry.'

'I'm not,' she told him quietly. 'Now, there's your money. Do take it, I have a lot to do.'

He walked across to the side table. Under an onyx-and-gold paperweight was a fifty dollar bill. He looked at her.

'That's correct,' she said, without changing her expression.

'Okay,' he nodded, and tucked the bill in his shirt pocket. 'I'll see you soon, huh?'

She smiled at him, that terrible lonesome smile of those who know how little they're loved, and have grown to accept it. He paused for a moment, and then he walked across to the settee, leaned down, and kissed her on the forehead.

'You're very special, Mrs Benduzzi. Don't forget it.'

Then he turned around and went back to join Vicki for lunch.

At two o'clock, the silver Grand Prix was parked on the corner of Sepulveda Boulevard and Pigott Drive, under the shadow of the San Diego Freeway. The tall black-haired man was sitting in the driver's seat, smoking a cigarette and listening to the Modern Lovers on his FM radio. Beside him on the seat were the crumpled-up wrappings of a Jack-in-the-Box cheeseburger, which had been his lunch. He waited with a frigid patience that showed he was used to waiting. Waiting, as he was well aware, is a specialized talent.

Sometimes the man looked as if he were asleep, but his eyes, though slitted, were never completely closed. He was keeping a constant watch on the corner of Sepulveda just ahead of him, and also in his mirrors. Once or twice, his fingers drummed briefly on the steering wheel, as if he were exercising them.

'*Massachusetts when it's cold outside ...*' sang the radio. '*With the radio on ...*'

Down by the side of his seat, tucked against the centre console, was his Colt .38 automatic, the same gun he had used on the hooker, in a greasy chamois-leather holster. Although it could penetrate through nine one-inch pine boards at a range of 3,000 feet, and had a muzzle velocity of 1,050 feet per second, the man was planning on hitting a target that, when the moment came, would not be much more than fifteen feet away.

He glanced up. In his mirror, he saw a black-and-white police car turning the corner of Pigott Drive behind him, and cruising slowly his way. His eyes flickered, but he didn't move. His mirror sunglasses lay on top of the console.

The police car drew alongside him, paused for a moment, and then turned left on Sepulveda and disappeared. The man's fingers drummed briefly on the wheel. The digital clock on his simulated-walnut instrument panel read 2 : 04.

FOUR

They ate tuna salads at Butterfield's, sitting outside by the fountain. It was cool in the shade of the trees, although the November sun played jigsaw shadows across their faces, and sparkled in the frosted carafe of white wine that stood between them. At the next table, a woman with a tight silk headscarf and a face as tanned as Shane's second-best saddle was insisting to her balding escort that *Nippon Chiobotsu* was the most uplifting sci-fi movie ever made.

Vicki raised her wine, and said: 'Here's to Daddy. I'm dying to see what he's like.'

John smiled, and clinked glasses with her. 'Pretty much like me, only a few centuries older. I'm surprised you're so enthusiastic about him coming. I didn't think you believed in relatives.'

'I don't believe in my own,' she said archly, as she nibbled around the fringes of her curly lettuce. 'Why do you think I left Minnesota? When your mother's a Sweet Adeline, and your father's big in the Cannon Falls Elks, then I don't really think there's much hope of meaningful parent-child communication, do you?'

'It depends,' he grinned. 'Didn't you ever want to sing with the Sweet Adelines?'

'Oh, schmooey,' she said.

He watched her affectionately. He hadn't seen her in

21

such a pepped-up mood for weeks. He finished up his tuna salad, sipped some more wine, and asked the waitress for coffee. He could have hocked his left leg for a cigarette, especially when the woman in the tight headscarf lit up one right next to him, and the smoke began to drift his way; but he put on a cheerless smirk and resisted it.

'Are you suffering?' Vicki asked him.

'A little. Does it show?'

'Only when you lean forward to vacuum up the passing smoke with your nostrils.'

He picked up a match folder and began to twist the matches around. 'I can tell you one thing, I'll never say a harsh word against dope addicts again.'

She said, in a noticeably different tone of voice, 'And I'll never say a harsh word against *you* again.'

He stopped fiddling with the matches and looked up. 'What does that mean?'

Vicki lowered her long eyelashes. 'It means that we've been pretty cat-and-dog lately, haven't we? But I hope we've come through it.'

'You sound like you have something to tell me.'

'Well,' she said, 'I guess I have.'

'You've decided you love me after all? And I can play my Rod Stewart albums whenever I like?'

'I love you,' she said, looking up with unexpected softness in her sky-blue eyes. 'I'm not sure about the albums.'

He picked at the matches again. There was a stray shred of tuna between his teeth, and he had to send his tongue to worry it out.

'Do you want to tell me about it?' he asked her.

'I don't know. Will you be jealous?'

'Is it as bad as that?'

'I don't know,' she said, with a faint shrug. 'I guess it could have been worse.'

He sat back, crossed his legs, then uncrossed them again and leaned forward. 'Well, don't keep me in suspense. *What* could have been worse? Don't tell me you've been dating Warren Beatty.'

She didn't look at him when she spoke. Her dark red

fingernails brushed along the edge of the table, and then back again, as if she was reading a rosary, or braille.

'It was about three weeks ago, that day you were out with Philip at Encino. I had a call from an old boy-friend of mine from Minnesota. He said he was coming to L.A. to live, and he wanted to see me again. I guess he'd gotten the number from my mother.'

John said dryly: 'Go on.'

She let out a breath. 'His name was Ed Tucker. I guess you could say that he was my childhood heart-throb. All the girls at school used to swoon whenever he went past, and send him love notes and stuff. He was real tall and good-looking, and he was always the best at everything. Athletics, football, you name it. He didn't notice me at first, he was too busy dating some Italian girl named Annette Marino. But when I was fourteen my boobs started to grow, and they grew and grew and made every other girl in school look like Olive Oyl, in-cluding the wonderful Annette Marino, and that's when he suddenly realised that I was around. Annette was jilted, and Ed and I went steady for almost five years. He was the second person I slept with.'

'The *second*? Who was the first?'

'What does that matter? I'm telling you about Ed.'

At that moment, John felt more like a cigarette than he had all week, if only to smoke his jealousy out.

'Okay,' he said, finding it extremely difficult to smile. 'It doesn't matter.'

Vicki reached across the table and held his hand. She looked very serious. 'I must admit I had a fantasy about Ed. I had this brilliant vision of some kind of athletic superstud, all bulging jockey shorts and gleaming teeth. And I must admit,' she said, so quietly that he could hardly hear, 'the idea of it turned me on.'

John slowly shook his head in disbelief. 'Are you tell-ing me that we went through all these arguments, all this fighting, just because you thought you fancied some childhood superjock from Cannon Balls, Min-nesota?'

'Cannon Falls.'

'Falls, balls, who cares.'

Vicki was silent with embarrassment for a moment, and then she nodded.

'He called me Monday,' she said. 'He asked me to come out for dinner.'

'So instead of going to see Phoebe, like you told me, you went out with him?'

She nodded again. 'It was terrible to lie. But I didn't know what else to do. I had to see him again. I had to find out if the fantasy was true.'

'Well,' he asked her, 'what was he like?'

She looked up at him, her expression full of regret for deceiving him, but bursting with amusement at her own absurd attempt to rekindle a long lost love affair.

'He was terrible,' she said. 'He was so terrible. He was about as casual as H. R. Haldeman in his Sunday best. I met him at Dino's and you know how damned dark it is in there. I didn't spot him when I first walked in, because if I had, I would have turned right around and made a run for it. He was such a nerd, I can't tell you. In the end, I told him I was a lesbian, just to get rid of him. I told him I was madly in love with a girl from Mishawaka, Indiana, and that our only problem was that our busts were both so healthily large that we couldn't get near each other.'

John stared at her for almost a minute, saying nothing. Then, quite softly, he said: 'You know something, I'm beginning to love you like I never loved anyone before. You lesbian, you.'

She leaned over and kissed him. 'I know,' she whispered. 'It shows.'

They finished their wine, and then they climbed up the stone steps to the street. John's powder-blue Chrysler Imperial Crown was parked a little way down, its roof gleaming in the afternoon sun. John opened the door for Vicki, and then walked around the front of the car and climbed in himself.

As he sorted out his ignition key, he chuckled. 'I wish I could have been hiding in Dino's when you walked in and saw that childhood sweetheart of yours. I think I would have ruptured myself laughing.'

24

Vicki pretended to look annoyed, and tilted her nose up.

'Aw, come on,' he told her. 'You weren't to know that he'd grown up a nerd.'

She kissed him. 'I think we'd better drop the subject, or we're going to be late for your dear papa.'

He started the motor, and pulled out into the traffic of Sunset Boulevard. This was one of his favourite cars of the Fifties; he had spent two years finding one and two thousand dollars restoring it. It had an immense grille of chrome teeth, an eleven-foot wheelbase, and twin fins at the back with torpedo-shaped stoplights. It bounced and glided along on air suspension, and their next-door neighbour up in Topanga Canyon, a sad and dedicated environmentalist called Mel, had christened it U.S.S. *Enterprise*.

John used the forecourt of the Hyatt Hotel to turn the car around and head west, into a dazzling sun that was already beginning to fall. Vicki turned on the radio, and snuggled up next to him, her hand ruffling his hair and her big breasts pressed against his arm. The tangerine light of mid-afternoon crisscrossed them in bright slices as they drove along Sunset through Beverly Hills, past the pink Beverly Hills Hotel and the gates of Bel-Air, until they reached the curve that took them down to the overpass where the San Diego Freeway ran.

The freeway was busier than usual, and John had to weave from lane to lane to keep his speed up. They were headed south, towards the airport, and the freeway was a glittering river of traffic, rising and falling over the hills and valleys of West Los Angeles and Mar Vista. The radio was playing: 'You're a native New Yorker ... you should know the score by now ...'

Smog still hung in the air in dim veils as they passed Palms and Culver City. John coughed, and wondered how long you went on aching for a cigarette before the craving died away.

Vicki said, 'What's your father like? Is he a fatherly father, or a buddy-buddy father?'

'Oh, positively a fatherly father,' said John, overtaking a brace of Hell's Angels and a custom ranch wagon crowded with Chinese children. 'I was expected to call him "sir" until I was twenty-one. But he's a friend, too. He's very understanding, you know, and he doesn't have any prejudices about anything. One of nature's real kind people.'

He turned off at Sepulveda Boulevard, and drove in towards the airport. Then, with Vicki giving imaginative and confusing directions, he located the parking lot, and took a ticket at the booth. The parking attendant leaned out of his window, surveyed the Chrysler, and said 'Who sold you that? Batman?'

They were twenty minutes early. The flight from JFK wasn't expected until ten after four, and so they ambled around the bookstalls, and then went to the bar for cocktails, a bloody mary and an old-fashioned, served by mini-skirted waitresses who looked like suburban America's answer to Hugh Hefner.

John said: 'Isn't it crazy? All of a sudden, I feel nervous.'

He was waiting behind the wheel of his silver Grand Prix at the junction of 83rd Street, Westchester, and Sepulveda Boulevard. The time by his digital clock was 3:57. He had seen the powder-blue Imperial pass by on its way to the airport, and he had called the United Airways desk from a phonebooth to check when the flight was due. He gave them twenty-five minutes after the flight touched down to pass this way again: disembarkation, baggage claim, parking lot, exit.

Now it was time to lift the automatic out of its chamois holster, slide out the magazine, and carefully reload it. One cartridge went into the chamber, seven into the magazine. Each cartridge contained $4\frac{1}{2}$ grains of powder, and 105 grains of lead. Loaded, the automatic weighed 32 ounces. He hefted it in his hand, and slid it back into its holster.

He lifted his mirrored sunglasses and rubbed his eyes. He hadn't slept too well last night, because his neighbour's dog had been barking. He'd been thinking of moving out of San Juan Avenue for a few months now, but somehow he never seemed to be able to get around

The Sweet Man Curve

to finding a new place to go. At least his part of Venice was quiet, and nobody bothered him. He could sit on his bed all evening, dismantling and cleaning his guns, and watching *Kojak* repeats on television, and that was the way he liked his life to be. Secure, private, orderly. He took his sheets to the laundromat every Thursday afternoon, ate a Chinese take-away every Saturday night, went to the sex movies Mondays, and spent all day in bed Sundays reading *The Los Angeles Times*, right down to the advertisements for cut-price rococo bedroom furniture. Once a month or so, he drove up to Hollywood and picked up a whore, the younger the better, and blew fifty or sixty dollars indulging his fantasies. He had an electric ring for cooking, and on the back of his wardrobe door was Scotch-taped a photograph of Chesty Morgan, the lady with the 76-inch bust.

He glanced at his clock. It was 4:04. Through the tinted glass of his car window, he could see people shopping, and a bunch of scruffy kids sitting on the steps of a rundown apartment building, chewing bubblegum and tossing jacks. He yawned. It was the first indication he had given all day that he was bored.

FIVE

Vicki caught sight of him first. She said, 'Is that him? He looks so much like you!'

And there he was, coming across the baggage hall, a tallish, grey-haired man in a brown herringbone tweed jacket, a fawn raincoat over his arm. He wore rimless eyeglasses, and his face had the thinness and softness of age, but he was unmistakably John's father.

They walked towards each other, John and his father, and Vicki didn't want to do anything else but stay by John's side and watch them, because she'd never seen such open affection between a son and his father before.

27

John held out his arms, and embraced his father close, feeling the roughness of his tweed jacket and smelling the lingering aroma of his favourite tobacco, Jacob's Golden Returns.

'Dad,' said John. 'It's so damned good to see you.'

His father held him tight, and looked at him proudly. 'You've grown younger,' he said. 'Is it California that does that to you, or giving up architecture?'

'It's good, clean living,' smiled Vicki, and John's father turned and saw her for the first time.

'Aren't you going to introduce me?' he nudged John. 'It looks like you've found yourself a little bit more than sunshine around here.'

John grinned. 'Still the rampant old goat I know and love. Vicki, this is my father, William Cullen. *Doctor* William Cullen, to be strictly accurate. Dad, this is Vicki Wallace.'

William Cullen, with his copy of *Newsweek* rolled up in his jacket pocket, bent forward and took Vicki's hand, and kissed it.

'Us doddery old fathers are always supposed to do chivalrous things like that,' he smiled. 'And besides that, it's the only way we can get our rocks off.' They all laughed, Vicki without a trace of embarrassment.

They went to collect William's luggage. They didn't say very much as other people's bags, trunks, plaid hold-alls, fishing-poles, buffalo-hide matching suitcase sets, and baby strollers went around and around on the carousel, but there was a warm feeling that surrounded them all, as if there was plenty to talk about later, and right now they just wanted to be out of this public place and alone together.

At last, William's battered green suitcase appeared, and John heaved it off the carousel. They walked out of the doors into the heat of the afternoon, and John led the way towards the parking lot.

'Oh, this is bliss,' said William. 'Do you know what the temperature is in Jersey? Eight below, and still dropping.'

'Don't count on it staying like this,' remarked John. 'We're having a heatwave.'

'I don't care if it snows,' said William. 'I haven't had a vacation since your mother died.'

'You can have the loft,' John told him. 'I know you like 1940s architecture, and it has a fine view of the back of Topanga fire station. Trash cans, worn-out firehoses, rusting ladders, everything.'

They reached John's Chrysler, and stowed the suitcase away next to Vicki's motorbike. William took an admiring stroll around the car, and then said, 'This is some kind of transport, huh? I know you sent me a Polaroid, but this thing has to be seen to be believed, doesn't it?'

'It's the triumph of money over good sense,' said John, opening the door. 'That's what I like about it.'

'You never did have any taste,' said William, as he climbed in beside John and Vicki, and closed the car door. 'I hate to think what would have happened to America if you'd have made the grade as an architect. Vulgar wouldn't have been the word.'

'Oh, I think everybody needs a little vulgarity now and again,' said Vicki, snuggling up to John as they glided out of the car park and headed north on Sepulveda Boulevard.

William wound down his window, and leaned his arm on the sill. 'The trouble with your generation is that you think the Fifties were all rock'n'roll and high school crushes and borrowing your suffering father's car keys. You never thought about anything that really mattered. You were too busy combing your pompadours and leaning on juke boxes.'

'Are we going to get into a generation argument our first day together?' asked Vicki, as they stopped for traffic signals at Manchester Avenue.

'I'd rather get myself into a tub, to tell you the truth,' said William. 'I feel like I've been wearing the same shirt for five years.'

'Hmm,' said John, sniffing. 'Maybe you should have sat in the back.'

They were still laughing about that as they passed 83rd Street, six minutes ahead of the schedule that the tall man in the Grand Prix had estimated for them.

29

John, driving his Imperial Crown through the mid-afternoon traffic and feeling buoyant with pleasure, didn't notice the silver car emerge from the intersection behind them and follow them cautiously northward along Sepulveda.

'Actually, I'm leading a very docile life these days,' said William, taking out his briar pipe and his old leather tobacco pouch. 'I think the trouble is that I'm too young for most of my senior colleagues' wife-swapping parties, and too damned old for my sexy female students.'

'So how do you pass your time?' asked John. 'Weaving macramé dictionary covers?'

William smiled. 'I wish I could. There's probably more money in it than politics.'

'You're back with the equal rights crowd?'

'Kind of. They've matured and developed now. We're trying to work towards what we call a society of mutual respect. That is, we want individuals to be respected by their government, legally and morally; and we reckon that, in return, individuals will slowly grow to respect and trust their government. It's going to be a long, slow process, but it has to happen. Government has gotten so impersonal today that it has to make a supreme effort to make contact with the folks who elect it.'

'Pretty idealistic,' remarked John, pulling up at the traffic signals just before the San Diego Freeway. He checked his mirror, and saw the silver Grand Prix drawing right up behind him. He couldn't see the driver's face, though – it was obscured by a triangular reflection of the concrete freeway overpass.

The lights changed to green, and John drove under the bridge and turned up the freeway approach ramp. The Grand Prix followed.

'I've been writing quite a few articles on the kind of conditions that we ought to impose on our next government,' said William. 'I brought some along to show you, if you're interested. Thought they might appeal to that journal of yours. The *Trenton Liberal* liked them.'

'L.A.'s kind of weirder than Trenton,' said John, crossing two lanes of freeway traffic and putting his foot down. 'I mean, they're more into TA and mystic cults around here, rather than straightforward liberal politics. We met a guy at a party the other night who claimed he was Tutankhamun back from the dead. He even offered to show me his discarded bandages.'

William grunted. 'That's nothing. I met a lecturer's wife at a party and she offered to let me feel her corsets.'

'I hope you took her up on it,' grinned Vicki.

John glanced at his rear view mirror. The silver Grand Prix was just emerging from behind a truck, and slowly overhauling them. John reached for the radio and said, 'How about some music?'

'Anything you like, so long as it isn't country-western,' said William.

The Grand Prix was now drawing alongside them, on their right. John was touching sixty miles an hour, and the silver car was matching his speed. They drove neck-and-neck as far as the Santa Monica Freeway crossover, and then a Coca-Cola truck pulled out in front of the Grand Prix and forced it to slow down. John, oblivious, kept up his speed.

William was sitting back comfortably, his hands in his lap, watching the concrete scenery flash past. 'The last time I visited L.A. this freeway didn't even exist,' he told them. 'Getting around was comparative hell.'

John moved across out of the left-hand lane, overtook a string of trucks, and then moved across, yet again to pass a dawdling ranch wagon with a trailing exhaust. He crossed back to the left-hand lane, and he glimpsed the silver Grand Prix again in his mirror.

'It's crazy, isn't it?' he said to his father. 'I was real nervous about seeing you again. I didn't know what I was going to say.'

'*You* were nervous?' laughed William. 'I was having an acute attack of the sweaty palms.'

'Now I'm *convinced* you should sit in the back.'

The Grand Prix was catching up with them now, and as they passed the Santa Monica Boulevard exit ramp, it was almost alongside. Then, it stayed where it was, on John's blind side, a few feet behind them, not overtaking, not falling back. John glanced in his mirror and said, 'What's that creep doing?'

They drove for a half-mile, side by side, and all the time the Grand Prix was hovering just out of John's line of sight. William turned to look at it, and remarked, 'That guy's pretty damned close.'

Abruptly, they heard a heavy metallic bang, which made John swerve out of nervous response.

'What the hell was that?' he yelled. But instantly, there was another bang, and the car flinched as if it had been struck by a ten-pound hammer.

'He's shooting! John! He's shooting!' Vicki screamed.

Desperate, John hit the gas hard, and the huge Chrysler surged forward. But the Grand Prix accelerated after them, and kept pace, even while John's speedometer needle climbed through eighty, ninety, ninety-five.

Ahead of him, a camper was driving at half his speed in the same lane. The Grand Prix raced beside him on his right, determined to box him in. On his left, the concrete-and-steel divider zipped past, only three feet away.

'What's he doing? John, what's he doing? He's trying to kill us!' Vicki shrieked.

Desperate, John slewed the Chrysler in towards the Grand Prix, and there was a shuddering grind of metal and plastic as the two cars collided and bounced. Vicki screamed, and fell heavily against John's shoulder. There was a long, drawn-out, horrific howl of tyres as the two cars skidded away from each other, and then came back together in another jarring collision. John couldn't see anything but hurtling concrete and cars; he couldn't hear anything but crunching bodywork and the drone of other drivers' horns.

He felt for a stomach-turning moment that he'd lost control of the Chrysler altogether, and he spun the wheel frantically, trying to correct its endless, graceless slide. But even as the car seemed to straighten, he saw the Grand Prix coming in again, like a battered silver shark worrying a whale, and with odd and frightening clarity, so close that he could have tossed him a cigarette, he saw the face of a man with mirrors for eyes.

William shouted hoarsely, 'Pull over! Step on the brakes and then pull over! There's an exit up there!'

Clenching his teeth, John jammed his foot down on the Chrysler's power-assisted brakes, and the car's tyres shrieked in protest as it bucked and nosedived.

What happened then was so unreal and slow that John could remember it later as if it had taken a week, or even a month. As he braked, the Chrysler was hit from behind by a massive green truck, crumpling the trunk and the fins and pushing the whole car helplessly past the Grand Prix and into the steel dividing rail. John twisted uselessly at the steering wheel as his car was ground against the barrier, wrecking its fenders and crushing its hood. He could see Vicki shielding her face, and he knew that she was screaming, even though the hideous noise of mashing metal blotted out any kind of sound. He could see his father clinging on to the windowsill, his face alarmed and wide-eyed.

But just as he thought it was over, and that they'd survived, he felt something spraying through the car, sparkling and bright, and realised that it was thousands of tiny fragments of shattered glass. He pushed Vicki down towards the floor, and he was reaching for his father when the back of his father's grey hair flapped upwards like a toupee, and in front of his eyes, his father's cheek and nose seemed to swell, as if a terrible black boil was growing on his face, and then burst open in a geyser of mucous membrane and blood. His father's hands were rising towards his face in surprise, but then he pitched forward and collapsed on the floor of the car.

There was an extraordinary silence. Then he heard someone tugging at the twisted door of his car, and saying: 'Are you all right in there? Jesus, are you all right?'

SIX

He had waited in the hospital reception area for more than five hours, under a flickering fluorescent light that hurt his eyes. There was a low table with a stack of dog-eared *National Geographic* magazines and an ashtray, but he couldn't concentrate on the hunting rituals of the Dayak Indians, and somehow it didn't occur to him to smoke. A homely nurse with higgledy-piggledy teeth brought him a cup of coffee, and he drank it without tasting it. He knew that he was probably in shock, but as long as his father was still in the operating theatre, he wanted to keep awake.

About a half hour ago, they had let him look in on Vicki. She was white-faced, as white as the stack of pillows that propped her up. Both of her eyes were bruised, and there were lacerations on her arms, but she had suffered no serious injuries, and the doctor had told her that she could probably leave the hospital in a couple of days. John had kissed her, shakily, but when she had tried to ask him what had happened, and why, he put his finger to her lips, and shook his head.

'I want you to get some sleep,' he told her gently. 'We'll talk about it tomorrow.'

From where he was sitting, he could see the duty nurse's desk, and the elevator. Once or twice, he had seen senior-looking doctors emerge from the elevator doors, and go to talk quietly to the nurse on duty, but the hours went by and nobody came his way. He shifted himself on the blue vinyl upholstery, feeling empty and devastated and hopelessly tired.

Just before ten o'clock, a thin man in a green jacket and badly-pressed pants appeared, murmured something to the nurse, and then walked towards him. The man was charcoal-chinned, dark-eyed, and he wore a small green hat that didn't fit him. He came up to where

34

John was sitting, and produced a leather wallet with a silver badge.

'My name's Morello, from the LAPD.'

John shrugged. 'I told your officer everything I saw, and everything I heard. You want something else?'

'Just a couple of minutes. But I could always come back tomorrow.'

John shook his head. 'No, sit down. I could use the company.'

The detective sat opposite him, and tidily straightened the stack of magazines. 'You said in your statement you didn't see the guy's face too good. Just sunglasses, you said.'

'That's right. Those sunglasses that have mirrors for lenses.'

'And that's really all you saw? No facial features? No idea of the guy's general build? No scars?'

John rubbed his forehead tiredly. 'I was trying to keep control of a crashing automobile. I wasn't out on a nature walk.'

The detective sat back in his seat and crossed his legs, revealing thin white ankles. 'You're pretty sure it was just the one guy, though? He didn't have any passengers with him?'

'Not that I noticed. But, as I've told you, I was more interested in keeping my hands on the wheel.'

'We think it was just the one guy,' said Detective Morello.

'Oh, yes?'

'Well, it seems to figure that way. He fired four shots at you. One hit the front fender, that was the first one; then another hit the front door, just by the hinge. The third one went through the rear window after the truck hit you, and the fourth one struck your father.'

John coughed. 'And that means there was only one guy?'

'It seems to point that way. He fired two wild shots for starters, and considering he was only thirteen feet away, that was pretty bad shooting. The weapon, incidentally, was a Colt automatic .38 calibre. They're not celebrated for their accuracy, but even an amateur

35

should be able to hit a man's head from thirteen feet. Our supposition is that he was driving and firing at the same time, and in that event he was probably alone.'

John nodded. 'I see. So you're looking for a lone maniac.'

'We believe so. A homicidal maniac who selects any car at random and slaughters the occupants.'

'This has happened before?'

'Don't you read your papers? We've had eleven random shootings on the freeway in as many months. Some from passing cars, others from overpasses or out of the bushes at pull-offs. It's an epidemic.'

John stood up, and walked across to the hospital window. Through the venetian blinds, he could see the night-time traffic crawling past MacArthur Park eight floors below. 'You think it's just this one guy, this homicidal maniac?'

'Not for certain, but out of eleven shootings, we've retrieved only three different kinds of bullet. Colt automatic, like the one that hit your father; and two Army rifles, an M-14 and an M-16.'

'Then it could be three homicidal maniacs.'

Detective Morello took out a cigarette and lit it. John watched him, but didn't ask for one. Maybe he'd go out and smoke a whole pack if he heard that his father was going to live. Maybe he'd never smoke again.

'It could be *eleven* homicidal maniacs,' said Detective Morello. 'But in each case, some guy's called *The Los Angeles Times* the following day, given a code name, and claimed credit for the killing. He calls himself The Bald Eagle.' He paused. 'We call him The Freeway Fruitcake.'

John turned away from the window and stood over the detective like a tired attorney who has almost run out of questions to ask his witness.

'Do you have any clues?' he asked him. 'Any idea who might have done it, or for what reason?'

Detective Morello shook his head. 'People don't seem to need a reason to kill each other any more, not like they did in the old days. I took a kid in last week, and he confessed to stabbing an old hobo up at Cahuenga Peak, because he was bored. He took an afternoon off from school, and he was bored.'

'What about this shooting? What are you going to do about it?' John asked.

'Follow it up the best way we can. We'll catch him one day.'

'How many people have to be shot before you find out enough to arrest him?'

Detective Morello looked pained. 'We're dealing with a headcase,' he protested. 'Headcases have patterns of behaviour, but most of the time they don't make any sense to anyone except themselves. I had a homicidal headcase last year, and he was only strangling women in Chemin-de-Fer jeans. Don't ask me why. But we're obviously dealing with the same kind of nut right now.'

'There's no pattern at all?' asked John. 'Nothing you can pin him down to?'

Detective Morello shook his head. 'The victims have nothing in common at all. None of them had any enemies. All of them were happy, well-balanced people. They happened to be sitting in the wrong car at the wrong time on the wrong freeway, that's all. This guy is a random killer. He does it for the sheer pleasure of it.'

John bit his lip. 'I haven't seen my father in three years. He may have had enemies.'

'The same enemies that Ken Galozzo had. Mr Galozzo was a notions salesman from Pasadena. Then there was Mrs Helen Walker, a housewife from Sherman Oaks. And Juan Fernando, a car-wash attendant from downtown L.A. Not to mention Mr Ben Oliver, who was a retired airline pilot on a visit from Missoula, Montana. All of those folks were shot, Mr Cullen, and there wasn't a single damned reason why, except some lone freak picked them out at random and decided it was their day to die.'

John was silent for a long time. Then he said, 'Okay. I guess you're up against a stone wall. I'm sorry.'

'We'll get him, don't you worry,' said Detective

Morello. 'But we can't work miracles. We're human beings, trying to track down someone who's a damned sight less than human.'

At that moment, a nurse came down the corridor and said softly, 'Mr Cullen?'

'What's happened? Is he out of surgery?' John asked nervously.

The nurse gave him a gentle smile. 'Please come this way, Mr Cullen.'

John glanced down at Detective Morello, but Morello simply nodded and said, 'You go ahead. If I want anything, I'll call you at your house.'

The nurse was already walking down the corridor, her rubber-soled shoes squeaking on the polished linoleum floor. John hurried to catch up with her, and she led him around the corner, past the duty desk, and through a pair of double doors. He was suddenly and poignantly reminded of Mrs Benduzzi's doors, but that seemed like a lifetime ago.

A doctor in a white coat and heavy tortoise-shell spectacles was standing up from behind his desk to greet him. He was a very small doctor, almost like a precocious child dressed up, with hair as black and curly as astrakhan.

'I'm Doctor Nathan,' he said. 'Would you like to sit down?'

John, uneasily, sat. 'How's my father?' he asked, in a whisper.

Doctor Nathan came around his desk and laid a hand on his shoulder. 'I want to tell you the truth,' he said. He carried with him the smell of antiseptic and non-allergenic soap.

'The truth? What does that mean?'

'The truth is that your father will not recover. We have done all within our power to save him, but the bullet damaged his brain beyond repair, and he is dying.'

John felt a harsh constriction in his throat. 'There's no hope at all?' he heard himself saying. He felt as if he was someone else altogether. Could it really be *his* father? He couldn't understand it.

'I'm sorry.'

There was an awkward pause. Then John said, 'Can I see him?' He was suddenly so near to tears that he could hardly speak.

'Of course. Come this way, please. Nurse, would you help?'

It was a strange dream about hospitals. It couldn't possibly be real. But his legs seemed to carry him along the corridor, past trolleys of surgical equipment, and past a group of interns, who turned and stared as he went by, and finally down to a door at the end of the building, a door which led into a blue-painted room.

His father lay on a white-draped bed in the centre of the room, connected to intravenous drips and a panel of diagnostic equipment. The sound of his heartbeat, electronically amplified, paced out his last few moments. His face was heavily bandaged on the left side, and his right eye was closed up with bruising.

John went up to the bed. He said, 'Father?'

'He can't hear you,' Dr Nathan said. 'He's in a coma.'

'Will he regain consciousness? Will I be able to say anything to him?'

Dr Nathan shook his head.

John looked back at the bed, where this frail damaged man lay dying. He thought of all the days in his boyhood when this man had taught him and cared for him and helped him. The day they went down to the river to net pollywogs, and John had fallen in, and his father had carried him home, dripping wet, along a sunny dusty road. The day they had flown kites together, with the grey clouds tumbling overhead. The day his father had told him about sex, in such a warm, understanding way that he had been aroused as much by the possibility of loving as he had been by the idea of copulating. Days of laughter and Hershey bars and baseball and friendship.

The tears ran down his cheeks. He couldn't stop himself from feeling more desolate and more miserable than he ever had in his whole life.

'Father,' he said. 'Oh, Father. Oh, Christ.'

He took the cold hand that lay on the white sheet. It

didn't seem like a real hand at all. But he bent his head and lifted it up to his lips, as if he could squeeze life into it.

The heartbeat signal skipped, and then faltered.

The nurse said, 'He's going, doctor.'

John kept his eyes on his father's face, as if at the last moment he might miraculously wake up, and at least give him the chance to tell him that he loved him, and that he would miss him for the rest of his life.

The heartbeat signal skipped, and then faltered.

There was an aching silence.

John pressed his lips tight together to stop himself from sobbing, but a muted sound of hopeless pain still wrenched forth, and there was nothing he could do to check his tears. The nurse put her arm around him, and led him gently from the room. John sat on a small folding chair in the corridor and cried.

SEVEN

The air-conditioning inside the white Fleetwood was so chilly that she sat wrapped in her white fur stole, cuddling it up to her neck with fingers that sparkled with sapphires and rubies and pavé-set diamonds. She liked it cold. She liked to think of herself as the Snow Queen, the frigid erotic empress who froze men's hearts until they shattered into tiny pieces. And even after all these years, even after *Across the Yukon* and *Passionate Pretenders* had been repeated so many times that most TV channels relegated them to two a.m. or later, and most of her movie roles were 'special guest appearances,' she was still disturbingly attractive, still carnivorously feline, and still deserving of one gossip columnist's off-the-record remark that she was 'the haughtiest woman ever to leave off her dance pants.'

Adele Corliss, at fifty-nine, was all that her cosmetic

surgeon could make her. Her well-sculptured face, with wide-apart eyes and sharp straight nose, was as smooth and free of laugh lines as a twenty-five-year-old. Her neck was soft and firm, and her hands were clear of liver spots or wrinkles. Under the furs and the close-fitting white satin dress, her breasts had been lifted, her stomach had been trimmed, and her thighs were slender and smooth. She didn't believe in growing old, gracefully or disgracefully. She believed in whatever youth money could buy.

She appraised herself in the gold-backed mirror she took from her purse. Her hair was ashblonde, curled and braided and tied at the back with a white silk bow. Her clear brown eyes looked back at her out of a deep golden tan. She could have been looking at her own daughter, except that her own daughter wasn't half as finely-preserved. All that disturbed her was a faint sense that she was looking at a transparency of a young face superimposed on a hauntingly elderly one.

Behind the wheel, her black chauffeur Mark sat in his crisp white uniform, gently humming to himself as he drove up Laguna Canyon Road towards Interstate 5. It was a brilliant sunny afternoon, and the sky was that dense inky blue of summer, even though it was mid-November. That Friday morning, they had travelled all the way from Palm Springs to Laguna Beach to pay their monthly homage to Adele's eighty-three-year-old mother at her retirement home. As usual, they had sat out on the balcony, watching the sun glittering on the sea, while old Mrs Corliss, all fraying white hair and magnifying spectacles, had mumbled and muttered about the days gone by, and her house in Anaheim, long since demolished, and the night that Uncle Richard had caught his foot in a zinc pail, and had to walk all the way home in the middle of the night, bomp-clang, bomp-clang, down Brookhurst Avenue.

Adele didn't like to be reminded of those days. They were days of poverty, and shabby rooms, and apart from that they were disconcertingly long ago. Since those days, she had risen to fame as a child celebrity, and then a star. She had married four times, borne two

41

children, attempted suicide three times, owned seven houses, drunk thousands of bottles of champagne, broken countless mirrors, ridden in fleets of Cadillacs to dozens of premières, travelled, wept, argued, screamed, pleaded and laughed, and if all she had now was her mansion in Palm Springs, a comfortable income, her looks and her sanity, then she was well satisfied. Always provided, of course, that she had enough men.

'Did you enjoy yourself, Mark?' she asked, semi-sarcastically, as they left the last blue view of the ocean behind them.

'Just as usual, Ms. Corliss,' Mark responded, glancing at her in his rear view mirror.

Adele smiled. 'You're very diplomatic. Still with a dingus like yours, you can afford to be.'

'Thank you, Ms. Corliss,' said Mark flatly.

Adele sat back in the soft white hide of the seat. 'You don't have to be so modest,' she teased him. 'Doesn't the Bible say that the well-endowed shall inherit the earth?'

'The meek, Ms. Corliss, begging your pardon.'

She raised an eyebrow. 'Well, in that case, you win out both ways.'

'Thank you, Ms. Corliss.'

They were approaching the intersection with El Toro Road. Adele was reaching forward to open the Cadillac's burled-walnut bar and take out a split of champagne, and she nearly missed seeing the hitchhiker altogether. But he waved from the roadside as they went by, and she turned quickly, and said, 'Mark, stop. Mark!'

The shining white Fleetwood drew up against the dusty roadside. Mark, as silent and obedient as ever, switched off the engine. Then there was nothing but the gentle hum of the air-conditioning, and the sound of the hitchhiker's desert boots as he came loping along the pavement to catch up with them.

The hitchhiker looked in at the tinted window, and Mark courteously lowered it from the switch console by the driver's seat. He was young, with curly sun-bleached hair, eyes the colour of faded violets, and a football player's strong jawline. His red plaid shirt was open to the waist, baring his muscular chest and his hard, flat belly. There were three gold chains around his neck, and a gold band around his wrist, but the canvas kitbag he carried over his shoulder was battered and worn.

'Thanks for stopping,' he said. 'I've been waiting there for quite a while.'

Adele looked him up and down with cool, aloof appraisal.

'It wasn't a very intelligent place to hitchhike, was it?' she asked him. 'I almost missed seeing you.'

The boy rubbed at his nose with the back of his hand. 'What happened was, the ride I picked up from Laguna Beach was forking off for El Toro. I told him I'd rather hop off here, and try for a ride straight to Santa Ana. I don't like to thumb for rides on the freeways, the heat always pick you up.'

'Is that where you're headed?' she asked him. 'Santa Ana?'

He shook his head. 'San Bernardino, really. But I can get myself another ride at Santa Ana if you're heading north.'

She smiled, her famous frosty movie smile. 'You'd better get in,' she said. 'We're going all the way to Palm Springs, and we can drop you off at the Riverside cloverleaf. Mark, would you unlock the doors, please?'

Mark flicked the door-lock switch, and the doors released. The boy opened up, and climbed into the back of the car, twisting his pack off his back and setting it down on the white-carpeted floor. Mark locked the doors again, raised the window, and drove off.

'I sure appreciate this,' said the boy, wiping his sweaty forehead with a grey handkerchief. 'I thought I'd be standing out there all night.'

'It's the least I could do,' said Adele, wrapping her fur stole around her more tightly as the temperature dropped.

The boy sat back. 'By the way,' he told her, 'my name's Ken Irwin, from Butte, Montana. I'm pleased to make your acquaintance.'

'I'm sure I'm charmed,' replied Adele with sarcasm the boy missed.

'I've been down here looking for work. I'm what you might call a male domestic. That's what I do to eat, anyway. My real target is to make it in the movies.'

'That's everyone's target,' murmured Adele.

Ken began to button up his shirt.

'What's the matter?' she said.

He gave her a confused, nervous smile. 'Well, nothing, ma'am. It's just a little cold in here, that's all. I've been standing out in the sun.'

Adele looked at him, her brown eyes liquid and deep. He shifted uncomfortably in his seat, and didn't seem to know whether to carry on buttoning up his shirt or not.

'Go on,' she said at last. 'We don't want you to catch a chill, after all.'

'Thank you,' he said, and buttoned himself up to the neck.

They joined Interstate 5, the Santa Ana Freeway, and headed north over the glaring concrete. On their right, the Santa Ana moutains rose into ragged crowns of white cloud. Mark commented: 'Maybe the heatwave's going to die off tomorrow, Ms. Corliss.'

Ken Irwin glanced at her. She looked back at him, her haughty expression almost daring him to speak.

'You're not *the* Ms. Corliss, are you?' he asked her. 'Not *Adele* Corliss?'

She crossed her long legs. Her white satin dress was slit up the side, and he could see her bare, perfectly-tanned thigh.

'Of course,' she said, trying to sound amused. 'Didn't you recognise me?'

Ken blushed. 'Well, yes, I mean I thought I did when you first stopped. But it just seemed that –'

'That what? That I was too young?'

'Well, shoot, no. But you're very –'

She reached across with her left hand and held his wrist. 'Very *what*?'

He swallowed. 'You're very classy,' he said, clumsily.

'I mean, you're terrifically good-looking, close to. Just like your movies.'

She watched him for a while in silence. He cleared his throat, and sat forward in his seat, his hands twitchily clasped, throwing a quick look at her now and again to see if she was annoyed.

In the end, she gave a tinkly little laugh.

'Ken,' she said, 'you're really very cute. Do you know that?'

'I don't know. Nobody ever called me cute before.'

She reached out with her fingertips and touched his forehead, his nose and his lips. He didn't attempt to kiss her fingers, as many men had. He just seemed to be awkward and confused, and overwhelmed by her fame and her cold sexuality. She leaned towards him until their faces were only inches apart.

'*I'm* calling you cute,' she whispered. 'Is that good enough for you? The great Adele Corliss, calling you cute?'

He shifted uneasily in his seat. 'Well, it surely is. I'm flattered.'

'Don't be. It's the truth. Now, why don't you open that bar for me, and take out a couple of splits of champagne.'

Ken, with relief, let go of her hand, and knelt down to open the bar. It was refrigerated, with racks of Krug champagne, and ready-mixed sours and martinis.

'Use the tulip glasses,' she told him. 'Only Hollywood starlets and Canadians use saucer glasses. They dissipate the bubbles.'

'Sure thing,' said Ken, and carefully, with an amateur's frown, poured out two glasses of champagne.

'Well,' smiled Adele, 'here's to our celebration.'

Ken lifted his glass. 'I'm not quite sure what we're supposed to be celebrating.'

She sipped the tingly, dry champagne. 'We're celebrating your employment, of course. You said you were a male domestic, didn't you?'

'Well, sure, but –'

'But what? Do you want the work or don't you? I

have a twelve-bedroom house at Palm Springs that needs constant attention. Dusting, waxing, vacuum cleaning, polishing. Isn't that the kind of thing you do?'

'Yes, but –'

She touched his shoulder as if she were conferring a knighthood on him. 'In that case, everything's perfect. You can be my man.'

Ken bit his lip. 'The truth is, Ms. Corliss, I have a couple of jobs lined up already.'

'Cancel them.'

'Ms. Corliss, I really did promise these people.'

'Cancel them. I like you too much to let you go. The second I saw you by the side of the road, I thought, there is a boy with fire. And what finer combination can a man and a woman have than fire and ice?'

'Ms. Corliss –'

'*Look* at me,' she commanded. She sat up straight, and let the mink stole slide from her shoulders. In the front of the car, Mark glanced up at her in his rear view mirror, and then turned his eyes impassively back to the highway. Mark wasn't jealous. Adele's body, after all, belonged to her, and if she happened to share it with him on nights when she felt fifty-nine and lonesome, well, that was nothing to get possessive about. He would just as soon spend the afternoon tinkering with the Cadillac's air injector reactor system as lie naked on her white silk bedcover while she moaned and sighed about the beauty of black balls between white thighs.

Ken Irwin, though, was embarrassed and aroused. He knew how old she must be. I mean, Jesus, she was in movies with Douglas Fairbanks Jr. But he couldn't help himself from looking downwards at her clinging white satin dress, and the deep V-shaped neckline that exposed a firm, perfect, siliconized cleavage. She had paid thousands of dollars to have a startling body, and it was impossible for anyone, whatever their sexual tastes, to ignore it. He looked up again. Her eyes were distant and frigid, and yet their coldness, in itself, was unnervingly erotic.

'Ms. Corliss,' he said throatily, 'I don't know whether you're trying to make a fool out of me or not. I'm not

46

truly smart enough to tell. But the truth is that I've already signed on with a domestic agency in San Bernardino, and the work's regular and honest, and what you're offering is kind of wild to say the least.'

She wrapped herself up in her furs again. Her cold expression did not alter. 'Don't you like being wild?' she asked him. 'Don't tell me you like to dust and wax and nothing else.'

He looked sheepish. 'Well, sure. I'm as red-blooded as the next guy. But I've kind of worked out this plan, the way I'm going to do things, and I was figuring I'd stick to it.'

Adele watched him for a while, and then she reached out and gently placed her hand on his blue denim thigh. He looked nervously down at it, as if it was likely to scurry up his leg like some Arctic scorpion, and sting him where it hurt most.

'You're afraid, aren't you?' she asked him. 'That's what it is – you're actually afraid.'

He coloured.

She raised her champagne glass to him. They were driving through Orange now, on their way to the Riverside Expressway. Whitewashed houses and palms and telephone poles flowed past.

'If you're afraid,' she whispered, in a voice which froze him, 'then we shall have to do what we can to restore your confidence.'

Mark, inaudibly, sighed.

Ken Irwin said, 'I'm really not sure, Ms. Corliss. I think I'd rather get out at the Riverside cloverleaf.'

Adele laughed. 'You are stolid, aren't you? A real mountain man from Montana. Have some more champagne, for God's sake. It helps you forget who you are.'

It was already dusk by the time the Fleetwood bounced through the wrought-iron gates of the hacienda which Adele Corliss had been given in settlement after her fourth divorce. The desert sky was grainy and purple, and Ken Irwin had to strain his eyes through the tinted automobile windows to see the private manicured paradise of lush clipped lawns, orderly yuccas, carefully-

47

trained dragon trees, poinsettia, magnolia and oranges. A haze of multi-coloured moisture hung in the air from the garden sprays.

Mark, humming to himself, swung the car around on the gravel drive in front of the house, killed the engine, and then opened the doors for them. Ken climbed out cautiously, and the air of a Palm Springs evening was fragrant and warm after the sterile frigidity of the Fleetwood. He looked up at the house, an E-shaped imitation of a Spanish wine-grower's mansion, with two enclosing wings. It was rendered with rough plaster, and colour-washed in primrose yellow, and its walls were a riot of wrought-iron balconies and grille-covered windows and arches and verandahs, with flowering creepers trailing from its red-clay roof. A fountain of plump concrete cherubs splashed softly in the twilight, and across to the left, Ken could make out the bright lilac reflection of a swimming pool, mutely surrounded by simulated Roman statues of naked nymphs and sultry discusthrowers.

Somewhere in the gardens, someone was clipping a hedge. The patient *peck-peck-peck* of the shears sounded like the call of a plaintive bird.

Adele stepped out of the car, and stretched out her arms to the fading warmth of the sun.

'This is a pretty nice place,' said Ken.

'You sound as if you don't approve,' Adele said.

'Oh no, it's great, really,' he quickly said.

Adele came around and grasped Ken's hand. He was surprised, when she stood next to him, how short she was. Even in her white stiletto-heeled shoes, she couldn't have topped more than five feet two or three. On the movie screen, she always appeared so lissome and tall, but maybe she was like Alan Ladd, and stood on a box. Despite himself, despite his real reasons for being there, he felt an urge to put his arm around her and protect her, this petite and sexy blonde who was old enough to be his grandmother. But she tugged his hand and said, 'Come along inside. We can freshen up and have something to drink. You like tequila?'

'I prefer beer, to tell you the truth.'

48

An elderly butler in a cream tuxedo and brown tie was waiting by the carved Spanish oak door. His nose was as curved as a toucan's beak, and grey hair was laboriously greased down. Adele said, 'Good evening, Holman. Have a quiet day?' and the old man nodded and then abruptly took out his handkerchief and blew his nose with a loud snort. He ushered Ken inside as if Ken was a brush salesman, or the man who comes to clean out the Jacuzzi.

The hallway was flagged with brown Mexican tiles, and the rough-plastered walls were divided into archways, through which Ken could see a spacious living room, with a crackling log fire, and a sombre but impressive dining room with a swamp oak table. There was an aromatic smell of sandalwood and polish and expensive leather upholstery.

'My ex-husband, that was Roger Sumter, rather fancied himself as Emiliano Zapata,' she remarked, handing her mink stole to the butler. 'We used to have dreadful paintings of Mexican folk heroes and bullfights all over the walls before the divorce. I let him have them back, and believe me that was an even greater relief than getting rid of *him*.'

A Mexican maid in a dowdy black dress appeared through one of the archways. She was stern-faced and stolid, and wore elastic support hose. She said, 'Your bath, Ms. Corliss?'

'*Our* bath, yes,' corrected Adele, turning to Ken in her tight white satin with such a girlish smile that he almost felt as if he were a new bridegroom, brought home to mother on his wedding night.

'Whatever you say, Ms. Corliss,' replied the Mexican woman sourly, and flapped away on plastic sandals to do her duty.

'You like the house?' Adele asked Ken. 'We'll take a look around when we're all freshened up. Actually, the whole place is sickeningly bogus, but don't you think that sickeningly bogus is better than nitpickingly stylish?'

'Well, uh, possibly,' said Ken.

Adele took his hand, and led him across the tiled

49

hall, and through the archway that took them to the main staircase. It was oak, each step of which had been glasspapered down and then abused with hammers and chisels to make it look as if Spanish servants had been shuffling up and down them for three centuries.

Adele said, 'Awful, isn't it? But Roger preferred custom-made antiques to the real thing. He didn't understand the difference between the slowly acquired patina of age, and beating the hell out of something in ten minutes. He approached our marriage in the same way.'

They climbed the stairs, and reached a long galleried landing. The windows along the gallery were all thrown open to the warm dry desert air, and Ken could smell the strange coolness of the garden sprays.

'Don't you get lonesome here?' he asked her.

She led him onwards, down the landing, towards a lighted doorway at the far end.

'My analyst says that being lonesome is simply the social manifestation of my uniqueness,' she said. 'That, of course, is typical analyst's bullshit. Being lonesome is an expression of the fact that when you're a movie star, you only have two kinds of people in your life, greedy sycophants and jealous enemies.'

'I'm not a sycophant, and I'm sure not an enemy,' Ken stated.

She gave him a fleeting, half-thawed smile. 'Well, dear, we'll see about that. At the moment you scarcely know me.'

All the same, as she gently pushed him ahead of her through the door, he felt her hand linger on his back, caressing his muscles through his shirt. The ice-queen, complicated and regal as she was, appeared to be in heat.

The bedroom was a huge vaulted hall that had been designed to make Adele's last husband feel as if he were a Spanish nobleman relaxing after a hard day horse-whipping the grape-harvesters on his bodegón. There was a carved four-poster bed, draped in white silk, as high and stately as an altar. The rugs were deep white shag-pile, and everywhere Ken looked, there were tall mirrors in gilded frames. Two grotesque hanging lamps of pierced brass suffused the room in soft yellow light.

Through another archway, Ken could smell bath oils and steam. Adele said, 'Let me see if Dolores has finished. She's such a tartar, you know. She'd stand over us and scrub behind our ears if I let her.'

Ken waited in the bedroom while Adele dealt with the maid. He carried out a quick reconaissance of the top of the bureau, where there was a large colour photograph of Adele, ten or fifteen years younger, against a background of Swiss mountains; a small silver beauty-patch box; and a gold-and-tortoiseshell comb and brush set. Then he swiftly opened the bedside cabinets, and ran his eyes down fifteen or twenty paperbacks, a Dristan nasal spray, a box of tissues, and two crumpled tubes of K-Y.

He stood up, and turned around, and as he did so all of his reflections in all of those mirrors turned around too, and gave him a heart-stopping shock. Then he looked back at himselves and grinned lopsidedly at his nervousness. Eighteen reflections grinned lopsidedly back.

Adele came through from the bathroom, followed closely by the stern Dolores, who glared at Ken from beneath her unplucked eyebrows before going out and closing the door behind her with firm displeasure.

Adele laughed. 'You mustn't let Dolores upset you. She's reached the age when the only men she approves of are priests, and not all of them.'

'How about you?' Ken asked.

It was a provocative question in all kinds of ways, and for the first time Adele sensed that Ken Irwin might not be as much of a hitchhiking hayseed as he made out. 'I'm at an age when the only men I approve of are silent and sexual,' she said.

He peeled back his shirt, and dropped it on the floor. 'Do you have a bathrobe?' he asked her.

'Do you really need one?'

He shrugged. 'I don't want you to think that I'm immodest.'

'Immodest? Where did you learn a word like that?'

'Church.'

'Well,' she said, 'you're not in church now, so you needn't worry about it. Now, unfasten my gown, will you?'

He stepped up to her. Close to, she was fragrant with musk. He lifted her ash blonde hair at the back, and slowly pulled down the zipper of her dress, all the way down to the small of her back, and the swelling curves of her bottom. She turned around, and peeled the white satin away from her body like plastic shrink-wrapping off a fresh nectarine.

Ken stood there, only a couple of feet away, and looked at her. Her figure was trim and curvy, and yet it had an unreality about it that reminded him of those inflatable vinyl women. Her breasts were high, hard and round, with nipples that stuck on top of them like cherries on a cake. Her stomach was flat, with no sign of sagging muscles. Her vulva was shaved like a child's, which added to the unreality, and her pubic bone was as flat as if she had never given birth in her life. She was tanned all over, a gentle glowing tan that spoke of expensive sun preparations and long nude days by the pool.

'You're pretty amazing, aren't you?' he said, in a soft voice.

She raised an eyebrow laconically.

'What did you expect? Grandma Moses?'

He smiled, and shrugged. She stepped up to him, and unfastened the big silver buckle of his belt. He didn't know whether he wanted to be aroused or not, but he couldn't help himself, and when she tugged down the metal zipper, and opened up his jeans, she had to prise out his erection with both hands.

He stepped out of his pants. She held him close, one hand still clasping his stiffened penis. 'Time for your bath, little boy,' she whispered in his ear.

Naked, they walked through to the bathroom. The tub itself was dark blue enamel with gold-plated faucets in the shape of leaping dolphins. The walls were mirrored in gold-veined glass, and there were plants hanging everywhere, in baskets and woven rope planters.

Adele stepped down into the foam, and then swirled around and held out her hand for him. He went in, cautious and apparently shy, but then she pulled him in, and he splashed up to his neck in perfumed water, breathless and spluttering.

'I'm going to soap you,' she said, kissing his nose. 'So you'd better stand up.'

'Anything's better than drowning, ma'am,' he told her. When he said 'ma'am' she gave him a quick, intense glance, but he stood up then, his muscular body slick with water, and she decided to leave any doubts and questions until later.

She stood up beside him, and began to lather his shoulders with strawberry and glycerine soap. She kissed and bit his lips, and then pushed her wet tongue into his mouth, and licked his teeth. He felt her caressing, sudsing hands rub down his back, and around his buttocks. Then she soaped his chest, and his stomach, and worked her way down to his pubic hair and his red, rigid erection.

Kneeling, she stroked his tight scrotum with soapy hands, and then worked her fingers in slippery strokes up the shaft of his penis. He groaned, even though he didn't want to, even though he believed he didn't care, and didn't want to get involved.

Just when he felt a feeling between his thighs like mercury rising in a heatwave thermometer, she let him go, and curled herself back in the tub, her eyes mocking and erotic.

'Come on,' she teased him, 'rinse yourself off. Then you can soap me.'

He knelt down, unsmiling, and took a sponge from a basket beside the bath to squeeze water over his shoulders and back. Then he picked up the soap, and rubbed it between his hands until it worked up a rich lather.

Adele again stood up, and gently rested her hands on his shoulders.

'You're a very beautiful boy,' she said carefully, looking down at him. 'You're almost too beautiful to have come from Montana.'

53

He reached up and began to soap her stomach and her back. Her skin felt much younger than he had imagined it would. It was almost like caressing a teenage girl. His fingers ran down her sides, around her thighs, and she shuddered with pleasure.

'Some pretty good-looking folks come from Montana,' he told her. 'Evel Knievel for one.'

'He's a biker,' she said. 'What do you do?'

'When I'm not being a male domestic?'

'That's right.'

He stood up, and took her breasts in both his hands, and soaped them until the nipples stood tight and stiff.

'Well,' he said, 'I'm an obliging kind of guy, I guess. I'll do anything.'

She opened her brown eyes wide. 'You're lying,' she said. 'I don't know why, but you are.'

He kissed her. 'Does that feel like a lie?' he said, in a warm, husky voice.

Her eyes were still wide. 'All kisses are lies. People only kiss when they don't want to bother to show how they really feel.'

He soaped her back, and ran his fingertips down the cleft of her bottom and between her legs. He touched the smooth lips of her vulva, and then parted them with one hand, a magician opening an orange, so that he could slide his middle finger up her.

She clung to him, her arms around his waist. His finger worked deeper, caressing her inner folds. She said 'Ohhh ...' under her breath. Her firm breasts, slippery as pet seals, pressed against him.

Suddenly, she reached down and held his wrist. His eyes, which had been almost closed, opened. There was that calculating smile on her face again. A smile unsettled by her feelings of passion, but still tinged with frost.

'What's wrong?' he asked her.

She lowered her eyelashes. 'You are,' she whispered.

There was an uneasy silence. 'Well. What makes you say a thing like that?' he asked her nervously.

She lifted her face up to him and kissed him with open lips. 'I want all of you,' she said. 'Not just one

54

finger of one hand. I want to see you shiver, and suffer. I want to ride you into the ground.'

She stepped out of the tub, wet, and held out her hand. 'Come on,' she told him. He paused for a moment, and then silently climbed out after her.

They didn't say a single word as they went back into the bedroom. Ken sat on the edge of the bed, and all around him, eighteen reflections sat on the edge of the bed, too. Adele pushed him back on to the white silk cover, and he could feel it sticking to his wet body. Then she climbed astride him, and took his erection in her small fist.

'Isn't this what you wanted?' she said. 'Isn't this why you waited by the roadside so long?'

'You think I was waiting for you?'

She watched his face for a while. 'I'm not certain,' she said. 'But it all seems to be too wonderfully good to be true. You look too much like Roger and Janoscz and Harry and Mike all mixed up together.'

'Maybe you're seeing ghosts,' he told her.

She didn't answer. Instead, she carefully guided his erection up between her slender thighs mantling the swollen head of it with her parted lips. Their eyes were locked in a curious encounter that didn't seem to have much to do with affection or human friendship, but more to do with the rising cold excitement of mutual fear. But then she slowly sat on him, sensually rotating her hips, until he was as far up inside her body as it was possible for him to reach. She was almost as tight as a virgin, and he knew that her surgeons must have been practising their art in unseen places, too.

She leaned forward, and kissed his face all over. His eyes, his cheeks, his forehead, his mouth. Her breath came in tight, controlled gasps.

'You're very honoured,' she murmured. 'You're now fornicating with the greatest screen actress of the century, with the possible exception of Garbo.'

He didn't say anything for a while, didn't even move, although his penis involuntarily flinched inside her.

'Garbo was nothing on you,' he told her throatily. 'Nothing at all.'

She began to move up and down on him, as if she were elegantly riding bareback on some well-broken stallion. Her eyes closed, and he couldn't even guess what he saw behind her eyelids. Her movements were supple, and she lifted herself so high with each upward stroke that she almost lost him, but she kept him there just, and gave him a little squeeze with the ring of muscle around her vagina. He began to feel waves of heat through his body, and a growing tension that he could not control.

She rose up and down faster, and deeper, and more savagely. Her long fingernails gripped the muscles of his stomach until he winced. She leaned forward again and bit at his neck and his face and his nipples, until he cried out. Then, as her body rippled with the first waves of her first orgasm, she seized his hair and twisted and wrenched it until the tears started in his eyes.

There was a moment when it seemed that the world had gone. A suspended moment of everything and nothing, like a house about to fall off the edge of a cliff, a hand about to wave, a bomb about to explode, a mouth just opening to speak.

Then he felt himself go and she screamed and screamed out loud, the scream of a woman of fifty-nine, and her body shook as if she were going to fall apart.

He had never seen anything like it. She lay on her own on the white silk bedspread, shifting and twisting and crying out, having orgasm after orgasm, long after he had sat up, and then stood up, and gone to empty the tub and take a shower. He came back in from the bathroom to watch her, and as he stood there the mirrors in the room made it look as if he had been painted eighteen times that afternoon by El Greco.

Eventually, she lay silent and still.

He said, 'Are you okay?'

She nodded.

He came around and sat on the edge of the bed. Her face was beaded with perspiration. She smiled at him, and affectionately held his wrist.

'I have to call my agency in San Bernardino,' he told her.

'At this time of night?'

'It's twenty-four-hour.'

She bent her head across and kissed his hand. 'I don't trust you one bit,' she told him. 'You seem like a boy with – what can I call them? Ulterior motives.'

'Ulterior motives? What kind of ulterior motives?'

'I don't know. But I sense them.'

He coughed, and said, 'I'd like to eat soon, if that's all right.'

'Of course. The cook will be making dinner now. You like saddle of lamb?'

He stood up, and scratched his scalp. 'Do you have some pants?'

'Pants? Sure. How do you like them cooked?'

He turned to look at her, ready to smile. But Adele wasn't smiling at all. She had been through too much betrayal and too many husbands to fail to recognise what men were and what men weren't. Even if Ken Irwin really *was* an obliging stud and a carefree male domestic from Butte, Montana, he was something else as well. Something unusual, unsuspected, and possibly dangerous.

She said, 'You can borrow Roger's tuxedo. We always dress for dinner here. I suppose you could call it a last vestige of civilisation.'

Before dinner, in Roger's one-time dressing-room, sitting at a desk that was clustered with photographs of Adele's mother and late father, Ken Irwin made his phone call to San Bernardino.

The phone rang for a long time before it was picked up, and even then there was almost a minute's silence.

Ken said: 'T.F.?'

A voice answered, 'Hi, Ken.'

'T.F., I'm in. She's a touch wary, but nothing to sweat about.'

More silence. Then the voice said, 'Okay, I'll meet you. Same time, same place we talked about.'

'That's fine,' said Ken. 'Any news from you-know-who?'

'Nothing so far.'

57

'Good. I'll keep in touch.'

The phone at the other end was set down, and Ken heard nothing but a long, continuous tone. He laid down his own receiver, and then stood up. Adele was standing in the doorway.

'Did you make your call?' she asked him.

'Sure thing. They said it was okay if I ducked out of those jobs. They have another guy to fill in.'

Adele looked at him, coldly but sweetly, with an expression like sugary grapefruit sorbet. 'I'm sure nobody fills in as magnificently as you do,' she said. 'Now, come eat your dinner. You want to keep your precious strength up, don't you?'

EIGHT

A warm salty wind was blowing in off the Atlantic, and the palms along Miami Beach rustled and tossed. It was eight o'clock on Saturday morning, the most unsettled time of day, and the pale sun was sliding between layers of low-lying cloud. A flock of seagulls wheeled and screamed in the shallow surf.

On the flat rooftop of the Doral Hotel gymnasium, in his purple and yellow Bermuda shorts and his old blue undershirt with CXC embroidered on the breast, Carl X. Chapman was jogging around and around with solitary doggedness. This was what he called his 'dice-shaking hour' – the time when he could juggle around in his mind all the day's upcoming problems and pressures, uninterrupted by his aides, his secretaries, his telephones, his teleprinters, or even his wife. 'I need an hour in the morning to shake those dice the same way other folks need bacon and eggs,' he used to say, too frequently for most of his friends to laugh.

He was a heavy, paunchy man with steel grey hair and a broad, rough face that reminded people of the blunt-

58

speaking, self-made politicians of the Thirties. People said he had somewhat of a fatherly personality, the kind of father who puts his arm around you and tells you to hand half of your candy to your friend, because friendship is greater than all the candy in the world; and you'd hate yourself for loving him so much that you actually did what he said.

It was his paternal manner that had won Carl X. Chapman his second term as Republican Senator from Minnesota. He seemed to be everywhere at once, joking and chiding in his deep, gravelly voice. He seemed to know all of the problems that worried his supporters the most, and when he sat down next to a farmer or a housewife or a factory worker, he could drink beer from the can and eat chicken out of the box, and make them feel that he was prepared to dedicate the whole of the rest of his life to solving their personal anxieties.

His Republican admirers back in Minneapolis-St Paul thought that Carl X. Chapman was the closest they had ever had to a private visit from God. They came up and shook his hand in the street. They sent his family gifts at Christmas. They worshipped him with such fervour that one sarcastic political columnist had asked when he was going to walk on the waters of Lake Minnetonka, and feed the entire population of St Paul Park (five thousand five hundred) on two Mounds bars and a pack of Hamburger Helper.

Carl X. Chapman didn't enjoy sarcastic criticism. In fact, he didn't enjoy any kind of criticism at all. In his view, what he was doing was above judgement, because his cause was the American dream, for every one of those Americans who had earned it. He saw himself as a huge, rugged patriotic figure, under whose stern but kindly eye the people of America would re-learn their very first principles: work and prayer.

He could handle criticism, of course, and although he rarely spoke about it, that was what made him a politician with staying-power as well as popularity. In Washington, he was known as a hard, dirty fighter, and *Rolling Stone* had remarked of his last electoral campaign that 'he heaped so many complex charges of bribery, infamy, hanky-panky and plain old jiggery-pokery on his adversary's head that some voters began to ask if a man who knew so much about all these underhand practises might not conceivably have employed some of them himself.'

But Carl X. Chapman believed in hitting his opponents first, and hitting them so damned hard that they didn't even finish round one. As he jogged around on the roof of his Miami hotel, he occasionally tried a flat-footed Ali shuffle, and shadow-boxed the morning wind. A left, and a right, and a jab in the kidneys.

He had turned sixty-six in May, and he liked to keep himself fit. His father had been allergic to almost everything, including horsehair and shellfish, and his mother had died of pleurisy when he was eight. He had spent a sad, shy childhood in a rundown side-street in Rochester, Minnesota, not far from St Mary's Park, and his father had worked as assistant manager in the Kress dime store. In his mind's eye, he could still see his father arriving home every evening after a ten-hour day, grey-faced and narrow-chested, hanging up his derby on the cheap varnished hall stand. He could picture his mother, too, in the days before she died, her face as pale as soap on the pillow. He still couldn't stand the smell of menthol, because it always brought back the lingering fumes of Leininger's formaldehyde-and-menthol inhalers, which his mother swore to God, right up until the morning she died, had saved her life.

But what stuck sharpest in his mind was the day he had walked nine blocks to the dime store to bring his father his eyeglasses, which he had left behind on the mantelpiece. Carl had wandered around the vast, crowded emporium, stacked floor-to-ceiling with mops and zinc pails and vegetable racks, its counters piled with cheap glittering jewellery and candies and notebooks with multi-coloured pages and combs and plastic ornaments and garish towels so thin and threadbare he wondered how anyone could get dry on them; and at last, in an alcove where they sold locks and door-knobs and latches, he found his father weeping.

He had never known why, and he had never asked.

He had simply handed over the eyeglasses, and run home. But when he grew older, he vowed that the world would never make him hide in a corner, and weep. No bastard was ever going to grind *him* down, no bastard on earth.

He punched at the wind again. A hard left to his father's memory. A harder right to all the creeps and morons who had laid his father so low. His father had done Carl one favour that was beyond price, and that was to put him through college. As a student, he had been awkward and touchy and aggressive; but he was lucky enough to come into contact with an equally belligerent tutor, an Irishman, who butted heads with him hard enough and often enough to make him understand that, without an education, aggression was wasted. He had graduated with honours – one of the toughest, brightest young Republicans around, and by the age of twenty-six, in a pinstriped suit with a vest to match and a well-brushed derby hat, he was elected one of Minnesota's youngest-ever senators.

He found support for his dream of a hard-working America from industrialists and banks and giant corporations, and during the Republican sweep of 1946, heavily financed and supported by Horace Ossenbacker of Ossenbacker Steel, he was returned to the Eightieth Congress, fierce, youthful, splenetic, and raring to make his mark.

Horace Ossenbacker had died in 1951, but not before he had gotten his money's worth out of Carl. Ossenbacker Steel was cleared of anti-trust charges in 1948 in a manner which *The Wall Street Journal* described as 'almost miraculous.'

For his part, Carl X. Chapman plunged into the dirtiest of political fights with the greatest gusto. His name came up in scandals of big business payoffs to Representatives; in Communist witch-hunt trials; in vote-rigging investigations. Now there remained only one honour that Carl X. Chapman wanted, to crown a career that had been brawling, spectacular and profitable. He wanted to be President in 1980. He wanted to be President so deeply that he had never once seriously considered that he wouldn't be. Art Buchwald had once remarked that he had 'a mental mortgage on the White House.'

'Will Carl Chapman be President in 1980?' Carl asked, at receptions and dinner parties. 'Does the Potomac flow to the Chesapeake?'

This morning, Carl jogged around the roof of the Doral-on-the-Ocean Hotel, his belly jumbling up and down with every step, and he turned over the moves he was already making to take him up to the White House door in 1980. Some of the key supporters he was counting on were still perched on a variety of fences, and he knew that his foreign policy wanted licking into much more attractive shape. But these were problems he could tackle as the primaries came closer, and as the issues of the next Presidential contest began to clarify themselves.

What worried him, though, was what he considered to be an unhealthy grass-roots changing of America's political feelings. He claimed he could sense it in the wind; the wind that blew across the Midwest from the Rockies, and the wind that chilled the East. It was a gradual turning-away from national ideals to personal ideals, a laying-down of shared responsibility for America as a family, a weakness of society's spirit.

Carl abhorred this change, and he also feared it. The people who would elect him into office in 1980 would have to be people who believed in a collective national dream, America's dream, Carl Chapman's dream. Those who dreamed their own dreams, at the expense of the greater ideal, were his enemies.

It was almost nine. The low-lying cloud had frittered and fizzled away in the sharp heat of the sun, and he was sweating now. Down below, on the pool deck, the first of the Miami widows had ventured out, an eighty-year-old woman in a harlequin-coloured beach-robe and sunglasses like the back end of a '59 Buick.

He kept on jogging, until he reached the low parapet that overlooked the beach. Then he slowed down, and stopped, and touched his toes a couple of times. He was breathing hard, and he could feel his heart rising and falling like someone wading through the shallows of the sea. He picked up his striped towel from where he had left it on the wall, and dabbed at his face.

A dry, ladylike voice behind him said, 'Good morning, darling.'

Across the roof, with a faintly supercilious smile on her face, came his wife Elspeth. She was wearing an embroidered white kaftan that ruffled in the breeze like the sail of a boat, and her black hair was curled into loose bubbles. Her face, under her huge light-tinted sunglasses, was pinched and lined. It was the face of a political and social huntress; a woman whose eyes are forever peering towards far horizons, and who will never quite believe, even in the presence of royalty and Rockefellers and Huntingtons, that she has actually arrived.

She leaned against the parapet and looked down at the surf.

'I thought I'd find you here,' she said. 'Working off the excesses of the night?'

Carl didn't answer, but folded up his towel and hung it back on the wall.

Elspeth turned towards him. 'How was Henry?' she asked him. 'Did he promise the extra funds? Or did he tell you that you were past it? Presidents are supposed to require a great deal of stamina, you know. Like adulterers.'

Carl looked back at her with a tired, set face. 'Are we going to have this conversation again? Don't you think it's time we talked about something fresh? About the weather, maybe, or the state of the nation?'

She smiled, quite unfazed. 'All you have to do is stop doing it, and then I'll stop talking about it.'

'Elspeth – you're trying to make out that I'm some kind of rampant satyr. I wish I had half the energy to satisfy half the women you think I'm screwing. It's all in your head, Elspeth. It's all up there, in that nutty noddle of yours.'

'Like Helen Pruitt, I suppose. Helen Pruitt, twenty-four-year-old secretary, was just a figment of my fevered imagination.'

Carl gave a short, testy sigh, but he didn't answer. Helen Pruitt was a sensitive subject.

Elspeth said, 'Listen, dear, I know what you're going to say. I'm a scheming, suspicious woman, and I never loved you, and I'm only along for the ride to the White House. Well, believe it or not, that isn't true. I happen to be quite fond of you, and if you ever gave me the chance, I might even be able to like you.'

He grunted. 'You're very generous this morning. What's gotten into you?'

'Oh, spare me the sarcasm, Carl,' she retorted. 'I mean what I say, even if you don't believe me.'

'So what's this adultery talk?'

She took off her sunglasses, and screwed up her eyes against the glare. She had cornflower-blue eyes, and precisely-pencilled eyebrows. A long time ago, back in Minnesota, she had been almost beautiful.

'It's only worth my sticking around if you're going to make it as President, dear, and make it as a husband, too. Right now, I'm not sure you're going to do either.'

'Oh, yes? On what grounds?'

'Cheating will do for starters. Especially cheating as flagrant as yours.'

Carl rubbed his eyes. 'I look down a secretary's cleavage and that's cheating? I'm a man, Elspeth, and it's about time you realised it. I'm a big man with big appetites. Just because you feel inadequate, don't take it out on me. It's not *my* fault you feel inadequate. Haven't I told you enough times that you're adequate?'

'*Adequate?* That's a compliment?'

'It's not an insult.'

Elspeth sat down on the parapet and took out a cigarette, which she knew would annoy him. She cupped her hands over her gold-and-platinum lighter to shield it from the morning breeze, and then blew twin grey flares of smoke from her nostrils.

'I thought we flew down to Miami to do business,' she said. 'That's if you can call coaxing money out of Henry Ullerstam "business."'

'There's nothing wrong with Henry. He's backed us up for years.'

64

'Oh, sure. Just so long as he's gotten a dollar-fifteen's worth of favours out of every dollar he's handed over.'

'He hands over the money, and that's all that counts.'

Elspeth drew deeply at her cigarette, and looked at her husband with a mixture of affection and disappointment. 'So the oil at Waurika didn't count?' she asked him. 'Letting Henry drill in the plumb centre of an environmentally-protected area, that didn't count?'

'It was a deal.'

'A deal?' she asked. 'It wasn't a deal that the environmental protection agency knew much about.'

Carl looked at her hard. 'Elspeth,' he said, 'what are you trying to tell me? You're not getting at Henry, are you? Because if you are –'

She turned her face away. 'I just thought we flew down to Miami to do business, that's all. I guess I forgot that business has its little favours and its little gifts. It was silly of me, really. You've done so many favours for Henry, it shouldn't surprise me so much when he does a favour for you.'

'Favour? What favour?'

'A shapely dinner companion, for instance.'

Carl pursed his lips. 'The only remotely shapely dinner companion we had last night was Olive Ullerstam. And damn it, Elspeth, at least she came along, as *you* should have done.'

She shrugged. 'Those money-grubbing affairs always give me migraine.'

'Your migraine is a pain in the ass.'

Elspeth laughed delightedly. 'You're wonderful. You talk in real life just like you do in the Senate.'

'And you talk just like you do in analysis. You think I have a Jungian urge to screw collectively the brains out of every girl in America.'

'He's Freudian, my analyst, not Jungian.'

'Whatever, he fills you with enough crap to choke the Panama Canal. I can hardly bring myself to pay the stupid bastard's bills.'

Elspeth was furious. 'And what about your precious Dr Lipman? What has he ever done, except pour out two glasses of Old Crow, hand around the cigars, and charge you two-hundred-fifty dollars for two hours' talk about marlin fishing?'

Carl took a long, controlled breath. 'Dr Lipman is a genius. Dr Lipman sorted out all of my identity problems and all of my virility problems.'

'What did he tell you? That sleeping around with young girls restores an old man's self-confidence? If he said that, he's wrong. A thousand million times wrong. Young girls will drain away whatever manhood you happen to have left, Mr Ernest Hemingway Chapman, and bring you face to face with the dotard you really are.'

'Elspeth,' said Carl tiredly, 'this is pretty heavy stuff for nine in the morning. Apart from that, it's totally untrue.'

'What's totally untrue?'

'Whatever you're suggesting.'

'I'm only suggesting that young girls are bad news for old men like you. What did you think I was suggesting?'

Carl looked at her steadily. 'You're suggesting that Henry provided a girl for me last night, aren't you? That's what you're really trying to say – that I was unfaithful again.'

She slowly shook her head. 'I don't know how you've got the damned nerve to look so wide-eyed and innocent,' she said with a bitterness that was as soft as decaying fruit. 'I don't know how you can do what you do and protest that I'm misjudging you.'

'Elspeth, if you think that last night –'

She jerked her head away as if flinching from a horsefly. 'Of course I do,' she told him. 'Last night and a hundred other damned nights. What do you take me for? You come back to my bed at three in the morning smelling of some strange woman's perfume and you don't think I notice? You have dinner in the same damned hotel where I'm lying sick, and you sit by the window with Henry and Olive and some damned floozie with a gold evening gown and red hair and tits that practically poke your eyes out, and you don't think I'll find out?'

'Elspeth, for Christ's sake!'

'Oh, don't be so damned childish,' she begged him. 'I know you don't love me any more. I know you don't even like me very much. But you need me, Carl, for your career; and for whatever I want out of life, I, God help me, need you.'

Carl said, as evenly as he could, 'All right, a redhead *did* sit at my table last night, but only for a while. She happened to come from back home, in Northfield. She wanted to know what I was doing to help out the local welfare programme.'

Elspeth stared at him for a moment, and then laughed at the top of her high-pitched voice. It was like listening to glass breaking.

'The *welfare* programme? Carl, what are you saying? Girls with gold evening gowns and pointed tits are interested in the *welfare* programme! If you'd said abortion, I might have half-believed you. Even dope addiction. But welfare! You want to be President, and you can't even think of a good lie!'

Carl stepped forward and gripped her shoulders. 'Will you quit provoking me?' he warned her, with eyes as hard as industrial diamonds. 'Will you just quit it!'

She looked up at him with undisguised sadness. 'Never,' she said. 'Not for as long as you hold yourself up as an example to other people. Because if I ever did quit provoking you, you'd go your own sweet way, and this country would follow you all the way down to the pits.'

He clenched his fist as if he was about to hit her in the face, but she didn't flinch.

'You wouldn't dare,' she said softly. 'The would-be Presidential candidate, punching the would-be First Lady?'

He let her go. 'I'm going for breakfast,' he said in a cold voice. 'Are you coming?'

She shook her head. 'I want to know that you're going to be faithful before I eat breakfast with you, Carl. I want to know that you're going to be honest and true in whatever relationship we have.'

He looked down at his frayed, worn-out sneakers. 'Elspeth,' he said huskily, 'we have to think of our country as well as ourselves.'

'What does that mean?'

He looked back up at her. 'It means that I've got myself a heavy burden to carry through life, Elspeth, and that sometimes I may stumble and slip. I'm not a saint. I freely admit that. But I'm always going to do my best for you, and I'm always going to do my best for America, and if I fail to live up to your expectations once in a while, or my country's expectations, then I can only beg forgiveness.'

She sat on the parapet in silence for a long, long time. Then she said: 'Go have your sugar-frosted flakes, Carl, before you make me seasick.'

NINE

Carl Chapman showered, shaved, and changed into a red-and-green plaid sports coat, light green pants, and white shoes. Smelling of Aramis aftershave, he went up in the elevator to the twelfth floor, where Henry Ullerstam was staying for the weekend in his permanently-reserved suite. A bulky security officer from Bayshore Oil was standing by the door in a crumpled beige uniform, his expression as stolid as a fire hydrant, and he barred the door as Carl approached.

'Mr Ullerstam home?' asked Carl.

'Who wants to know?'

'Tell him it's the next President.'

When Carl was admitted, Henry Ullerstam, the forty-eight-year-old chairman of Bayshore Oil, was standing by the window in a peacock blue silk bathrobe, eating an English muffin and looking down at a girl in a very small brown bikini on the sundeck of the adjacent hotel.

'Hi, Carl,' he said. 'What do you make of that?'

Carl glanced down. 'Thanks all the same, not this morning.'

Henry raised an urbane eyebrow. He was a tall, good-looking man, with swept-back hair and a hawkish nose. His wife, Olive, always said he looked more like Basil Rathbone than Basil Rathbone, although she herself looked remarkably like Barbara Stanwyck, but couldn't see the similarity at all.

'Young Lollie was all right, wasn't she? She did her stuff? Showed you her specialty?' Henry inquired.

Carl nodded. 'Lollie was fine. She's a lovely girl. But the trouble is Elspeth. She found out about it, God knows how, and she's doing her aggrieved but dignified number. We just had a spat on the gymnasium roof, of all places.'

'I'm surprised at that – her finding out,' said Henry. 'I had Shapiro keep an eye on her door all evening, and he swears she didn't appear once. Maybe she shinned out of the window on a rope of knotted sheets.'

Carl sat down heavily in one of the yellow plush armchairs. He was beginning to feel the strain of his last-minute flight to Miami, his six hours of hard nego-tiation with Henry, his rich dinner of lobster tails and marinated steak, and his strenuous struggling in Lollie's bed, all breasts, legs, arms, and a greedy mouth that wouldn't let him alone. And on top of that, jogging.

'Maybe one of the waiters tipped off Elspeth at break-fast,' Henry said. 'That's possible. But if it's true, I'll have his bow tie snipped in half, his menus torn up, his shoelaces tied together, and make sure he gets dis-charged with dishonour. '

Carl coughed. 'It's not a joke, Henry. Elspeth can make or break me.'

Henry brushed muffin crumbs from his bathrobe. 'I know it's not a joke. But maybe you're letting her scare you too much. She's only a woman, you know, and whatever she says, she wants to be First Lady just as desperately as you want to be President.'

Carl bent forward gloomily. 'I wish I had your con-fidence in her.'

Henry smiled, and sat in the chair opposite, propping his bare feet on the low, glass-topped table. His toes were crooked and there was a prominent bunion on his left foot. 'Perhaps you should pay her a little more attention,' he suggested. 'Woo her with diamonds and furs and frequent kisses. Make love to her now and again.'

Carl sighed. 'I have a feeling you may be right. I wish you weren't.'

Henry reached for the Indian marble cigarette box on the table, took out a cigarette, and lit it. Through the twisting blue smoke, he said, 'It has never ceased to surprise me how the men who yearn to handle the lives of two hundred fifty million people have such elementary difficulty in handling their own. Roosevelt, Kennedy, you name them.'

Carl did not answer. There was nobody else in the universe he would allow to speak to him like that, and even with Henry he didn't trust himself to respond with anything jovial or witty. Instead, he said harshly, 'Did you speak to your finance people?'

Henry blew smoke rings. 'Oh, sure. I had them all out of bed at five this morning.'

'And?'

Henry made a *moue*. 'They like you, and they like what you say. They particularly like your promise to allocate drilling rights in most of the federal oil fields to private operators.'

'But?'

'But, well, they do have *some* reservations,' said Henry.

'What reservations?' asked Carl. '*You* didn't have any reservations, last night.'

'No,' said Henry carefully, 'but then I'm not an accountant. I don't have one of those grim, unimpressible accountant's minds.'

'What's making them feel so grim and unimpressed?'

Henry smiled again, more distantly this time. 'It's hard to put this kindly, Carl, but please understand that it isn't a reflection of my personal feelings towards you as a politician. *Or* as a man. But my accountants feel that your estimate of your popular support in 1980 is a little on the high side. They think you're – well, how shall I put it? – overconfident.'

Carl did not reply. His fingers drummed on the arm of his chair.

'They couldn't understand,' Henry went on, 'how you could expect a voting swing of six to seven percent in your favour. You don't even know what the major voting issues of 1980 are going to be. And you don't have any kind of an opinion-poll profile on how people might accept you as President.'

Carl looked at Henry Ullerstam for a long moment, and then he said, 'What are your accountants trying to tell me, Henry? That the people may not like me?'

Henry raised his hands guardedly. 'You have to understand that accountants always look on the black side. I mean, they're professional pessimists. But they point out that you've been linked in the past with some pretty – I guess you'd call them discredited postures. And because of that, they're not entirely convinced that the voters are going to support you.'

He added, as gently as he could 'Your home state is one thing, Carl, but the nation is another. George McGovern found that out the hard way.'

Carl felt a tight-chestedness that was only partly due to physical exhaustion, and at that, a small part. 'Last night,' he said, 'I told you that I guaranteed my success. I didn't just estimate it, or guess it. I *guaranteed* it.'

'Hmm,' said Henry, finding a fragment of muffin in his lap and popping it into his mouth. 'I'd like to know how.'

'I can't tell you how. Not yet, anyway.'

'Carl,' Henry said with an edge on his voice, 'this isn't just a question of phoning up American Express and checking your credit rating. We're giving you thirteen million dollars, one way or another, and for thirteen million dollars you *have* to tell us how. Do you know what risks we're running, washing that money? We have a trading corporation in Canada, and we have a whole offshore oil-rig project, both specially and specifically set up to launder your campaign funds.'

71

Carl was silent for almost a minute, his hands clasped across his belly. He appeared to be thinking deeply, and Henry Ullerstam watched this process with an expression that was both sardonic and cautionary. As he watched, he puffed away at his cigarette.

Eventually, Carl said, 'There's a tide, you know, in politics, and that tide is the will of the people. First they want one kind of life, then they want another. First they want censorship, then they want free speech. First they want welfare, then they want every man-jack to stand up for himself.'

'Yes, yes,' said Henry, flatly.

'This tide isn't regular, like the tide of the sea. It doesn't seem to have any predictable ebb and flow. It may flood in support of the GOP for ten years, and then unexpectedly turn overnight, and dredge up the Democrats.'

'Nicely put,' said Henry.

'Up until now,' Carl continued, warming to his subject, 'candidates have tossed themselves into this tide like a collection of bottles with messages inside them, and hoped that the tide would take enough notice of their messages to wash them safely up on the shore. Getting elected has been a random, haphazard, helpless kind of business, with no real science applied to it at all. A little marketing, yes. But not science.'

Henry listened to Carl patiently. He had eight houses across America, including two sprawling antebellum mansions in Virginia and North Carolina. He had six private airplanes, fifteen automobiles, two hundred and nine servants, a wife, and three authenticated Van Goghs. He was regarded by most Americans with a sort of suspicious fondness, especially after his practical joke of inviting a prominent Republican statesman and his family to a 'fancy dress' ball, where they discovered on their arrival as five leafy cabbages that they were the only ones in costume.

Henry was witty, pithy, usually charming but unusually astute, especially for a millionaire, and that was why he deemed it a necessary chore to listen to Carl X. Chapman.

Carl stood up, and went across to the window. The girl in the brown bikini was lying on her back now, and there was a tantalizing cleft in her tight briefs. He reluctantly raised his eyes towards Collins Avenue, and the slow-moving morning traffic between the palm trees. He wished, with intense fervour, that Elspeth didn't always make him feel so guilty.

'I found out, Henry, about a year-and-a-half ago, that there *are* ways of predicting how and when popular political opinion will turn in future years.' Carl said this as if it were an announcement of such importance that Henry should applaud. He did not.

Henry Ullerstam merely said, without any of the irony he felt, 'You found out about this, but nobody else did?'

'Nobody else in politics. You see, the trouble with political forecasters and pollsters is that they think in political terms. They forget that their voters are people, not abstract decisions on a voting machine, and because they forget that they're people, they forget that their voters live, and grow, and change their minds, just like people do.'

Henry was silent for a while. Then he said, 'Is that all? Just tides, and beaches, and bottles with messages, and people?'

'I'm trying to explain it simply,' said Carl. 'It's a little more scientific than that.'

'How much more?'

Carl turned. Behind him, the sun shone through the salt-misted window to form an aurora, and Henry almost wondered if he was receiving a divine hint to trust in Carl X. Chapman's political future. But Henry was an oilman, and a financier, and he didn't believe in divine hints.

Carl said, 'You're not doubting my word, are you? You're not saying that Bay Oil doesn't have any confidence in me?'

Henry shook his head. 'Carl, we have confidence. We have faith. But you're asking us to spend thirteen million dollars, and the majority of that is outside the strictest bounds of the law. A sanction for that kind of

73

political investment needs to be supported by evidence. As it stands, we may be better off putting thirteen million dollars on a horse at Santa Anita.'

Carl was about to say something peppery, but then changed his mind. He gave a small smile that meant, 'Okay, you win,' and walked back to his chair.

'Listen, Henry,' he said as he sat down, 'every presidential election has its wild, unpredictable factors. Who can ever tell if a candidate's health is going to stand up to the strain, or if some headcase is going to step out of the crowd and assassinate him? Nobody. But what I've been able to do is reduce the number of unpredictable factors involved and in particular I've cut out the most unpredictable factor of all – the will of the people.

'I promise you that I can predict within a margin of five million votes how this country is going to respond to its presidential candidates in 1980.'

'That's presuming that the presidential candidates are Jimmy Carter and you,' Henry said.

'Well, that's right. I mean, there's still a percentage of doubt about the result of the primaries, but when you look at the potential opposition for nomination, it doesn't really amount to much. There's Mullins, of course, but he's already gotten his feet wet in this hydro-electric scandal in Iowa. Then there's Krolnik. But whoever heard of a President called Krolnik?'

'Don't be so sure,' Henry put in. 'Krolnik's smart.'

'Smart, sure. But not so smart enough. He's done well in Colorado, but he's too young. He's all Adam's apple and cloaked socks. The East doesn't like him, and the South believes he's a junior Richard Nixon.'

Henry said, 'I'm going to have myself a drink. Join me?' and tinkled a small handbell that stood on the table.

Carl looked at Henry narrowly, then said, 'You're going to have to trust me, Henry, at some point or another. I'm asking you to trust me now. I'm asking you to go back to your finance people and say, "Carl X. Chapman is going to be up there in 1980, and that's all there is to it."'

Henry smiled. 'I wish I could. Unfortunately, you've

missed a couple of convincing points.'

'Such as?'

'Come on, Carl, you know what they are. Such as, whether this tide of public opinion which you say you can predict so well is going to turn in your favour or Jimmy Carter's favour? And such as, what are you doing to do about it if it turns against you?'

Carl was silent for a while. Then, in a soft voice, he said, 'I've been thinking about that, and working on that, for quite a while. You're right, of course. The problem isn't predicting the future so much as controlling the future once you've predicted it.'

'And how can you?' asked Henry, smiling but humourless. 'We'll have to know, Carl, before we can pay you the money.'

Carl looked at Henry Ullerstam wearily but keenly. In the would-be President's face, Henry saw a lifetime of political experience, years of in-fighting, decades of disappointments, success, ambition, argument. He knew Carl set himself up as a father-figure, but Henry hadn't been much more than a schoolboy in knee britches when he had first divined the motive forces behind his own father, Albert Ullerstam, and he knew more about the complicated urge for power and wealth than Carl could ever guess.

Carl said, 'How far can I trust you, Henry? Can I trust you with my whole life?'

Henry shrugged. 'If you're elected President, I'll be trusting you with mine.'

A Nordic-looking blonde in a short blue dress and a freshly pressed maid's apron came into the room and said, 'You wanted something, Mr Ullerstam?'

Henry nodded. 'Bring us a jug of dry martini, Trudy. Martini suit you, Senator?'

Carl sat back, appraising the maid. 'I think you're out to kill me before I make my inaugural speech,' he joked. 'Sure, martini's fine.'

Henry lit another cigarette and looked at Carl with new seriousness. 'If we didn't have some trust between us, Carl, we wouldn't have gotten this far. Come on, now, I'm already as deeply incriminated as you are. It's the way that friends have to work. I just need to know how you're going to predict your 1980 result, and if it isn't in your favour, how you're going to make sure that it will be.'

Carl lowered his eyes. He felt strangely humble in front of Henry, as if Henry were his conscience. He had already gone a long way along the road to convincing himself that everything he was doing to get himself elected in 1980 was justified by the crying need of America for a strong, protective President; but this was the first time he had had to convince someone else.

'Before I tell you, I want you to understand that what we're talking about is nothing less important than the destiny of America. I want you to understand what I say in that context.'

'Okay,' replied Henry. 'I'm ready for you, in that context.'

Carl looked uneasy. He hesitated for a while, as if he wasn't sure whether he ought to tell Henry anything or not. But he had worked forty years for this, and his mother had died for this, and his father had wept in a dime store in Minnesota.

He said, thickly, 'It's going to sound shocking, and it's going to sound outrageous. But it's the first positive, long-term action that anyone ever took to save this country from itself.'

TEN

She came awkwardly down the steps of the thirty-foot cruiser, and peered into the gloom. The venetian blinds were angled so that only a few bars of sunlight lit the interior, and the man himself was sitting in the far corner, his face clouded in cigarette smoke.

'Mr Radetzky?'

'Come on in. You're late,' he said.

She clattered on her stacked heels down the last few steps, and then walked into the cabin and looked around. She was chewing gum loudly, and she had the incongruous lack of self-confidence that characterizes very pretty girls with very poor educations. After a couple of turns of the cabin, she sat herself down on a bench seat opposite her host, and crossed her long legs with a lack of grace that was almost hilarious.

'I never went on a boat like this before,' she remarked, chewing gum and grinning.

The man gave a polite little cough. 'If you can help me out, you might even get to own a boat like this for yourself. There's a lot of money in it.'

She giggled, for no apparent reason. She was a tall girl, with striking red hair, a splash of freckles, and green eyes that sparkled as bright as 'go' lights. She had a white cotton bolero top that almost burst its buttons, a bare midriff, and scarlet shorts with a Popeye decal and a white rope belt. As the doorman of the Doral had noted: 'Sex she's got, but class – never.'

The man said, 'You had a good time with Senator Chapman last night, I believe?'

The girl frowned. 'What does that mean?'

The man waved away the cigarette smoke with his hand. He was young, not much more than twenty-seven or twenty-eight, with an oval, blue-chinned face that looked like an egg that had been dipped in writing ink. His black hair was cut in a college crop, and he wore a shiny blue Nixonite suit, with white collar and necktie. There was a calm, composed, professional air about him, as if he knew exactly what he was doing at all times, and why.

He said, 'We don't have to play hide-and-go-seek, Miss Methven. I know what you did, and I can prove it, and I'm not here to report you for it, or run you in for it, or even snitch to your mother about it.'

The girl looked a little twitchy. 'I did it fair and square,' she said. 'I just did what I was told. The man paid me, and I just did what I was told.'

'Sure,' said Mr Radetzky calmly. Behind him, through a row of parallel chinks in the blinds, she could see the water of Biscayne Bay, and the noon traffic moving to and fro along Collins Avenue.

The girl said, 'What does "sure" mean? If you're not going to report me for it, or snitch about it, why did you ask me here? You're going to give me a medal of commendation or something?'

Mr Radetzky almost smiled. 'For your performance, you deserve one. Look at this.'

He pressed a button beside him, and with a quiet hum, a white movie screen descended from the bulkhead. Then he pressed another button, and a projector started to whirr, filling the screen first with brilliant white light, then with flickering numbers, then, to the girl's fascinated horror, with a grainy but explicit film of two naked people on a wide, king-sized bed, a red-headed girl in nothing more than black stockings and black garters, and a heavy-bellied man with grey hair.

'Oh my God,' she whispered. 'I'm in the movies.'

On the screen, the red-headed girl caressed and fondled the elderly man, and straddled him with stretched garters and swinging breasts. Then she kissed him all down his grey hairy belly, and guzzled at him with obvious relish. The grey-haired man kept his eyes tight shut and his face contorted until it was all over, until the girl looked up at him with creamily anointed lips and chin. There was no soundtrack.

The film faded, and finished. Mr Radetzky switched off the projector, and pressed the button which retracted the screen. Then he looked at the girl with a patient smile.

'Your name is Dolores Methven,' he said. 'You are a part-time go-go dancer, part-time hatcheck girl, part-time lady for hire. You live with your widowed mother in El Portal. You were employed last night by men working for Mr Henry Ullerstam of Bayshore Oil. They paid you three hundred dollars to go to Room 1126 at the Doral Hotel and give an unidentified old gentleman the time of his life.'

Mr Radetzky coughed, and took out a pack of Luckies. He offered them to Lollie Methven, but she shook her head and kept on chewing her gum.

'What neither you nor Mr Ullerstam nor your old gentleman knew was that your old gentleman was under close surveillance by me. Your time of arrival at the hotel was logged, as was your time of departure. Everything you did in Room 1126 was recorded on film.'

Lollie Methven blinked uncomfortably. She said, 'I was doing my job. I was doing what they asked me. Would you turn down three hundred dollars for sucking some old guy's dork? Well, maybe you would.'

Mr Radetzky raised his hand. 'I'm not accusing you of anything. I'm not blaming you, I'm not running you in. I'm a private investigator, not a cop. I'm working for Mrs Chapman on divorce evidence against Senator Chapman, that's all.'

'Well, isn't that all the evidence you need? The movie?'

Mr Radetzky shook his head. He seemed to Lollie like a horribly cold fish, the kind of john you went to bed with, and then discovered he had freezing feet. She could imagine him getting his rocks off by balling a girl when he was dressed up in rubbers and a raincoat, his pockets filled with mackerel.

'What you did last night with Senator Chapman was sufficient evidence for a successful divorce in law,' said Mr Radetzky. 'But it wasn't enough for Mrs Chapman. She wants incontrovertible evidence of adulterous intercourse before she's going to feel satisfied that the Senator is seeking more than, well, casual relief.'

Lollie's gum-chewing slowed down. 'What do you want *me* to do about it?' she asked him. 'Ball the guy in front of his wife?'

'You don't have to go that far. All I want you to do is agree to fly to Las Vegas next Wednesday, meet up with Senator Chapman at the Scirocco Hotel, go to bed with him, and make sure that you have intercourse. All the surveillance and collection of evidence you can leave to me.'

Lollie's eyes narrowed. 'This isn't some kind of set-up, is it? I'm a girl doing what she does best, Mr Radetzky, that's all.'

Mr Radetzky shook his head again. 'You don't have

anything to worry about. All you have to do is go when you're called, do what you're told, and one thousand dollars, in cash, is all yours.'

He took out a maroon Cartier billfold, and produced a pair of hundred dollar bills, both freshly minted.

'These,' he said quietly, 'are a small expression of our confidence in you.'

Lollie Methven stared at the money for a long time. Mr Radetzky then placed the money on the cabin table. Beneath their feet, the cruiser gently rose and dipped in the swell of Biscayne Bay.

'You'll call me?' Lollie asked uncertainly. 'And you'll pay for my fare to Las Vegas?'

Mr Radetzky nodded.

'Okay, then,' said Lollie. 'The guy's a goddamned bourgeois anyway. I'll do it.'

She picked up the bills, expertly folded them, and tucked them into her tight cleavage. Mr Radetzky sat back, and smiled. 'I can promise you won't regret this,' he said. 'I can really, truly promise that.'

ELEVEN

On Tuesday morning, John came to collect her from the hospital. It was cool and overcast, and the smog had draped downtown Los Angeles in sad veils of grey. He drove into the parking lot in a dented orange Volkswagen with a long waggling CB antenna and a lipsticked mouth painted on the hood.

He wearily climbed out of the car and wedged the door shut with a sharp thump from his hip. He was over the worst of the shock now. Since Friday, he had drunk four bottles of whisky, listened to Santana at such earsplitting loudness that his ears hurt, taken long and solitary walks up the canyon until it was too dark to see, and even smoked joints of sneezeweed yarrow, which his next-door neighbour Mel had described as 'like waking up in the morning and finding you've eaten your herbal pillow in your sleep.'

He looked white and grieved, but those hideous moments on the freeway were already becoming memories, instead of fresh, clamorous impressions. He was beginning to cope with what had happened in spite of his need for mourning, and even seek out some kind of reason why it had.

She was waiting for him in the hospital entrance-hall, in a dark blue sweater and white jeans. Her dark hair was tied back under a yellow scarf because it wanted washing, and she still had a yellowish bruise under one eye.

He kissed her, and held her tight for a long, wordless moment. Then he stood back and looked at her.

'I guess if there's anything to be thankful for, it's just that at least two of us survived,' he said hoarsely. He knew there were tears in his eyes, and he knew how sentimental he sounded, but it was the way he felt.

'Let's go,' she said. 'I can't take much more of this place.'

He picked up her suitcase, and they walked down the steps to the parking lot, under a sky the colour of pearls.

'What car did you bring?' she asked him.

'Mel lent me the Volkswagen.'

'Did the repair people tell you anything about the Imperial?'

He shrugged. 'They're not very optimistic. In fact, they're downright gloomy. The guy from the spares department said that he used to stock air suspension parts for the Chrysler Imperial, but they got lost during the Great Flood.'

They arrived at the shabby, battered Beetle, and John kicked the driver's door to open it.

'This car is masochistic, like all Germans,' he said. 'If you dig your fingernails into the upholstery, it gives you an extra five miles an hour in third.'

Vicki held his arm. He turned and looked at her, and her wide brown eyes were very serious.

'You don't have to crack jokes, John. Not if you don't want to. I can get along with a little sadness, if that's the way you feel inside.'

He nodded. He had to clear his throat before he could answer her.

'Thanks,' he said quietly. 'There will be one or two moments. But mostly I'm okay.'

He let down the driver's seat, and wedged Vicki's suitcase into the back. They climbed in, and sat there side by side, looking out through the dusty windshield and wondering what to say next.

Vicki said, 'Doesn't this car have CB?'

John shook his head. 'All Mel could afford was the antenna. He's saving up for the rest of the stuff next year.'

Vicki touched his hand. 'What are you going to do now? About your father?'

'Bury him first.'

'And then?'

He took a deep swallow of air. 'I don't know. The police keep telling me it's all in hand, they know what they're doing. But they don't seem to have any leads to work on, not one. And if they can't catch the Strangler, what hope do they have of catching this guy? The Freeway Fruitcake, they call him. Good old police department humour.'

'Come on, John. They're only cops acting like cops. They're doing their best.'

He turned the ignition key, and the motor whinnied like an old mare. He revved it once or twice, and a black cloud of smoke rose from out of the tailpipes.

'How Mel has the goddamned nerve to call himself a committed environmentalist and drive around in a travelling pollution crisis like this, I will never understand,' said John, as they backed up, and turned to manoeuvre through the white hospital gates.

He was still arm-wrestling with the gear-shift when there was a brisk rap at the car window. Vicki said, 'John.'

John looked up. It was Detective Morello, in a linen

suit that looked as if he had slept in it, and then lent it to his grandfather, who had slept in it as well. John wound down the window, and said: 'Yes?'

'Hi there, Mr Cullen, how are you? And that's Miss Wallace, isn't it?'

'That's right.'

'I thought I recognised her. You're looking better, Miss Wallace. You, too, Mr Cullen.'

'Well, thanks,' said John, uncomfortably conscious of the Beetle's racketing engine, and the oily smoke belching out of the back.

Detective Morello said, 'We turned up the killer's car this morning. It was an Avis rental from Hollywood. A boy scout found it way up in Big Dalton Canyon. The forensic boys are looking it over now.'

'Do you think they'll find anything?' John asked.

'Hard to say. There's nothing obvious. No prints, or anything like that. But you can tell a lot about a man from the car he drives, even if it's only a rental.'

'Is there any chance of catching him?' Vicki said quietly.

Detective Morello pulled a face. 'Who knows? It depends on whether he does something careless and stupid. So far, he's managed to cover his tracks pretty good.'

'But you still believe he's a psycho?' John asked.

Detective Morello's eyes narrowed. 'What do you mean? What else could he be?'

'I don't know. It just seems pretty strange to me that a guy with a mental disorder can kill twelve people on three different freeways and still manage to cover his tracks.'

'You think, because he's a psycho, he's going to leave clues all over?'

'You tell me. That's what *I'm* asking.'

Detective Morello hunkered down beside the car, and his face appeared at the open window as if he were putting on a puppet show.

'Let me tell you something,' he said gravely. 'Your average psycho kills because he believes he has some kind of mystical mission in life to destroy others. Because of that, he kills without a conscience, and because he kills without a conscience he is hardly ever flustered or hurried in what he does. Your average psycho thinks about details that most sane killers wouldn't even dream about.'

'For example?' Vicki asked, in a hushed voice that she wasn't even sure Detective Morello had heard.

'For example, we had a hit-and-run headcase about six or seven years back. He washed off the tyres of his car with soap and water after every homicide, and then drove through a special patch of dirt he kept in his back yard. He'd brought that dirt all the way down from Sausalito, and the Sausalito dirt on his tyres was supposed to prove that he'd been visiting his mother in Mill Valley at the time of the killing. We broke his story in the end, though. One of our forensic people pointed out that he would have had dirt on his tyres from every inch of Interstate 5 between here and San Francisco if he'd really been there, instead of just one particular dirt.'

John gave a tight smile. 'I see.' He didn't really feel like talking about police procedure at this moment. The Volkswagen was rattling and shaking, and uncomfortably hot inside, and he was beginning to break out in a sticky, feverish sweat.

He kept seeing his father's face in those last seconds before the killer started shooting, and hearing that gentle, humorous voice saying. '*You* were nervous? I was having an acute attack of the sweaty palms.'

He said to Detective Morello, 'Will you let us know if you hear anything?'

Detective Morello nodded. 'Sure thing. We'd like you take a look at some more ID pictures some time during the week in any case.'

'But if you find out anything about the guy's motive, you'll let us know then?'

Detective Morello took out his handkerchief, and began to fold it into a pad in preparation for blowing his nose. 'I'm not sure that I understand you.'

'Detective Morello,' John said, 'I need to know that

my father didn't die because of some stupid outrageous twist of bad luck. I need to know that he died for some purpose. Because of what he was, or what he believed in.'

Detective Morello blew his nose. 'Not many people die like that, Mr Cullen. I'm sorry.'

John stared at him. Then he turned away, and rubbed his neck tiredly, and said, 'Sure, you're right. I didn't mean to make you feel that you weren't doing your job. I guess it's a little hard to accept, that's all, dying for nothing.'

The detective said, 'A young woman was driving home in her Pinto this morning along Santa Monica Boulevard, and a drunk in a custom van came speeding at sixty miles an hour across the stop signals at La Brea and smashed her to death. Just think about it.'

Vicki said to Detective Morello, 'I believe he has enough to think about right now, officer. We'll be on our way.'

Detective Morello stood up. 'I'll keep in touch,' he promised. 'And do me one favour, will you?'

'What's that?'

'Have your exhaust fixed. I don't want my prime witnesses picked up for emission violation.'

John nodded, and engaged first gear. As he drove out of the hospital gates into the traffic of downtown Los Angeles, he didn't know whether to laugh, or stay silent, or bury his face in his hands and weep for all the people who die because of carelessness, and random malice, and for all those confused and bitter friends they leave behind.

TWELVE

They finally reached their steep curving driveway on Topanga Canyon with the orange Beetle coughing and sighing like an old asthmatic. John parked under the trees in front of their green verandah, and climbed out. He stretched, and took a deep breath of the canyon air, and looked up through the leaves at the hazy blue sky.

'John – the car's slipping backwards!' Vicki yelped.

John turned, tugged open the driver's door, and wrenched up the handbrake just in time. Then, gripping the brake tight, he told Vicki, 'Bring me a couple of those housebricks, will you? I forgot that Mel told me to chock the wheels on a gradient. Worn brakes, you know? It once ran all the way through a parking lot and halfway across Sunset, and didn't hit another car once. So he says, anyway. You know what Mel's like.'

'What *is* Mel like?' asked Mel, coming across the sloping drive with a large frosted flagon of Chablis. He was squat, and bearded, with horn-rimmed glasses and a belly that stretched his checkered cowboy shirt to the limit.

'Mel is generous and thoughtful to a fault,' said Vicki. 'Mel is also wonderful and wise, and the best neighbour anyone could wish for, provided they want to lose their life in an orange Volkswagen.'

Mel came up and kissed her. 'You keep your life, honey. It's too precious to lose any place at all. Hi, John. How are you?'

'On the way upward, thanks. Is the wine for us?'

'A little coming home present. I know that hospital wine is lousy.'

'What hospital wine?' asked Vicki. 'I didn't know they had hospital wine.'

'That's what's lousy about it.'

John pulled Vicki's suitcase out of the car, and the

three of them went up the flaking green steps of the house, across the verandah, and inside. The house was a quiet, dignified old place of weathered wood. It had been built by a retired set painter almost twenty years ago, as a retreat from the rest of the world, and a place where he would work on paintings that were only a few inches square, instead of acres. It had escaped one serious fire after another because of its unusual location in an isolated hollow, and it was one of the oldest dwellings in the canyon, with a gambreled roof, a balcony of carved Tyrolean-style railings, and shuttered windows.

John and Vicki had been working with patience and care to restore the house, and the living room into which they walked this morning was already finished. There was a high carved mantelpiece, crowded with Staffordshire figurines, a pine floor that was polished like glass, and elegant antique chairs upholstered in velvet the colour of dark grapes. Through the wide French windows, there was a green shady view of trees, and dappled daylight, and flowers.

Vicki brought out three green-stemmed hock glasses, and John opened the wine.

Mel said: 'Do you know a guy with blond hair? Looks like a surfer, or a football jock?'

'No,' said John, pouring wine. 'Not unless you mean Sammy, and he's on vacation in Hawaii.'

'Well, I didn't recognise him either,' said Mel. 'But he was around here this morning, when you were out. He came up the driveway, looked over the place, and then left.'

John handed Vicki her wine, and she glanced at him apprehensively.

'You don't think it's anything to do with what happened on the freeway?' she asked him. 'I mean it couldn't be him again, could it?'

John shook his head. 'I don't think it's anything. Probably some tourist looking around. Just because some maniac decides to use us for target practice on the freeway doesn't mean he's going to follow us around wherever we go.'

Vicki sipped at her wine. 'I've had nightmares about

it,' she said. 'Nightmares of men with dark hair, and cars that kept chasing me, and trying to kill me.'

'Well, there you are,' Mel said. 'This guy was a blond. A harmless, ordinary, all-American blond.'

Vicki went to the window. Her pale reflection looked back at her from the green garden like a lost ghost of herself. 'I hope you're right,' she said. 'Right now, I feel as if I'm never going to sleep properly again.'

'What did this blond guy look like?' John asked. 'Was he young, or what?'

'It's pretty hard to say,' Mel answered, scratching at his gingery beard. 'He was rugged, you know, and pretty well-built. Athletic, I'd say, but more like throwing the javelin than running. Wore a plaid shirt and jeans. But I couldn't pick him out in a crowd. Half the guys in California look like that, and the other half look like me.'

Vicki turned nervously away from the window. 'I hate a mystery. I like everything to be explicable. I guess I'm just being Capricornian.'

John grinned. 'Why don't you start being Aquarian and run yourself a bath and wash your hair? Then you won't smell like Dr Kildare's second-string date any more. In the meantime, I'll fix us some good ol' home-cooked hamburgers. Mel, could you get yourself around a good ol' home-cooked hamburger?'

Mel chuckled. 'Asking me if I want one of your good ol' home-cooked hamburgers is like asking if I want to take my next breath.'

'Well, you can take your next breath if you prefer. It's cheaper.'

'I won't be long,' Vicki said. 'Don't eat all the pickles before I get back.'

Mel raised his glass to her, and as she walked across the room called: 'Vicki.'

She turned. A cloud crossed the sun, and dulled the house.

Mel said, 'I just want to drink a toast, to whatever fates there are, that you're safe and well. We'd have been pretty lonesome up here in the canyon without you.'

88

Vicki nodded, and her eyes were a little moist. She came over and kissed Mel's forehead, and whispered, 'Bless you, Mel. Bless all friends.'

John had refilled his glass, and walked through the carved pine archway nto the kitchen. He took the ground beef out of the icebox, and started chopping onions and herbs. He opened the kitchen window, and there was a warm fragrant smell of California fall, and a view down the valley between the trees towards Topanga and the road. Mel came in with his wine, and perched himself on a wooden stool by the breakfast bar.

'This thing's hit Vicki pretty hard, hasn't it?' he said.

John looked up. 'More than she's telling.'

'Can her shrink help her? Who does she see these days?'

'She's into natural reflective healing. We both are.'

'Natural reflective healing? I never heard of that.'

'Sure you have,' John said, beating an egg into the ground beef, and seasoning it with pepper and thyme. 'It's when you look at yourself in the mirror first thing in the morning, and say to yourself, "Good morning, you well-adjusted person, why does a well-adjusted person like you need to waste ten thousand bucks a year on a psychoanalyst?"'

Mel opened the glass jar of hazelnuts and shook a few into the palm of his pudgy hand. 'Maybe she'd like to join in my TA sessions. I mean, it seems to me that she's been traumatized by this shooting, and it's going to take some pretty supportive stuff to get her out of it.'

'You'll have to ask her. She's an independent lady.'

'I know it. It's real sad that it had to happen to her. And to you, too. Do you think you're over the worst of it yet?'

John slickered oil over the broiler pan, and lit the gas. 'I guess I've accepted he's dead. But it's not the killing itself that shocks me so much. It's how senseless it was. I can't come to grips with the mind of any person who kills at random, innocent people, for no reason whatever. I think of my father, you know, and he was nothing more than a mild, ordinary, kind person. That's all. I could have accepted his death a little easier if he'd worked for the Mafia, or the KKK, or if he'd been into unions. But he was just a guy.'

Mel said, 'Do you think the cops are talking sense about that?'

'About what?'

'About this Freeway Fruitcake. I mean, do you really believe he kills people at random?'

John frowned. The oil was spluttering now, and he took down a blue-and-white striped butcher's apron and hung it around his neck. There was a pungent aroma of scorched beef and herbs.

'I don't understand what you're trying to say. The guy's a psychopath, that's all. He kills people because he feels like it. Anyone who happens to be passing.'

Mel took off his spectacles and wiped the lenses. His eyes were pale blue and myopic. 'I did a course, once, in analytical thinking,' he said. 'Some of it was kind of weird, but they did teach me one useful thing, and that was to stop making superficial assumptions.'

'A guy shoots twelve totally unrelated people on the freeway, and it's a superficial assumption that he's a fruitcake?'

'It's a superficial assumption until you prove it. And it seems to me, from what you've said, that the cops aren't doing very much to prove it.'

'They're looking for the killer. What else can they do?'

'They could try a little analytical thinking, and look at the victims instead.'

John turned the hamburger patties over with his skillet. He said quietly, 'They won't have much trouble finding my father. He's lying in the funeral parlour right now.'

Mel nodded, in quiet acceptance. 'I know that, John. I'm not trying to rub salt in your wounds. But I've never believed in totally random events. I don't believe that a guy goes around shooting people for no reason whatever. That's why I think that the cops ought to take another look for what the victims were, and see whether they have anything in common.'

John looked up. He looked sad and tired, but Mel

knew how much he wanted to believe that his father hadn't been killed for no purpose.

'The first thing they have in common is that they were all shot by the same guy,' John said.

'And what else?'

'Nothing. Nothing at all. There was a housewife, a notions salesman, a garage mechanic, an insurance salesman. All different ages, all different backgrounds.'

'You're talking like a cop,' Mel said.

'What the hell do you mean, I'm talking like a cop?'

'You're talking like a cop because you're describing those people in terms of what they were on the *outside*, not what they were on the *inside*.'

John went to the green enamel bread-bin to fetch the buns. 'I don't understand what you're trying to tell me. Talk plainer.'

'Okay, I'll talk plainer. You're a dog-walker, right?'

'Right.'

'Okay,' Mel said, 'if you were filling out a computer-dating sheet to meet the lady of your dreams, would you describe yourself as a dog-walker?'

John thought about it. Then he said, 'Well, I guess not. I might wind up with some chick who likes dogs. I might even wind up with a dog.'

'So what would you put down?'

'Jesus, I don't know. Something like "sensitive, liberal, charismatic male, with fondness for bizarre automobiles, Stravinsky, and balling on the beach."'

'Well, that's precisely my point,' said Mel. 'A police description is completely superficial, having to do only with what a person is on the surface. So you've got a housewife and a notions salesman and a garage mechanic. But how do you know that they're not all Stravinsky lovers, or Dodgers supporters, or ballers on the beach? How do you know that they don't have something in common which made this guy want to kill them?'

'Mel,' John interrupted, 'if my father and all these people were shot because they had something in common, then what you're suggesting is that all their murders were premeditated, worked out, calculated.

91

You're suggesting that guy trailed us, and shot my father deliberately.'

Mel helped himself to another glass of Chablis, and topped up John's glass, too. 'I'm not suggesting anything. I'm just saying that it's a possibility. And so far, it's a possibility that the police haven't disproved.'

John sat down on the stool next to Mel. He let out a long breath, and ran his hand tiredly through his hair.

'I know this mood, Mel. It's the same mood you were in when you tried to persuade me to join that nude UFO society.'

'Well, *that* was a ball,' Mel said with a wry smile. 'I picked up that female wrestler there, you remember, Vivienne.'

'Who could ever forget Vivienne? She couldn't open a door without tearing the handle off.'

Mel grunted, with remembered amusement. But then he said, 'I'm not trying to pressgang you into doing something you don't want, John. I hope you know me well enough for that. But ever since your father was killed, I've been thinking about this psychopath, and somehow he just doesn't seem like a psychopath at all.'

'What do you mean?'

'I mean that a psychopath wouldn't go to all the trouble that this guy goes to. I've been checking back on all the cuttings in the *Los Angeles Times*. Here, I've brought most of them with me.'

He took out of his back pocket an untidily-folded collection of torn-out pieces of newspaper, and spread them on the breakfast bar.

'You see this one here. This was a housewife. She was shot by a bullet from an M-16 while she was travelling home on the Hollywood Freeway after taking her daughter to riding class. She joined the freeway at Buffside Drive, and she was only going as far as the next exit at Primera Avenue. The sniper who shot her had to get into Universal City Studios with an M-16, escape supervision long enough to reach a point overlooking the freeway, shoot the woman, and escape. He did it all, according to what the police said here, in less than fifteen minutes. It may have been quicker. In other words, he must have worked out what he was going to do, where he was going to do it from, and how he was going to do it, all in advance. Would a man who works all that out, and goes to that much trouble, just shoot any passing driver for the hell of it?'

John picked up the cutting, and read it silently.

'Here's another. This is the garage mechanic. He was shot on the Ventura Freeway from a red Chevy which had trailed him all the way from Pasadena to Sherman Oaks. The interesting thing here is that eyewitnesses saw the Chevy behind him in Pasadena, and more eyewitnesses saw the Chevy behind him at Sherman Oaks. But right here it says that he left the freeway for a while at North Hollywood to buy some gas. So the killer must have followed him off the freeway, waited for him to tank up, and followed him back on to the freeway again.'

John went back to the stove, and gave the hamburgers a final flip.

'That still doesn't prove that the killings were planned,' he said. 'It might just show that the guy's even more psychopathic than anyone imagined. Maybe he just picks someone out at random, and trails them.'

Mel shook his head. 'Uh-huh. If he gets psychopathic kicks from picking someone out at random and trailing them, then that's what he'd do all the time. But he doesn't. He chops and changes his method according to the person he wants to kill. If the victims have a behaviour pattern of passing a particular spot on a particular freeway at the same time every day, then he tends to snipe at them from a fixed position. But if they have irregular habits, then he tends to trail them and shoot them car-to-car. Like, I'm sorry to say, your father.'

John took the sesame buns out of the toaster and set them on Chinese bird-patterned plates. Then he dished up the hamburgers, sliced up an onion for garnish, and handed one to Mel.

'You've really been thinking about this, haven't you?' he said.

'Thinking is my hobby. Especially thinking about my friends.'

93

John looked at him for a long, serious moment. 'Do you really believe that any of this could be true? That any of these twelve people *do* have something in common?'

Mel bit into his hamburger, and munched it. 'Mmm. This is terrific. If God ever made hamburgers, this is what they'd taste like.'

John said, 'You're evidence is pretty thin on the ground. Just because this guy takes a lot of trouble, that doesn't prove that he wanted to kill anybody in particular.'

'No, it doesn't. But it's worth checking out, right?'

John nodded. It gave him a peculiar kind of pain, thinking that his father may have been killed because of some affinity with eleven other people he didn't even know, all extinct now, and stiff in their strangers' graves. But it was a more acceptable pain than the agony of believing that his father had died because of some lunatic chance, for no reason except to thrill briefly the hypothalamus of a homicidal madman.

They walked through to the living room. Vicki had just come downstairs from washing her hair, and she sat on the sofa in a black silk dressing gown that clung to her body with static. A red towel was wrapped around her head, and she looked strikingly pale.

They drew chairs up to the coffee table, which was too low for eating, and bent themselves over their hamburgers.

Vicki said, 'I didn't think I'd be hungry. But I could eat about five of these.'

'I always knew you should have lived with someone like J. Wellington Wimpy,' John smiled. 'I'm just too ascetic for you.'

'Do you think we might go talk to a couple of people?' Mel asked.

'What people?' John wanted to know.

'Well, the survivors. Relatives, friends, whatever.'

Vicki looked at John, worried and uncomprehending. 'The survivors?' she asked.

John put down his hamburger. 'Mel thinks that these killings on the freeway may not be random. He thinks

94

all the victims may have had something in common, something which led this maniac to shoot them.'

Vicki was silent for a while, shocked. Then she asked John, 'And what do *you* think?'

He shrugged. 'I'm not sure. I can't understand what my father could have had in common with any of those other people, but as Mel rightly says, we don't know what they were like.'

'They were just innocent people, weren't they?' said Vicki.

Mel nodded. 'Innocent, sure, as far as sanity and logic goes. But they might all have been guilty of some imagined crime in the mind of this psychopath. And if they were, then they were probably all guilty of the same crime.'

'Crime? What kind of crime?' Vicki persisted.

'Psychopaths can turn anything into a crime,' Mel said. 'I read about a case where a woman went around trying to kill anyone who looked like one of her high school classmates, because she always felt her classmates had borne her a grudge. And there was a guy in Medellin, Colombia, who stabbed eight people because their names came before his in the telephone book.'

'But surely the police know all this? Why do *we* have to get involved?'

'The police are too busy with conventional thinking,' John said. 'That's what Mel believes, anyway. And I guess I kind of agree with him.'

'So you're going to play detective?'

'It's no worse than walking dogs.'

'It's a damned sight more dangerous. What if this psychopath finds out what you're doing?'

'How could he?'

'How did he track us down and shoot your father?'

'I don't know. But I think I'd like to find out.'

Vicki set down her plate and reached across the table to hold John's hands.

'John,' she said quietly.

He lowered his eyes.

'Why don't you leave it alone, John? Why don't you just bury your father with dignity, and let the police deal with the rest of it? They know what they're doing. They must have dealt with hundreds of cases like this before.'

'They don't think analytically,' said Mel.

Vicki didn't answer. She just repeated huskily, 'Why don't you leave it alone, John? Please. For my sake.'

John paused, and then squeezed her hands. 'Let me go see just one. I have to know if there's a germ of truth in it, Vicki. I have to know that he didn't get killed for some totally inane reason.'

She let her hands drop. Mel looked at her, and then back to John. Outside the window, in the leafy garden, the sun came out again, and lit the quiet room in flickering shades of green and yellow.

Vicki put her hand to her mouth, and the tears began to slide silently down her cheeks.

THIRTEEN

He sat on a wooden chair in his room on San Juan Avenue, with the dismantled M-14 across his knees. He had tied the stained net curtain back so that he could look out over the flaking window-ledge down to the street, and watch the mid-morning traffic. The sun was still hazed by smog, but it was growing warmer, and the weather report had advised of temperatures up to the high 70s.

He knew and loved the M-14. For the particular task he was preparing it, the M-14 was the perfect weapon. An angled shot of about ninety feet through a very narrow aperture. Up in the mountains, practising, he had been able to snip single blades of grass with it, shoot petals off flowers.

On the television, in black and white, Clark Gable was saying something serious and passionate in *The Homecoming*. The tall man with the slicked-back hair

96

had seen *The Homecoming* four times already, but he found repetition comforting rather than boring. On the edge of his bed beside him, there was a copy of *Hustler* open at the centre-spread, and it occurred to him that it might be amusing to take it out with him next target practice, and see how many bullets he could shoot through that wide-apart, unnaturally pink pussy.

He began to re-assemble the M-14 with care and skill. He had modified the sights slightly to help him with a downward shot, and he had eased the trigger tension so that a light brush of his fingertip would fire it. According to his information, the aperture through which he was going to have to shoot was less than three inches wide, and the rifle was going to have to stay as steady as humanly possible.

He was going to take the M-16 with him, in case he needed power at close range. But he didn't like the M-16's horizontal drift, and he found the pistol-grip clumsy and awkward. He only used it for quick freeway sniping when muzzle velocity was more important than finesse.

On the street below, a police car passed, and he watched it until it had turned the corner into Electric Avenue. Then he raised the rifle and gave it a final inspection. It was immaculately clean, exquisitely balanced. Someone had once told him that all guns smell of death, but this one smelled of nothing but metal and light oil.

He began to think of food and sex. This was Tuesday, and he usually went up to Hollywood Boulevard on Tuesday, to see a blue movie. He liked the movies where girls were hurt, or tied up. He was also fascinated by golden rain movies, although his interest in them sometimes made him feel guilty. Afterwards, he would cross the street and have a chili dog and a cup of coffee, and then see what young girls were cruising the sidewalks. He wondered if one of the girls would do the golden rain bit for an extra ten. He coughed.

Upstairs, across the creaking floorboards of Mrs Santini's apartment, he heard the heavy high-heeled rhythms of the samba, accompanied by a kind of hesitant shuffling. The shuffling was Mrs Santini's pupil, as she tried to teach Spanish dancing. Mrs Santini had a face like an angry buzzard, and long decorative pins through her greasy black hair. Samba was five dollars, rhumba six-fifty, complete flamenco course fifteen-oh-five, with tax; a tussle on the groaning springs of her bed, with her red skirt pulled up to her waist and her hairpins stuck into the side of the mattress for safety, eight-sixty-five.

The tall man stood up, and untied the net curtain so that it fell back across the window. He stayed unmoving for two or three minutes, as if he was trying to come to an important decision. Then the telephone rang, and the sound of it unexpectedly evoked the taste of salt in his mouth.

FOURTEEN

It was one of those orderly, white-painted, one-storey houses on 6th Street between San Vicente and Fairfax. A slightly worn beige Cutlass was parked in the driveway, and a small boy with a serious face was playing on the verandah with a pull-along Fisher-Price toy dog. They drew up in Mel's dilapidated Volkswagen, and climbed out. It was just after three, and the afternoon was stuffy and warm.

John and Vicki walked up to the house hand-in-hand, with Mel a little way behind them. The boy watched them curiously as they came up the steps of the verandah, one of his eyes screwed up against the sunshine.

'Is your mother home?' asked John.

The boy nodded.

'That's a nice dog you have there,' Mel remarked, as John went up to the front door to press the bell.

The boy nodded again.

'Does he sit up and beg?' asked Mel.

98

The boy shook his head. 'Nope. But if you come too close, he'll bite your leg off.'

Mel chuckled. He was still chuckling as the front door opened, and a pale-faced woman with greying hair and a washed-out print dress stepped out on to the verandah. Her expression was one of such defeat and tiredness that his chuckling died in his throat.

'Mrs Daneman?' John asked.

The woman looked at them, her chin held high. She could never have been particularly pretty. Her hair was too coarse and her nose too large. But now she seemed to have been pressed between the pages of a heavy book, like a wild flower, and lost all of her colour and all of her substance. A dried memory of what she once was.

'I don't know you, do I?' she said.

John cleared his throat, embarrassed. 'We didn't mean to intrude. But we were hoping you could help us.'

Mrs Daneman's eyes squinted against the light as if she were used to rooms where the blinds were always drawn, or as if her evenings were filled with nothing but reading and watching television.

She said, 'Is this religious? You're not Mormons, are you?'

'We're just folks, ma'am, like you,' Mel said. 'Mr Cullen here has just lost his father the same way you lost your husband.'

Mrs Daneman looked at John with vague comprehension. 'In a shooting?' she asked.

'It happened on Friday. It was in the newspapers.'

'Oh, yes,' said Mrs Daneman. 'I think I remember reading about it. Your father was a teacher, wasn't he? I think I remember now.'

There was an awkward silence, and then Mrs Daneman said, 'Well, I'm very sorry. It's the hardest thing in the world, to lose a loved one.'

Mel said, 'The truth is, Mrs Daneman, we were hoping you could tell us a little about what happened in your case. You see, we think there might be some kind of connection between all of these shootings on the freeway, some kind of link.'

Mrs Daneman blinked. 'I don't understand,' she said hesitantly. 'I didn't know your father at all, and I'm sure Charles never did. At least, he never mentioned anyone called – what was it?'

'Cullen. William Cullen,' John said.

'No,' she said. 'Nobody by that name.'

'Mrs Daneman,' Mel said, 'we don't think that your husband *knew* Mr Cullen. But we do believe that they may have shared some interest in life. Some hobby, or some society. Maybe they were both fraternity members at college, or both in the Army.'

Mrs Daneman looked at them, and then looked away across the sun-burned grass of her front lawn. There must have been a time when it was green, and the edges were trimmed. She said, 'We weren't even going any place special, you know. We just went out for a drive, to get some air. Then Charles suggested we go to Descanso Gardens, you know, up by La Canada. We were driving past Griffith Park on the Ventura Freeway, and Andy here was singing.'

She sighed. Her hands, hanging loosely in front of her, twitched against each other like two sad squids.

'I don't even know what make of car it was,' she whispered. 'I never did know the makes. I know that ours was a Pontiac, but that was all. It was white, this car, and it came up alongside us, and the next thing I knew all our seats and windows were covered in Charles's blood.'

She almost smiled. 'The police told us that Andy and I were lucky to be alive. We went down a bank, and stopped against a wire fence. I knew that Charles was dead, but I still waited at the hospital until they came out to tell me officially.'

John said gently, 'Do you mind if we go inside and talk? It seems kind of public out here on the step.'

'Well, if you really want to,' she said. 'You'll have to excuse the house. I find it difficult to manage since Charles went.'

John glanced back at Mel as they entered the narrow hallway. It was dark and airless, and it smelled of disinterest, neglect, and soured milk. On the telephone table was an ashtray crowded with butts, a reminder of her husband's recent death as graphic as a plateful of maggots. Vicki held on tight to John's arm, and Mel stayed close behind. It was like walking into the family mausoleum to view the dead.

The front parlour was dim and silent. There was criss-cross yellow wallpaper, and a reproduction of a Balinese girl with bare breasts. In a glass-fronted cabinet were three small tarnished golf trophies and a cheap tea service that had probably been a wedding present. On top of the television was a photograph of a balding man with an untidy moustache, smiling against the sun. In the wastebasket was the aluminium foil tray of a TV dinner, scraped clean.

Mrs Daneman sat down first, in a frayed chair, and reached for a pack of cigarettes. She lit one up, and took a long, nervous drag from it.

Mel lowered himself into an ugly armchair with black splayed legs, while John and Vicki sat side by side on the dull green settee.

'I don't know what I can tell you,' said Mrs Daneman. 'He was kind and loving, but he was a very ordinary man.'

'Could you describe him?' Mel asked. 'I mean, can you describe what he was really like as a person?'

She looked down at the red and grey rug. 'I guess you could say he was mild and gentle. I don't know what else to say. He was forty-six, and he sold insurance, and that was all. He loved me, and he loved Andy, and he hoped that one day Andy would grow up to be better off than he was.'

'Where was he born?' John asked.

'In Acmetonia – that's just outside of Pittsburgh.'

'Did you ever meet his parents?'

'Oh, sure. His parents came to the wedding. His father was a surgeon for the Miners' Clinic. He did some wonderful work on silicosis, you know, that miners' lung disease?'

John nodded. He was beginning to realise how difficult it would be finding a common factor in the lives of twelve different people. Even the simplest and least

101

controversial of them, like Charles Daneman, insurance agent, was made up of a thousand places, ten thousand names, a thousand thousand times of day. Here was Charles Daneman at high school, with his spotted bow-tie and his spotted cheeks to match. Here he was in the U.S. Marines, with his forage cap and his over-confident wink. Here he was on the beach at Las Tunas with Betty Daneman, his new bride, and here he was with his fresh-born son in a garden bright with washing.

Here was his life, in faded Kodak photographs and clippings from small-town newspapers. But what possible connection could it have to the life of William Cullen, of Trenton, New Jersey, a man who had lived three thousand miles away and whose days were recorded in completely different albums, in completely other memories?

As the afternoon wore on, Mel's stamina outlasted them all, and he was exhaustively thorough. He noted down details of Charles Daneman's school, college, frat house, favourite subjects; his athletics record, service record, best friends, favourite songs, and his preferred breakfast cereal (Force). He found out where the Danemans had been on vacation for the past twenty-three years. He jotted down the titles of Charles Daneman's best-loved books, movies, magazines and TV programmes. He learned that Charles Daneman liked Jackie Coogan, angel-food cake, drank three pop-top cans of Coors every evening, filled his car with Getty gas, and attended Baptist church.

Then, when John was suffocated by the airless room and wearied by the dreary task of dredging up the life of the balding man on top of the television; when Vicki had already gone out on to the verandah to smoke a little grass and pull herself back together again, that was when Mel asked Mrs Daneman: 'What did Charles think of the world? I mean, the world in general? Where did he stand politically?'

Mrs Daneman shrugged. Fifteen cigarette butts lay in the ashtray beside her, and the room was stiff with smoke.

'He didn't stand any place at all,' she said. 'Not politically. He wasn't a political man. But he did have his views. He was a great upholder of human dignity. He believed that all men were created equal, like it says in the Constitution, but of course his father taught him that.'

'His father?'

'Well, his father used to have to work with miners who were dying of silicosis and emphysema. It used to make him so angry, watching those men die, when all the time they could have been saved. He used to say that if the mine-owners donated half the money they spent on their own private medical bills to research into lung disease, then they'd probably save more miners in a year than had ever been killed in all the mine disasters in American history.'

'And Charles agreed with that?' Mel asked.

'He wasn't fanatical about it. But when his father died last year, I think he felt that he should try and carry on with some of the work that his father did for social equality. He wrote some letters to the papers, which never got printed, and he held a garage sale in aid of civil rights.'

'He didn't belong to any kind of political society?' Mel asked her.

She shook her head. 'He didn't want to set the world on fire. He just felt that the bosses and the government and the TV stations had taken ordinary people for granted for too long. He thought they were too cynical. He said it was about time that everybody who swore allegiance to the flag got a little bit of allegiance back in return. A little bit of respect.'

John could almost picture his father's face in the car beside him, almost reach out and touch that lined cheek. Like the tiny voice from an old-time victrola, he could hear his father saying: *'We're working towards what we call a society of mutual respect. That is, we want individuals to be respected by their government, legally and morally.'*

John said, 'Mel, that's enough now.'

Mel turned. 'Something's clicked?'

'I'm not sure. I need to talk about it.'

Mrs Daneman looked from Mel to John and back again, bemused and uncertain. 'Would you like a cup of coffee?' she asked them. 'I'm afraid I don't have any beer. Although I might have root beer. Andy likes root beer.'

John shook his head. 'I think we know everything we need to know, Mrs Daneman. You've been really helpful. I just hope this hasn't upset you too much, talking about your husband this way.'

'Not at all,' she said, with half a smile. 'I think it probably does me good, to talk.'

John and Mel stood up, and Mrs Daneman followed them out into the hall. At the door, she said: 'I loved him, you know, but he really wasn't anybody very exceptional. He liked people to think of him as a good man, and a good husband. He was very proud of being just what he was.'

Mel took her hand, and squeezed it. 'For most people, the finest people, that's usually enough, Mrs Daneman. Thank you for talking to us.'

Mrs Daneman looked at them vaguely, as if she had already forgotten who they were. Vicki was sitting on the verandah rail, talking to Andy, and the day was growing cool and shadowy.

John said: 'Take care, Mrs Daneman. That's a fine son you've got there.'

'Yes,' said Mrs Daneman, in a tone which seemed to mean, fine, yes, but fatherless.

FIFTEEN

He was parked across the street, on the junction with La Jolla, in a tan Firebird, rented from Avis. He wore a green golfing cap with a long peak and a buckle at the back, and sunglasses with lenses like mirrors. He was feeling impatient and edgy, and he kept checking his digital watch. The early evening showing of *Swedish Ecstasy* started at a quarter after six, and he didn't want to miss it.

He could see them talking on the verandah – Mrs Daneman, the young Cullen guy, that dark-haired girl with the big boobs, and the fat schmuck with the beard. Every now and then it seemed as if they were going to make a move, and he'd reach towards the ignition key, but then they'd step back in the shadows again. He couldn't understand why they were taking so long, or what was so goddamned interesting about Mrs Daneman.

Resting on the tan vinyl seat beside him, loosely concealed under a swimming towel, was his M-16, fully loaded. The radio was turned on very low, and he could barely hear the whispers of 'The Girl from Ipanema.' His fingers drummed on the steering-wheel, a light tattoo of impatience.

At last, as the sun was beginning to sink behind the palms, the three of them left the verandah, with a wave to Mrs Daneman and Andy, and began to cross the front lawn towards their beaten-up orange Beetle. He couldn't hear what they were talking about, their voices were only slight smudges of sound on the wind, but whatever it was they seemed in no hurry. He was parked on a red line, and it would only take a black-and-white to cruise past and they'd move him along; or worse, ticket him.

He checked his digital watch. It was 5 : 17. The girl

from Ipanema went walking and when she walked she just didn't see ...

He saw Cullen open the passenger door and help the girl into the back of the car. The fat guy with the beard walked around, laughing about something, and climbed into the driver's seat. As the sun disappeared, the street was clotted with shadows, and there was that curious Los Angeles smell of exhaust fumes and tropical vegetation.

The Volkswagen's motor sputtered into life, and its headlights lit up. At once, the man twisted the key in the Firebird's ignition, shifted the car into drive, and waited for his quarry to pull away.

The Volkswagen moved off from the kerb, tooted its horn once, and drove towards San Vicente. The man U-turned the Firebird in the middle of the street, and followed it. He drove with his left hand, and reached across with his right for the M-16.

As they drew up to the traffic signals at the corner of San Vicente, he pulled up so close behind them that he could see the girl's head in the Volkswagen's rear window, and a side profile of Cullen. He could have taken the three of them out with three shots, and that would have been a finish to it.

The signals changed from red to green, and the Volkswagen moved away in a cloud of oily black smoke that came straight in through the Firebird's fresh-air ventilators and almost choked him. He laid down his rifle and wiped at his mouth with the swimming towel as he followed them north. They bugged him, these three. They were too goddamned holy and cheerful; like the three goddamned musketeers. He had never had a friend himself, not a friend to trust, and signs of friendship in other people irritated him in a way that he could hardly describe.

He trailed the Volkswagen's tail-lights northwards as far as Burton Way, where they turned off westwards towards Santa Monica and (he guessed) the San Diego Freeway. A couple of quick shots on the freeway and that would finish it off for good. He wished he was able to get hold of incendiary bullets, because then he could hit them once in the gas tank and nobody would ever know what the hell had happened. He had seen a woman burn to death in a crashed car on the freeway once, and he had never forgotten how fifteen or twenty people had stood around watching, only a few yards away, but unable to reach her because of the heat.

Only fifty feet apart, the orange Volkswagen and the tan Firebird drove slowly through the rush-hour traffic on Santa Monica Boulevard, stopping within inches of each other at red lights, starting up together, accelerating together. By the time they reached the ramp to the San Diego Freeway, it was almost dark, and the tall man had taken off his sunglasses.

He followed the Volkswagen as it noisily drove up the northbound ramp, and signalled that it was merging left. The tall man put his foot down on the Firebird's gas pedal, checked his mirror, and pulled across to the outside lane. He lifted the M-16 in his right hand, and rested the muzzle on the sill of the open passenger window, steadying his elbow against the passenger seat. He gradually began to overtake the orange Beetle.

He couldn't overtake as quickly as he wanted to because there was a Cadillac in front of him, travelling at a sedate pace. But yard by yard, he crept up alongside the Volkswagen, until his nearside front wheel was spinning inches away from the Volkswagen's dented off-side rear wheel. He could see the girl in the back window now, talking to the fat guy in the driver's seat, although he couldn't yet see Cullen properly. He released the M-16's safety catch, and carefully licked his lips.

The Cadillac slowed a little, and he was forced to slow down too, and lose ground. He glanced quickly from the Cadillac's tail-lights over to the Volkswagen, and back again, trying to assess if he could get a quick shot in, but the Cadillac slowed even more, and in desperation he saw the orange Beetle gain fifty or sixty feet, and disappear up ahead of him.

He tried to pull across into the Volkswagen's lane, so that he could switch his approach and overtake it on the inside, but an intolerant Buick blasted its horn at him, and he had to stay where he was, boxed in behind the Cadillac.

They were rising up the long curving gradients into the Santa Monica mountains now, and traffic in the outside lane was slowing down even more. On the radio, the disc jockey said, 'We've had all kinds of phone calls on the subject of crash diets, and we have one lady in Encino on the line who believes that you can go without food for two weeks and still feel great.'

Unexpectedly, traffic in the next lane began to lose speed too, and the tall man saw the Volkswagen only three cars away now, and coming closer. He raised his rifle again, flicking his eyes from the car in front to the orange Beetle, judging distance, speed, time. Once he'd shot into the Beetle, he wanted to cut across in front of it, because it would inevitably veer sideways and collide with whatever car was travelling next to it.

Now it was only two cars away, and he was making up distance faster. He put his foot down and nudged a little closer to the tail of the Cadillac, gaining two or three more feet.

He could see the fat guy now, and Cullen. The fat guy's elbow was resting on the window, and his pudgy fingers were tapping on the Beetle's roof. Cullen's head was silhouetted against the light grey rhomboid shape of the passenger window, and he was talking about something and waving his hand.

The tall man's Firebird was almost alongside the Volkswagen now. He was already in a position to let off a shot into the back seat, but it was the front he was aiming for. In traffic as heavy as this, the girl probably wouldn't survive anyway.

Gradually, inch by unsteady inch, the sights of the M-16 crept along the side of the Volkswagen, past the rear window, past the door pillar, past the seats, until they hovered in line with Mel's bearded face.

On the radio, someone was singing: 'A day of happiness was all we knew, and then I lost my baby blue . . .'

In a split-second, just as he squeezed the trigger, the Cadillac's brake lights brightened, and his foot jabbed for the brake pedal out of sheer nervous response. The rifle punched in his hand, and the Firebird slewed towards the median strip as he almost lost control of it.

For a few jumbled moments, he couldn't work out what had happened, but then the Beetle suddenly blared its horn, and swung away into the next lane. The tall man twisted the Firebird's wheel and swung after it, arousing an angry chorus of hoots and honks from the traffic all around him.

He lost sight of the Volkswagen for a moment, but then he saw it over on the inside lane, accelerating fast to overtake a heavy truck, with clouds of oily smoke billowing out of its exhausts.

The rental Firebird wasn't tuned up, but it still had the edge on Mel's '62 Beetle. It came nosing close up behind, alongside the truck, and as the Beetle pulled out again, trying to dodge into the densest clusters of traffic, the tall man pressed his foot on the gas pedal again, and overtook the Beetle on the inside.

He saw Cullen's face at the window, his arm raised to shield himself. He could see the girl, too, her head down against the back of Cullen's seat. He picked up the M-16, and awkwardly lifted it across his chest so that the barrel rested on the driver's window.

The Beetle braked hard. Behind it, the heavy truck let out a bellow of air horns. The tall man fired one shot, but it went totally wild across the freeway. The truck bellowed again.

The Beetle speeded up, passing the Firebird, and then abruptly swung right into the centre lane. The tall man jammed his foot on the gas to follow it, but the huge truck was coming up too fast on his lefthand side, and the gap where the Beetle had been was closed.

He tried one more desperate shot, in a sharp trajectory between the front of the truck and the tail of an Olds in the next lane. He could just make out the Beetle's back, a fast-disappearing curve of orange with a waving CB antenna, and the M-16 was so heavy and ill-balanced that he wasn't sure that he could even hope to hit it. But he fired one shot, and then manhandled the rifle back onto the passenger seat. Under his breath, he said, 'Shit.'

In the dusky Santa Monica twilight, he slowed down and pulled off the freeway at the Rimerton Road exit. On Rimerton Road itself, he drew into the side, and parked, and switched off his lights. He was covered in freezing sweat, and his mouth was dry. The radio was still whispering to him; he switched it off.

There was silence, except for the swishing, droning sound of traffic on the freeway. There were no insects, no voices, no winds. He wiped his face with the swimming towel, and then sat back in his seat and let out a long, tense breath.

Maybe he should have shot them as they came out of the house. Maybe he should have blasted their heads off as they sat at the lights on San Vicente. But that wasn't what these freeway killings were all about. That wasn't the way this divine retribution was supposed to happen. The cold breath of the angel of fatal disapproval was meant to take these people's lives openly and publicly, on the freeway, and yet inside the private sanctuary of their own cars. It was an invasion of the American womb, a mass abortion of those who took everything in which he believed in vain.

He gave himself five or ten minutes to cool off. Then he started up the car again, and headed east on Mulholland Drive, winding his way slowly across the mountains as far as Laurel Canyon. He didn't know whether he wanted to go to the sex movies any more or not. A much more demanding instinct than sex was still frustrated, and his mind surged with electric tension that had no place to go for relief.

It was 6:31. He decided to buy himself a Chinese take-away meal and eat it in the solitude of his apartment. He parked the Firebird on Yucca Street, just north of Hollywood Boulevard, and packed the M-16 away in a brown leather case he had kept on the back seat. Then he locked the car, tossed the keys into the nearest garden, and walked towards Hollywood Boulevard in search of a taxi.

SIXTEEN

The Volkswagen coughed up Topanga Canyon, and only just made the drive in front of the house before it let out a whirring sound, and stopped altogether. Mel held on to the handbrake while John groped in the dark for a couple of bricks to wedge against the back tyres, and then Mel and Vicki climbed slowly and exhaustedly out of the car.

Vicki put her arms around John and held him relentlessly close for almost three long minutes, saying nothing, just trembling with shock and relief. Mel took his flashlight out of the glove box, and examined the Beetle all over.

'Here it is,' Mel said quietly, after a while. 'This must have been the first one.'

They went over to take a look. There was a deep pockmark in the Beetle's roof, where a bullet had glanced against it and ricocheted off.

'I guess the second shot must have hit the engine someplace,' said Mel. 'There seems to be oil leaking all over, but I can't see where it struck. I'll have to take a look in the morning.'

'Are we going to call the police now?' asked Vicki.

'Sure,' said John. 'I know what they're going to say, but they have to know. Who's for a drink?'

Mel nodded. 'Jack Daniels, straight up, straight out of the bottle.'

They climbed up the wooden steps to the house, and John switched on the lights. While Mel and Vicki went through to the living room, he walked down the corridor into the kitchen, and opened the icebox.

For a moment, John closed his eyes and pressed his forehead against the cold top of the icebox. A feeling passed over him like a heavy black flag waved across a windy sky. It was a feeling of fear, but a feeling of survival, too – that extraordinary sensation of having come out of danger unscathed. He thanked God that he was still alive, and he thanked God that Vicki was safe, and he thanked God for Mel and his amazing driving.

He stood up straight and opened his eyes. He was sure now that Mel was right, and that this freeway psychopath wasn't just knocking people off at random. If he had been, why would he have bothered to follow them and try to kill them again? Maybe they'd seen more of the killer that first time than he would have liked, and he was trying to eliminate some possible witnesses. But that kind of after-sales service was far more characteristic of mob killings, professionally-arranged murders, than it was of random psychopathic butchery.

John rolled up the sleeves of his blue hound's-tooth shirt, and poured out three glasses of straight bourbon. He felt as if he'd stepped through the looking-glass, out of the world of fussing old women like Mrs Benduzzi and their pampered pet dogs, out of the world of sprinkled lawns and over-polished cars, into a strange existence where there was real fear, and real death, and all the stories you read about in the newspapers happened not to other people, but to you.

He took the bourbon into the living room. Vicki was standing by the window, looking out into the dark garden, and Mel was thoughtfully hunched on a chair.

'Do you have Detective Morello's number?' Vicki asked.

'It's right by the phone. I'll call him in just a minute. I just want to get my nerves knitted back together.'

Vicki took her bourbon, and swallowed a mouthful nervously. She coughed and her eyes watered, but she smiled again, and that was more than he'd hoped for. He kissed her cheek, and she briefly stroked his short-cropped hair.

'What interests me is how he knew where we were,' Mel said.

'I don't understand,' said Vicki.

'Well, he must have tailed us *before* we got onto the freeway. He wasn't just cruising up and down the freeway hoping that one day he might catch sight of us. He must have tailed us all the way from Mrs Daneman's, because he couldn't have known in advance which route we were going to take. We didn't even know ourselves. It was only a spur-of-the-moment decision we went up San Vicente instead of La Cienega.'

'So he knew we went to see Mrs Daneman,' said John. 'And if he knew that, he must have realised we were trying to check up on him.'

'More important, he must have *cared* about us trying to check up on him. And if he cared, that means there must be some common factor between all these freeway victims that he doesn't want us to find out.'

'That's pure speculation, isn't it? I mean, we don't have any proof,' Vicki said.

'Not yet, honey,' Mel said, 'but we have the beginnings of proof, and those beginnings are that Charles Daneman and William Cullen shared six or seven things in common. They both had connections with the marines, they both read *Newsweek*, they both attended church regularly, they both liked cheeseburgers, and they both had developed a particular political view about mutual respect between the government and the people.'

Mel took a hefty swallow of Jack Daniels, and went on. 'What we need to do now is talk to some more survivors, and find out whether any of those common factors was shared by the person that *they* lost. The political bit is obviously the most important, although I wouldn't discount the marine connection either, or the *Newsweek* bit. Magazines have mailing lists, and those mailing lists are usually for sale. It's possible that our psychopath is killing people just because their names appear on a particular list.'

'What about the cheeseburgers?' asked Vicki. Her voice had a noticeable barb in it.

Mel accepted her sharpness with good grace. 'A psychopath can kill for all kinds of crazy reasons. It may be that he just doesn't like people who like cheeseburgers. But I don't think so.'

Vicki was silent for a moment, and then she ran her

hand tiredly through her long dark hair.

'I'm sorry,' she said. 'I didn't mean to sound bitchy. It's just that I'm so scared for you. I'm pretty scared for myself, too.'

John put his arm around her. 'We'll find him. He gave himself away by chasing us today, and the more he gives himself away, the more vulnerable he becomes. One day soon, he's going to make a mistake that shows us just who he is, and then we can call the cops right in and they'll bust him.'

Vicki smiled wanly. 'Honest to God,' she said. 'I don't know which one of you is Starsky, and which one of you is Hutch.'

That night, for the first time in a week, on their big brass frontier bed with its home-made patchwork coverlet, they made love.

They were careful and tender with each other, careful with their bruised bodies and tender with their unhealed emotions. They kissed with the exploratory softness of children, and when he held her breast in his hand and took her wide nipple in his mouth, she let out little sighs that were quieter than he could ever remember.

He parted her legs with his fingers, and slid himself up inside her slowly and gently, until she stretched and sighed again. They were almost silent while they worked gradually towards a climax, and when it happened, it was like a drop of brilliant colour on the surface of a quiet pool, spreading wider and wider, until it faded into the night.

Above their bed was an embroidered sampler which read: 'We Are Made Perfect Through Sufferings.'

SEVENTEEN

In the bright glare of Wednesday morning, Detective Morello and two officers from the ballistics department crouched around the Beetle's open engine compartment and peered into its rusty pipework as if it was the latest V-8 from Ford.

The two officers from the ballistics department wore creased lightweight suits with open-necked shirts, and had matching droopy moustaches. Detective Morello, looking more dapper than usual, was dressed in a cream-coloured linen jacket and pale-blue sports slacks.

John was sitting on the bottom step of the house in jeans and T-shirt, watching. Vicki was on the verandah, rocking backwards and forwards in their turn-of-the-century rocking chair, and stringing up the last of her homemade Indian beads for Mrs Tadema. She wore skintight French jeans and a close-fitting sweater of thin white shiny wool. Mel waited patiently beside his injured Beetle, his arms folded over his big chest.

The morning sun slanted down through the trees in fluted columns, and the woods were alive with birds.

Eventually, one of the ballistics men said, 'I think I see where it's gone.'

He opened the Beetle's door, folded the driver's seat forward, and peered down into the back.

'Here it is. It's buried in the trim, right here.'

He took out a pair of pincers, and extracted the bullet from the Beetle's body, holding it up for everyone to see. 'That's the one, all right. It went straight through the rear engine cover, straight through the oil pump, straight through the back seat, and wound up in the fabric trim. You were lucky it wasn't six inches higher and six inches further to the right.'

Detective Morello scrutinized the bullet with his nose

wrinkled up. 'Do you know what it is?' he asked the ballistics man.

'Hard to tell, it's pretty flattened out. It must have been a rifle bullet, though, with that kind of velocity. Maybe M-14, or M-16.'

Detective Morello pulled a resigned face. 'Okay, get it back to the lab and report on it as soon as you can.'

The two ballistics men popped their find into a plastic bag, and left. Detective Morello came across to where John was sitting. He sat down, and took a small cigar from his breast pocket. 'Did you get a look at the guy?' he asked. 'Did you recognise him from last time?'

John shook his head. 'The last time he was wearing those mirror sunglasses. This time, he could have been anybody. He had a kind of peaked cap on, and you couldn't really see his face at all.'

'How about the car?'

'A tan Firebird. Plain metal roof. I didn't catch the licence.'

'It was a California licence, though?'

'I think so.'

Detective Morello lit his cigar, and tucked his lighter back in his pocket. He looked out over the sunny, leafy canyon, and puffed away thoughtfully.

'You seem like you're holding something back,' he said, without turning John's way.

'Like what?'

'You tell me,' said Detective Morello. 'You're the one who's holding it back.'

John shrugged. 'It's only an opinion.'

'So? Opinions can help.'

'Well, it's just that Mel here and I both believe that these killings are probably planned in advance. We don't believe they're completely haphazard.'

'What gives you that idea? The fact that he chased you last night?'

'Partly.'

'Let me guess,' said Detective Morello. 'You believe that all of the twelve victims may have had something in common which the unimaginative cops have overlooked.

116

You're not sure what it is, but maybe the killer is worried that you do. So last night he tracked you down and tried to bump you off before you lit up like a "Ford has a better idea" bulb and put the fickle finger of fate on him.'

John turned and looked at him. 'You're a better detective than you look,' he said quietly.

'Well, thanks for nothing. But why else did you go around to see Mrs Charles Daneman, except to establish that her dead husband had something in common with your dead father?'

'You knew we were there?'

'Mrs Daneman called us after you left. She just wanted to check that you were genuine. She does have a son to care for, after all.'

'I see.'

Mel had joined them by now, and said, 'All the same, we did discover that Charles Daneman and John's father had quite a few things in common. Things that *you* don't seem to have latched on to.'

Detective Morello examined the lighted end of his small cigar as if he expected it to do something unusual, like sprout paper flowers, or explode. Then, with what he obviously considered to be tremendous patience, he said, 'I have personally checked over the family details of every single one of our twelve victims, and I have done it with the kind of nitpicking care that most people usually reserve for picking nits.'

'And what did you find out?' John asked.

'I found out that every person in the whole wide world has a little in common. I found out that our twelve victims, comparatively speaking, had quite a lot in common. But I also found out that nothing of what they had in common was worth killing them for.'

He sucked at his cigar, and then continued. 'We haven't ruled out the possibility that all of our twelve victims were killed because of some common factor, even if that common factor, to anyone with a sane mind, appears to be totally crazy. But if they were killed because of something like that, then they must have been killed by a lone fruitcake, and the only time we're ever going to find out why he did it is when we catch him and ask him.'

'But what about politics?' asked John. 'My father was –'

'Your father was a slightly left-of-centre liberal, as were most of the other victims, and as are a generous percentage of people in the whole world.'

'You did actually consider a political motive?' Mel said.

'We considered every motive,' answered Detective Morello. 'But for someone to be killed for political reasons, they have to be politically significant. None of these people were. Only three of them were active members of a political group. Five of them had never cast a vote in their lives.'

Mel took off his glasses and polished them with his handkerchief. 'I guess I owe the police some kind of apology,' he said. 'You're not as dumb as I thought you were.'

'But wait a minute,' John interrupted. 'How did the killer know we were at Mrs Daneman's yesterday? That's where he must have picked us up, and started to trail us.'

Detective Morello relit his cigar. 'It's more likely that he followed you from here, all the way from Topanga. Or it could be that he passes Sixth Street regularly, on his way home, and spotted you by accident. If he uses Sixth Street every day, that might account for how he first tracked down Mr Daneman.'

John rubbed his chin thoughtfully. 'I don't know. That seems to be stretching rationalisation kind of thin.'

Detective Morello stood up. 'Not as thin as trying to cook up some political assassination plot. Take it from me, Mr Cullen, there's a lone psychopath out there, and he's killing people for kicks, or for some odd motive that neither you nor I could ever comprehend. Now, I'd really take it as a great favour if you'd keep well out of this, and not try to do our job for us. You could warn the killer away from a stake-out without realising it, or get yourself seriously hurt.'

Vicki came down the wooden steps. Her hair was clean and brushed, and it shone in the sunlight. She sat down beside John and put her arm around him. 'Thank you, Detective Morello,' she said simply.

EIGHTEEN

He lay on his back on his crumpled bed, fully dressed, feeling tired and sweaty. Next to him, naked, lay a girl of not more than thirteen or fourteen, with tangled blonde hair and freckles. She was sleeping with her mouth slightly open.

He wasn't sure what day it was. His usual routine had been thrown out of sync, and the memory of what he had done the night before – eating a Chinese take-away meal and then going out to find a girl – didn't seem to fit into his normal week at all. He sneezed twice.

They hadn't done very much last night, the tall man and the young blonde girl. He had been tired and dis-tracted, and even when she had tried to coax him, he had irritably pushed her away. She had shrugged, and gone to sleep. While she slept, he had watched a late night movie on television, eaten pretzels out of the bag, and cleaned his two Smith & Wesson hammerless .38 re-volvers.

He checked his digital watch. It was 7:23. It was also Tuesday. He had a heavy day up ahead, a day of hassles and arrangements and complications. For starters, he needed to rent a new car. He rolled out of bed, walked over to the cracked washbasin, and splashed some water in his face. Then, still dripping, he went to his bureau drawer and took out two hundred-dollar bills from the untidy heap of bills that was crammed in there.

He saw his face in the bureau mirror. His eyes looked dark and introspective, and his cheeks were deeply engraved with lines. He stared at himself, not moving, for a long time, and then he turned his head and blinked as if he had been dreaming.

His M.14 rifle was waiting for him, propped in the corner. He looked across at it, and smiled, as an indulgent father might smile at his son.

'How are you, old buddy?' he whispered.

NINETEEN

She would always remember, almost to the second, the moment she had fallen in love. He came down the steps of the Catholic mission on Merchant Street that Wednesday morning, surrounded by dancing, laughing black children, and even in his shabby black jacket and his unpolished shoes he looked like a man of dedication and sacrifice. But he was handsome, too, with a kind of bruised, sad-looking, fallen-angel face, with curly black Italian hair and a short Michelangelo nose.

The smoggy sun radiated over the street, and there on the broken-down steps, against a background of slummy bars and peeling houses, amidst the chatter and hooting of children, she understood that she was actually in love with him, as a woman loves a man, and not a priest.

He waved shyly, and said, 'How are you?'

'I came by to see if you wanted any help with the talk-in tonight,' she said. Her words sounded like someone else's, like stilted lines from a play. She wondered why he didn't stare at her and ask her why she was lying.

'Well, that's very kind,' he told her. 'There's always room for one of our more vocal ladies.'

She smiled. 'Is that what you think of me? A vocal lady?'

'That's only one of your attributes,' he said. 'You're active, as well as vocal, and that's what really counts.'

'Why, thank you, good priest.'

He said, 'I have a couple of minutes to spare. Would you like some coffee? There's a place two blocks up that does a pretty honest doughnut.'

'Do you judge doughnuts as well as people by their honesty?'

He shook his head. 'I don't judge people. God will do that when the time comes.'

They walked past rusty, dilapidated cars and abandoned garbage. A wino sitting on a dusty step across the street gave a jerky, spastic wave and called, 'Hey, father!'

They reached Sal's Coffee House, a noisy, cheap, corner premise with worn linoleum floors and sticky tables. Most of the customers were old experts at stretching out the consumption of one doughnut and one cup of coffee to last the whole morning. Sal himself bustled around behind the smeary stainless-steel counter with a paper hat on his head and a burned-down stogie permanently clamped between his teeth, and was tolerant of poverty.

Father Leonard bought two coffees and two doughnuts, and came across to the table balancing them carefully.

'I really should watch my weight,' she said, as he sat them down.

'Your weight? You're as slim as a traffic signal. And in any case, you don't have to be thin to get into the Kingdom of Heaven. Just humble.'

She stirred her coffee. 'I'm not even sure if I'm that.'

She was twenty-three, but it was only now that she was beginning to look as young as she really was. She was very petite, with a sharp triangular face and short straight hair that was bleached by the sun into a shinning blend of platinum and gold. Her eyes were wide, violet-blue like a midday sky, and her mouth always seemed to have the first traces of a smile.

Perri Shaw's twenty-second year had been lost, like pages wrenched from a calendar, to her estranged husband, Rick. She had admired Rick from afar during her freshman year at UCLA. He had been a junior then – long-haired, sultry, rebellious. During her sophomore year, she had dared (on the strength of two rum collins) to approach him, and tell him how much she desired him, and within a week they had become lovers. He had been strong, occasionally brutal, but always exciting. She had adored him, and almost loved him.

Their first affair hadn't lasted long. Rick had dropped out of his economics course early in his senior year, and disappeared out of Perri's life, too. She had heard later that he was fire-watching up in the Wenatchee Forest, in Washington. Two years went by, and she had been dating a serious young English student named Garth. In a distant way, like a train whistle on the other side of the mountain, Garth had been quite loving.

But forcefully and accidentally, she had met Rick again, at a party in Venice a year and a day after her graduation in political science. They had small-talked over their drinks with cagey lust, and then, without a word, he had claimed her again by taking her out on the balcony, tugging up her skirt, and rutting with her like a fierce male elk.

Despite the vivid unease of her parents (whom Rick always described as Brentwood Park's answer to Grant Wood) they had gotten engaged, and married, and moved with his guitar and her embroidered bedspread into a small duplex in Westwood Village.

The marriage was hell. She had found out, too late, that Rick was heavily addicted to cocaine, and he would spend hours in the bathroom snorting and gagging. He was violent, too, and used to hit her unexpectedly almost every day, seemingly without any provocation. He would disappear for nights on end, and then return for sex and food, unwashed, foul-mouthed, and almost mad with drugs.

It was during this year, at a university seminar on marriage guidance, which she had attended with patient hopelessness, that she had met Father Leonard. He wasn't much older than she was, but he befriended her and counselled her through weeks of beatings and fear, and given her such a direct window onto the possibilities of life without pain and without desperation that she had gathered the strength to challenge Rick on his own ground, to make him face up to what he was. He had punched her almost senseless, then left her without money, without a goodbye, with nothing to remind her of their marriage but bruises and torn-out hair.

She had continued to visit Father Leonard, however, and help him occasionally in his mission work in the slums of Los Angeles. It wasn't until this hazy Tuesday morning, however, that she began to understand how much she felt for him, and how much her seemingly selfless help for the battered wives of the 12th Street district was inspired by her need to be close to him.

He was godly, quiet and beautiful, with that kind of gaunt figure which she could imagine hanging on a cross, or pierced, like St Sebastian, with arrows. She watched him stir two spoonfuls of sugar into his coffee, and she felt such a surge of affection for him, and such a sexual stirring for him as well, that she hardly knew what to say to him.

He looked up. His eyes were dark brown, emotional, and full of warmth.

He said, 'I believe these talk-ins are doing some good. At least, some of the women are beginning to understand that they have a right to their own identity. They're not just ribs taken out of their husbands' chests; they're people in their own right, and in the eyes of God.'

'How do their husbands feel about it?' she asked him. 'Don't they get angry at having their manhood questioned?'

He bit into his doughnut, and chewed it carefully. 'Sometimes,' he said, taking a sip of coffee. 'But it doesn't usually last for long. Once they realise that their wives are people, but that they still love them, then they usually come to terms with it. Of course, we've had one or two incidents. Quite a serious beating on Industrial Street. But I think most of the women know that it has to get worse before it gets better.'

'I wish you'd go to the Women's Liberation Conference instead of me,' she said. 'You could explain what you've been doing here so much better.'

He shook his head. 'You're the delegate, not me. And in any case, they don't want to hear a man talking about women's consciousness-raising. Even worse, they don't want to hear a man making a case for women's sexual equality instead of women's sexual dominance. It needs someone like you to tell them that. If *I* started to argue that many husbands are reacting badly because they feel they're getting the thin end of the wedge these days, why, they'd tear me to pieces, limb from limb.'

She looked at him softly. 'I wouldn't let that happen,' she said.

'Anyway, I don't want to go before the Lord chooses to take me,' he said. 'I have better things to do than sacrifice myself to Hilary Nestor Hunter and her feminist horde.'

She smiled. 'I never heard you talk so sharply about anyone before. I thought you were always so saintly.'

'It's difficult to be saintly about Ms. Hunter, I'm afraid. Even the bishop admits to a certain feeling that he'd rather be somewhere else when she's around.'

'I guess she does tend to be kind of domineering.'

'Domineering is an understatement. In Hilary Nestor Hunter's universe, the middle-aged middle-class woman shall inherit everything, including her husband's scalp and her lover's income. That's what you're going to have to fight when you go to this conference, Perri, and you can bet it won't be easy.'

Perri bit into her doughnut. It was surprisingly crisp, and good. 'I'll do my best,' she said. 'It's about time that someone stood up to those right-wing dykes.'

Father Leonard's mouth twitched a little, but he didn't censure her. Instead, he said, 'All I ask is that you remember you are going as a representative of the church marriage guidance service, and that whatever you say will reflect back on all of us.'

'I know, father. I won't call her a dyke to her face.'

Father Leonard looked amused, and then laughed.

They ate their doughnuts and drank their coffee in silence for a little while, and then she said, 'I never asked you before – how long have you been here?'

He looked out of the grimy window at the derelict street.

'Eight years, give or take a month.'

'Haven't you ever grown tired of it, or despaired of it?'

'Many times. But each time, I've asked God to guide me, and for whatever purpose He has, He has always given me to feel that He wants me to remain here.'

'You've never thought about a ministry up in the mountains? In Hollywood, maybe, or Bel-Air?'

He shook his head. 'There is much more pressing work to be done down here.'

'But the rich have souls, too.'

'The rich are in a better position to save their own souls. They have the wherewithal to be holy, and to be charitable. These poor people have almost nothing except their faith, and very little of that.'

She drew a circular pattern on the formica tabletop with the tip of her finger, around and around and around.

She said, 'You've never thought of giving up the priesthood altogether?'

He frowned. 'Why do you ask?'

'I don't know. I just wondered if it had ever occurred to you.'

He sat back, perplexed by her question. 'There was one time,' he said slowly, 'after I was attacked by a gang of black youths in the street and beaten. It did occur to me then. But the wounds healed, and so did my doubts.'

'It hasn't ever crossed your mind to give it up for any other reason?'

'What other reason could there possibly be?'

She didn't want to press him too hard, didn't want to crowd him into a corner. But sitting there with that slight furrow in his brow and that questioning look on his face he was even more attractive than before, and she knew that her lips were going to say the words before her conscience could stop them.

'Haven't you ever fallen in love?' she said quietly.

He was silent for a long time. She could see by the

subtle expression of understanding in his eyes that he knew now why she was asking. He put his hand to his mouth and bit at his knuckle, his dark gaze never leaving her.

Unsettled, she said, 'I've heard about it before. In the newspapers. Priests falling in love.'

He nodded, slowly. 'Yes, it does occur.'

'But not to you?'

He leaned forward on the table, pushing his plate to one side. In a very careful tone, he said, 'Perri, have you been harbouring feelings about me?'

She laughed nervously. 'You make me sound like a criminal.'

'But I mean it,' he said. 'Have you had feelings about me? Feelings of affection?'

She drew her fingertip around faster and faster. 'I suppose I have,' she said, in a tight voice. 'Well, I mean it's more than just affection.'

'You mean sexual attraction?'

'More than that, father, I've fallen in love with you. Genuinely, deeply, and completely in love.'

'I'm sorry.'

'Father, you don't have anything to be sorry for, and neither do I.'

'I should have realised. It was stupid of me not to.'

'How could you have realised? It's been building up inside me for weeks. I've only just begun to realise it myself.'

Father Leonard took her hand across the table. He had long, pale fingers, like a violin player's, except that his nails were broken from hard work.

'As a man,' he said, 'I'm very flattered.'

She looked up into his eyes.

'But as a priest,' he said, 'I have to tell you that any kind of wordly love you feel for me is hopeless.'

It was such a strange feeling, holding this man's hand, and looking so deeply into this man's eyes, and yet knowing that his love of God made him impervious to her sexuality. It gave her an extraordinary urge to do something to shock him, like tear open her blouse and bare her breasts. Or reach under the table and grasp his genitals through his shabby black pants.

'Haven't you ever loved a woman?' she asked him. 'Not ever?'

He nodded. 'Once, when I was very young.'

'Was that why you decided to become a priest?'

'No,' he smiled. 'I decided to become a priest because God called me, and because I love God, and Jesus Christ, and Mary the Mother of Christ, above all.'

'And you never even feel the urge to –'

'The urge to what? You can say it, you know. I've worked in downtown Los Angeles for eight years. The only words that can still shock me are words of hate.'

She leaned towards him. 'The urge to make love to a woman,' she whispered. 'I mean, if I said to you now, you can have me, you can make love to me, wouldn't you feel even the slightest thing?'

He kept hold of her hand. 'Of course I would. You're a pretty girl. But years of self-discipline have given me the strength to say no.'

'But I don't understand why you should *want* to say no.'

'It's not a question of *wanting* to. I would say no because of what I am, a servant of God who can best serve his Lord by remaining celibate.'

She sat back, and gently tugged her hand away from his. She didn't even notice, but there were tears in her eyes. He stayed where he was, leaning forward on the table, the unfallen angel of Merchant Street.

She whispered, 'You saved my life once. You rescued me from hell.'

'I hope I shall save many more,' he said quietly.

'Can't I rescue *you*?' she asked.

'I don't need to be rescued, except from my human failings, and I shall be rescued from those by Jesus Christ who redeemed the sins of the world by His crucifixion.'

'But it's such a *waste*,' she said. 'You don't even realise how beautiful you are! You don't even realise what you're missing out of life!'

He took out a leather purse, and shook out a dime, which he laid on the table, under his saucer.

He smiled at her.

'I know what I'm missing, believe me. But I also have faith in what is waiting for me in the life hereafter.'

'But you don't have to be celibate to go to Heaven.'

'No.'

'Then why? You could still do all this social work as a layman, couldn't you, instead of being a priest? Then you could be just as dedicated to the will of God, and have a woman, too.'

'You don't understand, do you? Unless I dedicate myself completely to God, body and soul, I have no strength to do this work at all. I find my strength in self-denial and frugality. They bring me close to the power of my belief, without personal comfort, or erotic pleasure, or earthly love, to insulate me from the charge that my belief can give me.'

'You make yourself sound like a household appliance.'

'I am, in a way. An appliance through which the current of God's holy will continuously flows.'

'Oh, Jesus.'

They left the coffee shop, and went out again into the humid street. A police patrol car drove slowly past, and tooted its horn at Father Leonard. Father Leonard waved back.

He said to Perri, 'I have to go now. I'm visiting Mrs Paloma in the hospital. She fell down a flight of stairs last night. At least, that's Mr Paloma's story. Fractured collarbone, broken hip.'

Perri wiped her eyes with her handkerchief. 'I guess I should say that I'm sorry,' she said.

He put his hand on her shoulder, and shook his head. 'You're full of love, Perri, and you're a pretty girl. You won't find it hard to meet the right man.'

'I thought I'd met him twice,' she said, with a lump in her throat. 'But the first time he turned out to be a devil, and that was no good, and the second time he turned out to be a saint, and that was no good, either.'

He said, 'Still friends?'

'Oh,' she said, 'sure.'

'Well, give me a call this evening, and we'll talk about

the Women's Conference. I have a friend who works for CBS, and he says that if we come up with a real challenge to Hilary Nestor Hunter, he'll try to make sure we get some television coverage. And you know what prime time exposure would mean to what we're doing down here.'

'So you have a human weakness,' grinned Perri. 'You want to be famous.'

'*I* don't want to be famous. But I want the underprivileged women of this district to be famous, and I want to see the basic human rights of both sexes upheld.'

Perri reached up and kissed his cheek.

'Don't you worry,' she said. 'If you don't love me now, I'll make you so damned proud of me at this Woman's Conference that you won't have any choice.'

Father Leonard laughed. But after they had parted, and he was walking down the street towards the bus-stop, he was frowning to himself, and he paused for a moment outside a dusty pawnbroker's window to gaze at the reflection of the man she had so regretfully dubbed a saint.

TWENTY

She stepped out of the Las Vegas airport terminal carrying her white vanity case, teetering on gold high heels, her red hair back-combed into bouffant curls, her skimpy yellow T-shirt bouncing five different ways at once, and her scarlet satin jeans so close-fitting that the skycap who was hefting her enormous suitcase couldn't keep his eyes off her rounded rump.

She peered out over the concrete pick-up area like a comical Ziegfeld interpretation of John Paul Jones staring out to sea.

'I have a ride someplace,' she told the skycap. 'I was

definitely promised a ride.'

The skycap, who was short and had a lot of bright red pimples, said, 'That's okay, I can wait,' and made a show of looking around the airport, so that he could sneak quick glances at her breasts, as big as beachballs, and her tight scarlet satin mound of venus.

'It's so *hot* here,' complained Lollie. 'You wouldn've thought the guy would have gotten his act together and arrived on time. My lipstick's melting.'

'Well, uh, he's, uh, bound to get here in a moment,' said the skycap, wishing furiously that her ride would never arrive, and that she'd be stranded here, and have to accept an invitation to go back to his one-room walk up, and fuck him until his ears rang.

But then there was the brief hoot of a car horn, and a white Monarch drew up alongside them, and David Radetzky climbed out.

'How are you doing, Lollie?' he said, and opened up the trunk so that the skycap, whose dreams had now been crushed beyond repair, could heave her suitcase into the back.

Lollie got into the car, chewing gum noisily.

'I'm okay. Do you want some Bubble Yum?'

'No, thanks. Wasn't there some kind of health scandal about that stuff?'

'A dumb rumour, that's all. It's cataclysmic.'

'Cataclysmic?' asked David, raising an eyebrow, as he pulled away from the airport terminal and headed towards Interstate 15. 'Where did you pick up a word like that?'

Lollie turned the car's air-conditioning to cold, and tucked her sunglasses up in her red curls. The drop in temperature made her nipples rise up under her T-shirt, but David Radetzky either didn't notice or wasn't interested. He was still wearing his shiny Nixonite suit, and his chin was still bright blue, as if he shaved with last year's blades.

'Senator Chapman taught me cataclysmic. Lollie, he said, you're cataclysmic.'

'You'll be meeting him again this evening. Maybe this time you ought to ask him what it means.'

They drove towards the skyline of Las Vegas, the sun shining hot and purple through the tinted car windows. The time on the Monarch's clock was 4:45. Lollie looked out across the hazy desert, and chewed her gum, and wondered if life had any particular purpose at all.

'We've booked you a suite at the Scirocco,' said David. 'We've had two cameramen and a sound-recording specialist working on it since six this morning, and there's no place in the whole suite that anybody can go without being filmed and taped.'

'Even the little girls' room?'

'That's right.'

'But supposing I want to go?'

'Supposing you do?'

Lollie chewed, and blushed. 'Well, I usually get paid a little extra for that, I mean, usually.'

David Radetzky sighed. 'Okay, if you need to go, we'll add twenty bucks to the fee. But that's only if you go.'

They arrived at the hotel, a gleaming curve of white concrete with the name Scirocco written in scarlet neon against the afternoon sky. David led Lollie straight through the wide marble lobby into the mock-rococo elevator, and pressed the button for PH.

'Is Senator Chapman here already?' Lollie asked.

'He arrives in about a half-hour. He has a meeting with some development people here. Something to do with hotel building in Minneapolis.'

'So how do I get to meet him again? I don't bump into him in some casino, do I?'

David shook his head. 'You call Senator Chapman at his hotel, you can tell him you came to·town because you heard he was here, and you're just aching to meet him again. You can even tell him he's cataclysmic, if you like.'

'You don't have to talk like a smartass,' complained Lollie.

The elevators doors opened, and they stepped across the corridor to a pair of gilded double portals marked 'Pompadour Penthouse.' David unlocked them, and ushered Lollie inside.

The main room was high, bright, and decorated in a style which the designer had fancifully believed was French 18th-century elaborate. The ceiling was suspended with a tent of pale blue satin, hung with golden tassels, and the bed had a gilded head of carved cherubs, dolphins, naked nymphs, and oceanic billows. The carpets were dark blue, and thick; and all around were hangings and drapes and tasselled cords.

Two men in overalls had pulled up a corner of the rug and were tacking a wire along the skirting. One of them was squat and Mexican-looking; the other was lean and mournful, with a thin curved nose.

'How's it going, Duke?' David asked, peeling off his coat and throwing it on the bed.

The thin man said, 'Okay, I guess. We've just been testing the reception from the bed, and I'm kind of worried we may not be getting the best.'

'What's the problem?'

'Well, it's the noise of the sheets and the bedcovers. When you get two fair-sized people humping at full gallop, you'd be surprised how much extraneous sound you pick up.'

'Duke used to work for Clay McCord, the porno film director,' David told Lollie. 'He's the best in the business.'

Duke stood up, and let the rug fall back over the wire.

'What we could do is conceal a transmitting microphone on the girl's body. We did that once on a movie called *Hard As Nails,* when we had about six people on one bed, and the sound came out pretty good.'

Lollie wrinkled up her nose. 'You want to put a microphone on my body? Like, where?'

'Well, it won't be up your snatch,' Duke said caustically. 'These things cost a hundred and fifty apiece, and we wouldn't like to lose it for ever.'

Lollie turned to David Radetzky and said, 'Who is this asshole?'

'Will you calm down?' asked David. 'We need to get the best reception possible, and if that means planting a microphone some place on your body, then that's what we'll have to do.'

'The navel is okay,' said Duke. 'We push the transmitter in, and then cover it with flesh-coloured latex. Then the thing to do is encourage the mark to go down on you. And when it's all over, get him to rest his weary head on your stomach, and engage him in conversation.'

'I have to get him to talk into my *navel*?'

'He doesn't have to talk *directly* into your navel,' Duke said impatiently. 'I mean, you don't have to stick out your stomach and say "Would you mind just saying a few words into here, Senator?" All you have to do is make sure you don't lie flat on your stomach and muffle the reception.'

'Is that what they teach you in the porno movies, sarcasm?' asked Lollie.

David looked at his watch. 'The Senator should be here soon. Lollie, I want you to call him almost as soon as he checks in at his hotel. Otherwise he's going to fix himself up with some other girl. His wife is at home in Minnesota this week, and he's making pretty full use of his freedom.'

'I thought the people who governed this country were supposed to be moral,' said Lollie, taking out her chewing gum and parking it under a simulated marble sidetable.

'Juan, will you bring me the Mullard remote transmitter from the blue case?' said Duke. 'And that latex make-up stuff. That's right. In the box that says MGM Make-up Department.'

David went to the window and parted the net drapes. 'It looks like the Senator's arriving now,' he said. 'There's a black Fleetwood just drawing up outside the Xanadu Hotel, and there's a bunch of people out there to meet it. Wait a moment. Yes, that's him.'

'I forgot what he looked like,' said Lollie. 'I just remember he wheezed a lot.'

'Would you take off your T-shirt,' asked Duke. 'I want to get this transmitter in before you make that call. Juan, will you go check that wiring?'

Lollie crossed her arms and tugged off her skimpy yellow T-shirt. All three men watched her with a kind of dispassionate relish. Her breasts were rounded and high, with a wide pink aureolas and prominent nipples There was a little spattering of pale freckles between them, which a boyfriend of hers had once described as 'seasoning.'

Without being asked, she unbuttoned her tight red satin pants, too, and eased her way out of them. Her pussy was scarcely covered by a scanty floss of gingery hair. The pants slid to the floor.

There was a silence, and then Duke said: 'Juan, will you *please* go check that wiring?'

Lollie lay back on the bed, and Duke got to work inserting the tiny transmitter. He stuck it into place first with a cyanoacrylate adhesive which actually bonded it to Lollie's skin, so that there was no chance of it falling out, no matter how sexually athletic she was. Then he carefully covered it with skin-pink latex rubber, and moulded the rubber into the curled shape of a navel.

'Your mother couldn't tell,' he said, when he was finished. 'Now let's test it out. Juan – do you want to get close to this lady's stomach and say something?'

Juan looked up from his wiring check. 'You bet your ass, Mr Duke.'

After Duke and Juan finished the final equipment tests, David Radetzky picked up the pale-blue rococo telephone and dialled the private number of Senator Chapman's suite. 'Come on,' he said to Lollie, and she obediently came across the room and took the receiver.

'It's still ringing,' she said.

David whispered, 'Duke – the amplifier.'

Duke went over to a makeshift amplification system on the table, and switched it on. Over the loudspeaker, they heard the phone ringing, and then they heard it picked up. There was a lengthy silence, and then Carl Chapman said gruffly, 'Hello? Who is this?'

'Senator Chapman?' Lollie said in a little-girl voice.

'That's right. Who are you? Who gave you this number? This is a private number.'

David whispered, 'Go on, tell him who you are. Tell him why you're here.'

'This is Lollie, Senator Chapman. Lollie Methven, from Miami, Florida. Don't you remember the Doral Hotel, room 1126? You said I was cataclysmic.'

'Lollie Methven?'

'That's right, Senator darling. Don't you remember that beautiful suck? Schlup, schlup, schlup, until you couldn't hardly stand it?'

There was an awkward pause, and then Senator Chapman said, 'I remember. But what the hell are you doing here?'

Lollie blinked at David Radetzky in bewilderment, but David hissed, 'Tell him you love him. You've been reading about him in the papers. You followed him here.'

Lollie gave a synthetic little giggle, and then said, 'The truth is, Senator darling, I couldn't get you out of my mind. I know it's silly, but I've fallen ass over curls in love with you.'

'That's romance?' asked Duke, throwing up his hands.

Lollie giggled again. 'I read in the *Miami Herald* you were flying to Las Vegas, and so I hocked my quad stereo to pay for my airfare, and here I am.'

There was another ruminative silence. Then Senator Chapman said, 'All right, you followed me here. What do you want?'

'Oh, Senator darling, I want you. I want to take off all your clothes and kiss you all over. I want to take your big stiff dork in my lips again, and schlup you till you're bone dry.'

Senator Chapman cleared his throat. 'I'm, uh, pretty busy tonight, Lollie. I have a couple of heavy meetings. I'm not so sure that I can –'

'You must,' insisted Lollie. 'I've missed you so bad, and there are so many things I want to do for you. Senator, I love you. You're the most masculine, sexy man that ever drew breath.'

Senator Chapman said, 'You really mean it, don't you?'

'Oh, yes, Senator. A thousand times over.'

'Well, uh, where could we meet? Where are you calling from?'

'I booked the Pompadour room at the Scirocco,' Lollie told him, while David Radetzky fiercely pointed to the name on top of the room service menu. 'It's all ready for you, Senator.'

'A nest of love,' whispered David.

'A nest of love,' repeated Lollie.

Senator Chapman was silent for a moment. Then he said, 'I can be there at twelve-thirty. How's that?'

'Oh, Senator, I'm going to count the hours,' said Lollie, coached by David.

'Well, that's wonderful,' answered Senator Chapman. 'I'm looking forward to it, too. How does that go again? Schlup, schlup, schlup?'

'That's right, darling. Schlup, schlup, schlup.'

David took the receiver and put the phone down.

Duke said, 'More like schmuck, schmuck, schmuck. Is that what makes our country great? Dummies like him?'

David took out a clean handkerchief and wiped his fingerprints off the telephone. 'We're not here to judge his politics, Duke. We're just here to get his wife divorced.'

Lollie said, 'How did I do? Was I okay?'

'Lollie, you were terrific. Now, you've got time to shower, and change into something sexy, and have yourself some dinner on room service. The steak here is passable, the clams farci are farcical, the cheeseburgers are better than nothing.'

'Will I see you again, Mr Radetzky? When it's over?'

David picked up his jacket. 'Not unless something goes wrong, and we have to try again. The less we see of each other, the better.'

'What about my money?'

'When you're through with Senator Chapman, take a taxi to the airport. Go to the United Airlines desk and ask for a package addressed to you. All your money will be there, plus a bonus if you're extra-specially good.'

'And twenty dollars if I –?'

David nodded. 'Sure. Twenty dollars if you –'

Duke said, 'We're all ready here, Mr Radetzky.'

'Okay,' said David. He put his arm around Lollie Methven's naked waist, although it was no more affectionate than a boss putting his arm around the stout middle of an elderly secretary.

'Do a nice job here, Lollie,' he said. 'And try to enjoy yourself, too.'

Lollie leaned over and kissed him. 'It's a job, Mr Radetzky, that's all. But you, I could go for.'

He took his arm away and grinned uneasily. 'Maybe you could,' he said, buttoning up his jacket. 'But that's not what we're here for, is it?'

TWENTY-ONE

Ken Irwin was lying on the surface of the pool on an inflatable airbed, his eyes closed against the afternoon sun, his hair dried into spikes from swimming. The airbed circled slowly around and around on the still water, and he appeared to be asleep. The Roman statues watched him with blind solemnity, and down in the gardens there was the monotonous hiss-hiss-hiss of a lawn sprinkler.

She had been watching him for some time from an upstairs window. He appeared to be asleep but she was not sure. He was naked, and getting very brown, and she liked the way his penis was curled up against his thigh.

She stepped back into the cool of the air-conditioned bedroom. It was a guest room, decorated in green, and it was hardly ever used. There was a single bed with a rounded oak bedhead, an oak chair, and a painting on the wall of a mustard field in France. For some reason, it reminded her of a room from her childhood.

Her ash blonde hair had been swept up in curls today, and covered with a fine lace cap with dangling pearls all around it. She wore a billowing white gown of cotton lace as transparent as smoke, which had been specially designed for her by the Moroccan dress designer Abid. Underneath it she wore nothing but tiny white cotton briefs.

There was something about Ken Irwin which nagged her, and disturbed her sleep. He was a willing, silent lover. He helped the staff to clean the house with efficiency and calm. And yet, considering he had been taken off the roadside and elevated into a life of luxury in one afternoon, considering that he was now the pet stud of one of Hollywood's most glittering ladies, he was strangely unimpressed and matter-of-fact.

The boy lovers she had taken before Ken Irwin had invariably been starstruck, and had followed her everywhere, delighted to bask in her ageing but still erotic charisma. But Ken went about his household duties without paying her any attention at all; and here he was, in the middle of the afternoon, lying on an airbed in the pool, apparently asleep.

Adele left the room, closing the door behind her. She went down the spiral oak staircase which served the back bedrooms, across the tiled hallway, and out through the back door. The sun was intensely hot and bright, and she wished she had remembered her sunglasses. She stepped on tiptoe across the scorching stones of the pool patio, until she was standing by the edge.

Ken, on his airbed, slowly circled the pool.

Adele said, in a clear, thespian voice: 'Consider the lilies, how they grow. They toil not, neither do they spin.'

Ken circled a little more, and then opened his eyes a fraction.

'You look very sexy,' she said, 'But if you stay out here much longer your little ding-a-ling will catch sunburn, and what will I do for pleasure tonight if that happens?'

Ken grinned. 'I was just waking up anyway.'

'I'm pleased about that,' she said. 'I was beginning to think that you might have grown tired of me.'

He rolled off the airbed, and splashed into the water. Then he swam with long, even strokes to the side of the pool. He lifted himself a little out of the water, and kissed her bare toes.

'You are a goddess,' he said, 'of whom no man could ever grow tired.'

'I wish my second husband had known that. It would have saved an awful lot of legal expense.'

He climbed out of the pool and shook himself like a wet dog. Then he reached for the thick Turkish towel that he had hung on the upraised arm of a Roman nymph, and wrapped it around his waist. He kissed her, and her thin dress clung to his wet body.

'Holman tells me you're very useful around the house,' said Adele, as they walked across the patio. 'He says you're very efficient.'

'I'm glad.'

'I don't know whether he's told you, but we're having a party on Saturday night. It's in honour of Tony Seiden. You know Tony Seiden the film director, don't you? He's finishing his new thriller on Friday, and we thought it would be nice for him to get away from Hollywood for his wrap-up party.'

'He directed *Secret Nights*, didn't he?'

'Directed and produced. The same with this one. It doesn't have a title yet, he calls it Number Seventeen.'

'He's kind of political, isn't he? I never saw *Secret Nights*, but I heard it was kind of political.'

Adele wafted in through the open door of the house. 'Tony's always political. He did that scathing picture on Mayor Daley of Chicago. That's why he always produces. He doesn't like other people telling him how to direct.'

Ken rubbed his hair with the towel as they walked through to the living room. Holman the butler was there, decanting the sherry, and Adele said, 'Holman, bring us two mint juleps, will you? Make them tart.'

Holman said, 'Yes, ma'am,' in a noticeably aggrieved tone.

'And Holman?'

'Yes, ma'am?'

'Mr Irwin is working for me, Holman, but he is also my guest and my friend. As well as yours, I hope.'

Holman kept his eyes on the floor. 'I'll bring the juleps right away, ma'am.'

After the butler had disappeared through the archway to the kitchen, Adele swirled about the room, her dress floating around her. Ken saw shadowy and tantalizing glimpses of her flat stomach, her perfect breasts, her slender thighs. She said, as she swirled, 'You mustn't mind Holman. He doesn't feel happy unless he has something to complain about. It's the butler's disease.'

Ken sat down in a heavy Spanish-style armchair, his towel draped loosely around his middle. He took a cigarette from the box on the table beside him, and lit it with a lighter in the shape of a conquistador's helmet.

'And what's the famous movie star's disease?' he asked her.

She smiled, but didn't stop dancing.

'I know what the sullen young gigolo's disease is.'

'Oh, yes?' asked Ken. 'And what's that?'

'It's over-confidence. An unshakeable belief in his own beauty. A firm conviction that his older mistress is so passionately fond of him that she could never bear to·throw him out.'

Ken stayed very still in his chair.

Adele twirled around a couple more times, and then came across the polished floorboards towards him. She leaned over him, and touched the tip of his straight young nose with her sharp pearl-painted nail.

'You've forgotten something already,' she said. 'I'm the ice queen. I have a heart of frozen stone.'

Ken licked his lips. He glanced up into her deep brown eyes, and he saw all of the years of pain there, all of the years of experience and fame and disappointment and of dragging herself out from under. His cigarette sent rags of blue smoke across the dim Spanish room, and outside he could hear one of the gardeners singing *Cuando caliente el sol* as he trimmed the herbaceous border.

'I didn't mean to take you for granted,' said Ken, in a husky voice.

'No,' said Adele. 'But you did.'

'What are you going to do?' he asked her.

She stood up straight, and walked a few paces back across the room. Her bare feet made a soft kissing sound on the floorboards.

'I'm not going to do anything,' she smiled. 'I happen to like you too much. And anyway, if we're having a party on Saturday, I'd like to show you off as my new stud. There are several ladies invited who will be absolutely emerald green with envy.'

'I hope you don't think that I've been trying to rip you off, just because you're a movie star,' Ken said. 'It hasn't been like that at all.'

She shrugged. 'It doesn't matter. You're not that important. I like you, I think you're cute, but just remember that you're not that important.'

Ken took a long, slow drag of his cigarette. He looked as if he might be about to say something, but didn't.

'I want to *parade* you on Saturday,' said Adele. 'I want you to look ravishing. A white silk shirt, open to the waist. White silk slacks, so tight that they can tell if you've been circumcised or not. White rope sandals. The ice queen's personal snow slave.'

'Who do you think I am? Liberace, or something?'

She gave a laugh that was like a carillon of small bells. 'Not at all. But I'll tell you something. For some reason I don't completely understand, you want to stay here much more than you've been trying to let on. You *need* to be here for some strange reason or another. Well, that's all right by me. You're a pleasantly decorative piece of flesh, and you're good in bed. But it's supply and demand in this world, Ken, buyer and bought, and if you want to stay here so desperately, then you're going to have to stay here on my terms. And my terms are that you strut around for me on Saturday with your shirt open and your pants tight, working my middle-aged lady friends up into a lather of jealousy.'

Holman came in with the mint juleps on a small silver tray, and then left again, like a shabby and disgruntled toucan.

141

'There's one alternative, of course. You can leave,' Adele said.

He looked at her. He said, in a thick voice, 'You really don't love me at all, do you?'

'Love you? Why should I?'

'I thought you might. Just a little.'

'My darling Ken, how can you think such a thing? I don't fall in love with people.'

He stood up, holding the towel around him. Against the light that strained through the living room window, his profile was dejected and sad.

'I guess the reason that I've been taking you for granted is because I've been trying to stop myself falling in love with you,' he said quietly.

She was sipping her mint julep, and she slowly lowered it.

'*What* did you say?'

He turned and gave her a brief, regretful smile.

'I didn't mean to. I was only looking for a few days of luxury living. Back where I come from in Montana, this kind of life is a fantasy. Folks wouldn't believe it existed for real if you showed them photographs. But I guess I got more than I bargained for. I fell in love with you, Adele. Instead of ripping *you* off, you went right out and ripped *me* off. You ripped off my heart.'

Adele stared at him. Then she set down her drink and walked across the room, her dress flowing around her magnificent body, her pearls glistening. She came right up close, so that her breast was touching his arm through the fragile lawn.

'I can't believe you sometimes,' she said. 'I really can't believe you. I don't think I've ever heard anyone talk such complete bullshit with such a completely straight face in my whole life.'

He didn't say a word. His brown chest rose and fell with his tense breathing. Somewhere in the house, a clock began to chime the hour of four.

Adele said, more softly, 'But you can stay, for as long as you like. I can't wait to see Hilary Nestor Hunter's face when you walk into the room on Saturday, and that's going to be worth a million bucks whether you love me or not.'

Ken gave her a small, secretive smile. Then he let the towel drop from his waist, and she saw that the thick, root-like veins in his penis were already swelling.

A little less than an hour and a half later, on the dusty road between Cathedral City and Rancho Mirage, under a wide velvety sky, a red AMC Jeep pulled off the road and stopped. Ken Irwin, in his jeans and his plaid shirt, was sitting behind the wheel with a cigarette between his lips and his easy-rider shades on the end of his nose. The radio was on very loudly, and it sounded oddly distorted out there in the open.

He didn't have long to wait. From the direction of Rancho Mirage, a primrose-yellow Pinto appeared, and drove gradually closer. As it approached the Jeep, it slowed down, and flashed its headlights once. It pulled over on to the opposite verge, and stopped.

Ken switched off his radio, swung down from the Jeep and walked across the road. There was a faint wind, but apart from that, there was only the sound of his desert boots on the ground.

The Pinto door opened, and out climbed a tall man with greased-back hair and sunglasses with mirrors for lenses. He was wearing a red open-necked shirt and black cord pants.

'How are you doing, Ken?' said the tall man.

'I'm fine, T.F. How are you?'

'Stiff in the butt. This was the largest car I could rent. I got it from AAA. Can't show my face around Avis or Hertz for a while.'

Ken leaned on the Pinto's hot yellow roof. 'I went up to the Cullen place,' he said. 'Madam's been pretty free with the use of her Jeep.'

'What did you find out?'

'Not much more than we already know. Cullen spends most of his weekdays out walking dogs and waxing cars. The girl stays home usually, making beads and artsy-crafty stuff to sell.'

'What about the fat guy with the beard?'

'Name's Mel Walters. His place is back in the trees a way. They're pretty good friends, apparently, and he comes down to supper once or twice a week. Usually Tuesdays and Thursdays.'

'So all three of them could be home tomorrow evening?'

Ken took a pack of cigarettes out of his shirt pocket. 'That's right. And it's real secluded up there. You could pitch Barnum and Bailey's circus in their front drive, and nobody would even see an elephant's ass from the road.'

T.F. leaned into the back of the Pinto and pulled out a long leather case. He lifted it on to the roof of the car, and clicked open the catches. Inside, its barrel wrapped in soft cloth, was his M-14.

'You're going to be able to get this into the house okay?'

'Sure thing. She never watches me. As long as I shove it up her once a day, and go around the house acting moody, she's happy.'

T.F. closed the case. 'You look after this. I've had this baby for years. It means something to me, you know?'

'Sure, T.F. Cigarette?'

T.F. took a cigarette and stuck it in his mouth. 'I really hate to be parted with it, you know?' he said, keeping his eyes on the horizon.

'Don't worry. I'll look after it.'

T.F. bent his head forward to accept a light from Ken's Zippo. He blew out smoke as if it was bitter, and said, 'The people I've nailed with that baby, you wouldn't believe. It means something to me.'

'For Christ's sake, T.F.'

T.F. looked at him, and Ken saw his own face, curved and dopey-looking, in the twin lenses of the tall man's sunglasses.

'I'd better be leaving,' said T.F. 'I have to get down to San Clemente tonight, for a job there.'

'I'll call you at three tomorrow,' said Ken.

'Okay, take it easy.'

T.F. climbed stiffly back into the Pinto, slammed the

door, and drove off. Ken stood by the side of the road until he had disappeared into the waves of reflected heat that shimmered on the horizon, a primrose yellow mirage that dwindled and shrank to nothing. Then he walked slowly back to the Jeep, carrying the long leather case. He covered the case with a tartan travelling rug, and then swung himself up into the driver's seat and started the motor.

TWENTY-TWO

In the first light of Thursday morning, Carl X. Chapman lay in the arms of Lollie Methven, his grizzled head resting on her breasts. She was stroking his temples with the tips of her fingers, soothing him. The blue and white bedroom was bright with desert sunshine.

'You're a girl in a million, you know that?' he said.

She stopped stroking for a moment, and looked down at him. 'I'm nothing special. Just a working girl.'

'There are working girls and working girls,' he insisted. 'And you're the best I ever met.'

'You must have met quite a few, huh?'

He chuckled. 'Hundreds. I reckon since I've been married that I've met hundreds. Tall ones, small ones, black ones, white ones. Blondes, brunettes, and redheads like you.'

Lollie eased herself up the bed a little way, to make sure that Carl was talking close to her navel. She said, 'You had sex with them all? I mean, intercourse?'

'What do you think I did? Played midget golf?'

She laughed. 'You're a beautiful person, Carl. I really want you to know that. A beautiful, beautiful person.'

He propped himself up on one elbow. 'You're damned beautiful yourself, Lollie. Apart from which, you have the sexiest mouth in the whole of the Western hemisphere. If I could take you back to Washington with me, all packed up in my luggage, I would.'

She gently pressed his head down against her breasts again.

'I wish I could come with you, Carl. I really do.'

He sighed. 'A politician who wants to succeed has to be married, honey. Or at least he has to *seem* to be married. It's the nation's guarantee that he's reliable, Christian, and heterosexual.'

'It really matters that much?'

'It does when you're aiming for the White House. I'm going to be President one day, Lollie, and a President needs a First Lady. That's why my wife and I have stayed married so long. It's not a marriage of love, although God knows it used to be. It's more of a business partnership these days. I don't think we've made love for more than a year, and then she told me I was behaving like an animal. A *hog*, she said. A Minnesota hog.'

Lollie said, 'You're going to be President? Is that for real?'

He propped himself up on his elbow again. 'Just about as sure as the sun's going to rise on Friday.'

'Wow,' said Lollie. 'You mean I'm in bed with the future President of the United States?'

He chuckled.

'You're really not joking?' she badgered him.

He lay back. 'No, I'm not joking.'

'But how do you know? Don't you have to get elected first?'

'Sure you have to get elected first. But there are ways of knowing how elections are going to turn out.'

'You mean you can predict them in advance? Like fortune-telling?'

'Something like that.'

Carl rolled over and stood up. Lollie tried to reach out for him, to keep him within range of her microphone, but he walked heavy-bellied and naked to the window, and looked out over Las Vegas and the desert. Lollie thought that he looked like a wise old orangutan, an elder statesmen from The Planet of the Apes.

'When I'm President,' he said, 'this country is going

to be great again. It's going to be strong, and proud, and pure.'

Lollie, anxious to pick up everything he said, climbed out of bed and twined her arms around him. She kissed the grey hair on his shoulders.

'I never met a President before,' she said. 'Not to talk to.'

'Well, it'll be something to tell your children, when you have them.'

'I'm so *proud*. You don't have any idea,' she gushed.

Carl put his arm around her, and gave her a squeeze. 'This country is crying out, do you know that? It needs a man who can tell it what to do, instead of compromising and backing down. It needs a man who can set it an example. A country is like a family, you know, and just like any family, it needs a father.'

He took a deep breath, and looked at her. His eyes were glistening with the emotion of his own rhetoric. 'Believe it or not,' he said, 'but I am that father.'

Lollie smiled, and then saw that he was deathly serious, and stopped smiling. 'Why don't you come back to bed?' she suggested. 'It's only six. Maybe we can do it once more. You know, once more with feeling.'

'You want *more*?'

She giggled. 'I like it with you, that's all. If you didn't have to work, I could stay in bed and do it all day.'

He beamed, but he shook his head. 'I don't have the time. I have a breakfast meeting in a half hour. I've got to get dressed, and haul my ass back to the Xanadu.'

'Not even a teensy one?' Lollie coaxed him in her little-girl voice.

'Not even a teensy one. I have three aides over there, and they'll be going bananas already.'

He sat down on the edge of the bed and looked up at her. The morning sun was behind her, and it glowed through her fine red hair, and gleamed on the pale skin of her breasts and her thighs.

She stepped forward, and stood in front of him, and laid her hands on his shoulders. He kissed her flat stomach, and his lips were within a half-inch of the microphone transmitter concealed in her navel.

147

'I'm going to tell you something, Lollie, and I hope you remember it in years to come. I'm going to be the greatest President that America ever knew, and that's because I was *born* to be President.'

'You mean you knew right from the time you were a kid?'

He nodded. 'I've never doubted it, not once. Not even when I've lost campaigns, or suffered setbacks in the Senate. All these years, I've never lost my belief in myself, and my fitness for the great task of leading America.'

She stroked his face. 'You're amazing,' she said. 'You're really and truly amazing. You have such confidence in yourself.'

He smiled. 'I have confidence because I know that I'm going to win. I have confidence because I'm the first President in history who's going to be elected because the people *need* him, rather than just because they *want* him.'

She gave a little, confused smile, and Carl said, 'You don't understand that, do you?'

'It doesn't matter,' she said. 'I was never much good at school. I just like hearing you talk.'

He lifted his chin and looked up at her. Her pert, pretty face looked down at him between the pale moons of her breasts, and that sprinkle of freckles called 'seasoning.'

'There're elections and elections, Lollie, just like there's working girls and working girls.'

He was speaking directly into her microphone now, enunciating each word as if he was a TV newscaster.

'Elections don't often give a fair representation of the real desires of the people. There are too many pressures from the media, too many pressures from fashion, too many pressures from the tides and the currents of time.'

Lollie said, 'That's Greek to me.'

'Well, look at this way,' said Carl. 'Television and newspapers tell people what they want. National moods tell people what they want. Emotions tell people what they want. But what people should vote for is what's going to be best for them, and what's best for them is not very often what they want.'

'But how do you make people vote for something they don't want?' asked Lollie, still baffled. 'I mean, how can you make them act that way?'

Carl smiled patiently. 'It's very simple,' he said. 'In any society, all these emotions and moods I've been talking about are generated by a comparative handful of people. There are people in any group who are leaders, and everyone else in the group takes their cue from them.'

'I know,' said Lollie, 'like a flock of sheep.'

'Well, it's a little more complicated than that. What you have a society, say, like Los Angeles, you have leaders on all kinds of levels with all kinds of different ideas. You have ethnic leaders, local political leaders, PTA leaders. You even have people who are leaders simply because everyone else on their block likes them and respects them.'

'Is that so?' said Lollie, trying to look as if she understood what he was saying.

He gently lifted her hands from his shoulders and stood up. 'It's not really the kind of thing you should bother yourself about,' he told her in a warm voice. 'Why don't you stick to what you do best?'

'But it's fascinating,' she insisted.

He picked up his shorts from the floor, where they had been provocatively tugged down the previous night. As he stepped into them, he said, 'It's the leaders who sway the way that everybody else votes. So if you can work out how *they're* going to vote, then you know how the country as a whole is going to vote. As the leaders go, so goes the nation.'

He located his undershirt. 'These days, you can work out how the leaders are going to vote with something very scientific called the Sweetman Curve.'

She giggled. 'The Sweetman Curve? That sounds kind of cute.'

'It's cute all right, because it works. And because once you know for certain how an election is likely to turn out, you can use that information to make sure that it turns out the way you want it to, instead of the way the nation wants it to. That's what I mean by making people vote for what they need, instead of what they want.'

Lollie came up and put her arms around him. 'You get to the leaders?' she asked him. 'You bribe them or something?'

He kissed the tip of her nose. 'Something like that.'

'Supposing they say no?' she whispered, nuzzling his ear.

'Then we try something else.'

'Like what?'

Carl's eyes suddenly went cold. He took hold of Lollie's wrists and held them with unrelenting tightness.

'You're asking a hell of a lot of questions.'

She blushed. 'It's only because I'm interested.'

'What makes a working girl like you so interested in politics?'

'You're hurting me,' she protested.

Carl snapped, 'I asked you a question, honey. What makes you so all-fired interested?'

'I'm not going to tell you until you let me go.'

'You'll tell me now or I'll break your fucking jaw.'

She glanced at him, confused and frightened. He had lost his temper and his self-control so quickly, without any warning at all, that she thought for a moment that he was acting, playing around with her. But his grip on her wrists was so painful that she knew he meant it.

She said, 'If you're going to be President – I mean, if you're really going to be President – then it's worth being your friend, right?'

'That's right.'

'Well, that's why I wanted to know. I just wanted to know if you really were, or if you were kidding.'

He kept hold of her wrists for a few moments, and then released her. Standing there in his underwear, he told her darkly, 'I never kid. And I don't believe you.'

'It's true, Carl. It's really true. It's what's really important, right? I mean, all this divorce stuff, that doesn't mean anything, right?'

Carl had been casting around for his socks. But he

jerked his head towards her, and stared at her as if she was crazy.

'Divorce stuff?' he demanded. 'What divorce stuff?'

She backed off. 'Just divorce stuff, that's all. You know, with your wife and everything. You do *know*, don't you?'

'Know *what*? I don't know a damned thing!'

Lollie reached for her baby-pink satin wrap, and pulled it around her protectively.

'Well, it's really nothing,' she said nervously. 'It's just that I thought you knew.'

Carl stepped across the bedroom towards her with three fierce strides, and seized her hair in his fist. He bent her head back and glared at her from less than an inch away, so close that she couldn't focus on him.

'You thought I knew *what*?'

'It's nothing, Carl, it's just a joke.'

'A joke? What kind of a joke?'

She tried to twist her head away, but he clenched her hair tighter, and forced her head even further back.

'Oh, Christ, you're hurting me,' she told him.

'That's the intention. I want to know more about this joke. Like, who's playing it, and why.'

'It's – it's only your wife,' gasped Lollie. 'She wa – wanted divorce stuff against you. This place is – wired for sound – and movies –'

Carl raised his head and looked around the bedroom. '*Sound?*' he whispered. 'And movies?'

'That's – that's right. It was a – private detective. His name's David – Radetzky.'

'Radetzky?'

'That's right. Oh, Christ, let me go, will you?'

Carl released Lollie's hair and pushed her roughly towards the bed. 'Stay there,' he ordered her, and then went straight to the phone. He picked it up, and dialled his private number at the Xanadu.

There was a pause, and then he said, 'Umberto? This is Carl. Yes, I know we're late for the meeting. Forget the damned meeting. I want you to get right on over to the Scirocco. Because I damned well said so. Bring Val with you, too. That's right. And there's one more thing.

Call Mr Domani at the Lucky Stallion, tell him there's a private investigator in town name of Radetzky, David Radetzky. Tell him it would help if Mr Radetzky stayed within the city limits until we've had the opportunity to talk to him. That's it. And do it quick.'

He banged down the phone and turned towards Lollie.

'You cheap whore,' he snarled at her. 'Do you know where the cameras and the mikes are hidden?'

White-faced, she said, 'They didn't show me. It was all done by the time I got here.'

'Well, it doesn't matter too much,' breathed Carl. 'Because we're going to get hold of this Radetzky character and we're going to make *him* show us. And then we're going to put the movies and the tapes on a plate, and shake a little Heinz ketchup on them, and make him eat them. And if you think I'm joking, I'm not.'

'I don't think you're joking,' said Lollie, in a hushed voice.

As Carl got dressed, he said, 'You've heard me say one or two things today about politics, honey. Things about elections and votes and how they can be manipulated. Well, I want you to remember that they're only theories, okay? Not for real. Just theories. And when you've remembered that, I want you to forget that you ever heard a word of what I said, and if you ever breathe a single word about the Sweetman Curve to anybody, then I'm going to make sure, personally, that your neck gets broken.'

'I won't say nothing to nobody, Carl. I promise you.'

He tightened the knot of his tie. 'I just hope your promises are better than your grammar.'

There was a quiet knock at the door, and Carl went to answer it. In stepped two tall, dark men. One of them wore an immaculate white suit, and had carefully-greased hair, like Rudolf Valentino, and a small clipped moustache. The other, in scruffy jeans and a blue sweatshirt with *Franklin and Marshall College* printed on the front, had an unshaven chin and close set eyes which gave him the appearance of a mental defective.

'We've got a problem here,' Carl said. 'This broad lured me up here last night under false pretences. The whole room here is bugged for sound and vision.'

The man in the white suit lifted an eyebrow, and looked towards Lollie.

'Did you say anything?' he asked Carl.

'What do you think?' Carl snapped back. 'I want you to look the place over, see if you can locate the mikes. If you can't, stay here until Mr Domani picks up the private investigator for us.'

'And what about the girl?' asked the man.

'Do what you like. Give her a slight accident.'

The man nodded. 'Okay. Are you going to the meeting now?'

'I'm going to change first, and take a shower. If you have any problems, call Phil.'

'Phil's gone over to the meeting already.'

'In that case, come over to the meeting. But I don't want anything to go wrong. I want all the movies found, all the tapes found, and I want Radetzky found, and I don't want any fuss.'

'You got it,' the scruffy man said laconically.

Carl opened the door, and then paused.

Lollie, with her wrap tightly pulled around her, said, 'Carl – you're not going to leave me?'

Carl smiled. 'You'll be taken care of. Just the way you took care of me. So long, Lollie.'

Then he closed the door and he was gone.

The tall man in the white suit took off his coat, hung it on a hanger on the back of the door, and then brought a bedroom chair across to the bed where Lollie was sitting. He sat astride the chair, with his elbows resting on the back, and he looked at her with eyes as dark and shiny as the backs of bugs. The scruffy man stood a little way behind him, cleaning his fingernails with his front teeth.

'My name's Umberto,' said the man in the white suit. 'What's yours?'

'Lollie,' Lollie said anxiously.

Umberto nodded in appreciation. 'Lollie, that's a nice name. This is Val, incidentally. You mustn't mind

Val on account of Val was dropped by his mom when he was a kid.'

'What are you going to do to me?' asked Lollie. 'Carl said an accident. You're not going to give me an accident, are you?'

Umberto's eyes closed and opened like a sleeping cat's. 'Accident? No way. Everything Val and me do, we do on purpose.'

'Stand up, kid,' Val said quietly.

Lollie looked at Umberto for help, but Umberto simply said, 'Go ahead. Do like the man says.'

She stood up. She felt alternately hot and shivery, and she wondered if there was something wrong with the air-conditioning. Val stepped up to her, and walked around her, as if he was admiring a statue.

'Okay,' said Val, 'that's nice. Now drop the robe.'

Lollie clung to her wrap even tighter.

Val continued to walk around her, and then came up and stood in front of her. His expression was calm, but strangely irrational, and he kept licking his lips as if he was thirsty. There were cold-sores all around the side of his mouth.

'Um, I said drop the robe,' he repeated, almost politely.

Lollie didn't move, but she could feel her pulse speeding up.

Val, watched from his chair by a benignly smiling Umberto, came right up close to Lollie and stared into her face. He must have been eating onions for breakfast, because she could smell them on his breath.

With brutal strength, he seized the front of Lollie's satin wrap and tore it off her. Then he flung it across the room, and stood facing her, panting. She let out a little high-pitched breath, and stared back at him, wide-eyed.

'You have a lovely body, Lollie,' Umberto said pleasantly. 'Do you know that? A body like that, it's a genuine pity to waste.'

Val didn't say anything, but pulled his sweatshirt over his head, baring his hairy chest, and unbuckled his jeans. He stank of stale sweat, but Lollie found herself

154

thinking, thank God he only wants to have sex with me. Thank God it's only that.

'Umberto, you joining me?' Val asked in that same odd, polite tone, as if he was inviting his friend to take tea with him at the Bel-Air Hotel.

'If it's all right by you, Val, I'll just sit and watch.'

Val pushed Lollie towards the bed. 'Come on then, let's get it together.'

Lollie lay on her back on the bedcovers, and Val climbed astride her. He bent forward first of all and kissed her, and she could feel the coarse bristles of his chin scratching her face, and the crusted sores around his mouth, but all the time she kept herself in neutral shift, and told herself over and over, *it's only sex, it'll soon be over, it's only sex.*

Val squeezed her breasts, and sucked a bit at her nipples. She tried not to, but she couldn't help crying out, and then he bit her even harder. Then she felt his hand between her legs, tugging at her pubic hair as if he was going to wrench it out, feeling her and stimulating her. She could feel her cheeks flushing hotly as she realised that she was aroused.

He forced a finger up her, then another, and probed deeply into her soft, wet flesh. Then his thumb went up her bottom, and he began to tug at the thin skin that divided his fingers and his thumb, and she felt as if he were pulling her insides out.

He mounted her roughly, forcing her thighs wide apart, so wide that she was frightened they were going to crack. His erection pressed into her with his whole weight, huge and hard, and it went up her so far that she jumped in nervous response. She kept her eyes shut tightly, feeling the weight of his hairy, stinking body on top of her, feeling his penis ramming into her harder and harder, and she wanted so much to keep herself detached, to believe that it wasn't happening to her at all. But the sensations inside her wouldn't let her, and in shame and fear she felt herself beginning to shake with an orgasm, a tremor that came and passed, while Val still thrust and gasped and bludgeoned.

When Val himself finally climaxed, he twitched and

clawed at her as if he was having a fit. She felt the spasms of his ejaculation inside her, and again that shameful tremor began, but she didn't reach an orgasm properly. She turned her head sideways, and opened her eyes, and it was then that she felt something warm and wet splash on to her cheek, and slide stickily into her ear.

She looked up. Umberto was standing over her, with a faint smile on his face, his cheeks a little bright, and he was just putting himself away. She said, 'Oh, God,' and wiped at her face with the bedcover.

Val climbed off her and walked across to the other side of the room, breathing heavily. Lollie stayed where she was on the bed; she had learned already that with Val, you did what you were told, and only what you were told.

Umberto took out a dark green silk handkerchief, turned away from her, and blew his nose. Then he said, 'You see? We're men who appreciate a beautiful girl.'

Val pulled his jeans up, buckled the belt, and told Umberto, 'I'll go run the bathwater.'

Lollie, lying still and frightened, heard the faucets splashing. Umberto paced up and down, more restless now, and occasionally glanced at Lollie and gave her a little encouraging smile.

'This your first time in Vegas?' he asked her.

She nodded, without speaking.

'Yes, it's a place with its own character,' said Umberto. 'Some people say that it's America's Gomorrah. Other people find it fun.'

Val came out of the bathroom, and said, 'Okay, it's ready.'

Between them, they helped Lollie off the bed. She didn't even understand, as they guided her solicitously through to the bathroom, what they intended to do. It was steamy in there, and the walls were tiled in turquoise. She saw her pale body in the misted-up bathroom mirror, marked with red bruises and scratches where Val had mauled her.

They assisted her into the bath. She stood there, shin-deep, her arms held over her breasts, and said, 'It's real hot. I don't usually take a bath this hot.'

Umberto said, 'Come on, sit down, make it easy on yourself.' Lollie sat, and stared up at them, and then of course she knew.

She splashed, and struggled, and tried to get out of the tub, but her foot slipped on the bottom, and Val pushed her face-first under the water. It was very hot, and she swallowed a huge mouthful of it. She heard Val's knees striking the sides of the tub in great distorted booms of sound, and bubbles of air bursting all around her.

Somehow, she managed to force her head up out of the water again, and she let out a terrible gargling scream. But Val pushed her back under, until her nose was pressed against the bottom of the tub, and his strength was so overwhelming that she lay there with scalded eyes and nose, and knew that she was going to drown.

She held her last breath as long as she could, until her lungs felt as if they were cast out of lead. Then she let it out, in an agonized rush of bubbles, and drew in hot bathwater.

Val and Umberto waited in the bathroom for almost five minutes. They didn't say much, or even look at each other much. When the time was up, Val let Lollie go, and she lay there, face-down, her red hair floating darkly in the water.

'Let's get those mikes out,' said Umberto, and ushered Val out into the bedroom. 'You look for wiring under the rug, and bugs under the bed. I'll check the mirrors for cameras.'

Val looked back at Lollie just once. He said, 'You know something, when you think of the risks, you wonder why they do it. Dumb broads.'

TWENTY-THREE

When the painted wooden clock on the living room wall struck eight on Wednesday evening, John switched off his desk lamp, rubbed his eyes and stretched. Vicki, who was embroidering a bead belt across on the other side of the room, said, 'Finished for tonight?'

He looked wearily over the heaps of newspaper cuttings and papers in front of him. 'I guess so. But it's one of those problems you can never quite come to grips with. There seems to be some kind of connection, some kind of answer, but somehow there's never enough solid evidence.'

He stood up, and walked across to the centre of the room. 'I could do with a beer,' he told her. 'Do you want one?'

'If I have a beer, it's going to go straight to my head, and this embroidery is going to wind up a mish-mosh. Do you remember the time I tried to mend your socks when I was stoned?'

He went through to the kitchen and opened the icebox. 'I remember. How could I ever forget? They were the most beautifully darned socks in the history of needlework. What did it matter if they were sewn to the arm of the chair?'

'They made good record cleaners,' she retorted, as he walked back in with a cold can of Coors.

'Sure, and we were the only couple in Topanga with Ban-Lon record cleaners.'

He came over and kissed her dark, silky hair. It smelled of natural shampoo, and that elusive smell of her. 'Did I tell you that I loved you today?' he said.

She raised her head and kissed him on the lips. 'You just did,' she said quietly.

He sat down in a big Victorian rocking chair, and rocked backwards and forwards for a while. 'Is Mel coming over tomorrow?' he asked.

'I think so,' she said. 'That's if you haven't scared him off with all these conspiracy theories of yours.'

'*My* conspiracy theories? It was Mel who turned me on to the whole idea.'

She put down her embroidery and looked at him. 'And now he's scared. Can you blame him? The sweetest thing he ever heard in his life was Detective Morello saying that he'd checked out every one of those twelve people who died, and that the evidence *still* pointed to a lone fruitcake.'

John swallowed beer, and shrugged. 'I still think Mel was right in the first place. It's just inconceivable to me that all these people should have been killed for no reason.'

'Maybe Mel *was* right in the first place. But don't forget that Mel has an estranged wife and a little girl he loves very dearly, and when Mel got himself involved with this business he suddenly came face to face with death. So did we, for that matter.'

'You want to back out, too?'

'Sure I do. But I'm not going to back out until you do.'

He thought for a moment. Then he said, 'There has to be a reason for these killings. There has to be some common factor that explains them all. I thought it was politics at first, but maybe Detective Morello's right. None of the victims were particularly political, and even the ones that were had such *mild* opinions.'

He got out of the rocker, and walked back towards his desk. 'All the people I've checked had the same kind of middle-of-the-road liberal point of view. They were all teachers, or social workers, or college lecturers, or insurance salesmen, or housewives. All of them with a decent education, all thinking people, but people who weren't prepared to take anything for granted.'

'You're trying to tell me they were killed for that?' asked Vicki.

'Well, why else?'

She knotted a blue thread, and snipped it off. 'I don't know, John. I really don't. But even if it's only to keep

us out of danger, I think I'm beginning to believe Detective Morello.'

She added softly, 'I love you, John. You're the first
man who's ever given me real happiness. I don't want
to see you killed because of some crazy idea about a conspiracy. You can see that, can't you?'

He was silent for a moment, and then he nodded.

'Sure, I can see it. But I can also see that an awful lot
of people are getting killed out there, completely innocent people, and if it is some kind of weird conspiracy,
then it ought to be brought out in the open.'

He picked up some news clippings from his desk.

'Look at this one,' he said. 'A twenty-five-year-old
postgraduate student from Madison, Wisconsin. Inex-
plicably shot dead while he was pushing off his boat
early one morning on Lake Waubesa. Here's another.
A grocery store manager, forty-two, shot dead for no
reason while he was waiting at a stop light on his way
home in Pennsauken, New Jersey. And another one. A
nineteen-year-old Post Office trainee shot dead in Hat-
tiesburg, Mississippi, when he was out on his first letter-
carrying round.'

John dropped the clippings back on the desk.

'None of these people were robbed. All of them were
killed by unknown assailants for no known reason. All
of them were shot, usually by sniper fire, or from passing
automobiles.'

Vicki had put down her embroidery again, and was
sitting in the circle of light from the brass reading-lamp
with an expression of gentle sadness.

'I've called as many of the bereaved on the phone as
I've been able to trace,' John went on, 'and police de-
partments in fifteen states. It's always the same story.
Shots from military surplus rifles, usually M-14s. And
always the same kind of person. The quiet, unassuming
liberals. People who were liked and respected. It's
almost as if they're being shot because they're popular.'

'Are they really your responsibility?' Vicki asked.

'I guess it depends what responsibility means. If it
means looking after yourself, and to hell with your
fellow human beings, then, no, I don't think they *are*

my responsibility. But somebody shot my father, Vicki, and that somebody is going to shoot somebody else's father, and somebody else's mother, or brother, or sister, or lover. And even if I make myself think that responsibility ends at the front door, I can't let those people get killed without making some effort to save them.'

She came across to him. 'Hasn't it occurred to you that these shootings are just coincidence? There's so much crime, maybe this is just an ordinary national percentage of unexplained shootings,' she said.

He reached out and touched her hair, tugging it softly into separate strands.

'Yes,' he said, 'I thought of that.'

'And?'

'The number of unexplained shootings in the continental United States has *quadrupled* in the past two years, compared with a general rise in the homicide rate of seven percent.'

'So what does that mean?'

He let out a sigh. 'It means that a lot of innocent people are being shot for no apparent reason. It doesn't prove anything, or establish anything, but that's what it means, and I believe that a conspiracy is possible. Not certain, maybe not even probable. But possible.'

Vicki went across to the telephone and picked it up. She held out the receiver. 'Call the FBI. That's all you have to do.'

'Call the FBI? And what am I supposed to tell them?'

'Tell them just what you told me. Then you can leave *them* to investigate it. They probably know something about it already, if the crime figures have gone up the way you say they have. Come on, John, that's what they're there for.'

'And what if they just laugh at me? Or what if they don't laugh, but don't do anything about it?'

'John,' she insisted, 'call them.'

He took the receiver from her, and laid it back on its rest.

'I want to make one more check. There's a woman in Mar Vista whose son was shot on the Santa Monica Freeway. I called her this morning and promised to go talk about it. I'll make that one check, and then I'll call the FBI.'

Vicki lowered her eyes, and then said softly, 'All right. As long as you promise.'

'Cross my heart and hope to fall off Mount Baldy.'

She put her arms around him and kissed him. A slow, sensitive, lingering kiss, both provocative and tender.

'I just want to keep you alive,' she whispered. 'You're no good to me dead. No good at all.'

TWENTY-FOUR

It was a corner house overlooking Mar Vista playground. A bunch of neighbourhood kids were out skateboarding and playing ball when he pulled up outside. They stared at his car with blatant curiosity. He climbed out and locked it.

The car was a '58 Lincoln Capri that had been loaned by the custom bodyshop where his Imperial was being repaired. They specialised in 1950s automobiles, and he was a favoured customer. He had picked it up this morning on his way to Mar Vista district, and he was already wishing he had walked enough dogs and waxed enough cars to be able to afford to buy it. It was Pepsodent-white, with whitewall tyres, and a front end that looked like a Chinese dragon, all slanted headlamps and chrome bullets.

A black kid in a Charlie Brown T-shirt came up to him and said, 'Are you an alien, or what?'

He grinned. 'I come from the planet Mongo, and here's a quarter to keep an eye on my spaceship.'

He went up the dusty steps of the house, and looked down the row of bell-pushes by the front door. He saw K. Perlman on the third floor, and he pressed it. A crackly voice on the intercom said, 'Who is it?'

John identified himself, and the door buzzed open.

He stepped into the stale-smelling hallway, stepping over bicycles and strollers and toys. He walked upstairs until he reached the third floor, and knocked at a cracked, brown-painted door.

He waited for a while, then the door opened a crack, and an old woman's face appeared. She was extravagantly made-up, with henna-red hair, plucked eyebrows, and a mouth of vivid scarlet lipstick.

'Mrs Perlman?' he asked. 'I'm John Cullen.'

'I know,' she told him. 'I was just checking to see if you looked suspicious or not.'

He smiled. 'I see. And what do you think?'

'You'll do,' she said, and unlatched the security-chain.

Inside, Mrs Perlman's apartment was hung with dozens of engravings and daguerrotypes of early American and European landscapes. In the living room, there was a circular table with a fringed velvet cloth, and a large mildewed rubber plant in the centre of it. Mrs Perlman led the way through, and pulled out a chair for each of them.

'Would you care for some coffee?' she asked him. 'I bought a fresh can of Maxwell House last Friday.'

'That's kind of you,' he said.

While he waited for her, he looked around the room. The cheap print drapes were drawn back, and the morning sunlight came through the dirty windows like bright fog. On the varnished sideboard, there was a hideous china fruit dish, and a framed photograph of a young boy of nineteen or twenty, an obvious studio portrait, and somehow all the more poignant for that.

In a glass-fronted bookcase, there were rows of bound copies of *Vogue*.

After a few minutes, Mrs Perlman came shuffling back in, carrying a wooden tray with two cups of pallid instant coffee and a saucer of coconut cookies. She set them down on the table, and then sat down herself, with a deep sigh.

'Sugar, Mr Cullen?'

'No thank you.'

She took a coconut cookie off the tray and dipped it into her coffee until it was soggy. She said, 'You'll have to excuse me. My dentist makes false teeth like a *klutz*.'

John sipped the tepid coffee, and then set the cup back on the saucer. 'Did the police tell you how your son died?' he asked.

She nodded, without looking at him. 'On the freeway, coming home early from work. He was a processor for movies, developing the rushes for big feature movies, you know? He worked on *Silver Streak*, with Gene Wilder, and Gene Wilder told him personally afterwards he was the best.'

'That's real nice,' John said politely.

There was a silence, and then Mrs Perlman said, 'The police said they couldn't think of any motive, why anyone should shoot him. He was just driving home, and some other car came up alongside him, and only one shot was fired. Straight at poor Nathaniel's head.'

'Were there any witnesses?'

'None. Everybody's blind when there's danger. So the *dybbuk* who killed my son goes free.'

'What were your son's political opinions, Mrs Perlman? Would you call him a liberal, or what?' John asked.

'A liberal, that's right,' she told him. 'Always a liberal. At work, he organised a club for movie process people out of work. He said the big studios and processors, they didn't care for the little people.'

John took a small notepad out of his coat pocket, and made a note of that. Nathaniel Perlman, thirty-one, film processor, liberal. Killed on the freeway from a moving car by an unknown assailant, for no obvious motive. In two days of telephone calls, and three personal visits, John had checked out twenty-seven of these shootings. He had chosen a random from the press clippings. Nathaniel Perlman was the twenty-eighth.

He talked to Mrs Perlman for an hour or two, until eleven o'clock, and then thanked her for the coffee and left. He guessed he was going to have to keep his promise to Vicki now, and call the FBI. He only wished he could have a little more time to analyse some of these homicides, to check up on more of them, to find out what kind of a fatal plague was systematically ridding

America of apparently innocent and well-liked people.

He was halfway down the stairs when one of the doors on the next landing opened, and a young blond man in a plaid shirt and jeans stepped out. John tried to get past, but the young man jerked out his hand and grabbed the rail, and stopped him. John cautiously took a step back, and looked the young man up and down.

'Are you going to let me pass?' he asked the young man.

The blond man was tanned, and looked athletic and fit. 'Are you John Cullen?' he said.

'What's it to you?'

The young man waited for a moment, and then said again, 'Are you John Cullen?'

'That's right,' John finally said. 'Now, who the hell are you?'

Without any warning at all, the young man punched him hard in the stomach. Totally winded, John fell back against the stairs, and cracked his head against the skirting-board as he collapsed. Then the young man kicked him in the legs and the ribs.

John lay there, his face against the worn linoleum, his stomach aching and his head ringing with noise. He could see the young man's feet, and he gingerly looked up towards his face.

The young man was impassive. He said, in a quiet but distinct voice, 'I'm sorry I had to do that, Mr Cullen. But I was told to put you into a co-operative frame of mind before we left.'

John wiped blood away from his lips with the back of his hand. 'Left?' he said hoarsely. 'Left for where?'

The young man reached down and pulled at his arm. 'You'll find out when you get there. Meanwhile, I'd appreciate your help. Just get yourself up off the floor, and walk downstairs a little way ahead of me. When you get outside, turn left, and walk as far as a brown Buick Century parked by the kerb in Rose Avenue.'

John painfully climbed to his feet, using the railing to support himself. He was still trying to catch his breath, and he felt uncomfortably nauseous. The young man jerked his thumb towards the next flight of stairs, and said, 'Faster, Mr Cullen. And please remember that I have a gun.'

He stared at the young man's face for a long, tense moment. The young man smiled, and said, 'Believe me, it's all the same to me if you live or if you die. So please get moving.'

John went down the stairs to street level, stepping carefully over the junk in the hall. He opened the front door, and outside, the street was glaringly bright. With a quick look back at his captor, he went down the steps, and turned left towards Rose Avenue. The young man with the plaid shirt and the blond hair followed twenty or thirty feet behind, glancing quickly and nervously around the street as he walked.

From across the street, the black kid who had been looking after his car came running. The kid skipped along beside him, and said, 'I took care of your space-ship, mister. I took care of it good.'

John quickly looked over his shoulder at the young man. The young man jerked his head at him urgently, telling him to keep moving.

John said, out of the side of his mouth, 'You want to make yourself a whole buck?'

The black kid nodded his head up and down enthusiastically.

'Well, here's what to do,' said John. 'You just go to that phone booth over there, and dial 625-3311, and ask for the police. When they answer tell them I've been kidnapped, and they've got to get here real quick, and put out a call for that brown Buick Century over there.'

'Are you kidding me?' asked the kid, dancing along beside him.

The young man called out: 'Keep going, Cullen. Tell the kid to scram.'

John said, 'He was just looking after my car, that's all. I was telling him to look after it a while longer.'

'Well, just tell him to scram.'

John said; 'Go on, scram.'

'What about my buck, man?' asked the kid.

'I'll pay you later, when I've been rescued.'

'Oh, sure,' the kid said sarcastically. 'I've heard *that*

one before. What do you take me for, a dummy?'

The young man in the plaid shirt caught up with them, and snapped; 'Keep your mouth shut, Cullen. Kid – you get out of here before I twist your legs off and use them for toothpicks.'

The black kid went running off, and the young man pushed Cullen roughly towards the parked Buick. He opened the back door, and hustled John inside. There was another man already sitting behind the wheel, a fat man with huge shoulders and ears like growths of red fungus. He held the wheel in his hands like a toy.

The young man said, 'Okay, Merton. Let's get out of here. Head for the Ventura Freeway.'

'Whatever you say, Ken,' and started up the motor. Merton pulled the car away from the kerb and U-turned in the street to take a right at Colbert. Then he spun the wheel towards Federal Avenue, took another right at National Boulevard, and drove up the northbound ramp on to the San Diego Freeway.

Both Ken and Merton were silent as they drove through West Los Angeles with the morning sun lighting the interior of the car.

'I've been wanting to meet you people,' John said.

Neither of them answered.

John looked out of the window of the car for a while, watching salesmen and families and van drivers cruising obliviously past him, all unaware that he was in danger of his life.

'I suppose you guessed what I was doing as soon as I went round to see Mrs Daneman,' he said.

Ken glanced at him, but said nothing.

'Well,' John continued, 'I guess it was kind of stupid of me to stick my nose in where it wasn't wanted. But you people are really acting obvious, aren't you? It can't be long before the FBI get on to you.'

Merton, the fat man in the front, said in a breathless voice, 'Will you shut up?'

'I'm sorry. I was only trying to make conversation,' John said.

Ken gave him a tired, humourless smile. 'This isn't like the movies, Mr Cullen. The victim doesn't sit in the car giving out with a bunch of crap which needles the hit men so much that they lose their cool. It just doesn't happen that way.'

'You're not even going to tell me what you're going to do?'

'Sure,' said Ken. 'We're going to kill you.'

'Are you going to tell me why?'

'You know why,' panted Merton. 'You just gave out with why.'

'You mean I'm right? You're actually going around knocking people off?'

'Don't answer that, Merton,' Ken said quietly.

'I wasn't going to,' Merton said. 'I have a date with Bea tonight, and I'm saving my breath up.'

Ken sat back in his seat and looked at Merton with an arch grin. 'I'd pay a million bucks to see you and Bea making it together. Talk about the collision of the Zeppelins.'

Merton wasn't offended by this remark at all, and let out a high-pitched, wheezing giggle.

'You won't even tell me why you're killing people? You killed my father, and you won't even let me know why?' John said.

Ken turned to him with a handsome, bored expression. 'Give it a rest, Cullen. It doesn't make any difference if you know or if you don't know.'

John stayed silent. He looked at his hands, clasping his knee, and he saw that his knuckles were spotted with white. His muscles were locked up tight like woodworking clamps, and he felt cold all over; he slowly began to understand, in a ghastly revelation, how frightened he actually was. These men, without any emotion, were going to end his life in cold blood. These men who didn't even know him, or what he was. They were just going to take him out and kill him.

They reached the Ventura Freeway, and turned east into the sun. Merton pulled down his sun-visor, and sneezed a couple of times. John looked across at Ken again, but Ken was watching him with complete impassiveness. They could have been anything, these men. Waiters, salesmen, out-of-work extras. It was their or-

168

dinariness that made them so frightening.

Merton switched on the car radio. There was a blather of news and commercials, and then he tuned to a schmaltzy music station. With a terrible wryness, John reflected that it was just his luck to go to his funeral to the sounds of Mantovani.

On their left, the blue-and-ochre San Gabriel Mountains were hazed in late morning mist, although the radio was predicting another hot one. Merton said, in a matter-of-fact way, 'Do you want to go fishing next week, after you finish up at Palm Springs?'

Ken shrugged. 'Did you line up a boat yet?'

'I can if you're interested. I know Bea wants to go.'

'You and Bea together in one boat? What are you going to rent? The *Queen Mary*?'

Merton cackled. He was still laughing as he turned off the Ventura Freeway at the Griffith Park off-ramp, and then took a left by Travel Town, where old Union Pacific and Southern Pacific locomotives and trains were parked out in the open for children to climb on. But they were hardly past the park when, without warning, a Hughes supermarket truck pulled out of the turn-off in front of them, and Merton was forced to jam on the brakes.

He put down his window, and yelled at the truck-driver, '*You asshole!*'

The truck snorted and shuddered to a halt across the highway. Then the cab door opened, and a beefy red-faced driver in greasy yellow coveralls climbed down from the cab and walked slowly back towards them.

The truck driver leaned on the roof of the Buick and stared at Merton with massive self-control.

'Did you say something, fat man?'

'I didn't say nothing,' wheezed Merton. 'I'm a sick man, now get out of my way.'

The truck driver didn't appear to be in any hurry. He said, 'I suggest you get out of that car, mister, and repeat yourself. Because if you said what I thought you said, I'm going to turn you into the thinnest fat man that ever was.'

John sat in the back, sweating. He looked at the truck

driver, at the back of Merton's neck, at Ken. Then he looked at his door handle, only inches away from his hand. Ken was probably ruthless to the point of insanity, but would he shoot in front of a witness? Would he shoot the witness as well?

Merton was saying, 'I'm sorry. It's a misunderstanding. If you want me to say I'm sorry, then I'm sorry.'

The moment was passing. The truck driver was looking as if he was mollified, and he had lifted his hefty forearm off the roof of the car. John had seconds, no more than seconds, to make up his mind what he was going to do.

It seemed like a slow-motion dream. He lifted his hand across to the door handle, and saw his fingers opening to clutch it. Then he pulled it open, and heaved his weight against the door. It swung open, and the next thing he knew he was rolling across the hot concrete of the road, grazing his hands and his face against it.

He picked himself up, and saw them turning towards him, the truck driver and the two killers. Then he was running as hard and as fast as he could back up the road towards the travel museum, along the wire mesh fence which separated it from the highway, searching for a way in, searching for people amongst whom he could hide himself.

The Buick, with its rear passenger door still hanging open, roared into life and backed up towards him, slewing from one side of the road to the other. John kept running, his body charged with fear, his lungs expanded, his muscles bursting with energy.

He saw the Travel Town parking lot entrance, and ran towards it. Merton wrested the wheel of the Buick around, shifted into drive, and mounted the sidewalk in an effort to run him down.

John dodged into the road again, and then back onto the sidewalk, and he heard the roaring of the car's engine and the banging of its suspension as Merton came after him. He turned the corner into the parking lot just in time – the Buick's front bumper, colliding with the parking lot fence, pulled the back of his shoe down.

Hopping, limping, he ran the length of the parking lot to the entrance, stared at by curious tourists and children, and hobbled inside. There were dozens of railroad cars to hide himself in, and he headed straight for a luxury Union Pacific car, and clambered up the wooden steps at the back of it. Over by the park entrance, he heard the squeal of brakes as the Buick pulled up outside.

Sweating, panting, he walked the length of the stuffy railroad car, and then walked through to a sleeping-car, trying the doors of the sleeping compartments to see if he could hide in any of them. They were all locked. He hurried through to the end of the sleeping-car, and through the dusty windows he could see Merton and Ken coming through the entrance, and looking around.

He went right through to the last car, and waited by the door to see which way Merton and Ken were going to start searching. He closed his eyes for a moment, and tried to get his breath back. His breathing and the pulse of his blood seemed to be the loudest noises in the whole park. Even the chatter of children, and the calling of parents to smile now, Clark, and look like an engineer, that's right, seemed muffled and diminutive in comparison.

He saw Ken, with one hand inside his plaid shirt, walking past a Grumman Cougar naval aeroplane in the distance. If Ken was over by that side of the park, then it was likely that Merton was close. He stepped quietly to the open door of the railroad car and peeked out.

Merton was right there, fat-faced and puffing for breath. He yelled, 'Ken! He's here!' as John popped his head out.

John jumped down from the railroad car into the dust, and began to sprint the length of the train, with Merton lumbering after him. He heard Ken shout, 'Okay, Merton, I'm on my way!'

John reached the giant black-painted Union Pacific

locomotive, and scrambled up the metal rungs into the engineer's cab. Merton yelled, 'I've got you now, Cullen! Come down out of there, you don't have a damned chance!'

Inside the locomotive cab, John kept down close to the metal floor. He could hear Merton panting and gasping down on the ground, and he knew that he could outrun him any day. But the fat man was probably armed, and even if he tried to jump down from the cab on the opposite side, he would find himself being shot at through the locomotive's wheels.

John waited, and tried to get his breath back.

He heard Ken come loping up. 'He's up there?' Ken asked.

'That's right,' answered Merton. 'Asshole just took three years off of my life.'

There was a momentary silence, and then Ken called, 'Cullen, you'd better come down out of there! I'm giving you three to step out with your hands over your head!'

John waited, and sweated, and knew damned well that if he tried to escape, they'd kill him, and if he gave himself up, they'd kill him. He said to himself, 'Forgive me for this Vicki,' under his breath, and began to edge his way to the opposite side of the cab.

'Okay,' said Ken, 'that's one – two –'

John threw himself ten feet from the cab on to the ground, jarring his shoulder against a railroad tie, and then he was up and away across the Travel Town park. He heard something snap and whine past his head, and he vaguely understood that they were firing at him with silencers. He ran towards the entrance, his foot throbbing and his lungs on fire, praying that Merton had left the keys in the Buick.

He didn't get a chance to try for the car. A party of small children was crowding the entrance, and he had to wade his way through them, pushing them gently but hastily aside, while Ken came running closer and closer across the park. By the time he was through the children, Ken was only a few feet away, and he had to run back up the length of the parking lot, hoping to God that he could get up in the rough hilly ground beyond the museum and lose his pursuers for good.

John was only a few feet from the parking lot entrance when he heard the Buick's motor start up, and the shriek of its tyres as Merton turned it around after him. He couldn't run much further. The sweat was running down him like blood, and his foot was swelling painfully.

He limped out of the parking lot into the roadway. The Buick came screeching after him, in a cloud of dust, and he knew that the grassy hills were too far away, and that Ken and Merton would shoot him down before he had the chance to get out of sight.

But then he heard the blast of a car horn, and a station-wagon appeared around the bend in the road from nowhere at all, a huge green Mercury with a laden roof-rack, and Merton had to spin the wheel to avoid it. The Buick skidded across the road, lurched tail-first into the ditch, and turned over on to its side.

There was a second's silence, and then the Buick exploded in a fierce orange-and-black billow of flame.

John saw the passenger door kicked open, and Ken struggling out of the car with his face blackened. Ken yelled out: *'He's trapped in there! He's trapped behind the wheel!'* But then there was another roaring spout of flame, and he had to jump down from the overturned car and back up on to the roadway.

There was nothing that anybody could do. Merton was wedged by his own fatness, and the heat was already too intense for anyone to go within ten feet. As the fire grew fiercer, they could hear him shrieking in a terrified, high-pitched voice. Blazing gasoline rolled through the car, smoking up the windows and setting fire to the vinyl seats. Black smoke was already heaping up into the hot morning sky. A crowd of people had come out from Travel Town, but all they could do was stand in a silent semi-circle and watch the Buick blaze.

The shrieking went on and on, but then there was another loud explosion, and it died away. In the distance, on the freeway, they could hear the warbling of a firetruck siren.

John and Ken stood amongst the crowd of awed tourists and frightened children, only ten feet apart, looking at each other with strange hostility and suppressed emotion. John took a step towards Ken, but Ken gave a quick, sharp shake of his head, and stepped back.

Finally, when the first firetruck turned the corner of Intervale Road, its blue lights flashing and its siren whooping, Ken turned away and elbowed into the circle of people, and disappeared.

An old man with a cardboard engineer's hat on said to John, 'Did you see what happened here, sir? Did you actually see what happened?'

John was given a ride as far as Hollywood by a talkative novelty shop owner who had been taking his children out for the day. Then he caught a taxi back to Mar Vista, where his borrowed Lincoln Capri was parked. It was nearly three o'clock now, and he was exhausted.

As he unlocked the Lincoln, the black kid who was supposed to have been looking after it came dawdling along the sidewalk on a bicycle. The boy stopped, and said, 'Hi.'

'How are you doing?' asked John. 'Too bad you didn't call the cops for me.'

'I would've,' replied the kid, 'but my pa says never to trust white folks, and never to trust the cops.'

'And what do you think?'

'I agree with my pa.'

John climbed in behind the wheel of the Lincoln. 'How old are you, kid?' he asked him.

'Ten.'

'Well, allow me to congratulate you. You're the youngest racial bigot I've ever come across.'

The black kid said, 'Ain't you going to give me that dollar?'

TWENTY-FIVE

By the time John got home, Mel was there, sitting on the verandah with a beer. He stood up and came down the steps as John swung the long white Lincoln around in the driveway, and killed the motor. It was a warm afternoon, and the air was fragrant with the scent of trees and the smell of Vicki's cooking.

'Is that a car or is that a car?' Mel said, walking around the glittering chrome-plated front end, a grin of admiration on his face.

'That's a car all right,' said John. 'Fifty-eight Lincoln Capri Landau, seven-litre V8 developing 375 brake horse.'

'Are you buying it or borrowing it?'

'Right now I'm using it to get the hell out of trouble.'

Mel looked at him. 'You've been shot at again?'

'Nearly. I was down seeing a woman in Mar Vista about her son who got killed on the freeway. A couple of weirdos jumped me and tried to kidnap me. Come on inside and I'll tell you about it.'

They went into the house. Vicki was in the kitchen, cooking a casserole for the evening. She was wearing her tight denim shorts with raggedy bottoms, and a V-necked red T-shirt. Deep in her cleavage nestled a gold Egyptian ankh that John had given her for Thanksgiving.

He kissed her, and then peered over the cooker at the casserole pot. 'That looks good,' he said. 'What are you going to call it when it's finished?'

She shrugged. 'Beef surprise. The surprise is that it's not beef at all, it's lamb.'

Then she said, 'What took you so long? You look kind of funny.'

'Funny?'

'Well, pale. What happened this morning?'

He went to the icebox and took out a beer. 'It wasn't anything much. But I've decided to take your advice.'

'John,' she said, setting down her ladle. 'Something happened, didn't it?'

He popped open the can, and took a mouthful of beer. Then he wiped his mouth with the back of his hand, and nodded. 'I was telling Mel on the way in. Two of them tried to kidnap me. I don't have any idea why. They took me out to Griffith Park and said they were going to kill me.'

'They *kidnapped* you? Oh, my God! Oh, John.' Her eyes filled with tears, and she suddenly began to shake uncontrollably. 'Oh, my God, I can't take any more of this.'

He held her in his arms. 'Vicki, it's okay. I got out of it. They got snarled up in a traffic argument and I ran away. I'm okay.'

She clutched him tight, kissing him. Her tears ran down his face, and it was all he could do not to cry himself. 'I'm going to call the FBI,' he promised, 'and Detective Morello, and I'm going to stay out of this. I promise you. Whatever's going down here, it's something really big and really heavy, and I don't want to be part of it.'

'They'll come back for you.' She said, 'I know it. They're crazy.'

'One of them might. But the other one's dead. They tried to chase me in their car and they had an accident. It was a fat guy called Merton, that's all I know.'

'Isn't that worse?' she said. 'I mean, won't they want to revenge him?'

'I don't know,' John said. 'I'm going to call the cops anyway. The whole thing goes much wider and deeper than I even guessed.'

'You mean you're really convinced it's a conspiracy?' asked Mel. He had come into the kitchen, and had overheard most of what John had said.

'It's much more than that,' John said. 'It's as if somebody's trying to wipe out a whole type of human being, all across America. Nice, liberal-minded, ordinary people, the more popular with their friends the better.

Jesus, Mel, it's like genocide. I have more than a hundred unexplained shootings in newspaper cuttings on my desk and that's for last month alone. How many don't get reported? How many get logged as suicide, or traffic accidents?'

'I just don't see the point of it,' Mel said. 'I'll grant you these victims have all got something in common. That was my basic doubt about this business in the very beginning. But now we've got some idea of what the common denominator is – like, it's mildness, and niceness, and political moderation – and it just doesn't make any sense. Who kills people like that? And what for?'

'John, you've hurt your foot,' Vicki said.

For the first time, John took a look at his ankle, where Merton's Buick had struck it at Travel Town. It was badly bruised and swollen, and the back of his shoe was split.

Vicki made him sit down, and examined his ankle carefully. John winced as she pressed in at the sides of it. She said, 'It could be fractured, but I don't think so. It's more like you've sprained it, or the ligament's torn.'

'Why don't I run you down to the doc?' Mel suggested. 'Vicki here can finish the casserole, and then when we come back we can try out some of my home-made chablis. I brought along a couple of gallons.'

'What are you trying to do? Drink us into oblivion?' John said.

'It's worth having your ankle checked,' Vicki said. 'You go along now, and I'll have everything done by the time you get back.'

Doctor Pickaway's house was a mile or two up the canyon towards Woodland Hills. The doctor palpated and probed John's ankle and foot, and then said, 'You're fine. It's nothing worse than a bad bruise. I'll give you a spray to ease the swelling, but it shouldn't worry you for longer than two or three days.'

Mel said, 'Do I have to keep him in bed and feed him with beef tea?'

Doctor Pickaway smiled. 'You should get him to run up and down the canyon a few times. He should do that anyway. Being fit is the best preventive medicine there is.'

'I couldn't bear to give up my cars,' John said, swinging off the examining table and resting his foot tentatively on the floor. 'Exercise is fine, but people don't turn their heads when you go by in running shoes like they do when you go by in a 'fifty-nine gas guzzler.'

Doctor Pickaway shrugged, a little prissily. 'Well, Mr Cullen, I've always been a believer in people taking care of the human machine. Most of the ailments that I have to deal with here could have been avoided by people in good physical condition. People eat too much, drive too much, smoke too much, drink too much. Look at you, Mr Walters, you're at least sixty pounds overweight, and that's going to tell against you when you grow older.'

'Oh, come on, doc,' said Mel. 'Different people have different physiques, different ways of life. Some fat people last for ever.'

'That's true, to a certain extent. But these days, you can tell which fat people are going to die at an early age, and which ones are going to survive. In fact, you can predict medical life expectancy within a three-year bracket.'

'How do you do that?' John asked.

Doctor Pickaway raised his eyebrows indulgently. castered chair and examined his bookcase with a slight frown. He pulled out a copy of a medical magazine, and then wheeled himself back to his desk.

'This is *Analytical Medicine*. It only has a circulation of two or three thousand, but I like to keep in touch with some of the really advanced medical techniques.'

'I'm a *Rolling Stone* man myself,' said Mel, with a grin.

Doctor Prickaway raised his eyebrows indulgently. He leafed over the pages of the magazine, and said, 'This issue came out about a year-and-a-half back, but there's been correspondence about it in every issue since. Mind you, it only appears once every three months.'

'We really have to go now, Doctor Pickaway. We

have a meal waiting for us back home,' John said.

'This won't take a moment,' Doctor Pickaway said, 'and it's really very interesting. Here it is. "Demographic curves for the accurate prediction of human physiological and psychological development." '

Mel looked across at John, and pulled a face.

'What it means in simple terms is that computerised graphs can be prepared which can predict the probable life expectancy of any individual, according to his or her parentage, physical type, life-style, medical history, home environment, and about two hundred other factors. You can even tell which diseases are most likely to occur in any individual body, and when.'

'So that means you can predict the week before you go on vacation that you're going to come down with the grippe, which you knew anyway?' Mel said.

Doctor Pickaway gave a small, dry snort which they guessed was a kind of laugh. He said, 'It's potentially much more sophisticated than that. You can tell when you're five years old if you're going to die of cancer when you're seventy-two, give or take eighteen months in either direction.'

'That's incredible,' John said, now interested.

'It *is* incredible, but all the research has been done, and tested over a period of thirty years, and so far the accuracy has been eighty-six percent, which is quite remarkable. One of the doctors on the project predicted in 1954 that he himself would die from bone cancer in 1967, and he did. A woman subject was told that she would live until she was eighty, in spite of the fact that her parents had died young, and she expected to die young herself. She survived until she was eighty-two.'

'You mentioned psychological as well as physiological. How does that work?' John asked.

'Much the same way,' said Doctor Pickaway. 'You can draw up a demographic curve which predicts how people are likely to think in future years. It could be pretty useful for commercial companies, I should imagine. They could tell in advance how people are going to react to a new kind of cereal, or a new model of automobile, and they could adjust their designs and their sales promotions accordingly.'

'Isn't that kind of pie-in-the-sky?' Mel asked. 'I mean, any computer programme needs information, and who's going to be able to find out that much information about any particular person?'

Doctor Pickaway peered at the article in the magazine. 'It says here – and I'm only quoting, mind you – that if you know someone's age, racial origins, occupation, education, and most of the particulars on their credit rating assessments, then you have almost enough information to be able to predict what washing powder they're most likely to buy in five years' time, and even how they're going to vote.'

'*Vote?*' John repeated.

Doctor Pickaway nodded. 'That's right. It says here specifically: 'A demographic curve could be prepared for those members of our society who are politically influential, and the pattern of this curve would show quite expressly how the nation is likely to vote in forthcoming years, provided there are no political scandals of Watergate proportions.' Then there's a footnote which reads: "politically influential does not necessarily mean politically active. It means those people whose personality is sympathetic enough to influence the thinking of their immediate neighbours and friends."''

John felt as if he had woken up in the night to find himself covered by a wet, ice-cold sheet. 'Who wrote that article, doctor?' John asked quietly.

'It's written by Professor Arlnikov, from Berkeley, but most of the work on the curve was done by Professor Aaron Sweetman, from San Diego. A dear old boy. I met him once at a medical convention in Atlanta. Quite charming, and brilliant, too. That's why all this correspondence here refers to the Sweetman Curve.'

They could tell something was wrong as they came around the bend in Topanga Canyon just above the firehouse. There were people running, and there was a dim, unhealthy glow above the treetops. Mel said, 'Christ, that's a brush-fire. Right by the hollow, too, by the look of it.'

He put his foot down, and the orange Beetle rattled and coughed as it speeded up. They took the next curve with the worn-out tyres howling, and John holding on to the handle to keep his balance. Through the trees, they could already see the sparkling of burning bushes, and the thick smell of smoke was already tainting the wind.

'Oh, God,' said John, as they arrived at their driveway. 'It's the whole damned hollow.'

There were two firetrucks already parked halfway up their drive, and firemen were beating at the scrub and sending four or five tall arches of spray into the bushes. John scrambled out of the Beetle and ran up the slope with Mel close behind him.

A fireman blocked his way. 'You can't come up here, sir. We want to contain this thing and we don't want anyone hurt.'

'What do you think I am, a sightseer?' snapped John. 'That's my house up there!'

'I'm sorry, sir, you can't go up there. I'll have a word with the fire chief.'

'Will you get out of my way?' John yelled. 'That's my house and my girlfriend's in there!'

'Well, sir, I'm –'

Mel pushed his way forward and grabbed the collar of the fireman's jacket. He said, 'I'm not normally a violent man, officer, but we have to get up there, by force if necessary.'

John said, 'Come on,' and they pushed their way past the fireman and up the driveway, jumping over a tangle of hoses, almost ankle-deep in black, sooty water. The noise of the fire was enormous. A huge, ravenous roaring like endless rolls of thunder, almost drowning the yells of the firemen and the crackling, electric voices that came over their walkie-talkies.

'Get those bushes down there!' shouted one of the firemen. 'I want a break there, and I want it fast! If the wind gets up, this is going to be a wiener party!'

'Get those beaters over here!' came another hoarse voice. 'Get those goddamned beaters over here!'

Another firetruck came howling and warbling up the

canyon, and as he ran through the heat and the smoke and the foul-smelling water, John heard the firemen calling for a helicopter water-drop.

'If we can contain the worst of it in the hollow, we're okay!' shouted the fire chief. 'Now, move your ass!'

John and Mel reached the crest of the driveway. To John's cold horror, his own house, his own old-fashioned wooden house, was fiercely ablaze. The downstairs windows had already broken, and curtains of flame were flapping from them wildly. The verandah rails were charred and burning, and most of them had already collapsed. There was a hot, funnelling sound as the flames ate away at the wooden weather-boards, and cedar-fragrant sparks were whirled up into the smoky sky.

Three firemen were plying water on the roof, but the house was burning so intensely that there was nothing they could do but damp down the sparks, so that the fire didn't spread out of the hollow.

John sprinted up to them and yelled, 'Where's the girl? There was a girl in there!'

One of the firemen glanced at him. 'We didn't have a chance, mister. This place was already going like a torch by the time we got here. We haven't been able to get near it.'

'*But Vicki's in there!*' he screamed. His face was already scorched red by the heat of the fire. '*She's in there! You have to get her out!*'

Mel's strong hands held his arm. He said, 'John, there's no way. It's too late.'

John twisted himself free. 'Mel, she's in there! Maybe she's trapped!'

The fireman said, 'I'm sorry, mister, but nobody could live through that. If your girl was in there, I'm sorry, but that's it.'

'We managed to move your car,' put in another fireman. 'The big old white Lincoln? That's down at the pull-off now.'

John stared at his crackling, blazing house. He felt such a sense of dread and grief that he couldn't speak or think or move. The whole house was wobbling like something out of a nightmare, as the heat distorted the air, and sparks whipped upward with hectic and unnatural speed. It was so hot now that he had to pant for breath.

With a wrenching, lurching noise, part of the roof collapsed, and fiery rafters fell through the house into the downstairs rooms. Then the staircase went, a ladder of flames, and part of the brick chimney dropped into the living room with a heavy crash.

Mel put his arm around John's shoulder, and held him tight. There were tears in his own eyes, behind the dancing orange flames that were reflected in his glasses, and he couldn't speak any words of comfort that would have meant anything.

The fire chief came up, a hard-faced blue-eyed man **in a black helmet.** 'I hear this is your house, friend,' he said.

John lowered his head. He closed his eyes for a moment, and behind his eyelids, in the darkness of his mind, he prayed that he wasn't here at all, that none of this was true, and that he'd open his eyes again and find he was standing next to Vicki at the stove, and asking her what was for dinner. Mel said to the fire chief, 'Yes, sir, it's his house. It was his girlfriend in there.'

The fire chief looked at the house for a while, and then up at the smoke-dark sky, and the way the sparks were flying.

'I'm sorry,' he said. 'If there was any chance at all of getting into the house, we would have taken it.'

'Do you know how the fire started?' Mel asked.

The fire chief shook his head. 'Could have been anything. We've had all this dry weather lately, and a heatwave. Cigarette butt, maybe.'

'Jesus Christ,' said Mel, and there was a catch in his voice he couldn't hide.

The fire chief said, 'You'd better get out of here now. We've had a forecast the wind's going to turn, and if it does, we're going to have a bad one. Do you have someplace to stay for the night?'

'Sure,' nodded Mel. 'We can check into a hotel.'

'Okay,' said the fire chief. 'Leave your number with

the fire department when you've settled in, and we'll call you if there's any news.'

'Thanks,' said Mel. Then he squeezed John's arm, and said, 'Come on, John. There's no reason to wait around here. Let's go.'

John stared with smoke-watering eyes at the ruins of his house, black and smouldering like the ashes of a ritual cremation. He couldn't believe that Vicki was lying in those ruins, burned and dead, but he knew that she was nowhere else, that no matter what he did now, or where he went, he would never see her again, or touch her again, or talk to her again.

He waited for almost a minute, with tears streaking the smuts on his cheeks, and then he said: 'Okay, Mel. Let's go.'

TWENTY-SIX

That night, the sirens warbled and screamed until dawn, as Topanga Canyon was ravaged by one of the worst fires in years. A hot wind fanned the flames, and the glow from the burning trees and brush could be seen for miles. On his way back to his room in Venice, driving his primrose-yellow Pinto, T.F. was passed by three firetrucks from Anaheim, their lights flashing and their hooters blaring.

He parked on San Juan Avenue, locked his car, and went upstairs to his room. He propped his long canvas rifle-case up against the wardrobe, and threw on to the bed four sex magazines that he'd bought that morning in Hollywood. He switched on his television, without any sound, and sat down to take off his shoes.

The telephone rang. He let it ring for a little while, and then he picked it up.

'Who is it?' he demanded.

'T.F.? It's me, Ken.'

'What's happening?'

'We had some trouble with that Cullen guy today. He was round at Mrs Perlman's this morning, snooping and asking questions.'

'So?'

'So I checked back with you-know-who, and you-know-who said waste him straight away.'

'And?'

'Well, we were going to take him out to the park and get rid of him, but we had a foul-up on the way. He made a run for it, and we had a smash-up in the car. Merton's dead. Burned in the wreck.'

T.F. took a cigarette out of his shirt pocket and lit it carefully. Then he testily blew smoke, and said, 'Who is this guy? Shazam or something? He's unarmed, and on his own, and he smashes your car and kills Merton?'

'T.F., it was an *accident*. A freak accident.'

T.F. put his feet up on the bed. 'Did the cops ask you what happened?'

'Sure, but I said it was just a traffic smash-up. They're not making a case out of it.'

'That's one relief. So what's happening now?'

'We fixed Cullen tonight like we originally planned. I went up there at five and torched the house. That's what all this big fire is about. I torched it so damned well the whole canyon's burning.'

'That's good. I like it. A guy I knew in Seattle always used to say that if you wanted to knock someone off and hide the evidence, then the best thing to do was knock *five* people off.'

'Anyway,' said Ken, 'the three of them must've gotten roasted. Cullen, the girl, and the fat guy. All on one broiler.'

'Pity about the girl,' T.F. remarked absently. 'She had just the kind of figure I go for.'

Ken said, 'I got your baby into the house okay. She's hidden under the floor in my dressing room.'

'Fine, 'said T.F. 'I miss her.'

'Do you want me to call you again before Saturday?'

'Not unless it's urgent. I'll see you then, okay?'

'Okay, T.F. Go easy.'

'Go easy yourself, Ken.'

T.F. set down the telephone, took another drag at his cigarette, and then went over to the bed and inspected his sex magazines. One of them was called *Wet Party*, and was full of colour pictures of girls in black stockings and garter-belts peeing all over themselves. Another one was titled *Canine Lovers*. He looked through them with a strangely dispassionate expression, smoking as he did so. He paused for a while at a photograph of a pretty brunette with her mouth wide open and her eyes closed, drinking from two busty black-stockinged girl friends; and then he closed the magazines altogether and put them away in the bottom of his wardrobe.

He decided he felt hungry, but he couldn't make up his mind what he wanted to eat. These days, the hunger in him had been growing fiercer, and he wasn't altogether sure that it was simply for food.

TWENTY-SEVEN

John woke up just before dawn with a hangover that rose up inside him like a ton of wet gravel. He opened his eyes and realised he was lying in a strange, narrow bed, and that sunlight was slanting across the ceiling at an unaccustomed angle. His eyes felt swollen and he had a headache that was pounding at so deep and low a frequency that it was hard to recognise just where the pain was coming from.

The first things he remembered when he sat up were that Vicki was really dead, and that he was sitting in bed in Room 21 of an apartment hotel on Franklin Avenue, in Hollywood. Mel had driven him there last night in his borrowed Lincoln Capri, and then gone out to the supermarket at the corner of Franklin and Highland to bring back two bottles of Jack Daniels and a six-pack of Old Milwaukee to wash it down with.

They had drunk a lot, talked a lot, argued, wept and grieved. At two in the morning, sick and dizzy, and so drowned in whisky that he didn't know what was real any more and what wasn't, John had collapsed on the floor, and Mel had put him to bed.

He swung his legs around, and put his feet on the shag-pile rug. The apartment was small and neat, with a simulated-log fireplace, a table and two chairs in dark Mexican wood, and a sliding picture window that gave out onto a balcony. All he could see through the window was the back yard of the house next to the hotel, with flowering vines, a chicken coop, and a few stunted palms. He stood up, his head swimming, and shuffled into the kitchenette.

Mel, with his usual forethought and consideration, had remembered to buy Alka-Seltzer and coffee. John filled the kettle, put it on the stove, and searched through the kitchen cupboards for a glass. While the Alka-Seltzer fizzed, he kept his hand clamped over his eyes, and wondered if Vicki's death would have been easier to take if he had stayed sober.

'Good morning, John,' came Mel's voice.

He peeked through his fingers. Mel looked as rough as John felt, and without his glasses he appeared oddly vulnerable and unfamiliar. He came into the kitchen, shook out a couple of Alka-Seltzers himself and dropped them into a glass.

'How do you feel?' asked Mel.

'Like hell. How do you feel?'

'Like hell.'

'I'm making coffee,' said John. 'Do you want some?'

Mel shook his head. 'No, thanks. I think I'd puke if I drank any coffee.'

'Maybe it would do you good.'

Mel pulled out a chair and sat down at the table. He said, 'I woke up and couldn't believe it had really happened. I kept thinking that it had to be a dream.'

'Me too,' said John. 'But it isn't. She's actually dead.'

They drank their Alka-Seltzer in silence for a while, and then Mel said, 'What are you going to do now?'

'I don't know,' said John. 'I haven't even buried my

father yet, and now this. My house, everything I ever owned, my furniture, my paintings. And, more than anything, Vicki.'

'It wasn't your fault, John. You had some real mean guys after you, whoever they were. You couldn't have done anything to stop them.'

'I could have gone to the FBI, like Vicki wanted. I could have asked for police protection. But oh, no, I had to be a goddamned one-man detective bureau. I had to be a great hero. What I didn't realise was that heroes are always heroes at someone else's expense.'

'John,' insisted Mel, 'it wasn't your *fault*.'

John slid aside the picture-window and stepped out onto the balcony. The sky was beginning to lighten, and the morning air had an uncomfortable chill to it.

'Are you going to the FBI now? You've got some pretty good information to go on, and you know that I can back you up.'

John shrugged.

'You can't handle this on your own,' protested Mel. 'If you keep on crowding these people, they're going to kill you, too.'

'And if I *don't* crowd them? How many more people are they going to do away with?'

'John, it isn't up to you to track down these killers. It's not your job. It's up to the police and it's up to the FBI.'

'Except that *they* think he's a Freeway Fruitcake. A lone psycho. And *I* think that there's somebody out there who's organizing these killings for a purpose. Somebody who's doing it for their own very good reason.'

Mel sighed. 'You're getting ahead of yourself, John. We haven't even established that there's any kind of sensible connection between the victims yet, let alone that somebody has a reason for killing them, and certainly let alone a very *good* reason.'

'That's where you're wrong. There is a connection, and that's their political point of view.'

'Most of them didn't have a point of view.'

'That's exactly it. They're middle-of-the-roaders,

188

slightly tending to the left. But if they were offered the right kind of options at an election, they could go either way. They would have voted for Kennedy, but they would also have voted for Eisenhower.'

Mel said, 'John, I don't get this. We don't have an election for years.'

'Sure we don't. But remember what Pickaway was talking about, how you can draw up demographic curves to predict how people are likely to vote in future years. And remember what he said about politically *influential* people not necessarily being politically *active* people.'

'Yes, but –'

'But nothing. That's the whole point. All of these people who died were nice people. Ordinary, friendly, nice people. They were influential because people liked them, and come election time, whatever they thought about the candidates, their friends would have felt the same way. Or tended to, at the very least.'

'Okay,' Mel said, 'it's a good analytical theory. But you're forgetting what Doctor Pickaway said about that magazine of his. Only a few thousand people read it, and I bet half of *them* don't understand it.'

John shook his head. 'He said the article had stirred up a lot of interest, and that makes it likely that people outside of medical circles got to hear about it.'

'But *who?*' said Mel. 'And even supposing they did, would it occur to them to go around knocking people off?'

'It might. That's what I want to find out.'

Mel scratched at his beard. 'It seems way off target to me. I mean, what kind of person systematically shoots down ordinary people just to influence a political trend?'

'It's been done before, and it's being done now,' said John. 'Maybe it's more blatant in places like Uganda, but why should the minds of men who want to seize power and keep power be any different here than they are in Africa?'

Mel was silent for a long time. Then he said, 'John, do me a favour, please.'

'What is it?'

'Call the FBI. Don't get involved. I don't want to see you hurt.'

John said, 'I'm sorry, Mel, I can't.'

'John, it's your duty.'

'Duty? Duty to whom?'

'It's your duty as a citizen. You can't catch these people. The FBI can.'

'What about my duty to my father? And what about my duty to Vicki?'

Mel banged his fist against the wall. 'And what about your duty to yourself? The only surviving member of your family?'

'I'll take my chances. My father had to, and Vicki, too.'

'They didn't walk into it with their eyes open, like you're doing. They never knew what hit them.'

'Nor will I, if I can't get to the bottom of this.'

'So what are you going to do?'

John sat down at the table, and rubbed his eyes tiredly. 'I'm going to buy myself a gun, first of all, because I think I'm going to need one. Then I'm going to go have a talk with Professor Aaron Sweetman.'

'Don't you think that's dangerous?'

'I think it's dangerous if I don't.'

Mel regarded him carefully for a while. Then he said, 'Well, I can only say this once, because you seem to have made up your mind. But you and Vicki were always my best friends, and now Vicki's gone, there's only you. I wish you wouldn't, that's all.'

'I have to,' said John.

Mel nodded. 'I know.'

BOOK TWO

THE FALLEN

ONE

She had once been described (by *People* magazine) as a 'marriage between Charlie's Angels and the Ride of the Valkyries.' She was nearly six feet tall, with blonde hair swept away from her face in a Farrah style that was at least two years out of date. Her shoulders were as broad as a man's, and she wore tweed hacking-jackets and corduroy pants tucked into high leather boots; yet her wrists jangled with bangles, and her fingers were covered in rings with huge amethysts, sparkling diamonds, and tiny gold bells.

Her face was sharp and square, and her chin was always raised high. She possessed those pale blue eyes that could pierce through everybody around her like lasers. Her belt buckles could have kept the gates of Bel-Air locked together, but under the tweed jacket she always wore floating filmy chiffon blouses through which (as she walked, or postured, or pranced) you thought you might be able to see the nipples of her very small breasts, although you never actually could. Hilary Nestor Hunter, thirty-seven years old, honours graduate in law, president of the Women's Liberation League, did not believe in giving anything away to men, not even a glimpse of her body.

She appealed to women because she frightened men. Yet she also appealed to men because she frightened men. As her friend and patron Carl X. Chapman had often told her: 'Too many politicians make the mistake of being nice guys, and then get hurt because nobody loves them. The only way to make people love you is to scare them to death. Then you'll have them running around in circles, looking for where your ass is, so they can kiss it.'

She appeared at the fifth Women's Liberation Conference, which was held at the L.A. Convention Centre on Figueroa Street, to a flashing accolade of press photography, stalking across the sidewalk with her sulky escort of beautiful but consciously unkempt girls, all unplucked eyebrows and home-cut hair. She didn't disappoint the photographers as she turned at the entrance and raised her hand in clenched-fist salute.

The hall was already crowded, and the air was buzzing with women's voices, a nest of bees eagerly awaiting their queen. But they had to wait a little longer while television reporters crowded into the convention centre lobby and surrounded Ms. Hunter with microphones.

She turned and faced the glare of television lights with a remote, condescending expression. One reporter asked her, 'Ms. Hunter, you've been under a lot of pressure from your gay supporters lately – mainly to have the Women's Liberation League take a firm **stand** on lesbian rights. What are you going to say to those ladies today?'

In a clear, penetrating voice, Hilary Nestor Hunter said, 'I'm going to remind them that the Women's Liberation League is a *sexist* movement, but not a *sexual* movement. We are concerned with women's political and social inferiority, not with their personal problems.'

'That sounds kind of unsympathetic, doesn't it?'

'Women don't join this movement for sympathy. They join it because they want to achieve the kind of political dominance that so far has been the sole prerogative of men.'

A leading female TV reporter pushed forward with her microphone to ask the most crucial question of all, and the rest of the microphones followed Hilary Nestor Hunter's lips like a shoal of pilot fish.

'Ms. Hunter, it seems to me that you've got one or two pretty determined opponents out there today – ladies who think that your movement is too politically extreme. What do you think about them?'

Hilary raised one of her perfectly-plucked eyebrows. 'There are always dissident voices to every great idea. There are always moderates who want to dilute the essence of originality and genius. But I don't mind about that. A great social idea like female dominance *should* stir women up. It *should* make them think. It should even make them angry. I'm pleased that women are dissenting. It's the measure of the greatness of everything I stand for.'

'You're aware that some of your moderate opponents are trying to oust you from leadership?' the reporter asked.

'Of course. But they don't worry me. They're my children, and I expect my children to squabble and fight and challenge authority. All they have to remember is that I have their best interests at heart, and I'm going to make sure that they get what's best for them, whether they like it or not.'

'How are you going to do that?' asked another reporter, a man. 'Slap their tushies and send them to bed without any supper?'

Hilary Nestor Hunter brushed back her Farrah curls and looked down at him with utter disdain.

'I'm an influential woman. I'm not an oddball liberationist turning out cyclostyled newsletters about babyminding facilities and lesbian bridge parties. I have the backing of people of considerable power, and I am convinced that many of my ideas are going to be made law in future years. '

'Would you consider public office, Ms. Hunter?' asked the female reporter. 'That's if you were offered one, of course.'

'The question isn't *if*, but when,' Hilary said archly, and then beckoned her aides and supporters to gather around her. As a last word, she turned and said to the microphones and the cameras: 'I always bet on certainties, ladies and gentlemen, and right now it's a certainty that a little sanity is going to return to the administration of this country.'

Then, closely surrounded by her bevy of lady bodyguards, she pushed through the crowds and the lights, and entered the auditorium. The buzz rose to a highpitched scream, washed along on a roar of applause, and she walked down the aisle towards the stage with both hands held high in the clenched-fist salute as adoring women stood on their seats clapping and shrieking. The television cameras followed her as she stepped up on the stage, and stood there alone in a brilliant spotlight, her head thrown back and her arms wide, the applause rising like an ocean up to her feet.

'*Domination!*' she called, through the booming, echoing microphones. 'Domination!'

And back came the scream of: '*Domination!*' from every side of the hall, and thousands of clenched fists, most with braceleted wrists and painted nails and rings, rose up and proclaimed their loyalty to Hilary Nestor Hunter.

From the lobby, now almost empty and littered with crumpled programmes and cigarette butts, Perri Shaw watched this Messianic entrance and felt as weak and transparent as a ghost. She turned to Father Leonard, who had been observing her closely. He was dressed up today, in his best sport coat, and he had slicked down his hair with water. He looked like a small boy who had been smartened up for a Sunday visit with his rich aunt and uncle.

'Frightened?' he asked Perri.

She nodded. 'I guess I shouldn't be. But they think she's the greatest woman who ever lived. How can you fight that?'

'With God's help,' said Father Leonard. 'And with your own courage.'

'I never did anything like this before.'

He took her arm, and pressed it affectionately. 'You'll get through. You'll come out of there and they'll be applauding you the way they did for Hilary Nestor Hunter when she walked in. You'll see.'

'I wish I could believe you,' she said.

'You think a priest would lie?'

She turned and looked at him gently. 'I think a priest would lie to encourage someone he was fond of.'

He didn't say anything for a while, but then he bent forward and very softly kissed her on the forehead.

'Yes,' he said quietly, 'I am fond of you. I will ask God to aid and protect you today. I will also ask Him to give us both strength to fulfil our allotted tasks.'

There was another roar from within the auditorium, and Perri looked inside to see Hilary Nestor Hunter with her arms wide, as she made her opening speech. Women were rising to their feet to applaud her, and cameras were flashing in a crescendo of flickering blue light.

'They'll be asking for motions soon,' said Father Leonard. 'You'd better get in there.'

'Will you say a prayer for me?' she asked him.

He smiled. 'I'll say a prayer for all those men and women who would benefit from political enlightenment.'

'And for me, too?'

'Yes, Perri,' said Father Leonard. 'For you too.'

She kissed him, with lightness and tenderness, on the cheek. Then she turned and walked down the aisle into the auditorium, just as the magnified voice of Hilary Nestor Hunter was demanding: 'A *committed* acceptance of women as political candidates ... a *committed* acceptance of women as administrators and leaders ...'

Perri found her seat, next to Ann Margolies from the Chicago branch of the Women's Liberation League, who had been pressing for months for a moderation of the league's political views. Ann Margolies was a plain, long-haired girl with thick-lensed eyeglasses and a seemingly inexhaustible wardrobe of beige and black turtlenecks. Perri had met her at a regional conference in Phoenix once. 'I'm glad you could make it,' Ann said as Perri sat down. 'We're in for a tough time today.'

Hilary Nestor Hunter finished her opening speech to screams and whoops and almost five minutes of solid applause. Then the chairperson, Agnes Frohauer, a middle-aged Republican lady who had buried three husbands and vengefully divorced two more, lifted her short arms for silence.

'We have some motions before us,' she said, looking down at her papers through half-glasses on golden chains. 'We don't have time to discuss them all today, so we have selected some of them out of a hat. The first is a proposal from the Idaho branch that we produce some kind of guidelines for women living on their husbands' farms and holdings in rural areas, where it is difficult for them to escape male domination, or assert themselves politically or economically. The second is a motion from New York that we should affiliate ourselves openly with a political party. The third is a call from the Los Angeles delegates for what they describe here as 'moderation of the league's political aims.' In other words, they want *equality* rather than *domination*.'

There was a disturbed rustle and murmuring throughout the hall. Perri, in spite of herself, blushed and felt a sudden urgency to go to the john. Ann Margolies touched her hand comfortingly, though, and whispered. 'They've let us speak, at least. They couldn't deny us that.'

Perri said, 'I don't feel very confident about carrying enough delegates along with us. They seem so delirious about Hilary. I've never seen her get so much applause.'

'Delirium is usually short-lived,' Ann insisted, 'and it's usually the prelude to a rude awakening. Just get out there and give them hell.'

The discussion on rights for women in rural areas took over an hour, and by the end of it they still hadn't really worked out a satisfactory code of sexual self-assertion for isolated wives. As one woman from Kansas said, 'If I say that I'm his equal, he laughs in my face. If I don't let him make love to me, he beats me black and blue. And there isn't a soul for sixteen miles to help me.'

The motion on affiliation with a political party was postponed for further discussion by the league's political committee. And then, just before the mid-afternoon break, it was Perri's turn.

She was dressed today in a light, flowing dress of pastel pinks and blues, and her hair was pinned back with red combs. There was a flush of pink on her cheeks as she left her seat and walked up to the stage, followed by a smattering of applause. Ann Margolies was the only woman to rise to her feet and cheer, and her voice sounded desperately alone and thin in the huge theatre.

Perri went up to the microphone, and looked out over the rows and rows of intent faces. There was coughing.

and an expectant rustle of programmes, because they all knew that Perri was directly challenging Hilary Nestor Hunter, and they all anticipated verbal slaughter.

'Sisters,' Perri began, 'my name's Perri Shaw and I represent one of the seediest, seamiest districts of Los Angeles. The women aren't physically isolated where I come from, the way they are in rural regions. But they're culturally isolated from anything that could give them consciousness of their own womanhood and their own birthright. They are as oppressed by their husbands and brothers as black slaves were in the South. They have to work to keep a home, they have to raise children, they have to give their bodies, and if they ever dare to protest, they get hurt.

'Talking of female domination may be an amusing idea in middle-class circles where women are wealthy and bored, and where they already have the fundamental rights of a good education and money of their own. But the women I'm talking about aren't interested in dominance. They're only interested in being recognised as people. They're only interested in being treated as equals.'

Perri paused, and the auditorium was very hushed. 'In the slums of Los Angeles,' she continued, 'I've seen women burned with cigarettes because it amused their husbands to torture them. I've seen women beaten almost to death because they dared to express an opinion. I've seen women who were forced to share their marriage bed with another girl because their husbands felt like a bit of sexual variety.

'You can't talk to women like these about dominating their men. And you can't educate their men to accept the idea that women might be superior. It's difficult enough getting them to understand that women are human beings, let alone that women might be capable of ordering their lives.

'We have to raise the consciousness of *both* sexes if we're going to succeed in liberating women. It's no use telling a prisoner that freedom is wonderful unless you also convince the jailer to let her out. So far, it seems to me that the Women's Liberation League hasn't succeeded in doing very much except frightening working-class husbands into adopting a rigid and uncompromising posture towards it, and it's the women who are suffering. Right now, we need to come out and say that we're not *not* right-wing female dragons. We're *not* political harpies. We need to say that we're sensitive and sympathetic women who can understand the problems of men as well as the oppression of women.'

Perri spoke for almost twenty minutes. She didn't look at Hilary Nestor Hunter, who was sitting at the side of the stage with her legs crossed and her face set in a glacial expression of contrived boredom. She looked instead at the women in the audience, because she was beginning to sense that they liked her, and that they liked what she was saying. To hear about the agonies of poverty-stricken wives in downtown Los Angeles startled and thrilled them. It was hard reality, instead of wordy political rhetoric. It made them feel as if they could do something practical to help downtrodden women, instead of devising high-flown schemes at fundraising wine-and-cheese parties.

Perri finished by telling the story of a woman rescued by Father Leonard, a wife who had been offered by her husband to any stray man he happened to bring home from his night's drinking. She had been forced to have sex with teenage boys, street-sweepers, derelicts and drunks, while her husband looked on. After months of tedious and often heartbreaking counselling, Father Leonard had at last persuaded the man to understand the grossness of what he was doing to his wife, and had gradually helped them to reconstruct their marriage.

There was a long silence after Perri had finished speaking. Then, all on her own, Ann Margolies began to clap. She was joined by another woman, and then another, until the whole audience rose to their feet and applauded her. Out of protocol, even Hilary Nestor Hunter had to stand and clap, although her face was as hard and displeased as Perri had ever seen it.

The women didn't shriek and whoop as they had when Hilary had appeared on stage. But their earnest, serious applause was more encouraging. It meant that they believed and accepted what Perri said.

Perri stepped down from the stage, and Hilary Nestor Hunter came up to the microphone. She waited with an indulgent smile until the applause died away, and then she said, 'That was one of the prettiest little contributions I've heard for a long time. I think we should all be proud of sister Perri Shaw.'

She raised her head, and her pale eyes looked around the audience like the eyes of a witchfinder, daring any of her women to meet her stare with anything but humility.

'Of course,' she said, 'we cannot seriously *agree* with what Perri Shaw has been saying. Her case histories are moving, and her convictions are genuine, but she seems to forget that we are waging a civil war. And a war, a real war, can never be fought successfully if we treat it like social work in a sadly deprived but very small part of Los Angeles.

'We aren't fighting to mollify a few brutish husbands. We're fighting for what, after all these centuries of male mismanagement, we're really entitled to: power, money and influence. We're fighting to get out from under. We're fighting the whole world, not just a few shiftless men.

'I know what sister Perri Shaw is trying to say, but sister Perri Shaw is thinking too small. So, while I thank her for her speech in support of the motion, I really think that to vote in favour of equality rather than domination would be to betray everything that we have fought for, and everything that we are fighting for.'

The applause this time was loud and long, and there were whistles of approval. Perri looked worriedly around the auditorium, and knew that Hilary Nestor Hunter's magnetism had easily outweighed her own persuasiveness. She hissed to Ann Margolies, 'Can't we delay the vote? I feel if we could talk to some of the delegates privately, we might be able to convince them that we're right.'

'I'll try,' said Ann, and raised her hand.

Agnes Frohauer said: 'Do you have a motion?'

'Yes, sister. I propose we postpone a final vote on the

motion of equality until tomorrow morning. I believe it would give us all time to consider and weigh the arguments.'

'Seconded?' asked Agnes Frohauer.

A girl from South Carolina put up her hand.

'Let's have a show of hands, then,' said Ms. Frohauer, and a thick forest of hands went up.

'In that case, we'll vote on the motion first thing tomorrow morning. I think it's time we adjourned for today, in any case. Thank you all for your attention. There are Women's Liberation League buttons on sale in the lobby.'

Perri met Father Leonard outside. He looked pleased and shy. He held out both his hands, and said, 'You were wonderful. Even better than I thought you were going to be.'

'Are you going to buy me a celebration cup of coffee?'

'You can even have a celebration drink.'

'A cup of coffee would do. I don't want you to lose your place in Heaven in too much of a rush.'

They walked along Figueroa in the purplish light of evening, almost oblivious of the hurrying women delegates who jostled past them on the sidewalk. They went into a snack bar and ordered two cups of coffee, and they sat at their table and hardly ever took their eyes away from each other. It was as if they could watch their affection flowering, second by second, in each other's face. Father Leonard's was grey with anxiety, the wrenching doubt and questioning that had plagued him ever since Perri had first spoken to him of her feelings. He couldn't help himself, and he didn't know what to do about it.

At six-thirty, they parted on the corner of Figueroa and Pico, and Father Leonard took her hand in his and held it tight.

'I have to make up my mind, you know,' he told her. She nodded.

'I thought it would weaken my resolve to serve God, and my ability to do my work, if I had feelings about you. But I think I was wrong. I seem to feel more strength now than I've felt in my life. I seem to have even more purpose. I have God, and I also have you.'

'You mustn't let me influence you. I love you, Leonard, but you mustn't give up your vocation because of me. Perhaps I'm selfish, but I couldn't bear the responsibility of that.'

'It's my responsibility,' he said. His eyes were dark and sad. 'It's between me and God and nobody else.'

TWO

Perri walked alone to the parking lot, and unlocked her saddle-brown Toyota. She tossed her pocketbook on the seat beside her, and drove home through the rush-hour traffic to her small apartment near Plummer Park in Hollywood. The radio warned of high smog levels tomorrow, and announced that the Hillside Strangler had claimed another victim. Boy scouts had discovered her body in bushes near Griffith Park.

Perri parked along the wide concrete sidewalk outside her apartment building. It was quiet and cool as she climbed out of the car and walked through the front yard, and the dusty palms rustled in the dusk. Through one of the downstairs windows, she could see Mrs Ramonez cutting up red peppers on her kitchen table, and the sound of Spanish music, like the memory of some gaudy and romantic love affair, twanged all around the yard. She climbed the steps at the side of the building and walked along the balcony that led to her pink-painted apartment door.

She took out her key, and was about to insert it into the lock when she paused, and listened. It sounded as if music was playing from inside her apartment. She wondered for a moment if she had left the radio on when she went out, but then she remembered that she had been playing a record that morning, and that she had switched off the stereo.

The music was Odyssey singing: '*It was de woman behind de man ... de woman behind de man ...*'

She felt frightened. Supposing she had interrupted a burglary? Almost all of these apartments on Norton Avenue had been broken into at one time or another, mostly by dope addicts looking for score money, although a Mexican woman across the street had been beaten and raped as well as robbed.

Perri paused for a moment, and then decided to ease the front door open and take a quick glimpse inside.

She pushed the key slowly and quietly into the lock, and gently turned it. She had never realised before what a loud clicking noise it made. The Spanish music from downstairs mingled with the Odyssey record, and created an oddly unpleasant disharmony. A white cat was sitting at the far end of the balcony, watching her with half-closed eyes.

She opened the front door about an inch. She could see now that the lamps in the living room were lit, and she could hear the music more clearly. It seemed like a weird kind of burglary. She always thought that burglars just came in and took what they could and left. She didn't think they sat down and made themselves at home.

With her heart beating at uncontrollable speed, she called out, 'Who's there?'

She waited. There was no answer. The record ended, and she heard the radio disc-jockey babbling something about a traffic snarl on the San Diego Freeway. Then there was more music. Frank Sinatra singing 'My Way.'

Perri took one cautious step into the hallway. There was her familiar hall table, with this morning's mail lying just where she had left it. There was the barometer she had picked up in a secondhand store downtown. There, inside the living room door, was her coffee table, and the same criss-cross yellow wallpaper, and even her coffee cup, undisturbed.

She called again, 'Who's there? Who is that in there?'

There was no answer. She took two more steps into the hallway, glancing nervously into the bathroom on her left to see if anybody was hiding in there. Ever since she saw *Psycho* on television, she had harboured a niggling fear about bathrooms and showers, and stabbings.

At last she reached the open living room doorway. Frank Sinatra was still halfway through 'My Way,' so it couldn't have taken her as long as she thought it had. She stood there for a long time, her arms by her sides, her fingers clenching and unclenching, her heart running a dark and frightened steeplechase.

She entered the room. She gasped in fright.

Sitting on her white vinyl settee was a young girl with long chestnut-coloured hair. She was sprawled there quite casually, as if it was her own home, and Perri was a visitor. She had been reading a *TV Guide*, and as Perri came in, she looked up and blandly said, 'Hi.'

Perri slowly put down her pocketbook, staring at the girl in disbelief. She wasn't more than sixteen or seventeen, with a pretty, snubnosed face, and tiny gold earrings. She was wearing a frayed denim vest and frayed denim shorts, and her thin arms and legs were very tan. She looked as if she had only just shaken the sand out of her shoes and come back into town from a day's sunbathing. The shorts had been cut from a pair of Levis, so brief that as she sat there with her thighs spread carelessly apart, she was covered by nothing more than a ragged string of blue cotton.

Perri said, 'Hi yourself. Is it too much to ask what the hell you're doing here?'

The girl's calm, innocent expression didn't alter. 'I was waiting for you.'

'Waiting for me? You don't even know me.'

'Oh, I do. I saw you at the women's conference today.'

'You mean you're a delegate?' asked Perri.

The girl shrugged. 'Not exactly. But I was there.'

Perri approached her. 'Listen,' she said patiently, 'I don't know who you are, or what you're doing here, but I suggest you get the hell out.'

'My name's Star,' said the girl, as if that answered everything.

'Star? Star who?'

'Just Star. That's what my friends call me.'

'I'm surprised you've *got* any friends if this is the way you treat other people's apartments. Breaking in like a burglar.'

Star smiled. An immediate, and somehow threatening smile. 'You left your bathroom window an eensy-teensy way open,' she said.

Perri looked her up and down. Star made no attempt to get up and go, nor to close her wide-apart thighs. Perri was disturbed and strangely frightened, not least by Star's overwhelming self-assurance.

She said, 'You're going to have to leave. I have a great deal of work to do.'

Star smiled again. 'You're very beautiful,' she told Perri. 'That's why I came here.'

'Don't talk such garbage.'

'I'm not. It's true. You were like Joan of Arc out there today.'

'Listen, Star, whether I'm like Joan of Arc or Cloris Leachman, you're still going to have to leave.'

Star got up off the settee. She was very petite, even smaller than Perri, and almost too attractive for her own good. She was wearing one of those musky perfumes that only smells good on young girls.

'I think I love you,' she told Perri, in a simple, sincere voice. 'I saw you at the conference and I fell for you. You were so beautiful, and so proud, and you stood up for what you believed in. I found out where you lived, and came here straight away.'

Perri went nervously to the bureau and took a cigarette out of a half-empty pack. She lit it, and quickly puffed out smoke.

'I'm sorry,' she said, 'but I'm straight.'

Star's eyes were wide and dreamy. 'That doesn't matter,' she said. 'I still love you just as much, if not more.'

'Maybe you do, but I'd really appreciate it if you left.'

Star smiled. 'You can't be completely blind to women. Isn't that why you joined the Women's Liberation

League, because you thought that women were so beautiful?'

'Of course women are beautiful. But I could never
have a sexual relationship with a woman. Now, please
leave, because I have to shower and change and get to
work.'

Star came up close. Her moist lips glistened in the
lamplight. 'Couldn't I stay and watch you?' she said.

'*Watch* me? Of course you can't watch me. Just leave,
that's all. I don't want you here.'

Star frowned. 'Don't you think I'm pretty?'

'Will you please leave? I simply want to be alone.'

'I won't say a word. I'll just watch.'

Perri crushed out her cigarette. 'How many times do
I have to tell you? I'm straight. I'm in love with a
wonderful guy. I have nothing against lesbians, and I'm
sure what you feel about me is genuine. You're very
pretty and very sexy. But I don't want you to watch me,
and I don't need your love, and I think the best thing
you can do is put your shoes on and get the hell out.'

Star blinked. 'I never wear shoes. Just like I never
wear panties.'

'Well, it's very unhygienic,' said Perri. 'Not wearing
shoes, I mean. You could pick up all kinds of foot diseases.'

Star looked at her. She was mesmerically pretty, and
Perri felt that she could almost have drowned in those
wide, slate-grey eyes.

Star whispered, 'I shall be as quiet, as quiet as a tiny
mouse.'

Perri took a deep breath.

'Please? Pretty please?' Star said.

Perri, for a moment, felt at a loss for words. She never
had had anyone make such an openly sexual advance
to her before, and in spite of her uncertainty and her
irritation, she found herself fascinated. Star had something about her which was so erotic that it didn't seem
to matter if she was a girl or a boy. She had a magical
magnetism, as if she was a changeling, or the offspring
of some forbidden love between goblins and humans.

Perri found herself wondering what it would actually be like to be lesbian, or at the very least bisexual, and touch a girl like this. Kiss her, and hold her small rounded breasts in the palm of her hand.

It's my vanity, she thought. My vanity, and the tension and fears of being in love with a priest.

'I really think it's better if you leave. I'm sorry.'

Star lowered her long eyelashes. 'I see. Then you don't really like me.'

'I don't *know* you. How can I tell if I like you or not?'

Star lifted her face. 'You could trust me. That's the first step to liking somebody.'

'Why should I trust you? You broke into my apartment,' Perri asked.

'Yes, but I didn't steal anything. And I waited for you.'

Perri sat down on the vinyl settee, and Star knelt down beside her. They looked at each other carefully and warily. Then Perri said, 'I'm sorry. I'm flattered if you find me attractive, I really am. But if I let you get involved with me – well, you'd only wind up getting hurt. I'm in love with a man, and that's all there is to it.'

Star leaned close to Perri. 'I love you, Perri. Doesn't that count for anything?'

'It's crazy. You don't even know what I'm like. How can you love me?'

'Kiss me, Perri,' she whispered. 'Kiss me once, and then I'll go. Just kiss me once so that I can remember it.'

Perri shook her head. 'No, Star. All I want you to do is go.'

'Oh, God, kiss me once, just kiss me once,' moaned Star, with her eyes closed. She began to tug at her shorts, pulling them up so that they cut even deeper.

'For God's sake –' Perri said.

It happened in a split second. Perri started to rise up off the settee, but Star lunged forward and kissed her full on the mouth. More than that, she seized Perri's right hand and pressed it right up between her legs.

Urgently, instinctively, Perri tried to pull her hand away, but Star held her wrist tight, smearing her fingers against her moist flesh.

At that moment, the room was blotted out by the brilliant blue light of a photo-flash.

Perri slapped at Star, and tugged her hand free. She turned around just in time to see a man in a light-coloured linen suit and a Panama hat walking unhurriedly down the hallway towards the front door. He opened it, and stepped out into the darkness. Perri stood in the centre of the room, appalled and frightened, and then she turned back to Star.

Star was already pulling her shorts down so that they didn't reveal as much of her pubic hair as they had before, and straightening her denim vest.

Perri said, 'Star –'

Star looked up, and gave her a mischievous grin.

'You set me up for that, didn't you?' demanded Perri.

'Sure.'

'You admit it? You actually have the barefaced nerve to sit there, in my apartment, and admit it?'

'Sure.'

'All right, why?'

Star smiled, but the smile was matter-of-fact now, and all the pretended passion had vanished.

'It wasn't my idea, Perri. It really wasn't.'

'You really think I'm going to believe you?'

'You have to believe me.'

'Why? You broke into my apartment and set me up for some cheap blackmail picture and you expect me to believe you?'

'Perri,' Star said, soothingly. 'Can't you guess who thought of it?'

'I'm damned if I can. Who would have the gall to –'

She stopped herself. Star was smiling at her, gentle and fey and still outrageously erotic.

'It wasn't Hilary, was it?'

Star only smiled.

Perri sat down again. 'Now I get it. Hilary Nestor Hunter. She paid you to come here, right? She even gave you my address.'

'She gave me fifty bucks. But you're real nice, you know. I would have done it for nothing if I'd known how nice you were.'

Perri felt chilled. 'Does Hilary really think that I'm *that* much of a threat? Can't she be satisfied with voting me down, instead of dragging me down? There was only a thin chance of my winning that motion tomorrow, and she knows it as well as I do.'

'Well,' grinned Star, 'I just don't know about all that. All I know is what Ms. Hunter told me to do.'

Perri looked at her frigidly. 'I see. Well, since you've done it, and very successfully, you'd better get out of here before I have you thrown out.'

Star said, 'There's one more thing. A message.'

'What message?'

'It's simple,' Star told her. 'Hilary says that if you don't withdraw your motion tomorrow, then she's going to make sure this picture gets around.'

'Well, you can tell her I don't give a damn.'

'Hilary says you have to remember that if the gay delegates see the picture, they'll probably vote against you because they'll think you've been hiding your lesbianism in the closet. And if the straight delegates see it, they'll vote against you because they'll think you're gay.'

Perri shook out another cigarette. 'I'll take my chances, thank you. Tell her to show the picture to anyone she likes.'

Star brushed back her long shiny hair, and smiled ruefully. 'Hilary said to remind you that none of this would do Father Leonard much good, whoever Father Leonard is.'

Perri stared at her. 'What does Hilary know about Father Leonard?'

'I don't know,' shrugged Star. 'But she told me to make a point of mentioning him.'

Perri's mouth felt dry. She just stared at Star as the girl picked up her purse from behind the settee and blew Perri a kiss. 'So long,' she said, and padded off up the hallway on her bare feet. She opened the front door, and was gone.

THREE

Early Thursday afternoon they caught David Radetzky as he was crossing the state line from Nevada into California, on highway 52 through the Pahrump Valley. He had been driving his white Monarch at ninety miles an hour for three hours, a high tail of dust rising behind him as he sped away from Las Vegas.

The day was dazzlingly hot, and David drove with the air-conditioning at full blast, his eyes screwed up against the dusty glare of the road. His short-sleeved shirt was soaked in frigid sweat, and he chewed gum like an animal trying to bite its own leg off to get out of a trap.

On the seat beside him lay the spool of tape on which he had recorded Senator Chapman's incriminating conversation with Lollie Methven. On the centre console, rattling slightly as he drove, rested a Smith & Wesson .38 police revolver.

David and Duke and Juan had abandoned their room just below the Pompadour Suite as soon as they realised that Lollie was giving the game away. Duke had taken the videotape and headed back to California on Interstate 15. Juan, with the movie films, had headed northwest to Reno so that he could cross the state line at Lake Tahoe. David had opted for a fast but (he hoped) unexpected escape through the Nopah mountains to Shoshone.

The highway was deserted for miles, except for occasional trucks. His hands perspired on the steering-wheel as he slewed the Monarch around long mountainside curves with its tyres shrieking and its suspension bucking. He counted the miles to California, and chewed savagely at his gum, and prayed to God that the wrath of the senior Senator from Minnesota wouldn't be able to catch up with him. He had heard Chapman mention the name 'Domani,' and he knew what that meant.

Eugenio Domani was one of Las Vegas's inner circle of mobsters, with a fondness for horseracing, maiming, and blinding, in that order. If Chapman had a man like that for a friend, then David felt he would rather be out of Nevada and into California as fast as he could. California was David's home turf, and there were plenty of people there to help him, not least amongst them the Highway Patrol.

He was tempted to put out a call for assistance on his CB, but until he crossed the state line, he thought it was wiser to keep radio silence. He didn't know how wide Chapman's influence was cast, but he knew that Domani ran the southwest corner of Nevada as if it was his own vegetable patch.

He glanced at his gas gauge and saw that it was reading a little under half-empty. But he should be able to make Shoshone without any difficulty, and tank up there. He suddenly realised his chewing-gum was all chewed out of flavour, and he put down the window and tossed it out on to the road. He wished he wasn't so damned tense.

This was the kind of situation he had always feared. For years, in his single bed in his neat, tobacco-coloured apartment in West Los Angeles, he had had nightmares of getting involved with hoodlums and big-time mobsters. He was a precise, experienced private detective, with a systematic way of working which sometimes took longer but almost always brought results. He didn't want to get himself tangled up in those dangerous and unpredictable cases that usually ended up in injury or death.

He looked across at the spool of tape. He was almost tempted to throw it out in the desert and forget about it. But that wasn't going to solve any problems, neither America's problems nor his. It seemed that what he had on that tape was at least as deadly and volatile as Watergate, and somebody was going to have to be told about it. He was scared, but it gave him a strange kind of high, thinking that he was responsible for something so important. Maybe, when everything was tied up and Chapman was arraigned for criminal conspiracy, the newspapers would write about this ninety-mile-an-hour drive from Las Vegas like the ride of Paul Revere. He just wished it was all over, and he could stop sweating.

He switched on the car radio. Reception wasn't too clear out here, because of the mountains and the heat. But through the fizz of static, he could hear President Carter talking about the neutron bomb. He listened for a while, as the desert flashed past him and the road unwound beneath the wheels of his car like a dusty black ribbon, and then he switched over to an easy-listening station.

He was ten or twelve minutes from the state line.

What he didn't see was the Bell B-47 helicopter skirting the hills behind him from the direction of Potosi Mountain. It was flying fast and low, glinting in the afternoon sunlight, tracking the tail of dust that rose from the back of his car, but keeping well out of sight. As the Monarch zigzagged down a long series of bends that took the road down into the Pahrump Valley, the helicopter hovered and danced behind the rocks, and then sped off again like a dragonfly as the car reached the straight highway on the valley floor.

Val, in a garish red-and-orange sport shirt, was piloting. Beside him, in well-pressed white slacks, clean white shoes and a white half-sleeved shirt, sat Umberto, with a .47 calibre big game rifle held upright between his knees.

Umberto pointed a few miles across the valley to a rising curve in the road, and told Val, 'There. Take me down behind the curve, where he can't see me.'

'I don't know why we just don't swoop right down and blow off his head,' Val said.

'Because it's dangerous and stupid, that's why,' Umberto said coldly.

'We never do anything with style. We're always playing it safe,' Val grumbled.

'That's because Senator Chapman wants it that way.'

'Senator Chapman! What does he know?'

Umberto shrugged. 'He knows enough to be President, and that's good enough for me. Now, let's get over there before we lose our chance.'

Chased by its shadow across the scrub, the Bell sped

213

towards the distant rise in the ground. Umberto glanced across the valley from time to time, checking the distant white speck of David Radetzky's car. They had over-hauled it in a matter of seconds, and then they clattered over the rising ground and circled around towards the highway.

Umberto indicated a left-hand curve in the road, still out of David Radetzky's sight. 'Set me down here. Then back off and land behind those hills,' he ordered.

Val brought the helicopter down by the roadside, whipping up a hurricane of dust. The deafening *chock-chock-chock* of its rotors gradually slowed, and Umberto unbuckled himself and opened the door. He clipped a radio-transmitter to his belt, and took six extra shells, which he buttoned neatly into his top pocket. He checked his Seamaster watch.

'Radetzky should be here in two or three minutes. Make sure you're well out of sight. I don't want the heli-copter damaged if there's any shooting. If I don't report back in ten minutes, come looking for me.'

Val grinned. 'You're going to blow his head off, huh?'

Umberto lifted the rifle out of the helicopter. 'That's right. Just for you, I'm going to blow his head off.'

He closed the cockpit door, and then loped quickly for shelter as the helicopter's motor roared, and the rotors beat at the hot, dusty afternoon air. He waited until the Bell had risen a hundred feet, and clattered away towards the hills, and then he walked along by the roadside until he reached a solitary road sign which read *Dangerous Curve*.

Umberto took out a clean white handkerchief and dabbed the dust and the perspiration from his forehead. Then he checked his watch again. At ninety miles an hour, David Radetzky's car would reach the curve in about one minute twenty seconds. He would be a fast target to hit – faster than any of the animals his rifle had been designed to bring down. But three factors would slow him up as he approached the spot where Umberto was standing: the curve, the rise in gradient, and the sun which would suddenly shine in his eyes as he came speeding into view. All these would make for an easier shot, although Umberto was not unduly worried. Even at a hundred miles an hour, David Radetzky's car would only be travelling at 140.8 feet per second, and that, in relation to a 300-grain bullet travelling at 1,861.5 feet per second, was almost standing still.

The road was suddenly quiet. The noise of the helicopter had dwindled and died now, as Val set it down behind the hills. The wind blew only softly, streaking the blacktop with dust, and there was only the muted chirping of insects in the scrub. Umberto chambered a round into the breech of his rifle. The sound of the bolt clicking into place was almost embarrassingly loud.

Barely audible in the distance was the murmur of a car engine, and the swishing of tyres on a dusty road surface. Umberto took out his handkerchief again and wiped the palms of his hands. Then he rested his back against the road sign, and raised the rifle so that it pointed towards the approximate area where David Radetzky's car would appear.

The sound of the car engine grew louder.

At that moment, only a half-mile away from the curve, Umberto was still hidden from David Radetzky by the wind-eroded rocks that bordered it on each side. David's foot was almost flat down to the floor now, and he was driving in the centre of the highway at a hundred and ten. He kept checking his rear-view mirror to see if anyone was behind him, but he knew that they couldn't have gone after him soon enough or fast enough to catch up.

He reached over and switched on his CB. In a few moments, he'd be speeding over the Nevada-California state line, and then he was going to put in a call to his friends of the Highway Patrol straight away. The sooner he offloaded that tape, the better he was going to feel.

He'd gotten hold of incriminating evidence quite a few times before, and he'd usually managed to sell it back to the guilty parties for a substantial profit. But this time, he knew that he didn't have the nerve to start making deals. He could have tried to blackmail Carl Chapman, or sell the details of the Sweetman Curve to the Democrats. He could have called up Woodward and

Bernstein, and asked them if they wanted the greatest news story since Watergate.

But Carl Chapman's whole career was tied up with the Sweetman Curve, and David knew that he wasn't going to take at all kindly to anyone who attempted to put the squeeze on him. David had a nagging fear, although he wouldn't really admit it to himself, that Lollie Methven was already dead, or at least maimed, and he wouldn't have bet much on Duke's chances either, out on the interstate highway.

Umberto raised his rifle, settled it against his shoulder, and took aim down the long barrel. One minute and thirty-seconds had elapsed since he had alit from the helicopter.

David eased his foot off the gas as he came nearer the curve. He was about to reach over to change radio stations but the sun suddenly dazzled him and he raised his hand to fold down his sun-visor instead.

It happened in seconds. Umberto was resting against the *Dangerous Curve* sign, tense and ready, when the white Monarch abruptly appeared. He squeezed the trigger once, and the .41 bullet, almost half-an-inch in diameter, burst through the car's windshield and exploded straight through David's upraised hand.

The car snaked across the highway in an agonized skid, and collided tail-first with the rocks at the side of the verge. Then it slewed back across the road, with David desperately wrenching at the steering-wheel with his one good hand. The car shrieked like something alive, scoring the dusty road with twisted curves of black rubber.

Umberto smoothly turned around, resighted his rifle, and fired again. The bullet punched into the trunk, but missed the gas tank. He fired once more and the rear window smashed. He fired a fourth time, and a rear tyre flapped into black ribbons.

The Monarch jounced and banged on ruined suspension and came to a halt beside the highway. The echoes of its crash re-echoed from the hills and then faded away. Umberto put down his rifle and stood by the *Dangerous Curve* sign, quite motionless, waiting for any signs of life.

After a while, when there was none, he walked quickly and quietly over to the Monarch in his soft white shoes. He circled the car once, looking warily into the smashed windows, but when he saw that David Radetzky was hunched in his seat with his face smothered in blood, he rested his rifle against the side of the car and tugged open the passenger door.

On the floor, in the welter of broken glass and bent trim, was the spool of tape. He picked it up, brushed off the fragments of glass, and put it on the car's roof. Then he made a quick search under the seats and in the glove box to make sure there was no other incriminating evidence. He picked up the .38 revolver and stuck it in his belt.

David Radetzky's face was already swollen and blue, but Umberto reached across the car and thumbed back his eyelid, just to make sure. The eyeball was solid crimson.

Umberto unhooked his radio transmitter, pulled out the aerial, and said: 'Val, it's all over. Come in and get me.'

As he shut the aerial away, the helicopter rose from behind the nearby hills like a noisy conjuring trick. Umberto waved it towards him, and for a few moments it hovered over the wrecked car, blowing up billows of dust, while Val took a few photographs for Senator Chapman's information and amusement. Then it backed off, and landed twenty-five yards away in a blizzard of grit.

Umberto hurried over to the Bell with his head bent and his handkerchief over his mouth. He wrenched open the door, slung his rifle inside, and then climbed aboard himself. Val pulled away, and within a few minutes they were nothing more than a droning spark of silver against the clear cloudless sky. The Monarch baked under the mid-afternoon heat in silence.

Two hours passed, and the sun dropped towards the distant blue horizon of the Nopah range. The car's shadow lengthened. The desert air began to cool slightly, and the sheet-metal hood ticked spasmodically as it contracted. Around five o'clock, David Radetzky stirred.

He was aware of thirst before he was aware of pain. He ran his tongue across his lips and felt the saltiness of dried blood. His head was pounding and there was a crushing sensation in his right hand. He opened his eyes.

Everything was blurry at first, but then he slowly made out the images of a broken car windshield, a badly bent steering-wheel, and his own surprisingly crooked legs. He closed his eyes again for a little while and rested them.

Half an hour later, he opened his eyes again. It seemed cooler now, almost chilly. He could see that the sky was growing dusky, and it occurred to him that if he stayed here until it grew dark, he was probably going to die. He wasn't aware that Umberto's second bullet had penetrated the trunk, the rear seats, and the back of the driver's seat, and that his spinal column was shattered into red jelly and splinters of bone.

A calm wind was blowing. He wondered what he was doing here and what could have happened. He knew that he was supposed to be driving to Shoshone, but he wasn't altogether sure why. He knew that it was something to do with the Sweetman Curve, but he didn't understand what the Sweetman Curve was. He thought about the name Sweetman, and all he could picture was a kind of gingerbread man made out of crunchy brown sugar.

Another hour passed. He woke up feeling freezing cold, and in terrible pain. He couldn't feel or move his legs at all. But somehow the pain had cleared his mind, and he was beginning to remember what had happened. He couldn't recall the final moments when Umberto had actually shot him, but he remembered approaching the curve, and thinking about putting out a call on his CB.

He looked across at the CB. It was still switched on.

He stared at it for a long time, and then tried to swing his left hand across to pick up the microphone. The first and second times he tried, his fingers couldn't close over it. But then he made a third strenuous attempt, and managed to fumble it up between his wrist and his chest. Then he worked it up into the palm of his hand, and said weakly, 'This is Blue Eyes requesting emergency assist in Pahrump Valley. Anyone in range, I'm in Pahrump Valley. Badly need assist.'

That was all he could say before pain gripped his back so mercilessly that his nervous system was paralysed, and the microphone dropped from his hand to the seat. He sat there with his teeth clenched and his eyes shut, and prayed that some angel would find him.

The angel was a fifty-four-year-old truck driver called Al Rippert, from Santa Barbara. He picked up David Radetzky's distress call from only two miles away in California, on highway 178. He was driving a pre-fabricated chalet up to the Lee Canyon Winter Sports area, and he was running three hours late because of a burst tyre.

He brought his massive Mack truck to a halt just a few feet away from David's wrecked Monarch, and walked across in the glare of his headlamps, pulling his waistband up over his pot belly as he came.

David Radetzky was barely conscious. When Al Rippert cradled his bloodied head in his arm, all David could manage to murmur was: 'Election ... it's the election ...'

He was silent for a while, and then he mumbled 'Road sign.'

FOUR

The phone rang, and Carl X. Chapman reached across his desk to pick it up without taking his eyes from the draft speech he was reading.

'Yes? Who is this?' he said.

There was a crackly silence, and then a voice said, 'Everything's fine, Mr Chapman. Everything's under control.'

'Are you sure? What about the tapes and the films?'

'All accounted for. One tape-recorder, one tape. Two movie cameras, two movies. One video machine, one videotape.'

'What about Radetzky?'

'Radetzky is suffering from Sweetman's disease. Umberto saw to that. Val caught up with that wetback, Juan, and Domani's men nailed the sound technician. Forced his car off the highway.'

'Okay. Get the tape and the films back here to me, and don't let them out of your sight. And make sure you pay off Domani. Maybe five thousand dollars or so, just for his trouble.'

'With all respect, Mr Chapman, I should make it ten. Hits come expensive these days.'

'Harris, don't talk like that on the open telephone.'

'I'm sorry, Mr Chapman.'

'You'd be a damned sight sorrier if this line was tapped.'

'Yes, sir. I'm sorry, sir. I'll have those tapes and films right over.'

'One more thing, Harris.'

'Yes, sir?'

'As soon as tomorrow's meeting is over, I want to get straight down to Palm Springs. Call Adele and tell her what time we're coming.'

'Very good, Mr Chapman.'

Carl sat down the telephone, and then ran his fingers through his wiry hair. He felt less unsettled now that David Radetzky had been caught. He had dozens of prepared contingency plans for dealing with accidental leaks of the Sweetman plan, from grandiose press statements to schemes for diverting the blame for the killings onto 'Communist agents.' But he felt safer if the plan stayed a secret, and the closer he came to the White House, the closer he came to keeping it a secret forever. Unknown to any of the twenty-two professional killers he was using across the breadth of the continental United States, it was Carl's intention, once inaugurated, to dispose of them all within twenty-four hours. He had documents already drawn up which incriminated each of them for breaches of national security, and he would use the FBI, and particularly his old college pal the deputy director, to hit them swiftly and legally.

That was when the killing would stop for good.

Carl had known when he embarked on the Sweetman plan that hundreds and possibly thousands of Americans were going to die. It had taken him weeks of agonizing to make up his mind to do it. Although the plan had seemed theoretically scientific and controllable, Carl was enough of a practical politician to know that theory and reality rarely coincide. If his scientific advisers prognosticated that they would have to kill eight hundred people to ensure a certain vote for Carl Chapman in 1980, then at the end of the day it would probably total three times as many. That didn't include the inevitable security killings like David Radetzky and Lollie Methven, and anyone else who stumbled accidentally on the truth of the Sweetman Curve.

But, in the final analysis, Carl had decided that it was better for America as a nation to regain her national pride than it was to consider the lives of only two or three thousand people. Why, more people died in auto accidents in a single month, and their deaths were more tragic because they were meaningless and wasted. At least the Sweetman plan had the virtue of having a political purpose. All those who were likely to threaten the American way could be weeded out, and with each weeding the strength of the country would grow.

He pushed back his chair and stood up. He knew that the people who were dying were more than abstract lines on a demographic chart. He was tough, and sometimes bitter, but he wasn't lacking in human sensitivity. He had seen his own father cry, and he knew that other people were crying because of what he had done, and that even more would cry in the months leading up to the primaries. But he felt no guilt. He felt instead the deep paternal sadness of a father who has to send his sons off to war. He only wished he could talk to some of them, and tell them why they had to die.

Every day, on the demographic charts that were printed out of the Sweetman computers, more and more thin blue lines rose up to meet the thick red line that represented the Sweetman Curve. Each thin blue line was the political life of an American man or woman, and as soon as it intersected the red line, that meant that somewhere in the United States, somebody had reached a stage in their political thinking that would probably lead them to vote against Carl X. Chapman in 1980. As soon as the blue line and the red line met, orders were immediately sent out from Carl Chapman's headquarters to erase the blue line forever.

Carl stared out of the window of the Xanadu Hotel, down towards the Las Vegas strip. One day soon, he would be staring out of the French windows of the Oval office on to the White House lawns, and then his sadness would be appeased. He watched cars lazily driving up and down, and people crossing the street, and he felt a sense of responsible power that was greater than almost anything he had ever experienced.

The phone rang again. He went across to the desk, and picked it up. The receptionist said, 'Your wife is calling you from Minneapolis, Mr Chapman. Do you wish to take the call?'

He paused, and then said, 'Surely. Put her on.'

Over the echoing long-distance line, he heard Elspeth saying, 'Carl? Is that you?'

'Yes, dear, it's me. How are things?'

'The weather's dreadful. We've had six inches of snow

this morning. I've changed my mind about Palm Springs, and I've decided to come down. That's why I'm calling.'

'You're coming down? I thought you were going to spend the weekend with the Delanceys.'

'Carl, it's really too awful here. And anyway, I'm already packed. There's a flight to Los Angeles at nine tomorrow morning.'

Carl bit his lip. He had been counting on Elspeth staying in Minnesota, and giving Adele Corliss's weekend party a miss. He hadn't seen Hilary Nestor Hunter for a month, and he hadn't been able to spend an evening alone with her for nearly a year. He had been looking forward to reviving the acquaintanceship that had begun so spectacularly at the last Republican party convention. Hilary excited Carl. She had excited him from the moment he first walked into the cocktail party, and saw her talking in the far corner of the room, tall and striking and obviously dominating the conversation. She excited him because she was so determined and aggressive, politically and sexually; and she excited him because she stirred up almost fanatical support among women, not with middle-of-the-road liberalism or left-wing idealism, but with intense right-wing fierceness. After that first cocktail party, they had gone out to dinner, and then to bed, and in the small hours of the morning, Hilary Nestor Hunter had talked female politics of a kind which stirred him and challenged him. He had determined that, when the time came, he would choose her to play a part in his 1980 administration. Elspeth could be his First Lady, and pick the wallpaper and place settings for the White House; Hilary would be his political empress.

He said, in a controlled voice, 'It really isn't worth your coming down, dear. It's going to be deadly dull, all movie people and British tax exiles, and you won't enjoy a moment of it.'

'Carl,' insisted Elspeth, 'I just feel like some sun. And nothing could be duller than Minneapolis on a snowbound Sunday.'

'I suppose you want to keep your eagle eye on me, too?' he asked her.

There was a short silence. Then Elspeth said, 'Should

I have any reason to? Apart from the usual floozies?'

'You tell me. You're the one who's been hiring the private detectives.'

There was another silence, longer. Elspeth said, 'I'm not at all sure what you're talking about.'

Carl gave an ironic grunt. 'Oh, come now, dear. You know exactly what I'm talking about. You've had film cameras rolling for months, recording every carnal sin that I've committed in sound and vision and stunning Cinemascope.'

There was no point in Elspeth denying it. She said, in a steady voice, 'How did you find out?'

'It wasn't very difficult,' Carl said. 'I just happened to bump into a friend of yours called David Radetzky, and David Radetzky and his little gang were having a whole lot of fun wiring up my bedroom for sound and pictures. On your instructions, of course.'

'Did they tell you why they were doing it?'

'The girl did. She said you were seeking a divorce. David Radetzky wasn't in much of a condition to talk to me himself.'

'You haven't hurt him?'

'Radetzky? I haven't laid a finger on him.'

'Well, thank God for that, Carl, because I'm *not* seeking a divorce.'

'You're not? You've hired private detectives, you've taken full colour movies of whatever I do in bed, and you tell me you're *not* seeking a divorce?'

There was a pause. 'I was seeking protection, if you must know,' she said.

'Protection? Protection against what?'

'Protection against you, Carl. You're dangerous. I know something of what you're doing to get yourself elected.'

Carl sighed. So Elspeth knew about Sweetman, too. He supposed it wasn't much of a surprise. Elspeth was beside him most of the time, after all, and she must have picked up fragments of conversation with his aides and his secretaries, and heard him on the phone. All the same, it disturbed him, and he was anxious to find out how much she knew. Elspeth could become as much of a security risk as David Radetzky. Inviting, of course, the same kind of retaliatory action.

'What have you heard?' he asked her, more gently.

'Enough,' she said.

'How much is enough?'

'Enough to make me realise that you won't let anything or anybody stand in your way, including me. Enough to make me realise that you will almost certainly be President-elect in 1980. And enough to make me realise that if I want to be First Lady, and stay First Lady, I've got to have some kind of reliable insurance.'

Carl sounded pained. 'Do you really think I'd ever hurt you?' he asked.

'Yes, Carl, I do. I can just imagine the political capital you'd make out of the sad and tragic death of your dear wife. I can picture you already, making your election speeches with tears in your eyes and a black armband.'

Carl took a deep breath to steady his temper. He said, as coaxingly as he could, 'Elspeth, it seems that you have some pretty wrong ideas about what I'm doing here. Now, do you think you could tell me what you've heard, and maybe who told you?'

'Oh, no,' Elspeth said, decisively. 'I'm not that much of a pumpkinhead. I'll tell you when it's all over, when you're elected and inaugurated and safe in the White House. And even then, I'll still have my films and my tapes to keep me warm.'

'What films and tapes? I took all Radetzky's films and tapes.'

'Including the films and tapes from the Doral?'

'The *Doral*? You didn't–'

He clamped his mouth shut in anger. Of all the people he hated to outsmart him, his wife came at the top of the list. Maybe it was his own fault. He always thought of her as superior and elite and elegant, but essentially dumb, and it was a constant surprise to him, a constant upleasant surprise, that she could work things out for herself. She wasn't all raised eyebrows and sarcasm and social graces.

'Are you catching the nine o'clock plane into LAX?' he asked.

225

'You don't have to sound so depressed about it, dearest.'

'How do you expect me to sound after finding out that you took goddamned snooping movies of me in Miami?'

'Carl, how do you think *I* reacted when I found out that you were romping around in bed with some red-headed whore while I was in bed with a sick headache?'

'All that's ever been sick about you is your sense of wifely loyalty.'

'On the contrary, Carl,' said Elspeth evenly, 'I think my loyalty has been my greatest virtue. Especially when you consider how often you've cheated on me.'

'Listen!' he yelled. 'If you want a divorce, you can have a divorce! I don't need to listen to you telling me how loyal you are!'

'I don't want a divorce,' replied Elspeth. 'I just want us to understand each other. I've told you before. The only difference is that this time I'm holding a far stronger hand.'

Carl let his temper slowly simmer down. Then he said, 'All right. Let's talk about it in Palm Springs. Perhaps we'll both be a little cooler by then.'

'I'm perfectly cool,' said Elspeth.

'Well, good,' snapped Carl, 'because I'm damned if I am.'

Just as he banged down the phone, there was a chime at the door of his suite. He shouted, 'Hold on a goddamned minute!' and stalked across to the glass-fronted liquor cabinet. He took out a whisky tumbler, slammed it angrily on to the table, and then unscrewed a bottle of Wild Turkey and splashed out four fingers of straight bourbon.

He sipped the drink back, swallowed it, coughed, and pulled a face. He closed his eyes, and let the burning sensation of it sink down inside him like a blazing funeral ship sinking in a dark ocean.

The door chimed again. Steadied, calmer, he went to answer it, and admitted Dan Harris, his press aide, carrying a briefcase and an aluminium movie can. Harris was a young, pale-faced man with a neatly-clipped moustache and an expression of irrepressible self-confidence, as if he had just thought of a great idea and couldn't wait to repeat it. The only trouble was, he never did repeat it, because he never did have any great ideas.

'Here it all is,' he said, tipping out a spool of video-tape, a spool of magnetic tape, and two reels of movie film.

Carl didn't even look at it.

'I think we did a pretty neat operation there,' said Dan Harris. 'All three of them wiped out, all the stuff recovered.'

Carl looked at him with tired eyes. 'Do you like the idea of killing, Harris? Do you really like the idea of gunning people down?'

Dan Harris went slightly pink. 'When I said we wiped them out, sir, I didn't mean –'

Carl sat down in a big velour armchair and stared at his empty whisky glass. 'I know what you meant. I wish I damned well didn't.'

FIVE

Adele was sitting on the edge of the pool, idly stirring the surface with her legs. It was a few minutes past midnight early into Friday morning, and the sky above her was warm and black and prickly with stars. The only illumination came from a floodlight at the bottom of the pool, which turned the water into glowing liquid glass. The light suffused Adele's face in a strange and magical way, as if she were a water-nymph, possessed of unusual powers.

She wore a small white bikini by the French designer Quéran, which turned completely transparent when it was wet. She was sipping a mint julep, and smoking a menthol cigarette. All around her, the night was silent and windless.

The door from the house opened and Ken Irwin stood

there, in jeans and a plaid shirt. Although it was the middle of the night, he was wearing dark glasses. He stayed in the doorway without moving and without speaking.

Adele let him stand there for a while, and then she lifted her head and said, 'You're back late.'

'I've been back for a while,' he told her. 'I've been looking for something.'

'Did you find it?'

He took a step or two out on to the pool patio. 'No, I didn't.'

Adele drew at her cigarette. 'It's a beautiful night, isn't it? Why don't you take off your clothes and come for a swim?'

'I'm not in the mood,' he said in a low voice.

'I thought you adored swimming. You haven't been out of the pool since you came here.'

'I'm not in the mood,' he repeated.

She splashed the water, and fluorescent ripples circled across the pool. 'I suppose you're sulking,' she said.

He came closer, and stood over her with his thumbs in his belt loops, looking down at her. 'No,' he said. 'I'm not sulking. I'm just looking for something.'

'I suppose you think I know where it is.'

'I'm damned sure you know where it is.'

She smiled. 'Do you want a drink? If so, you'll have to fix it yourself. The servants have all gone to bed.'

Ken hunkered down beside her, and unhooked his sunglasses. His eyes were tired and serious, and not in the mood for games.

'Adele, you don't know what you're getting yourself mixed up in.'

She challenged his eyes with her own, and smiled at him patronizingly. 'My dear young man,' she told him. 'In my lifetime I've been mixed up in more than you could even guess. Whom did you plan to kill?'

'Nobody. The gun was just for protection.'

'Protection? A high-powered rifle with telescopic sights? And in any case, protection against what? Against whom? You don't need protection against *me*, do you?'

'How did you find it?'

Adele reached out and touched his cheek with her fingertips, stroking it gently. 'Nothing goes on in this house that I don't get to know about, Ken. I think, right from the start, that you've misjudged me. Just because I'm a self-indulgent lady with a taste for too many mint juleps and too many horny young men, that doesn't make me dumb. I wouldn't have survived all these years if I'd been dumb.'

'I have to have the gun back, Adele,' Ken said quietly.

'Can you tell me why?'

'It's not mine. I'm looking after it for a friend.'

'Well, why does your friend want it back?'

'Adele, I want that gun.'

'I want to know what you're planning to do with it first.'

'Listen, I just want that gun.'

Adele cocked her head to one side. Her eyes were sparkling in the reflected light from the pool. 'Do you want me to call the police?' she asked him. 'I'm sure *they'd* be interested to ask you what you're planning to do with it.'

He was silent for a moment, crouched and tense in the darkness. Then, suddenly, he made a grab for her. But Adele ducked out of his way, and jumped into the pool, sending up a splash of illuminated spray.

She backed away from the edge of the pool, treading water. Her fizzled-out cigarette floated a few feet away from her. Ken stood looking at her.

'Well,' she taunted, 'aren't you going to come in and get me? Aren't you going to *force* me to give you your gun back?'

He didn't move. Adele kept on treading water, for a while, and then swam in a wide, lazy circle. 'You're really very ineffectual for a killer,' she told him.

Deliberately, slowly, Ken tugged his shirt out of his belt. He stripped it off, baring his muscular chest, and tossed it aside. Then he kicked off his sandals, and unbuckled his jeans. He stepped out of his jeans, and stood naked on the edge of the pool, his chest rising and falling with controlled anger. On either side of him, the mock-Roman statues gazed at him incuriously, and above him the stars sparkled in the deep dark sky.

'You look gorgeous,' called Adele, as she swam. 'You look like Ulysses about to face Circe.'

Ken dived, plunging right down to the floor of the pool, and swam underwater towards her with long, powerful strokes. Adele immediately struck out for the shallow end of the pool, her legs kicking up spray and her arms thrashing. Beneath her, in the depths of the water, she could see the dark outline of Ken's bare body rising towards her like a killer shark. She gasped for breath, and thrashed the water harder.

He caught her just as her feet touched bottom. She tried to wade for the semi-circular steps at the end of the pool, but his hands seized her legs and brought her down into the water with a splash. She shrieked and gargled as he momentarily pulled her under.

She pushed him, and managed to scramble to her feet again, and fight three or four steps through the water, to where it was only a few inches deep. But then he brought her down again, and they wrestled and panted across the width of the pool, kicking and splashing and rolling over.

He pinned her down against the steps, and slapped her wet face hard, first with the palm of his hand and then with the back. She jerked her head away, but he gripped her chin and forced her to look up at him. His hair was wet and plastered to his head, and dribbles of water ran down his face.

'You think this is all a big joke, don't you?' he gasped. 'You think that the whole damned world exists for your personal amusement. Well, this time you're way off beam.'

'You grade-school bully,' she spat back.

He let go of her chin. 'You spoiled bitch.'

He pushed her head back against the marble step. Her face was clear of the surface, but the rest of her body was half under water. Through the tight transparent material of her wet swimsuit, her nipples rose wide and red and rigid.

'You dirty, vicious, unprincipled whore,' he said.

'You bastard,' she breathed.

He reached around and gripped the elastic at the back of her bikini pants, and wrenched them downwards. She arched her back, and kicked and splashed water, but he pressed his weight down on her again, and she couldn't get free.

'You filthy pig,' she cursed him. 'You disgusting depraved swine.'

He pulled her pants down as far as her knees, then raised his leg and pushed them right off her with his foot. She managed to twist one of her arms free and clutch at his wet hair, but he slapped her again, and she let go.

'You deserved this, you slut,' he panted. 'You asked for everything you're going to get.'

'You shit,' she sneered. 'You moronic shit.'

He forced open her thighs by twisting his knee between her knees. She felt the water seethe and splash between her legs, and it gave her an oddly intense shivery sensation, as if a cold tongue had suddenly licked her.

'Oh God,' she said, 'you loathsome animal.'

'Shut up,' he said, and then he mounted her.

He was impossibly hard and big. When he thrust himself up inside her, she felt a harsh, searing pain, because the water had washed away all her juices. She clutched at him and winced, but he wouldn't stop. He thrust again, deep and relentless, and this time she cried out. Her fingers dug into the muscles of his back and buttocks, but he thrust again and again and again, with the water churning up all around them, a sparkling illuminated wash of bubbles and foam.

He went on and on, but somehow he couldn't reach a climax, and after almost five minutes his thrusting stopped. He drew himself out of her, and stood up.

She lay back in the water, her legs apart, looking up at him. Her cheeks were crimson from his slapping, and her body was marked and bruised where they had clawed and fought.

'What's the matter?' she said quietly. 'Don't I turn you on any more?'

He gave a brief shake of his head.

'Then what is it? Are you worried about something?'

'I have to have the gun.'

She sat up in the water and dabbed at her swollen cheeks with her fingertips.

'I have to have it,' he insisted. 'If I don't get it, they'll kill me.'

She said, softly, 'Is it really for protection? I mean, you're not a murderer, are you?'

'Do I look like a murderer?'

'Did Lee Harvey Oswald? Does anyone?'

He held out his hands to help her up. 'I'm sorry,' he said. 'I didn't mean to hurt you. I guess I kind of panicked.'

She hesitated for a moment, but then she grasped his hands and got to her feet. She put her arms around him, and squeezed him for a moment, and kissed his chest.

'You're very tasty,' she said, 'and there are times when I think you really *do* love me, in spite of yourself.'

He wiped water away from his face. 'The gun?' he asked her.

She nodded. 'Sure, you can have it back. As long as you promise me two things.'

His right eye twitched slightly. 'What are they?'

'That you don't use the gun for anything except self-defence, and that you take me to bed right now and show me what you can do when you don't have your mind on other things.'

He almost managed to smile. 'You drive a hard bargain, Ms. Corliss. A real hard bargain.'

SIX

The phone was ringing as he unlocked the door of his low-rent apartment over the Catholic Mission on Merchant Street. He hurried into the musty-smelling living room, and picked it up. The room was dark except for a blue neon sign across the street, which flickered because of faulty wiring. He stood there unbuttoning his coat and said, 'Yes?'

'Leonard,' she said softly, 'it's me.'

'Perri? Do you know what time it is?'

'One o'clock. I've been trying to call you since ten.'

'Just let me go switch on a light, and close the door. I only just got back from the hospital. Mrs Pokowski gave birth to triplets, and one was dead.'

He put down the phone, and went across to lock the door and switch on the table lamp. Then he sat down in his frayed brown armchair, and picked up the phone again.

'What's wrong?' he asked her.

She sounded hesitant and tearful. 'Leonard, the most dreadful thing. I'm going to have to withdraw my motion tomorrow. I'm going to have to say that I've reconsidered, and that I'm pulling out.'

He could hardly believe what she was saying. 'You're going to do *what?*'

'I'm going to quit. Say that I've changed my mind.'

'But why? You've got so much support! Give it a couple of years and we could have Hilary Nestor Hunter out of the league altogether.'

'It doesn't matter. I'm quitting.'

'I don't understand,' he said. 'I don't understand at all.'

'Well,' she told him, in a shaky voice, 'have you ever heard of a little thing called blackmail?'

'Blackmail? Somebody's blackmailing you? But what in heaven's name for?'

She told him, slowly and haltingly, about Star. He listened with an intent frown on his face, his eyes on the gentle picture of the Virgin Mary that hung on the wall opposite his chair. Once or twice he made a couple of notes on the cover of his telephone directory. Meanwhile, the blue light across the street flickered and dimmed, and then brightened again.

At last, he said, 'If only I'd known. I feel that I've failed you.'

'Leonard, you haven't failed me. Not once.'

'I should have been strong, Perri, instead of weak.

Every time we sin, there's a terrible and inescapable consequence. I've brought the consequences of this particular sin on both of us.'

'Leonard, you mustn't talk that way.'

'Why not? I believe it. But I believe something else, too. I believe that Hilary Nestor Hunter is ambitious and very ruthless, and that she's quite prepared to do anything to get the power she wants. I believe that it would be wrong of us to give in to her. I believe that we ought to fight her.'

'Leonard,' she said, 'it's *you* that I'm worried about. This could ruin everything you've worked for.'

'That's beside the point,' he put in. 'What I want to know is – *are you prepared to fight?*'

She took a breath, and then she said, 'It's no use, Leonard. There just isn't time. The vote's tomorrow morning, and if I don't quit now, Hilary's going to drag me down into the gutter, and you, too. She's going to bring me down, and Ann Margolies down, and all of those women who support us. What sort of chance do you think we're going to have if she says we're all lesbians?'

Father Leonard rubbed his eyes tiredly. Then he said, 'Perri, I'm going to make a call to my TV friends. I'm going to get them out of bed if I have to. I'm going to see what I can get done between now and the start of the conference tomorrow.'

'Leonard –'

'I'm going to fight this, Perri, because it's evil. It isn't just a bit of internal politics in the women's lib movement any more. It's to do with everything I believe in – the fundamental issue of people's rights and how they're recognised. Give me ten minutes. Then I'll call you back and tell you what's happened.'

'Please don't do anything that's going to hurt your work,' she begged him. 'Please, just promise me that much.'

Father Leonard smiled. 'My work is upholding the rights which God gave to every man and every woman,' he said. 'Anything I can do to further that work can never hurt me.'

'I love you,' she said softly. 'I don't deserve you.'

He held on to the phone for a while, saying nothing. The Virgin Mary was shadowed in flickering blue. 'I love you too, Perri. More than I could have dreamed,' he whispered.

SEVEN

Friday was a spectral morning of hazy smog. Along the Santa Monica Freeway between Palms and Highland Avenue, the traffic snailed along bumper-to-bumper through the dim polluted air. The early sun had barely risen above the horizon, and Los Angeles was an end-of-the-world landscape of orange and grey.

In a borrowed Plymouth Fury with dented fenders and a wire coat-hanger for a radio aerial, T.F. crept along in the traffic with everyone else. His mirror sunglasses lay on the dashboard in front of him, and he was listening to the morning news. He had a slight sinus irritation caused by the smog, and from time to time he gave a short, dry sniff. He was looking forward to going to Palm Springs.

Two cars in front of him was a white Thunderbird with Arizona plates. He had picked it up outside a house in Otsego Street in North Hollywood while it was still dark, and patiently tailed it as far as here. The driver was a twenty-seven-year-old auto salesman named Peter Hughes. He lived in North Hollywood with his wife Clare and his two-year-old daughter Sally. Clare Hughes was pregnant with their second child.

Peter Hughes organized outings for old folks in the district where he lived, and that was his worst mistake. He was known by most people in the streets around Laurelgrove Avenue and Magnolia Boulevard, and he was popular. Last Tuesday, his name had come up on the Sweetman Curve.

T.F. kept a laconic eye on the tail of Peter's car. The traffic was beginning to thin out a little, and in a while he would be able to close up on him. His .45 Colt automatic was lying on the seat beside him, loosely covered by yesterday's *Los Angeles Times*.

Last night had been a celibate night for T.F. He had been down to San Diego during the day for a shooting that didn't come off, because the target unexpectedly went out of town. T.F. didn't like unexpected situations. They jangled his nerves. He had spent a sleepless night playing records and leafing through pornographic magazines, and at four o'clock he had gone down to an all-night diner and eaten a greasy plateful of bacon and eggs.

On the radio, the news reporter was saying: '– is still being pressed to make a statement about the future of the neutron bomb, but in Washington yesterday he insisted that –'

T.F. sniffed. The trouble was, he was beginning to wonder if all these shootings served any purpose. Why knock off so many people, and what for? It seemed as if he was going to have to spend the rest of his life killing two or three people a day. It was depressing. It was like trying to bail out a flooding boat. Every day he shot someone, and every day twenty people were born in their place. He felt as if he was going against the whole tide of history.

Up ahead of him, the white T-bird began to flash its right-hand indicator and pull across to the inside lane. It looked as if Peter Hughes was going to exit on Venice Boulevard, and maybe make his way to work up Highland. T.F. signalled that he was moving across, too, and kept fifty or sixty feet behind the white car as it slowed down for the exit ramp.

This was going to make life difficult. He didn't like taking people on the streets. It was too exposed, too crowded, and escaping at any speed couldn't be guaranteed. He had once shot at a woman on San Vicente Boulevard, missing her by inches, and then had to stop at a red light a few feet further along the street. The woman, oblivious of what he had done, had pulled up alongside him and smiled at him, and there had been too many other cars close by to shoot at her again.

Peter Hughes turned onto Venice Boulevard and headed northeast, with T.F. right behind him. There was less traffic here than T.F. had feared. There was plenty of smog, too, which made it hard to read a licence plate at anything further than thirty feet.

The boulevard was clear ahead for two blocks. T.F. accelerated, and gradually pulled alongside the white T-bird, until they were driving neck-and-neck. He kept his eyes on Peter Hughes, but reached across for his .45 and felt the weight of it in his right hand.

He could see Peter Hughes quite clearly for the first time now. He was young-looking for twenty-seven, with high-coloured cheeks and a snub nose. His hair was cut short, and he was wearing a blue sports shirt. He must have been whistling along with the radio, because his lips were puckered.

The traffic signals ahead of them changed to red, and they drew up to the line side by side. Peter Hughes kept looking ahead and whistling, his elbow resting on the windowsill of his car. The passenger window, nearest to T.F., was closed.

Seconds passed. T.F. checked his rear-view mirror and saw that the block behind them was empty of traffic. On the block ahead, there was only a slow-moving truck, and he could use that to help a quick getaway.

He saw the cross traffic slowing down as the signals changed. He lifted the .45 and rested it in the crook of his left elbow, to steady it. Peter Hughes, only fifteen feet away, didn't even see him. He was whistling and thinking about Clare's birthday, which was on Wednesday the following week. He had bought her a watch and a bottle of Jontue. He hoped the perfume would suit her.

T.F. fired. The passenger window was blasted into smithereens of flying glass, and the bullet hit Peter Hughes in the right ear. It passed right through his head and was later found loosely lodged in a timber telephone post across the street. Peter Hughes slumped sideways, his head resting against the sill of his open window, and runnels of blood streaked the white door of his Thunderbird.

T.F. flung the .45 on the passenger seat and took off in a cloud of smoking rubber. He overtook the truck on the next block and swung in front of it so that any witnesses would find it hard to read his licence plate and even harder to see where he might have gone. He screeched around the corner into Burnside Avenue, and headed back towards Washington Boulevard so that he could rejoin the Santa Monica Freeway and go west to Venice as fast as possible.

He didn't hear the warble of police sirens until he was comfortably settled in the stream of westbound traffic. Then he sat back, sniffed, and turned up the news on the radio. The reporter was saying: 'There's big trouble at the fifth Women's Liberation League convention this morning, with charges from a Catholic priest that one of its most controversial delegates has been set up for a sexual blackmail picture. Here's Dick LaGorda with the story ...'

EIGHT

John Cullen was shaving when he heard the morning news on TV. It was seven o'clock, and the November sunlight, clearer up in the Hollywood hills, was slanting into his small bathroom.

Mel was brewing coffee in the kitchenette and humming quietly to himself. They had talked since dawn, worrying their grief like enraged hounds tearing at a jackrabbit, as they slowly came to grips with the pain of what had happened. John knew that there was more grieving to come, but right now, in the light of his first morning without Vicki, he felt too tired and too talked-out to cry. He knew, too, from his father's death, that tomorrow morning wouldn't be so painful, and that the day after that would be even less so. As his father himself had once told him about death: 'It's surprisingly easy to come to terms with it, easier than divorce, because the person you loved isn't around any more to remind you. You know that you could search the whole world over, and never find them.'

Whether he wanted to or not, he knew that he would eventually get over her. All he hoped for, because he had loved her so much, was that it wouldn't be too soon. His sadness was all he had left.

He shaved under his chin, and rinsed his razor in the basin. The television news reporter said: '– expects to go down to Camp David during the week for a private meeting with Israeli minister –'

Mel, from the kitchenette, said, 'You want some juice? I bought orange and grapefruit.'

John answered, 'Grapefruit.'

Then the news reporter said: 'Here in Los Angeles, where the Women's Liberation League has been holding a stormy fifth convention, a Catholic priest has made amazing charges against the league's founder and leader, Ms. Hilary Nestor Hunter.'

'I wonder what amazing charge that is,' commented Mel. 'Maybe someone's said she's a woman after all.'

John dried his face and came through into the living room. The news reporter said: 'In the early hours of this morning, Father Leonard Zaparelli, a social-working priest from the deprived Merchant Street district of downtown Los Angeles, said that delegate Perri Shaw, an attractive blonde divorcee, was set up last night for phony blackmail photographs. Apparently, a scantily-clad girl broke into Ms. Shaw's Hollywood apartment and, in Father Zaparelli words, "forced Ms. Shaw into a compromising situation." Whereupon, a hidden cameraman snapped the proceedings and made his escape.'

'John – your coffee's ready,' Mel called out.

'Okay, Mel. One minute.'

The reporter said: '– says he's naming no names, but challenges Ms. Hilary Nestor Hunter to deny that Ms. Shaw's withdrawal from the controversy would not be "substantially to her advantage." So far this morning –'

'Can you believe that?' John asked as he came into the living room.

'Believe what?'

'All this backstabbing in the women's lib movement. They're worse than men.'

'What backstabbing? I wasn't listening.'

John took his coffee and sat down at the table. 'It seems like Hilary Nestor Hunter set up some fake blackmail photographs, trying to prove one of her lady opponents was a lesbian.'

'I thought they were *all* lesbians.'

John laughed. 'Don't let Vicki hear you say that.' Then he suddenly realised what he'd said. He was quiet for a moment, and then he added, 'Well, she would have given you a couple of hours' pretty tough argument.'

Mel nodded. 'You don't have to pretend that she's lost and gone forever,' he said gently. 'Maybe she's not walking around, but she'll always be there, in your mind and your memory, so don't deny her that much.'

'I couldn't if I tried.'

'So the ladies of the Women's Liberation League are cutting each other's throats. I guess it was bound to happen. That Hilary Nestor Hunter makes women like Kate Millett look like Playboy bunnies.'

'She's pretty well connected, though,' John said. 'It seems to me that most extremists are. Jack McGuire at the *Liberal Journal* told me she was great buddies with Carl X. Chapman.'

Mel looked surprised. 'Chapman? He's the biggest chauvinist since Attila the Hun. How did Hilary Nestor Hunter get to be buddies with him?'

John sat back in his chair, sipping his coffee. 'Their political views are pretty similar, even if their social views are different. They both approve of a pure, strong America – all wagon trains and Baptist churches and no fornicating on Sundays. I guess they'd team up if they thought it was the best way for the two of them to further their political careers. Maybe they'd fight to the death later, but I think they could come to some kind of a compromise for as long as it suited them.'

'Didn't Chapman say he was going to stand for President in 1980?'

'That's right, in *Newsweek* or someplace. There was all that fuss about it. Teddy Kennedy said if Carl X. Chapman stood for President, then he'd be obliged to stand against him, just to stop a fascist getting into the Oval Office.'

Mel checked his watch. 'You're still planning on going down to San Diego today?'

'Sure. Have you changed your mind?'

'I guess I have. I mean, if you don't object. I just think I'd go stir-crazy sitting in this place on my own.'

John finished his coffee. 'Okay, then. Let's go.'

They tidied up, and then they left the hotel and walked across the street to where John's car was parked. It was almost eight o'clock now, and the day was beginning to warm up. The weather forecast said it was the hottest November in nine years. Mel lit up a thin black cheroot, and tossed the match in the gutter.

They got into the car, and John U-turned to take them west towards the San Diego Freeway. They didn't talk much. There had been so much talk lately, sometimes angry and sometimes bitter and always sad, and today they were quite content to sit in peace and let time heal them in its own way.

'I hope this Sweetman character is at home. I hope he's not too well protected, either,' Mel said.

John nodded towards the glovebox. 'I brought the .38 along, in case.'

'That doesn't make me feel much better.'

John smiled, then glanced up at his rear-view mirror. Three cars behind him was a dented, beige-coloured Plymouth Fury, with a wire coat-hanger for an aerial.

NINE

Father Leonard came down the steps of the Catholic
Mission into the street. He had been up at the TV
studios since early this morning, and he had only just
come back to change and shave. There were dark circles
under his eyes, and he looked even more martyred and
seraphic than ever.

He had managed to make a quick telephone call to
Perri, at the convention centre. As far as he could gather
(there was shrieking and shouting in the background),
the whole conference was in an uproar, and Hilary
Nestor Hunter had tried to have the vote on women's
equality indefinitely deferred, on the grounds that it was
now the subject of legal proceedings. It was, of course.
Two lawyers in creased suits had already been around
to the Catholic Mission that morning, with unshaven
chins and a writ for libel.

Father Leonard had accepted the writ, and placed it
in his letter-holder with all his other correspondence. As
far as he was concerned, there were far more urgent
priorities. He had to visit Mrs Jarvis on 16th Street, in
the shadow of the freeway, and read Thomas Wolfe
stories to her. She was dying of bone cancer, and Hilary
Nestor Hunter and her lawyers would outlive her by a
score of years.

He was just about to cross the street when a car horn
beeped, and a black Matador drew up alongside him.
He recognised the car at once. The window was lowered,
and Bishop Mulhaney, a small fat man in a dark grey
shiny suit and a black shirt, leaned across towards him.

'Father Leonard? Can I offer you a ride?'

Father Leonard opened the car door, and stepped inside. The bishop, as he pulled away from the kerb, gave
him an abstracted smile of greeting. There were clusters
of tiny beads of sweat on the bishop's cheeks. His air-

conditioning had broken, and he wasn't sure whether it was a simple mechanical failure, or whether God had meant him to suffer a little temporal discomfort.

'I'm going to Sixteenth Street, just across from the intersection with Essex Street,' Father Leonard said.

'You're not going to the convention centre?'

Father Leonard shook his head. 'What's happening there can look after itself for the moment.'

'Until you decide that your intervention is once more desperately needed?'

Father Leonard didn't reply. He knew why the bishop had come. Usually, whole months would pass between visits, and then they would be hurried and uncomfortable. It wasn't that Bishop Mulhaney was lacking in charity, or in sympathy for human suffering. It was just that he felt he was an administrator rather than a missionary, and that he could best deal with poverty from behind his desk. Face-to-face, the mean streets of downtown Los Angeles made him feel hopeless and worried.

'I hope you understand the gravity of what you've done,' Bishop Mulhaney said.

Father Leonard nodded. 'I went into it with my eyes open.'

'Going into it with your eyes open wasn't really enough,' said the bishop. 'You shouldn't have gone into it at all.'

'You don't think I should have stood up for the Bill of Rights? You don't think I should have stood up for the Christian belief that all men are created equal under God?'

'I notice you put the political principle before the religious belief,' the bishop remarked.

Father Leonard said, 'That's unfair. The Bill of Rights is Christian and humane, and you know it. What you're trying to say is that you don't believe priests should meddle with politics.'

Bishop Mulhaney took a left, and drove towards 16th Street. 'You're right, of course, in your obstreperous way. I *don't* believe that priests should meddle with politics. Particularly sexist politics.'

'These days, sexist politics are making and breaking

243

people's lives. I have to care for those lives, and that's why I meddle,' Father Leonard said with some acerbity.

'I know your ideals, Father Leonard. I know that your missionary work here is excellent. I would go so far as to say that it is inspired,' the Bishop granted. 'But in my opinion, and in the opinion of the cardinal, you have made a grave error in involving yourself in this particularly distasteful scandal. I came down here this morning to tell you how we felt, and to see if you had already understood the necessity of withdrawing your support for Ms. Shaw.'

They had arrived at the corner of Essex Street, and the bishop pulled over to the kerb.

Father Leonard said, very gently, 'I can't do that, I'm afraid. I must support Ms. Shaw. I've already committed myself.'

The bishop looked at him with regret. 'When you commit yourself, Father Leonard, you also commit your church. If your church cannot support what you have taken it upon yourself to promise, then I am very sorry to say that we must reconsider your position.'

'What does that mean?'

'Well,' said Bishop Mulhaney uncomfortably, 'a posting overseas to say the very least.'

Father Leonard looked at him with dark, sad eyes.

'Do I have some time to think about it?' he asked.

'Of course,' said the bishop. 'Perhaps you'd like to come around to see me this evening, at about eight. I must require you not to talk to the press any more today. No television, please, no matter how much they pester you.'

Father Leonard thought for a moment, and then nodded. 'Very well. I'll talk to Ms Shaw this afternoon. Thank you for the lift.'

He opened the car door. As he did so, Bishop Mulhaney reached over and held his sleeve.

'We need people like you,' he said sincerely. 'Please don't make a terrible mistake.'

Father Leonard placed his hand over the bishop's hand. 'I'm always prepared to admit that I might have strayed,' he replied. 'But I'm always prepared to fight

244

for what I think is truly right, too.'

The bishop let out a small sigh. 'I was rather afraid of that.'

Father Leonard shut the car door, and Bishop Mulhaney drove off.

Father Leonard was walking past the tyre warehouse, with its rusting corrugated doors and its spray-paint graffiti, when he heard the truck turn the corner of Essex Street and grind slowly towards him. He didn't know what made him turn and look at it. It was a beaten-up looking Mack diesel stacked with wooden pallets. He kept on walking, but he had the strangest feeling that he was close to a moment of great fearfulness.

The bellowing of the truck grew louder. Father Leonard looked over his shoulder again and saw that it was only twenty feet away. Then – just as he was turning back – he heard the truck's load rattle and shake. He glanced towards it, and saw to his horror that it had mounted the sidewalk and was bearing down on him.

He turned, stumbled, and tried to run. The truck's smokestack blasted out a funnel of black exhaust as it surged towards him. All he could hear was the deafening noise of its engine. It filled up his whole world.

The massive front bumper caught him in the side, and crushed him up against the corroded corrugated door of the tyre warehouse. In a moment of unbelievable agony and horror he felt his pelvis bend, then snap, and his stomach burst open. Then the truck roared, clashed gears, and backed off, and he slid down to the sidewalk and died.

They came to tell Perri an hour later. A policewoman in a smart grey tweed suit took her into one of the small conference rooms at the convention centre and gave her a cup of weak coffee in a polystyrene holder.

'I'm sorry, but there's been some kind of traffic accident. Father Leonard is dead,' she said.

Perri didn't know what to say. It was impossible to believe, and yet she believed it. She sat down at the conference table.

'How did it happen?' she said in a whisper.

'Nobody knows. A truck hit him, someone said.'

'A truck?'

The policewoman nodded. 'He was down on Sixteenth Street, visiting one of his sick ladies. We don't have any more details right now.'

Perri buried her face in her hands, and then suddenly the whole pain of it collapsed on top of her, and she sobbed and sobbed until her throat felt raw, and she could hardly cry any more. She looked up at the policewoman with reddened eyes. 'Oh God, why did it have to be him? He was so good. He was so perfect. He could have been a saint.'

'I don't really like to ask you this so soon, but do you think this accident could have been deliberate?' the policewoman said.

'Deliberate? What do you mean?'

'I mean that Father Leonard was very mixed up in politics. Especially this row at the Woman's Liberation League convention this morning. We have to consider that someone might have wanted him injured or dead.'

Perri thought for a moment, and then slowly shook her head. 'It just isn't possible. I mean, Hilary Nestor Hunter's a pretty tough cookie but she wouldn't kill anyone for the sake of politics. I mean, who kills people for the sake of politics?'

The policewoman gave her a gentle, lopsided smile. 'It happens.'

'But Hilary Nestor Hunter?'

'It didn't have to be her. It could have been any of her supporters. Is there anybody who comes to mind?'

Perri thought again, and then said, 'No. Nobody does anything without Hilary's express permission. If anybody killed him on purpose, then it was her.'

TEN

As they drove south on Interstate 5, the car filled with sunshine, Mel went through the morning's newspapers, drawing a red ballpen circle around anything that looked like an inexplicable death. A twenty-four-year-old mother had been shot dead on the driveway of her house in Watertown, South Dakota. A seventy-two-year-old grandfather had been shot from a passing car in Rolla, Missouri. A thirty-year-old teacher had died in Virginia when his car was forced off the road near Lake Barcroft.

'A heavy crop today. Maybe ten or twelve of 'em,' Mel said.

'All similar?' asked John.

'Most of them,' said Mel. 'It looks like our friends have been busy.'

They were approaching San Juan Capistrano. John pulled out to overtake an empty southbound fruit truck, and for a moment he glimpsed the beige Plymouth Fury in his rear-view mirror. He saw a brief flash of reflected light in the Fury's windshield, and didn't realise that it was the sun glancing off mirrored sunglasses.

Mel opened another newspaper, and began to comb through it. 'You remember we were talking about Carl X. Chapman this morning?' he said. 'Here's a picture of him in Vegas. Looks like he's just made some kind of multimillion dollar development deal.'

'Good for him. Do you want to pour some coffee? The flask's on the back seat.'

'Oh, sure.' Mel reached over and found the Thermos flask. He held the plastic cup between his knees as he opened up the flask, and carefully filled it with steaming black coffee.

'Say, here's another killing,' he said, as he passed the cup over to John.

'What does it say?' asked John, taking a quick scalding sip. He felt more like a shot of liquor than a cup of coffee, but he knew what would happen if he started on the whisky. All the sadness for Vicki that he was keeping suppressed in the back of his mind would well up again, all that desperate, lonesome sadness, and that would mean the finish of their day's work. He needed to keep on going, or else he'd wind up on the funny farm. And apart from that, he wanted to track down Professor Aaron Sweetman more than he wanted to give way to his grief. He wanted to avenge Vicki, really avenge her and his father. He could begin to understand someone who killed out of fury, or passion, or jealousy. But to kill for votes?

Mel read: ' "Private Eye in Probable Gang Slaying?" How does that sound?'

'Not particularly promising. Tell me more.'

'A private detective was found dying in his car in Pahrump Valley, Nevada, last night – victim of a shooting that police are convinced is connected with recent gang struggles over in Las Vegas gambling.'

'There you are,' said John, 'it's explicable. We're looking for the inexplicable.'

'Will you wait a minute? It goes on to say: "The private eye's last words, however, are still puzzling the Las Vagas P.D. According to 54-year-old Alphonse Rippert, a passing truck driver who discovered the detective dying in his vehicle, they were: 'Election, it's an election. Road sign.' " '

'*Road sign?*' asked John.

'Yeah,' said Mel. 'It says here: "The only road sign within six miles of the dying detective was a Dangerous Curve sign just fifty feet away." '

John was silent for a long while. They drove through San Juan Capistrano, past white-painted houses and palms and rooftops, and under Del Obispo Road. The highway curved southwest towards Capistrano Beach, and the distant glitter of the ocean.

John said, 'I gather you're trying to draw some kind of inference here.'

'I don't know,' Mel told him. 'I really don't know.

248

But look at what we have here. He's been shot for no apparent reason, he's talking about elections, and he mentions a dangerous curve. Also, he's a private detective. Maybe he's discovered something about the Sweetman Curve, and maybe somebody caught up with him in the way they've been trying to catch up with you.'

'Does it mention his name?' asked John.

'David Radetzky. A private detective well-known in California for his divorce work for famous TV and movie stars.'

'A divorce detective getting himself mixed up in Las Vegas gambling? That doesn't ring true. Not unless he was looking into the private life of one of those gangster types.'

'That's possible,' said Mel, folding the newspaper. 'But there's no reason for him to mention elections or dangerous curves, is there, unless he's into something political?'

'Las Vegas is always political,' remarked John. 'Any big-time hoodlum has to be well-connected with Washington to survive these days.'

They passed a supermarket truck and a pick-up stacked with chairs and tables like something out of the *Grapes of Wrath*. They glided over the intersection with the Pacific coast highway, and kept on south through the bright misty morning. A half-mile behind them, the battered Plymouth Fury kept up its dogged pursuit.

Mel circled the David Radetzky story and turned back to the front page. There, grizzled and grinning, was the face of Senator Carl X. Chapman during his visit to Las Vegas. Mel looked at it, and didn't say anything for a minute or two, but scratched at his beard and frowned.

'What's the matter with you? You look like you just remembered you left the gas on,' John remarked.

'It's just one of those funny kind of feelings,' Mel said. 'The sort of feeling I first had when your father was shot.'

'More analytical thinking?'

'Just a coincidence, that's all. Here's good old Carl X. Chapman, the ambitious right-wing Republican senator from Minnesota, the man who says he's going to be

President in 1980. And here's poor young David Radetzky, a private detective who's been killed because he
seems to know something about elections. And they're
both in Las Vegas on the same day.'

'You think *Chapman* could be ordering these killings?'

'It would figure,' said Mel. 'I mean, how many politicians do you know that are as hawkish as Chapman,
and at at the same time are as likely presidential candidates as Chapman?'

'Walstrom?'

'Oh, sure, Walstrom, but I can't imagine Walstrom
doing anything as systematically heartless as this, can
you? He's hawkish, all right, but he's all bluster and
brimstone. Chapman's always controlled.'

John finished his coffee and handed the plastic cup
back to Mel. He saw the Plymouth Fury closer now,
slowly overtaking him on the outside. He said, 'I think
Chapman's a possible, but I don't like to jump to con-
clusions. Not without some real hard evidence.'

'That's going to be hard to find. Chapman was under
investigation by two special senate committees a few
years back, because they thought he was taking back-
handers from the oil industry, but they never proved
anything. I mean, if a senate committee can't nail him,
how the hell can we?'

'Maybe Professor Sweetman will tell us.'

'And maybe he won't. And maybe he doesn't even
know.'

The Fury was almost alongside. John glanced across
at it, and saw its dented fender, and its patched-up
paintwork. Its tyres made a sizzling noise on the concrete
highway.

'We still have to admit the possibility that what we
really have here is a national craze for shooting people.
Nuttier things have happened,' Mel said.

John looked sideways at the Plymouth again. His
mind registered what he saw like a camera. *Click-snap.*
Behind the wheel was a dark-haired man with mirror
sunglasses. One arm was raised, and he was pointing
straight towards John's face.

250

John screamed, '*Mel – get down!*' and hauled the Lincoln's wheel over so that the huge white car slewed across two lanes of traffic. Horns blared on all sides, but he made it through to the inside lane, and then punched his foot down on the accelerator. With a deep whistling roar, the engine surged power through the car, and they took off along the freeway in clouds of burned rubber and exhaust.

The Lincoln reached ninety in seconds. John flicked his eyes up towards his mirror, and saw that the Fury was after him, but it had lost almost a quarter of a mile.

Mel raised his head cautiously and looked behind them.

'Was that guy after us?' he asked, a little shakily.

'It's the same one,' John said, tersely. 'The one with the mirror sunglasses. The one who shot my father.'

Mel opened the glove compartment and took out the .38 revolver. He opened the chamber to check that it was loaded, then snapped it shut and gave John a nervous grin.

'I never used one of these before.'

'Let's hope you won't have to.'

They were flashing along the highway now at a hundred-and-ten. They weaved in between the traffic, tires howling on the hot concrete, rousing up an angry flurry of car horns behind them. John checked his mirror again. The beige Plymouth was almost within a hundred feet of them now, leaving a trail of oily smoke behind it as it chased them. He saw the glint of those sunglasses again, and he felt both vengeful and scared.

Up ahead of them, all three lanes of the highway were blocked by two slow-moving trucks and a family camper. John muttered, '*For Christ's sake, get out of the way,*' and flashed his headlights. The trucks and the camper continued to trundle down the long incline through San Clemente, growing larger and larger as the Lincoln zipped along the highway towards them.

The Plymouth was close on their tail now. John leaned on the Lincoln't horn and flashed his headlights again, but he knew that the trucks hadn't even seen him. He was doing a hundred-and-fifteen, and the trucks were only two hundred feet away. They came towards him like a solid wall.

With seconds to spare, the camper overtook the truck on its nearside. Spinning the steering-wheel, John piloted the hurtling Lincoln right up behind the camper, and then zig-zagged through the narrow gap in between the truck's front bumpers and the camper's tail. The Lincoln's suspension bounced and kangarooed, and its tyres wailed on the road surface, but John held it through the skid, and pushed his foot down on the gas again as they straightened up.

Behind them, the camper had slowed in surprise, and the Fury was boxed off. John seized the moment to build up his speed again and put as much highway between them as he could. The needle strayed back up to a hundred-ten, a hundred-fifteen, a hundred-twenty. The highway flashed and wriggled beneath them like a rushing river of concrete.

Mel said, 'He's still after us. He's cleared the trucks. I can see his smoke.'

John looked in his mirror. 'Let's give him a damned good run for his money. If we can beat him into San Diego, we can lose him. This is his favourite killing ground, the open highway. Let's get him into the streets.'

'If you say so,' said Mel. 'But I hope he doesn't start shooting.'

'Me too. But shoot back, if he does.'

Mel examined the .38 unhappily. 'I never did like cowboys, when I was a kid. I was always the fat unpopular one who went off on nature walks.'

'Well, now's your chance to change all that.'

It was over forty miles into San Diego. They slammed along the highway with the Plymouth Fury burning along behind them. The traffic was sparser now, and John could really let the old car out, speeding past San Onofre beach like a meteoric reminder of 1958.

'How are we doing for gas?' asked Mel.

'Okay,' John told him. 'We've got a tank the size of the Dodgers Stadium.'

In spite of their speed, the gap between the Fury and the Lincoln was gradually closing. As they sped through

Camp Pendleton, the man in the mirror sunglasses was only two hundred feet behind. They sped past a long convoy of Marine Corps trucks with only a hundred feet between them. With Oceanside just a couple of miles away, the Fury began to overtake them again.

John swerved from lane to lane, trying to keep away from their pursuer. The Lincoln's tyres screeched and squittered on the highway, and the car's heavy tail slewed from side to side. But the Fury kept close, only feet away, even though it was blowing out black smoke now, and it must have been burning oil like an Exxon refinery.

'Mel!' shouted John. 'You're going to have to use the gun! See if you can hit his tyres, or his engine!'

'Supposing I hit *him*?'

'Supposing you do? What do you think he's trying to do to us?'

Mel put down his window, and the slipstream roared into the car, blowing his hair up into a fright wig. 'Okay!' he yelled. 'If you say so!'

He knelt on his seat, and held the revolver in both hands. The man in the Fury saw what he was doing, and swerved out of his line of fire, coming up on John's side of the car instead. In answer, John put down the rear windows, so that Mel could shoot across the car diagonally. The rush of air at a hundred miles an hour was so loud that they could hardly hear each other.

'*Shoot!*' John insisted, in a harsh scream. '*For Christ's sake, shoot!*'

Mel fired. The bullet must have dinged off the front of the Fury's hood, because the car kept going, nosing up beside them and almost touching the side of their long-finned fender.

'*Again!*' screamed John.

Mel fired, and the bullet pierced the Fury's radiator. A spray of water enveloped the front of the car, and then a blast of steam.

'*Again!*' John shouted.

The Fury nudged against them, with a screeching of metal. The Lincoln skidded and slithered, but John twisted the wheel and held it steady. The Fury nudged against them again, and this time he almost lost control. For a moment, the huge car was sliding sideways, its front fender locked against the Fury's bumper. Then John nudged the brakes, and the Lincoln spun free. Mel tried another shot, but the bullet went wild.

The two cars banged and collided against each other one more time. But then the Plymouth abruptly slowed, and fell back. Within a few seconds, they had left it far behind, and they could see it limping off the highway with steam rising from the hood. Mel's second shot had ruptured the cooling system, and the motor had overheated.

John put up the windows. Mel sat back in his seat, brushing his hair with his hand, and breathing heavily. He opened up the .38 and emptied out the spent cartridges. For a while, neither of them spoke.

'Do you think we ought to turn around and go back?' said Mel. 'I mean, do you think we ought to finish him off for good?'

'I wish we could. But the best thing we can do is to stop in Oceanside and call the cops.'

Mel raised the .38 and stared at it. 'You know something, I never knew what a feeling of power a gun could give you. It's frightening.'

They pulled off the road on the outskirts of Oceanside in a cloud of drifting dust, and John went across to a telephone booth and called the police. He waited for a long time for a laconic detective to come on the line.

'It's about the guy who's shooting people on the L.A. freeways,' he said.

'Oh, yeah?'

'Well, my name's John Cullen and my father was shot last week. The same guy that did it tried to shoot me today on Interstate Five a couple of miles out of Oceanside.'

'Are you spelling Cullen with a "K" or a "C"?'

'A "C". Listen, the guy's out there now, just a couple of miles out of town. His car broke down. A beige or a tan Plymouth Fury. Kind of beaten-up.'

'His car broke down?'

'That's right. He was tailing me out of Los Angeles, and he had a gun, but his car broke down. If you get out there fast enough, you'll catch him.'

There was a lengthy silence while the detective wrote all this down. Then he said, 'Are you making a charge against this man, whoever he is?'

'A charge? He's a mass murderer! He's the guy they've been looking for in L.A. for months!'

There was another silence, and then the detective said, 'Okay, we'll check it out. Where are you?'

'In a telephone booth just outside of town.'

'Stay right where you are. We'll have a couple of officers along in a short while.'

The line went dead. John stared at the receiver a moment, then set it back in its cradle. He walked slowly back to the car.

'Did you get through?' asked Mel.

'Oh, sure. I spoke to some half-assed detective. He talked like shooting people on the freeways was about as criminal as driving a Winnebago with bald tyres.'

They waited for almost a half-hour, listening to the radio and drinking the rest of their coffee. It was nearly eleven o'clock before a blue-and-white police car pulled off the road behind them, and stopped. A cop climbed out and walked up to the Lincoln at a leisurely pace. He leaned in to the window with his big freckled face, and said, 'How do. Are you the folks who called about the L.A. freeway killer?'

'That's right,' said John. 'Did you catch him?'

The cop slowly shook his head. 'We went back up the highway there and checked the car out. But there ain't no sign of the driver. The car was stolen from a used-car lot in Santa Monica round about a week ago, so there's no way of tracing who it might be. Do you want to give a description?'

'Detective Morello of the Los Angeles Police Department has a full description,' John said. 'All I can say is that it was the same guy who shot my father, and shot at both of us earlier this week.'

'Are you sure?'

John took a deep breath. 'When someone kills your father, officer, and then tries to kill you, you don't mistake his face.'

The cop smiled sympathetically. 'I guess you don't. Anyway, you'd best come downtown and make a statement about all this.'

It was almost three o'clock by the time they drove past the University of San Diego campus along the Pacific Highway, and into San Diego. The afternoon was hot, and the deep blue sky was streaked with horsetails of cirrus cloud. Overhead, a seaplane droned as it circled into the Coronado amphibious base.

They hadn't talked much on their drive down from Oceanside. They were both tired, shaken, and depressed by what had happened. Although the ocean was sparkling and the breeze was rustling softly through the palms, their fears of the Sweetman Curve and the men who were using it made them feel chilled. The both knew that it wasn't any use trying to pretend that America was being swept away by an epidemic of random shooting, or that some lone psychotic was flying daily from city to city, picking off all the good-natured liberals he could find. If they *hadn't* worked out the truth of what was going on, if they *weren't* a threat to the killer in mirrored sunglasses and the blond-haired man who had probably fired John's house in Topanga Canyon – then why were they being so doggedly pursued?

'Professor Sweetman lives on Fairmount Avenue, close to the state university,' said Mel, consulting his map and the scribbled notes he had made the night before. 'If you take a left on Mission Valley Road, that should take you there. Then right on Fairmount.'

John turned the Lincoln at the next intersection, and they made their way along the hot sunny streets towards the San Diego State University campus. Mel said, 'I hope the old boy's home today. I'd hate to have gone through this trip for nothing.'

John signalled a right, and turned into Fairmount Avenue. 'I'd hate to have been through *any* of this for nothing,' he said. 'If I woke up tomorrow and found out that there wasn't a Sweetman Curve, and that Vicki and my father had both died for no reason at all, then I think I'd go bananas.'

They found the house easily. It was an untidy three-storey Spanish hacienda, painted in flaking pink, with a red-tiled roof. It had a small front yard with a patch of crisp burned grass and a driveway of cracked concrete. The front door was solid oak, studded with black nails. One of the downstairs shutters was hanging off its hinges, and the whole house looked as if it needed fresh paint and good cheer.

John parked the car and he and Mel got out. He stood in front of the house, looking it up and down, trying to see if there was anyone at home.

'Well,' said John, 'here goes.'

He walked up to the front door. There was an un-polished brass plate that said 'Aaron J. Sweetman, Ph.D.' In the centre of the oak door was a tiny window of yellow hammered glass, but it was impossible to see anything through it except a faint light from the hall-way. A wind ruffled the creeper around the door.

John pressed the bellpush. He could hear it ringing somewhere inside the house. He turned and looked at Mel, and Mel, who was wiping his glasses, gave him a quick, nervous smile.

The door opened quite suddenly. Standing in the doorway was a tall, old man in a light grey suit and a crumpled cream-coloured shirt with no tie. He had silver hair that had been cut very close, and his skin was the yellowish colour of people who have lived in sunny climates for so long that they don't bother to keep up their suntans. He had a large fleshy nose in which were imbedded the marks of spectacles, although he wore none at the moment. His eyes were china blue.

He said, 'Yes?' in a dry, testy voice.

'I'm sorry to trouble you, sir,' John said. 'I'm looking for Professor Aaron Sweetman.'

'Ah,' said the old man. 'Then you have come to the right place.' He stuck out his hand. 'I am he.'

ELEVEN

The arrival of Anthony Seiden at Twentieth-Century Fox studios that Friday morning followed the usual dramatic and unexpected style. His long black Fleetwood with dark-tinted bulletproof windows swept through the entrance gate, swung around the corner by the administration block, and pulled into a parking space marked *G. Wilder*. The rear doors of the car opened, and two crew-cut men in lightweight suits climbed out. They quickly checked the parking lot for suspicious faces, and then Anthony Seiden himself, a small man in a green T-shirt and glasses, was allowed to get out of the car and hurry across to the double entrance doors.

He went up in the elevator to his third-floor office, flanked by the two crew-cut men, who said nothing. His secretary, a pretty young Californian with sun-blonde hair and big white teeth, said, 'Good morning, Tony, do you want some tea?' and took his briefcase for him. He said, 'Good morning, Trixie. Sure. And a piece of that raisin bread if they have some.'

The two crew-cut men sat themselves down in the outer office and produced dog-eared paperback books from their inside pockets. They would wait here, silent and patient, until it was time for Anthony Seiden to leave the office again. They appeared to be engrossed in their books, but every time the door opened, their eyes would flick upwards to check out who it was.

Anthony Seiden sat behind his huge desk, and reached for a cigarette. He lit it, puffed out a cloud of smoke, and then sifted quickly through his mail. Trixie came back with a glass of Russian tea and a piece of raisin bread, and said, 'Here's the sustenance. Is there anything there you want to answer straight away?'

He shook his head. 'Nothing that can't wait. I have

to see those last rushes this morning, and then I'm
going to go straight back home and catch up on some
sleep.'

'Is Dana home now?'

He sipped his tea, and nodded. 'She decided to stay
last night. I think she's coming out to Palm Springs
tomorrow, too. I guess we've more or less decided to
make another go of it.'

'I'm pleased,' smiled Trixie. 'I think the whole of
Hollywood felt sad when you and Dana split.'

Anthony shrugged. 'When you live under the kind of
pressure that we were living under, separation isn't
much of a surprise. You can take so many pills and so
much booze, and then the whole thing falls in on you.
But I'm real happy to have her back. The moment she
walked through the door, I remembered just what it
was I married her for.'

The phone rang, and Trixie picked it up. She talked
for a while, and then she put her hand over the mouth-
piece. 'It's Daniel. He says the cuts are ready to show.'

'Tell him I'll be down in five minutes.'

Anthony Seiden was wrapping up the final takes of
Number Seventeen, a political thriller about corruption
in government. There was already talk in *Variety* and
the *Hollywood Reporter* that it was his most abrasive
movie yet, and when it was released he didn't expect
to be able to pay off his bodyguards. His picture *Secret
Nights*, an exposure of bribery during the election
campaign of a Republican candidate, had brought so
many threats of murder and kidnap that the studio had
helped him to pay for round-the-clock protection. It
was part genuine fear and part publicity stunt, but it
was done professionally and rigorously. He never left
his house in Bel-Air at the same time in the morning,
and he never drove to the studio by the same route
two days running. His bodyguards always checked the
streets before he was allowed to leave his car, and they
kept him sandwiched between them in stores and
restaurants. Even on the set they weren't far away, reading their paperbacks assiduously and keeping their cold
eyes on everyone who came and went.

Anthony wasn't the kind of man who enjoyed being guarded. He was quiet, warm, and persuasive, and he liked to think that America was a land in which you could say that you wanted without fear of reprisals. He didn't believe that free speech was an inalienable right, but a right which a man earned through suffering. His father, Dan Seiden, had been one of the finest lighting cameramen that Hollywood had ever known, but his career and his health had been wrecked during the Communist witch-hunts of the 1950s. These days, Anthony hoped things were different. But it was only by keeping intolerance and extremism in check that they could stay that way. Maybe McCarthy himself was gone, but there were too many of the old guard left, too many friends and sympathizers of McCarthy, too many rich bigots. Anthony Seiden knew their names and directed the cutting edge of his movies against them.

The men he hated were men like John Walstrom, and Carl X. Chapman. The old enemies from two decades ago, who still wouldn't lie down.

His campaign hadn't done much for Anthony Seiden's marriage, nor for his well-being. His wife Dana, a statuesque Norwegian actress, had left him six months ago after saying she was sick and tired of living under glass. Anthony himself had taken to nursing a bottle of Jack Daniels wherever he went, and he had directed a crucial scene in Number Seventeen in a state of drunken paralysis. But the movie was almost finished, Dana had taken a chance on coming back, and he was gradually getting himself back into shape again.

He was a slight man, with a serious, good-looking, dark stubbled face. His eyes were grey and alert. He spoke softly, with engaging self-confidence. He liked wearing casual French sweaters and Italian slacks, and his favourite moviemaker of all was Bo Widerberg.

The phone rang again. Trixie picked it up; it was Adele Corliss. Anthony took the call.

'Adele, honey, how are you?'

'I'm fine,' she said. 'A little off-balance, but fine.'

'Off-balance?'

'I have a new lover,' she confided. 'He's alternately childish and threatening.'

Anthony smiled. 'I thought all lovers were.'

'That's what you know. But then you've been faithful to Dana for all these years.'

Anthony blew out cigarette smoke. 'You know she's decided to stay? She'd like to come to the party tomorrow.'

'I did hear it on the grapevine,' said Adele. 'I'm very pleased. In fact, we're *all* very pleased. You two are the nicest couple I know.'

'That's very kind of you to say,' Anthony told her. 'You're certainly the nicest person we know.'

Adele laughed. 'If we can finish this mutual self-congratulation session, perhaps I can tell you why I'm calling. I know you're a busy, busy movie director, but I am a little worried about tomorrow night.'

'What for? It's just a party, isn't it?'

'Well, sure, Tony. But that's the whole point. I don't want it to turn heavy. Are you sure that you're going to be able to get along with Carl and Hilary and the rest of that crowd? It's not going to turn into a doorslamming and shouting drama, is it?'

'Why should it?' asked Anthony.

'Why should it, he asks! Carl X. Chapman is only super-conservative, and you're only super-liberal! What happier formula can you think of for a nice, friendly party?'

'Adele,' insisted Anthony, 'they're your *friends*. Carl was a fan of yours way before you knew me. You can't give him the cold-shoulder from the biggest party you've held all year, just because of his politics. Anyway, it's the *type* I'm against, his politics, not him personally. I expect he's a wonderful husband and father, and gives generously to sickle cell anemia.'

Adele sighed. 'He's having a rough time with Elspeth, he doesn't have any children, and the only thing he regrets about sickle cell anemia is that he didn't invent it.'

'Come on, Adele, he's not that bad. I hate his guts, but he's not that bad.'

'No,' she said, 'and that's the trouble. There are times when Carl has been so thoughtful and caring that I've wondered why I didn't marry him when I had the chance.'

'You had the chance? Then why didn't you?'

'Oh, it was the wrong time. For a movie star to have married Carl X. Chapman in those days would have been like the Pope's sister marrying Attila the Hun. But he did ask me. Elspeth doesn't know, which is probably just as well, and I guess she's made him a better wife than I ever could. He's not actually the kind of man you marry, to tell the truth. He's more like a father than a husband.'

Anthony waved to Trixie to bring him some fresh tea. His first glass had grown cold, as it always did. He said, 'Adele, if you feel that way about Carl, then I'm sure we're not going to have any trouble tomorrow night at all. In any case, I think it's good ironic publicity. The arch right-winger arrives to celebrate the making of a left-wing movie. Let's face it – if he hadn't wanted to come along, he would have declined your invitation, sent you a dozen red roses, and ordered up *The Green Berets* for his home movie camera on Saturday night.'

Adele sounded uncertain, but she said, 'If you don't mind, then I guess it's all right.'

'Adele, of *course* it's all right,' said Anthony. 'I'm a liberal, right? And that's what liberalism is all about, being liberal. If you want Carl to come, who am I to say that he can't?'

'And Hilary?'

'Well, Hilary's not exactly sweetness and light combined, but why not? Perhaps she'll dress up like a woman for a change, instead of a British gamekeeper. I think Dana quite likes her, in a feminist kind of way.'

Adele laughed, still marginally uneasy but more relaxed than before.

'If you think you can take them for what they are, then I'm sure we'll manage all right,' she said.

They kissed over the phone, and promised a kiss for real on Saturday night, and then Anthony spent a busy ten minutes going through his mail. One of his letters was a threatening letter, and Trixie had attached a note which said: 'This is just a Xerox. I have called Detective Prince and he is sending officers around later today to collect the original. *Nil desperandum!*'

The letter read:

'Stinking traitor Seiden, this is your last day alive, tomorrow you're going to be wiped off the face of the earth like the maggot you are.'

Anthony held the letter in both hands for a while, staring at it. Then he crumpled it up and tossed it into his wastebasket. Even after hundreds of threats, and dozen of anonymous telephone calls, these fierce illiterate ramblings still gave him the creeps. Some day, some mis-guided lunatic was going to catch him unguarded, and then God knows what would happen. There was a revolver in his bedside table drawer, but he didn't have much faith in it.

He dictated quick replies to two of his most urgent letters – about financing and promotion – and then collected his bodyguards and went across the studio to the screening theatre to see the results of yesterday's takes. They didn't amount to much, just a few seconds of conversation between two minor characters in a White House office – but Anthony had insisted on re-shooting the scene twice to capture the nuances of political con-spiracy. Political movies were always the hardest to shoot. Whatever the implications, there was nothing visually exciting about middle-aged men in shiny blue suits talking to each other on the telephone.

Anthony was surprised to see Hilary Nestor Hunter there, sitting down at the front of the theatre with three or four sulky-looking girls. Hilary was looking as haughty and disdainful as usual, in a severe black suit and a black turban hat, and a jet brooch. Anthony said, 'Good morning, Daniel,' to his assistant, Daniel Kermak, gave a friendly salute to his executive producer, Joel Ford, and then came down the aisle to where Hilary was sitting.

'Well,' he said, 'I'm honoured.'

Hilary crossed her legs, slender and shiny in black stockings. She gave him an indulgent, scarlet-lipsticked smile.

'I twisted Joel's arm,' she said. 'He said this was your most marvellous movie ever, and I couldn't resist a peek at it.'

'I wouldn't have thought my pictures were quite your cup of tea,' Anthony said, in an even voice. 'Ideologically speaking, that is.'

One of Hilary's girls, an exquisitely beautiful dark-haired girl, gave him a feral grin. It wouldn't have surprised him if Hilary fed her young ladies on raw meat.

Hilary said, 'You mustn't get the wrong impression of me, Anthony. I'm not a political bigot. In fact, I'm not really very political at all. I'm what you might call a student of sexual opportunity, but not much else.'

'I wouldn't have thought there was much sexual opportunity around here,' Anthony answered, in a gently sardonic tone. 'You know what the movie business is like.'

'I know that it's very influential. Steven Spielberg only has to make a flying-saucer movie, and suddenly everybody's watching the skies. Anthony Seiden only has to make a political graft movie, and suddenly everybody begins to wonder if Karl Marx may have been right, after all.'

'I'm not a Marxist,' smiled Anthony. 'I'm not even Leninist. I'm a few degrees left of centre, that's all.'

Hilary smiled. 'I'm not criticizing you, my darling. I love your movies. I thought *Secret Nights* was positively orgasmic.'

Daniel Kermak called: 'We're ready when you are, Tony.'

Anthony waved back. He said to Hilary, 'I'll be surprised if you get an orgasm out of this one. But you can try. The scene we're showing now is when two White House chisellers get together to oust the Secretary of the Interior so that they can pull off a land deal that's going to make them a couple of million dollars each.'

Hilary raised an eyebrow. 'It sounds like fun.'

Anthony gave a small, appreciative nod. 'Four things

in life are always fun. Sex, politics, money and revenge.'

He went back to his seat at the rear of the screening theatre, and Daniel Kermak gave the signal for the projectionist to start the scene rolling. As the screen flickered and flashed into life, Anthony looked down towards Hilary Nestor Hunter and saw her staring back at him with a cold, thoughtful expression that strangely disturbed him.

On the screen, a jowly actor in a blue mohair suit said, 'We have a problem here, Bradley. We have a problem and we have just twenty-four hours to solve it.'

Half an hour later, Hilary Nestor Hunter was sitting at the desk of a borrowed office. Her girls stood around her, adopting poses of studied indifference, and talked about the movie in tired Hollywood drawls.

She picked up the telephone, and dialled a a familiar number 'Carl? It's me. Can you talk?'

She paused, then she said, 'I saw the cuts from the movie. It's worse than you said. And Seiden's going to promote it for all he's worth. Well, sure. Absolutely. It's the best thing you can do.'

She paused again, as she listened. Then she said, 'I know. But you'll never get him otherwise. He never goes out of the door without those two bodyguards. Well, sure. Sure. All right then, I'll see you tomorrow night. Yes, and me too. You know I do. Goodbye, Carl.'

She set down he receiver, and then she picked it up again and dialled quickly. She was obviously put through to a recorded message, because she waited for a short while, and then she said, clearly and slowly, 'Everything's going as planned. He's going to give the go-ahead. I'll meet you on Sunday evening when it's all over. Oh – and I've already paid off the cuckoo.'

She thought for a moment, in case there was anything else she wanted to add. But all she said was, 'I love you,' and then she set the phone down.

The girl with the dark close-cropped hair looked at her and gave a toothy, animal grin. Hilary reached for her cigarettes.

TWELVE

Professor Sweetman invited them into his dark tiled hallway. Through a decorative grille at the far end of it, they could see into a courtyard overgrown with vines, where a dried-up stone fountain stood. There was a musty odour of tropical fungus, and a pervasive smell like cough-drops or camphor, as if there was an invalid in the house. Professor Sweetman led them through to a stale sitting-room, where two empty chairs in chintz covers stood facing a sadly worn settee. There were some watercolours of Egypt on the walls, both walls and paintings spotted with damp and neglect. On a roll-top bureau was a collection of brass crocodiles, engraved penholders, paperweights, chewed pencils and tobacco tins marked 'paperclips' or 'thumbtacks' or '?' in magic marker.

'You were lucky to catch me at home,' said Professor Sweetman, patting his chest in search of his spectacles. I'm normally down at the laboratory these days. Very busy, you know. Big project.'

He found his spectacles on a circular copper table next to one of the chairs, and carefully wound them around his ears. He blinked first at John and then at Mel, and said, 'Well, do sit down. Now you've caught me, you might as well take advantage of me.'

They sat side by side on the creaking settee. The hot sunlight from outside was filtered through slatted blinds of bamboo, and there was a timeless gloom about the room, as if they had found themselves in an old photograph. From another room in the house came the sound of a radio.

'We're sorry to come down here without an appointment,' John said, 'but we felt it was urgent, and we also felt it would be safer for all of us if we didn't make any prior plans.'

266

'Safer?' asked Professor Sweetman vaguely. 'Would you like a glass of Madeira wine?'

'No, thank you.'

'Well, what do you mean by *safer*? I'm not sure that I understand.'

John took out his handkerchief and patted the sweat from his face. Professor Sweetman may have been a great scientist, but he didn't seem to believe in new-fangled scientific equipment like air-conditioning. The air in the house was still, and uncomfortably warm.

'I found out about the Sweetman Curve,' said John. 'I found out what it is, and what it's being used for.'

He hoped he wasn't overplaying his hand. For all he knew, Aaron Sweetman was the cold-blooded originator of the whole conspiracy. And if he wasn't, the odds were high that he was deeply involved, and wouldn't take kindly to interfering dog-walkers prying into his personal affairs.

There was a short silence. Professor Sweetman was pacing up and down the room now, searching for something else. He looked under magazines, and in drawers, and didn't seem to be able to find it at all, whatever it was.

'Go on, go on,' he said.

John glanced at Mel and frowned. Mel shrugged, and looked as if he could do with a long cold beer.

'That's it. I know what's going on.'

Professor Sweetman smiled. 'In that case, I'm very glad for you. It's a very interesting subject, isn't it? The possibilities are quite endless. Did you know that, with the right data, we can now predict the rise and fall of most of the world's stock markets?'

He sniffed. 'I don't suppose I ought to have told you that. It's extremely secret. But it doesn't really matter. Unless you know how to plot a predictive curve, it's no use to you at all, that information. No use whatsoever. Do you know how to plot a predictive curve, Mr — er —?'

'Cullen,' said John. 'John Cullen. And this is my friend Mel Walters. And I'm afraid that neither of us has much idea of how to plot a predictive curve.'

'Oh,' said Professor Sweetman. 'Pity.'

He sat down opposite, and crossed one leg over the other, revealing a bony white ankle and a white tennis sock with perished elastic. He laced his fingers together, and beamed at his visitors. 'Well, what can I do for you?' he said.

John took a deep breath. 'It's hard to put this into words, Professor Sweetman. When it comes down to it, it doesn't amount to very much more than a series of educated guesses, and we may be way off beam. The trouble is, we've been thinking about it so hard over the past week that it's become very convincing to us. Whether or not we've convinced ourselves mistakenly is something that nobody can tell us but you. That's why we're here.'

Professor Sweetman nodded slowly. 'I see,' he said.

'We're not here on any kind of frivolous errand, Professor Sweetman,' Mel put in. 'John here lost his father last week in a shooting on the Los Angeles freeway, and his girlfriend died earlier this week in a fire.'

'I see,' said the professor. 'Well, you must accept my condolences. You must be feeling very upset.'

'What upsets me most of all, professor, is the reason why they died,' John said. He looked at Sweetman as hard as he could. But all the old professor did in return was sadly shake his head, as if he was very sorry to hear the news, but quite innocent of any knowledge of killings or fires.

'Can you think of a reason why they might have died?' John asked him. 'I mean, can you think of any reason at all?'

Professor Sweetman took off his spectacles. 'Why, no. Of course not. I wasn't even aware that they were alive, I'm afraid, let alone that they might have died.'

'Oh, they were alive all right,' said John. Mel touched his arm, warning him. This wasn't the time for bitterness or anger or sarcasm. John said, 'Sure, it doesn't seem like your problem, professor. Not on the face of it. But Mel and I believe that somehow the Sweetman Curve was involved in my father's death and in my girlfriends' death, and in the deaths of a great many more people besides. In fact, we believe that the Sweetman Curve has been used to kill off hundreds of innocent people all over the United States.'

There was a stuffy, sweaty, and very awkward silence. Professor Sweetman coughed, and recrossed his legs. Upstairs, the radio burbled, and there was the added noise of someone vacuum cleaning.

At length, Professor Sweetman coughed again, and said, 'That, Mr Cullen, all that, is a most extraordinary allegation.'

'I know,' said John. 'But some pretty extraordinary things have been happening. It isn't every week you lose the two people most dear to you in all the whole damned world.'

'Yes, I understand that, Mr Cullen, but you must appreciate that the Sweetman Curve is not a weapon. It can never be considered to be *dangerous*, in any way. It is simply a means of drawing a line on a graph which will closely predict the physiological and psychological development of a human being during most of his life. That is all it is. Only that, and nothing more, as Poe would have it.'

'We know that,' Mel said. 'What we're saying is that someone is using the curve to pick out people to kill.'

'We're not trying to suggest that *you've* killed anybody, professor,' John quickly explained. 'We're simply saying that someone, somewhere, is using the Sweetman Curve as their plan of assassination. What we wanted to find out is if you could tell us how it was being done, and if you had any ideas who it could be.'

'It couldn't be anyone,' asserted Professor Sweetman, in a sere voice.

'Can you be sure of that?'

'Of course I can. I have written several articles on the curve in specialized magazines, and I have presented some of my reasearch papers to the University of California at San Diago. But there is nobody on the entire planet who knows, apart from myself, how to programme a computer to plot out a Sweetman Curve. If anybody is guilty of your murders, Mr Cullen, then it is I, and that, of course, is patently ridiculous.'

'You don't have any research assistants who might have gotten hold of the details and passed them outside of your laboratory? Maybe by accident?' John asked.

'I have a team of five working in the university computer laboratory. All of them are exceptionally trustworthy, but quite apart from that there isn't one of them who can prepare the necessary formulae without my guidance. This is rare stuff, Mr Cullen, highly progressive mathematics. It took an exceptional brain to work it out, if you don't mind my saying so, and it will be quite a few years before anything but exceptional brains will be able to use it.'

John sat back on the old settee. He was beginning to feel very tired and strained. He had been able to keep down most of his exhaustion and his emotional pain while he felt there was something to go for, something to hunt, but now it looked as if he may have been wrong. The problem was: if the killings *hadn't* been planned on a Sweetman Curve, then what on earth were they all for?

Professor Sweetman said, 'I can see the temptation you've been feeling to blame something unusual and scientific for your father's death, Mr Cullen. But I swear to you that I have never prepared a curve for the purpose of decimating the American people, and none of my clients' curves could be used in that fashion. Besides that, every one of them is reputable to a fault.'

'Clients?' asked John. 'I'm afraid that I don't understand.'

'Clients are clients. People who come here and ask for a service to be given, and who pay for it when they get it.'

'What kind of service?'

'Sweetman Curves, of course. What other service could I possibly provide?' the professor said with some exasperation. 'When I first published my articles in *Analytical Medicine*, I had one or two approaches from industry and other organisations, asking me to plot curves to help out their sales programmes, or whatever it was they were interested in. I said yes, of course. It means that I get a large quantity of interesting data to work with, and apart from that they pay me a consider-

amount of money. It's all tax-deductible to them, so they don't stint. I've bought two new computers on the proceeds.'

John looked at Mel. In the closeness of the sitting-room, Mel was very red-faced and hot.

'You'd be surprised at some of the household names I can count among my clients,' the professor went on. 'An automobile manufacturer, for instance, who wants to plan car designs for the next ten years. A cosmetic company. Two drug corporations, who want to know which illnesses are most likely to strike us down in the next twenty years. That kind of thing.'

'Are there any – political clients?' John asked, carefully.

Professor Sweetman slowly shook his head. 'I really couldn't divulge that. I'm not supposed to tell anybody anything, as a matter of fact. My clients do expect secrecy.'

'You can't even tell me if you have one client connected with politics, or with political sociology?'

'Well, no, I couldn't really.'

John said, as evenly as he could, 'Has it occurred to you that if you do have a political client, this might be the person we're looking for? Or have you carefully evaded any idea that you could be responsible for some of the most brutal killings this country has ever seen?'

Professor Sweetman pursed his lips. 'All of my clients are reputable. That's all I intend to say. Why, you can't expect –'

'I expect you to face up to what you could be doing, that's all,' insisted John. 'If you do have a politician for a client, then for Christ's sake tell us. You may not *think* that your curve is dangerous, but then you're a nice professor from San Diego whose mind doesn't work the way that politicians' minds do. What looks to you like nice, clean, useful information can look like a blacklist to someone else. Or even worse, a deathlist.'

Professor Sweetman stood up awkwardly. His face was pale, and he tugged off his spectacles in annoyance.

'Mr Cullen, you've abused my hospitality,' he said. 'When you came in here, I expected a discussion of my work and my progress, not this trumped-up harangue. You're talking absolute nonsense, and offensive nonsense, too. I must ask you to leave.'

Unexpectedly, a buzzer sounded in the hallway outside. Professor Sweetman turned towards it, and then turned back to John and Mel.

'I don't know what you're trying to prove against me, but I warn you that it's all quite ridiculous, and if you persist in this slander I'll have you in court.'

The buzzer sounded again. Professor Sweetman took a step towards the door, but then John said, 'Listen, Professor Sweetman, I don't think you realise how serious this is. I don't think you understand just how many people are dying. It isn't just my father and my girl-friend. It's hundreds of innocent people in towns all over America. People who don't even know that they've done anything wrong.'

'*I* haven't heard about wholesale killing in America, Mr Cullen, so I don't even know if you're telling the truth. Perhaps you're just trying to wring the name of my political client out of me. You could be anyone. I haven't even seen any proof of your identity.'

'So you *do* have a political client?'

'What?' blinked Professor Sweetman.

'You said I was just trying to wring the name of your political client out of you. You said it as if you actually had one.'

The buzzer sounded again, twice. Professor Sweetman said, flustered, 'This is all quite ridiculous, Mr Cullen. You'll have to go. My wife –'

'Professor,' threatened John, 'if you don't tell me the name of your political client right now, I'm going straight to the San Diego police to make complaints that you're involved in a murder conspiracy.'

Professor Sweetman said desperately, 'This is a nightmare! You can't go around saying things like that! I believe you're mad!'

Mel shook his head, slow and easy. 'He's not mad, Professor. He's just trying to find the truth in a pretty horrifying situation. Don't you think it's better to tell us?'

At that moment, a slight figure in white appeared in the doorway. It was a woman of at least sixty, in a floor-length nightdress. Her white hair was tied back in a white ribbon, which emphasised the waxy appearance of her skin and the unhealthy prominence of her cheekbones. Her blue eyes were faded, as if they had been bleached for years by the sun.

'Mima, you shouldn't have come down,' said Professor Sweetman, going to her side and taking her arm. 'You could have fallen.'

The woman gave a faint smile. 'I'm sure you would have picked me up, Aaron. I heard voices. Were you having an argument?'

'These gentlement were on the point of leaving,' said Professor Sweetman. 'They came here under a misapprehension. They mistook me for someone else.'

'It sounded like a very loud misapprehension,' said Mrs Sweetman. 'Did you offer them a glass of wine?'

'They're leaving,' insisted Professor Sweetman.

John turned to him. He didn't know for sure that Professor Sweetman had a political client, but it seemed like a sure bet. He said, in a low and level voice, 'A lot of people are counting on you for their lives, professor. Are you going to change your mind?'

Professor Sweetman lifted his head obstinately. 'No, Mr Cullen, I am not. Now, you must leave. My wife is seriously ill, and her doctors say that she has to rest.'

'All right,' John nodded. 'But don't think it ends here. And if you do change your mind, here's my telephone number in L.A.'

Professor Sweetman took the hotel card and tore it up into small pieces. Mima Sweetman looked at him with a concerned frown, but said nothing. She had obviously trusted him all her life, and her trust wasn't going to fail her now. She linked her arm through his, and watched John and Mel walk out of the sitting-room and back down the corridor.

From a green Buick Regal on the corner of Fairmount and University Avenue, T.F. watched them leave the Sweetman house and pause for a moment on the lawn.

He cursed softly under his breath. It had been a lousy day all round. First he'd messed up the hit on the highway, and now Cullen and Walters had chosen the exact moment a cop was giving them a parking ticket to walk out of the house.

He glanced across at the passenger seat where his Colt .45 automatic was hidden under a pale grey cardigan he'd found in the car when he stole it from a parking lot not far from Miramar Naval Air Station. He'd been lucky to hitch a ride off the highway, at least. But he was going to take great pleasure in blowing a hole in that fat bearded Walters. Nobody made T.F. look like an asshole and got away with it.

He saw Cullen and Walters talking to the cop. As he watched and waited, he thought about his M-14, beautifully oiled and ready for tomorrow night's job. He was looking forward to that. It had a touch of class, much more than these rough-and-ready hits on the freeway. He missed the M-14 more than he could have believed possible. He could almost imagine holding it in his hands, and squinting down that sight, and then *sque-e-zing* that trigger.

They'd told him that tomorrow night was the most important hit for months. They'd told him it was something special. He knew he would feel like being sexually purged afterwards. He wondered what it would be like to force a hand grenade up a young girl's ass, with only the pin protruding, and then pull the pin out so that she was keeping the trigger in place by muscular contraction alone. To make love to a girl like that would be out of this world. It made him horny to think about it. He guessed the only problem would be to retrieve the grenade afterwards. Maybe he'd just leave it in there, and say, 'Take it easy when you walk home.'

He gave two or three dry snorts at his own sense of humour.

It looked like Cullen and Walters had finished talking to the cop. They were climbing into that antique Lincoln of theirs now. T.F. started the Regal's motor, and nosed out of University Avenue into Fairmount.

Just as he did so, the cop walked towards him with

his hand raised. T.F. stopped, and glanced again towards the pale grey cardigan in case he needed to go for his automatic quickly. The cop came right up to the front of his car, and then turned his back on him.

For a moment, T.F. wondered what the hell was happening. Then, around the corner, came the first car in a funeral procession. Fifty cars, nose to tail, with their headlamps blazing in the four o'clock sunshine. A long black Cadillac hearse, followed by shiny black limousines, and then polished family sedans, and finally a few odd station wagons and beaten-up vans belonging to less affluent relatives.

The whole procession took ten minutes to pass, while T.F. sat stony-faced, his fingers drumming in spasmodic bursts and his temper rising fast. Whichever way Cullen and Walters had gone now, he'd lost them, and he was going to have to report that failure. He put on his mirror sunglasses, and scowled behind them until the cop turned, grinned and waved him on.

They heard the news on the car radio on their way back to Los Angeles. It was twilight now, purple and soft, and they were driving in a stream of red tail-lights. They both felt tired and disillusioned.

The radio report said: '– still searching for the truck which crushed and killed Father Leonard Zaparelli this morning, only seconds after Bishop Mulhaney had dropped him off on Sixteenth Street –'

John turned up the volume. 'Zaparelli? Isn't that the priest they were talking about this morning? The one who said Hilary Nestor Hunter had set up some lesbian blackmail pictures?'

Mel yawned. 'I think so.'

The radio continued: '– his involvement in the women's liberation controversy, police are "fairly satisfied" that his death was not the work of vengeful supporters of Hilary Nestor Hunter. Ms Hunter said today she was "shocked and grieved" to hear of Father Leonard's death, and added that she was all the sorrier because she had not had the time to prove her innocence to him.'

'That would have taken the rest of his life in any case,' put in Mel. 'She's about as innocent as John Wilkes Booth.'

The radio said: '– his close friend Perri Shaw maintained this evening that Father Leonard's death was not accidental, even though it was inexplicable. She said she had "a good idea" who had done it, and she wasn't going to rest until she brought the crusading priest's killers to justice.'

The news went on to talk about cooler weather and the possibility of storms. Across the northern states of America, snow was already falling heavily, and forecasters were predicting an unusually bitter winter.

'I wonder what Professor Sweetman's predicting, down there in San Diego?' John said.

Mel grunted. 'The same, if you ask me. An unusually bitter winter.'

THIRTEEN

Dana Seiden was waiting for her husband that evening as his limousine swept up the drive of his Italian-style house on Siena Way in Bel-Air. She was posing at the top of the marble steps that led to the front door, wearing a golden evening gown that was cut so low that it looked as if it was going to drop off her at any moment, her platinum blonde hair brushed back from her face and tied in a golden ribbon. Beside her, their shaggy Afghan hound Cecil was posing with equal *hauteur*.

The two bodyguards climbed out of the car first and glanced quickly around the front of the house. One of them said, 'Okay, Mr Seiden,' and Anthony followed them. He looked tired, and he wore a tweed jacket slung over his shoulders because he was beginning to feel the cold.

Dana held out her hand. 'Darling,' she said in her

throaty voice. 'I was beginning to worry.'

He came up the steps and kissed her. The kiss was a little uncertain, because he still wasn't used to having her back. 'It took a long time to select the right take,' he told her. 'But we've got it licked now. Did you get Franco to light the fire?'

'Two fires. One in the living room, and one in the hall. Would you like a tequila?'

'I think I'd like a bath first.'

He lay back in the tub in their Italianate bathroom with its genuine Venetian tiles and its Sienese floor, letting the tensions of the day soak out of him. Dana sat in a gold-painted chair beside him, drinking a martini and smoking a pink cigarette. For a long time, they looked at each other and said nothing, two people who had become strangers and were going to need time and sensitivity to become friends again.

He guessed he had probably known when he married Dana that they weren't right for each other. He was small, dark, energetic. He worked himself relentlessly, and he was known in the movie business as one of the most exacting of directors. He would shoot and re-shoot each take until his camera crews were screaming at each other, and the actors felt that they were going to spend the rest of their lives repeating this one scene. Dana, contrarily, believed that life was a golden opportunity to swim, sunbathe, go to parties, snort cocaine, dance, laugh, and flirt with as many young men as possible. She had married Anthony because he was intense, and because he was famous, and because there was something wonderfully martyred about him. He made movies that people respected, and she had never come across intellectual respect before. Unfortunately, once she'd savoured it, she realised it was founded on political dedication and hours of hard work in the studios, and that was boring. They had started to argue over the time he spent at the studio. Then they had started to argue over politics, and sex, and what colour to paint the conservatory. And most of all they had argued about the bodyguards, and their security restrictions, and everything about Anthony's life that made Dana feel hemmed in. In a Bergmanesque scene, he had walked into the kitchen during one of her parties (nobody ever thought they were *his* parties) and found her with her half-brother Tad, a surfer. The palm of her hand had been filled with his semen. That was when they had pulled their marriage down around them, and screamed at each other, and separated.

She had stayed away for five months. Then, two days ago, he had arrived back at the house to find her sitting on the steps. All she said was, 'Don't ask me why.'

Soaking in the bath, Anthony said, 'What did you do today?'

She smiled. 'I just wandered around the house. I think the word for it is refamiliarisation.'

'Did you think some more?'

'About what?'

'About us.'

She blew out cigarette smoke, and then stubbed the half-finished cigarette in a gold shell-shaped soap dish.

'Of course. I don't think I thought about very much else.'

'And?'

She smiled again, and shook her head. 'I guess I decided to play things the way they came. That was my problem the first time. I didn't take you for what you were, and I didn't play things the way they came.'

He settled back in the foam. 'You were bored, most of all, weren't you? You thought that living with a movie director was all parties and fun. Well, I guess it is with some movie directors, but it isn't with me.'

'I was younger then,' she said. For some reason he couldn't pin down, the way she said that implied some other meaning, apart from the obvious. For the first time since he had met her, he got the feeling that she was concealing something from him. In the early days of their marriage, she had always been so transparent. Now, he could sense that something else had entered her life. Her thoughts were orbiting around some other sun, apart from him.

He said, carefully, 'Do you think you're going to be

278

happy this time? I haven't changed much. I've just wrapped up a movie now, and I'll have some free time. But there are going to be others.'

She said, 'I'm going to be happy. I'm sure of it. Do you want me to scrub your back?'

He sat up in the tub. In her glittering gold evening dress, she knelt on the bathmat and soaped his back, slowly and caressingly. She massaged his neck and his shoulders with her soapy fingers, and then ran her hand down his spine. Her soft breasts, barely concealed in her thin-strapped gown, pressed against him. Her lips were slightly parted, and her brown eyes had taken on a dreamy, faraway look. She was probably high on Quaaludes, but he made himself stop thinking about that. She had come back, she had accepted him on his terms, and he was going to have to accept her on hers.

She kissed and licked his cheeks, his lips, his eyes. Her hands soaped his chest, pulling his nipple between finger and thumb. Then she stroked his stomach, and ran her fingertips down his sides. The crest of his hard and reddened penis rose from the foam, and at last she closed her fist around it.

As he lay back in the water, she slowly and teasingly pulled at him. He closed his eyes as the feeling between his legs began to tighten, and her hand stroked him faster. He thought of sexual fantasies, of being masturbated in front of an audience of naked girls, of being caressed during a business conference by a woman hidden under his desk. Dana began to croon to him, to whisper dirty words, and the bathwater splashed as she worked him quicker and harder.

At last, he felt a deep spasm, and he climaxed.

He floated for a while in the water, his eyes still closed. Then, gradually, he opened them. Dana was still kneeling beside the bath, and there was a curious smile on her face. He said, 'You haven't lost your touch. That was terrific.'

She kept on smiling, and it was only after a long time that he saw her smile had no humour in it at all, no love or empathy of any kind. He opened his eyes wide.

She was holding her palm upwards. She said, 'What does this remind you of?'

They ate a silent dinner by candlelight in the gloomy Italian-style dining room. The servants came, and served their food, and left them alone. There was no sound except for the clatter and squeak of their knives and forks on their plates.

As they were sipping their coffee, Dana said, 'I suppose you think I'm vengeful. I suppose you think I've come back to hurt you.'

Anthony lit a cigarette. 'I don't think that. I don't know what to think. I don't think you came back because you love me.'

She stirred her coffee, and set the spoon down in the saucer. 'I don't love you, not yet. I came back because I thought that I could. You'll have to give me a chance.'

'I'm prepared to.'

'Then stop acting so silent and hurt. I didn't mean what I said. What I'm trying to say is, I didn't mean it vindictively. I just thought that we ought to face up, right now, to what happened between us. Try to catharsize it.'

Anthony sighed, breathing out smoke. 'I'm going to have to take it more slowly than that, Dana. It was a tough marriage, and a hard separation, and I don't expect it to get any better. Not for a while, anyway. It's something we're going to have to work at.'

'Work, work, work,' she said, in mock-exasperation. 'That's all you ever do. You work at making movies, you work at eating your dinner, you work at making love.'

He shrugged. 'My father always told me that work was the practical side of prayer. A man is never closer to God than when he's working, he used to say.'

'I don't want you to be close to God, Anthony,' appealed Dana. 'I want you to be close to *me*.'

He stood up, and walked across to the leaded window. Outside, the lawns of the house were floodlit in greenish light. It looked like a set for a Shakespearean play. Enter Malvolio, from the pasteboard bush on the right.

'I sometimes wish we'd never met,' Anthony said. 'We seem to have about as much in common as the turtle and the hare.'

'The turtle won the race,' Dana reminded him.

Anthony turned to her, and smiled regretfully. 'Sure. But the hare had more fun.'

She stood up, and came over to him. She took his hand, and said, 'You can have fun, too, you know. Turtles are allowed to. You're going to have fun tomorrow, aren't you, at Adele's party?'

'Of course,' he said. 'I've been looking forward to that. Adele Corliss is the only person who makes me feel that I don't have to work so hard. I look at her, and I think, why worry about growing old? If I can look like that and act like that when I'm Adele's age, then there's plenty of time left to make all the movies I've ever dreamed of.'

Dana kissed his cheek. 'Is that all you think of? Movies and politics?'

Anthony kissed her back, on the lips. Their kiss lingered for a moment, and she ran the tip of her tongue across his teeth.

'I think of you,' he said softly.

'And movies, and politics.'

He gave a wry laugh. 'I'm a political moveiemaker. What else should I think about?'

She smiled, but didn't answer. He said, 'Anyway, tomorrow night's going to be a political occasion as well as a social one. Did I tell you that Hilary Nestor Hunter's going to be there, and Carl X. Chapman?'

Dana dropped her gaze. 'That sounds like fun, of a weird kind.'

'I thought you always had a sneaking admiration for Hilary Nestor Hunter. Or was that in the days when you got off on a woman's domination? She's a very powerful lady these days, so they tell me. The voice of the vociferous majority.'

'I'm into meditation these days, and jai-alai,' said Dana simply.

Anthony looked at her for a while. Her eyes reflected the swaying flames of the two candles in the table. 'Why did you come back?' he asked.

She was silent for a moment, and then she said quietly, 'I came back because of love. Maybe not *for* love, but because of it.'

'And do you really think we can make it? The turtle and the hare?'

'I don't know. But I'm trying, aren't I?'

'I guess so. I feel like a stranger with you, that's all.'

She went across to the carved oak sideboard and opened a decorative silver box. Inside was Moroccan marijuana, and cigarette papers. She said, 'Everybody starts off strangers. Everybody winds up strangers.'

He wasn't at all sure what she meant, and he looked at her with a frown. There was a rap at the dining room door, and the Mexican servants came in to collect the coffee cups. Anthony wondered what it was that made him feel so uneasy. It was as if an earthquake were imminent, or an electric storm. Something unpleasant, even frightening.

That night, while he slept, breathing evenly through the small hours of the morning, she went into the bathroom, turned on the light, and closed the door behind her. She tiptoed naked across to the tall upright mirror in its decorative gilt frame, and looked at herself. Wide-shouldered, big-breasted, narrow-waisted. Her skin brown and glowing. Her hair long and blonde and straight.

She went close to the mirror, and stared into her own eyes. Then, slowly and lovingly, she kissed her image. Her left hand, almost absent-mindedly, rolled a nipple between her fingers, until it rose stiff and crinkly and pink. Her right hand strayed down her body, and between her thighs. Her fingers probed inside her soft flesh, and she half-closed her eyes, and let out a long, almost silent sigh.

It didn't take long. As her orgasm came closer, she pressed herself against the cool glass of the mirror, panting and shaking. Her face and her breasts were glossy with perspiration. Then she shuddered and shook, and sank to her knees, wincing.

Maybe Anthony wouldn't have minded if he had seen her. After all, she had lain close to him and masturbated some nights when he was exhausted after sixteen hours in the studio. But he would have been shocked if he had *heard* her, because she whispered a name on her lips over and over, the way a woman whispers the name of a secret lover.

FOURTEEN

She came out of the double swing door of the mortuary, and he was standing in the corridor in a worn leather jacket and corduroy jeans, looking tired and unshaven under the yellowish fluorescent lights. It was a little past nine in the evening, and the biulding was echoing and empty, and smelled of formaldehyde.

She walked along the corridor towards him, and her heels went *click-click-click* on the green plastic tiles, that sound always reminded her of TV crime pictures, when the girl is being followed by the rapist through the dark streets of the city.

'Ms Shaw? Ms Perri Shaw?' he said as she approached.

She stopped. She was wearing a dark grey dress that didn't suit her, and her eyes were reddened. She said, 'Yes? What do you want?'

'They told me at the desk that you were here. My name's John Cullen. I was wondering if I could talk to you for a while.'

'What about?'

He glanced back down the corridor towards the double doors.

She licked her lips. 'I'm not sure there's anything to say,' she told him. 'I've already spoken to the television and the newspapers. And the police, of course. The police seem to think that I'm acting a little hysterical.'

'That's what they thought about me.'

'I don't understand,' she said. This tall, unkempt-looking man was beginning to make her feel uneasy. He was quite handsome, and he *looked* normal, but you could never tell. There were so many rapes these days, and who knew what the Hillside Strangler looked like?

'Can I buy you a cup of coffee?' he asked her. 'There's a good place open across the street. My friend's there.'

She said, 'I'm sorry, Mr –'

'Cullen, John Cullen.'

'Well, I'm sorry, Mr Cullen, but I'm afraid I have to get home. I've had a terrible day, and all I want to do is rest. If you'll excuse me.'

'I don't think you understand,' John said. 'My father and my girlfriend were both killed this week, in the same kind of way that Father Zaparelli was killed. For no apparent reason at all, except maybe a political one. I've been trying to –'

He paused. He was feeling exhausted. Perri Shaw was standing there looking at him, waiting for him to come up with answers, and he didn't really know any. Maybe Professor Sweetman had been right, and his ideas were nothing more than trumped-up fantasies. After all, grief affected different people in different ways. Perhaps his grief had given him delusions of political conspiracies.

He added, in a defeated voice, 'I've been trying to find out who killed them. So far, without much success.'

'Are you telling me the truth? Was your father really killed? And your girlfriend?'

He nodded. 'My father was shot on the freeway. My girlfriend Vicki died when my house was burned.'

'What makes you think there's any possible connection with Father Leonard's death?'

'A crazy kind of inspiration. That's all. I don't have any concrete proof. The only thing that makes me sure that I'm on the right track is that the same man who killed my father has been hunting me down all week.' This morning, he chased me all the way down to San Diego.'

Perri didn't know what to say. When the policewoman had first told her about Father Leonard's death, she had found it impossible to believe that anyone should have wanted him out of the way badly enough to kill him. All he'd done, after all, was speak out against a woman's liberation leader. She knew that Hilary Nestor Hunter was determined and ambitious, but Perri didn't think it conceivable that she could have been involved in a political murder.

The only trouble was, she couldn't think of any other reason why Father Leonard might have been killed, and from what witnesses had told the police, it was plain that his crushing was deliberate. Even if Hilary Nestor Hunter hadn't killed him, *someone* had, and that was what she had told the press.

'Just let me tell you this.' John said. 'I believe that a whole lot of deaths all over the United States have been arranged for someone's political benefit. I'm not entirely sure whose, or why, but from what I've discovered so far, it seems as if Senator Carl X. Chapman might be connected with it.'

'Are you suggesting that people are being murdered for some kind of political reason?' Perri asked with disbelief.

'I can explain it in detail later. But the reason I came to see you tonight was because Senator Chapman and Hilary Nestor Hunter are great political buddies, and from what you said on the radio, it sounded like you were pointing the finger Ms Hunter's way. '

Perri glanced down the corridor. A black janitor in a green shirt was labouriously polishing the plastic tiles. At least she wasn't entirely alone. She said, 'Is this some kind of a hoax? You're not a nut, are you?'

John took his wallet out of his back pocket. He showed her his driver's license, and his press card, and then he showed her a clipping from the *Los Angeles Times* which read: 'New Jersey Teacher Dies In Freeway Shooting.'

She looked at his evidence, and then she said, 'All right. Let's go have that coffee.'

They left the mortuary building and walked across the street to the Coronado Coffee Lounge. Inside, amid dusty palm trees and crudely-painted murals of Mexican jungles, Mel was eating tomato soup with crackers, and getting crumbs in his beard.

'This is Perri Shaw,' John said as they sat down. 'She was the women's liberation delegate that all that fuss was about.'

Mel said, 'How do you do, Ms. Shaw. I'm sorry to hear about your troubles,' and he warmly shook her hand.

They ordered coffee. Somehow, for all three of them, sitting here was the first normal thing they had done for days, and they all relaxed. Briefly, John explained about the Sweetman Curve, and everything they had either discovered or guessed.

'Well, there it is,' John finished. 'We're not sure if we're crazy or brilliant. I guess it all depends on whether there could actually be someone around who's ruthless enough to do it.'

'You really think it could have been Hilary Nestor Hunter and Carl Chapman?' asked Perri. 'I didn't know they were that close.'

'I guess common interests bring all kinds of people together,' said Mel. 'And those two have common interests. Power, power, and more power.'

'You know Hilary Nestor Hunter better than we do,' John said to Perri. 'Do you think she'd really team up with a guy like Chapman? That's one part I find pretty hard to swallow. He's such a chauvinist.'

'Hilary's a Pied Piper,' Perri told John. 'Only the difference is that when she reaches the Promised Land, *all* the people who danced behind her will be shut out. Only Hilary will get inside.

'So it's quite feasible they're in this together? Like, if Hilary wanted someone out of the way, it would be in Senator Chapman's interests to fix it for her?'

Perri looked from John to Mel, and gave a small shrug. 'I guess so,' she said. 'That's if this whole idea of yours isn't – well, that's if it isn't mistaken.'

John sat back. 'I don't know any more. I don't think I care any more. But trying to track down something is better than sitting in some hotel room staring at the wall.'

'I'd like to help you.'

286

'You've helped already.'

'No,' she insisted, 'I'd like to go along with you, and help you hunt these people down.'

'I'm sorry, Perri, that's out of the question,' Mel said. 'This is so damned dangerous. I guess the only reason that we're doing it is because now we want to get *them* before they get *us*.'

'I'm not afraid of danger. Father Leonard wasn't.'

'Perri,' John said, 'you've given us all the information we need to look into Hilary Nestor Hunter's involvement with Carl Chapman. We don't need any more. The best thing you can do now is try to forget that any of this ever happened.'

Perri shook her head. 'You forget you're dealing with a feminist,' she said. 'And feminists don't just sit meekly at home knotting macramé planters while the men go out and do all the dirty work. I want to help you, and I think you could do with some help. Look at you, you're both exhausted. You need a fresh mind to think things out for you.'

She added firmly, 'You need to eat properly, for starters. Why don't you order yourself a steak and salad, and we'll talk about this whole thing while you're eatin? You can't live on coffee.'

John looked at Mel and Mel looked at John. Then John turned back to Perri.

'Okay,' he smiled. 'Anything you've got to say will be welcome. And if you really want to come along, you're welcome to do that, too. But don't ever say that we didn't warn you.'

John ordered a steak and a green salad, and while he was eating, Perri talked about Hilary Nestor Hunter and the Women's Liberation League, and about Father Leonard, and about her ideas on the Sweetman Curve.

'From what you've said,' she told them, 'it seems like Professor Sweetman knows more than he's telling you. Why did he get so upset when you asked him about his clients? I think he *does* have a political client, and if there's any truth at all in what you're saying, then it's probably Carl Chapman.'

Mel said, 'The only thing that worries me about that

conclusion is that if it *is* Carl Chapman, then his security is shit. If *we* can work out that he's behind all these killings, then why haven't the cops and the FBI worked out the same thing?'

'Because they're obsessed with lone psychopaths, that's why,' said Perri.

'Do you think it would be a good idea to go see Professor Sweetman again?' John asked her.

'Certainly,' said Perri. 'Could we go tomorrow morning?'

John shook his head. 'It's my father's funeral, but if you want to go directly afterwards, I'll be glad of the break.'

She touched his arm. He looked at her.

'Would you mind if I came along, too? To the funeral?' she asked.

'I'd be glad to have you there. You're the first person we've met in a week who's believed us.'

FIFTEEN

Beside the pool at Palm Springs, Adele and Ken sat on sun-loungers while the stars came out, sipping martinis and watching Holman and Mark and some hired Mexicans string lights between the trees for tomorrow night's party. Adele was wearing a white gown with a low square-cut décolletage and puffy shoulders, medieval-style. She was smoking a cigarette in a ridiculously long holder. Ken wore red swim shorts and an open red shirt.

'I'm still wondering how you ever got yourself involved in guns, and things like that,' Adele said.

Ken didn't answer. He was still feeling embarrassed from last night. He had never failed to satisfy any of his girlfriends at any time, and to lose his erection in the middle of trying to prove his virility to a woman like Adele Corliss was more humiliating than anything that had ever happened to him. It made him feel inadequate in everything. As a man, as a lover, and worst of all, in an insidious way, as a killer. He knew that T.F. was pretty kinky in his tastes, but he would have bet fifty bucks that T.F. never had any hard-on problems.

'You don't seem the type, somehow,' she went on. 'You seem too gentle by half. Too soft. A muscular exterior and a marshmallow interior.'

'I'm hard enough,' growled Ken. He didn't like being teased.

'For some,' retorted Adele.

He shot her an irritated look. 'And what's that supposed to mean?'

She smiled beatifically. 'A stud should never have to ask what anything means. A stud should be beautiful, stupid, and permanently stiff.'

'I was worried. You took the gun. You know what happens when a guy gets worried.'

'*You* were worried? How do you think I felt?' Adele leaned towards him. 'I think it's time I had some answers, Ken. You planted yourself on me. You knew I was coming up the road from Laguna Beach. You knew that I would take you in. And for some reason, and in some way, you've brought a rifle into my house.'

She stood up, and stepped to the brink of the pool. 'I haven't asked you to explain who you are and what you're doing here before because I'm not that kind of a person. If I want to have you around, then I'll have you around, and both of us are entitled to our privacy. But I sense that something terrible is going to happen, and I want to know what it is.'

'I told you, Adele. The gun is for self-defence.'

'I don't believe you.'

'Why don't we go inside, and talk about it there?'

'No,' Adele told him. 'I want an answer now. It's time, Ken. I want you to tell me what the gun's for.'

'Adele, I have some personal enemies, that's all. People who want to see me hurt. That's the only reason I've got it.'

289

'Where did it come from? You didn't have it when I picked you up.'

'A friend brought it. I met him in town one morning, and he brought it to me.'

'You're lying,' snapped Adele. 'I'm sick of your lies, and I'm growing sick of you.'

'That wasn't what you said last night.'

'Since last night, my dear little boy, I've had a lot of time to think. And one of the things I've been thinking about is how weak and dangerous you are. If you could have managed to rape me last night, it might have been different. You might have proved you were a complete man, all the way through, no matter which way they sliced you. But you're not. You're not much more than a worm, and you've burrowed your way into this particular apple for some damned good reason.'

Ken swung his legs off the sun-bed, and stood up. He stood close to Adele. 'Are you going to keep on pushing me?'

He said it blandly, but somehow that made the words all the more threatening. Adele refused to be intimidated, though. She looked up at him with frosty disdain, and said, 'I'll push you as much as I damned well choose. This is my house, and you're my creature.'

Ken stared at her for a long time. His eyes were steady and expressionless. There was something about him which was disturbingly sub-normal, as if he had a history of mental sickness. He looked like a grown-up version of those children who sit in institutions, beaten by their fathers, tortured by their brothers, seduced by their mothers, betrayed by life before they've even lived it.

He said, 'All right, I'm here for a reason. I'm a security agent.'

Adele gave a high, ringing laugh. 'A security agent?'

Ken looked dull and serious. 'I'm here because we've heard that somebody might threaten Senator Chapman's life when he comes here tomorrow for your party. I'm here to protect him.'

'I still don't believe you,' Adele insisted.

Mark had come around the pool and was standing beside them. He was tall and broad-shouldered. His eyes glittered in the twilight. He said, slowly, 'If you're a security agent, Mr Irwin, sir, then I think we're entitled to see your badge.'

'I, uh, don't have it with me,' said Ken, keeping his eyes on Adele.

There was a pause. Then Mark said, 'Okay, Mr Irwin. In that case, I think I'll go call the Palm Springs police.'

Ken raised his hand. He still kept his eyes on Adele. He warned, 'I wouldn't do that if I were you.'

'Oh, no? You going to stop me?'

Ken turned to Mark at last. In a slow, tightly-controlled voice, he said, 'Have you heard of the Hillside Strangler?'

'Who hasn't?'

'Well,' said Ken, wiping his lips with the back of his hand, 'how would it sound if Adele Corliss, the famous movie actress, was found guilty of harbouring him? Even sleeping with him?'

Again, there was a silence. Then Mark said, 'Are you trying to tell us *you* are the Hillside Strangler?'

Adele glanced at her chauffeur, and then turned back to Ken and laughed. 'You're nuts,' she said. 'I do believe you're absolutely nuts. I should have seen it sooner. You're as nuts as a jarful of pecans. Mark, go call the police.'

'I am the Hillside strangler,' Ken repeated, in a high-pitched voice. 'I can name the names and I can tell you the places. And if you go for that phone, then I'm going to take great pleasure in telling the cops just how Adele Corliss knew what I was and what I was doing, and always let me come back to her place to hole up.'

Mark looked at Adele. But Adele simply nodded and said, 'Go on, Mark. The police.'

Mark moved towards the house, but Ken was quicker. He caught Mark by the shoulder, and smacked him a fierce karate chop on the bridge of the nose. There was a sharp *krakk!* as Mark's nose was broken, and the chauffeur dropped to his knees and fell over on his side. Ken pulled him up by his shirt, and punched him viciously in the mouth. Then he kicked him back against the concrete pool deck, and Adele heard his head bang against the ground.

Ken turned over the chauffeur, breathing heavily, and then he turned back to Adele. Across, on the other side of the pool, Holman and the Mexicans, with strings of coloured lights in their hands, were staring at them, but they did not move any closer.

'You listen,' Ken said to Adele, his voice low and threatening. 'You're going to go on with what you're doing, you're going to give this party, and you're not going to say nothing to nobody. Especially the cops.'

Adele was pale, but she kept her head raised, and when she spoke she sounded calm and collected.

'What are you going to do? Cut off my telephones? The second that happens, the police will be here. You're in a hopeless position, dear Ken, and you really ought to realise it. Hillside Strangler, indeed! The only thing you've ever strangled is your own intelligence, what small intelligence you ever had.'

'Adele,' said Ken, 'you're going to hold this party and that's all there is to it.'

'Of course I'm going to hold my party. It's too late to put people off, in any case. But I can assure you that *you* won't be there. Neither you, nor your rifle. I'm going to go call the police right now, and have you put where you belong, whether you're a security agent or a hitchhiker or the Hillside Strangler.'

Ken yelled, *'T.F.!'*

Adele blinked at him. She said, 'What? What did you say?'

Ken, his face active with fear, screamed, *'T.F.! For Christ's sake! Come down here!'*

Adele took a step towards him, but he backed away. 'You're being very stupid, you know,' she said. 'Whatever you're trying to do here, you'll never get away with it. I'm telling you right now.'

'T.F.!' yelled Ken. *'T.F.!'*

'Will you stop shouting?'

But he didn't have to shout any more. The door from the house opened, and a tall man in a black shirt and black corduroy jeans appeared, with mirror sunglasses and greased-back hair. He looked Slavic, and he walked with a long, easy stride. In the crook of his arm he carried the same rifle that Holman had discovered in Ken's closet.

T.F. walked up to them and looked around. He saw Mark lying stunned on the concrete pool deck, and briefly prodded him with the muzzle of his rifle. Then he glanced across at the silent, mystified servants, and finally at Adele.

'Well,' he said dryly, 'it looks like you've got yourself some problems here, Ken.'

'I told you she found the gun,' said Ken. 'She kept pushing me to tell her what it was for. I tried to shut her up, but she kept on.'

T.F., his eyes nothing but blank reflections, looked at Adele and grinned. 'Curiosity killed the cat,' he said, without changing expression.

Adele said, 'I demand to know what's happening. You can't simply force your way into my house and –'

T.F. came closer. The M-14 was over his arm, but his finger was on the trigger. Tall and dark and threatening, he stood over Adele, and she could feel the coldness of his personality like an aura of liquid oxygen. She had always considered herself frosty and haughty, but this man carried with him an utter indifference to everyone around him that could have cracked mirrors. He was still grinning.

'This is kind of a complication,' whispered T.F. 'We had hoped that all this would go off without any complications.'

'All *what*?' demanded Adele.

'We have a little business here, that's all. A little unfinished business. We had hoped to carry it off without your becoming aware of it at all. But, well, it seems like Ken here got careless, and too excitable, as usual. It can't be helped.'

'You're going to shoot Senator Chapman, aren't you? That's it, isn't it? You're going to assassinate the senator.'

T.F. shook his head, without answering her. His grin

looked as if it had been scratched on a frozen lake with an ice-skate. He turned to Ken. 'We'll hold him as hostage,' he said, pointing to Mark. 'I'll keep him up in your room. The party goes ahead as planned or else he gets his brains on the ceiling.'

Adele felt chilled. 'You can't do that. You'll never get away with it. Holman, go call the police at once,' Adele ordered.

Holman hesitated, and then took one step towards the house. Almost casually, T.F. raised his M-14 in the crook of his arm, and fired once across the swimming pool. The noise was deafening, and the echoes sounded loud and flat in the desert night. Holman, petrified, looked down at the string of decorative bulbs he had been holding. One of them, an inch from his hand, was shattered.

T.F. said softly, 'Miss Corliss, I don't want anyone hurt who doesn't need to be hurt. But I'm warning you here and now that if this party doesn't go ahead like it was planned to, without any kind of winks or nods or signals from you that there's anything unusual going on here, then your black fellow here is going to be shot dead at once, and you too, and most of your staff.'

'But you're going to *kill* somebody,' said Adele. 'If I hold the party, you're going to kill one of my guests.'

T.F. grinned. 'Maybe. Maybe not. And even if we are, you don't know who it's going to be. So what are you going to do – take a chance on the life of somebody who may not mean anything to you at all, or have someone you know and care about wiped out?'

On the concrete, Mark began to regain consciousness, and he groaned. There was blood splattered all over his face from his broken nose, and he looked grey from concussion.

'He needs a doctor,' insisted Adele.

T.F. raised a hand. 'He can get one Sunday morning. After the party. Meantime, he's coming on upstairs with me.'

'What shall I do?' Ken asked.

'Make sure the servants know the score. Then keep an eye on your lady friend here. Make sure she knows that neither of us have anything to lose.'

'What does that mean?' asked Adele.

'It means that if the cops come, we're not going to throw our guns away and come out with our hands high. We're going to shoot to kill and we'll probably get away with it.'

SIXTEEN

That night, in their two-hundred-dollar suite at the Century Plaza Hotel in Los Angeles, the Chapmans, together again after days of separation, both slept badly. At three in the morning, Carl rolled out of bed, shuffled his feet into his slippers, and went into the sitting-room. He switched on the desk lamp, took a sheaf of hotel notepaper out of the desk, and began to write.

A few minutes later, Elspeth followed him, her hair in curlers, dressed in a pink quilted bathrobe. 'Do you want something to help you sleep, Carl?' she asked. 'You've been tossing and turning all night.'

'I'll have a brandy in a while. I guess I'm just tense.'

'Tense about what? Not about me, surely.'

'A little.'

She went across to the tray of drinks on the bureau, and poured herself a dry vermouth on the rocks. She sipped it slowly as she walked to the window, and looked out over the lights of the Avenue of the Stars. So far, they hadn't spoken about her phone call from Minneapolis, or what she had said about protecting herself from him. Their conversation over dinner had revolved mainly around tomorrow night's party, and how bad Cousin Kate's sciatica was, especially now that it was snowing in the northeast. They had carefully skirted around threats, and elections, and anything to do with politics.

Carl sat heavily back in his chair, and turned towards

Elspeth with a serious, jowly expression. 'Elspeth, how does a married couple get into this kind of a conflict?' he asked softly.

Elspeth didn't turn around. 'It's not a conflict, Carl. It's a breakdown of trust.'

'Well,' he said, 'I guess a lot of that is my fault. The girls, and all.'

'Yes,' she said. 'The girls, and all.'

He was quiet for a while, and then he said, 'I don't suppose it's any use if I promise to stay faithful.'

'Why should you?' she asked him. 'Why stay faithful when you can have me, and the presidency, and all the sexy young girls you want? It doesn't make sense, staying faithful.'

'Elspeth, I don't like having things hanging over my head. Those films and tapes you hired that guy to take at the Doral – those worry me. They really worry me. I mean, it's okay if you keep them as your personal insurance policy. I don't mind that, because I know that I'm always going to treat you right. You're never going to have to use them. But supposing they got into the wrong hands? Supposing someone did a black bag job on the house, just to see what they could come up with, and found them? Where do you think the future President of the United States would be then, if people found out he was cheating on his wife, and not only that, but cheating on his wife with a dead girl?'

Elspeth turned around. 'Dead?'

'You didn't know she was dead?' he asked her.

'No. Of course not. How did she die?'

'Soon – er, soon after I left her. She, er, took a bath. It must have been too hot. Or maybe she was doped on pills. She, er, drowned. She drowned.'

'She *drowned*?'

Carl stood up, and came across to put his hands on Elspeth's shoulders. 'It was an accident,' he said. 'I made sure the police investigated very thoroughly. They checked everything. The Las Vegas coroner said it was an accident.'

She stared at him, alarmed. 'And what really happened to David Radetzky?' she asked. 'I called him today and all I got was his answering service.'

'Radetzky? How should I know? A future president can't look after the whole damned population individually.'

'Carl, I called him yesterday and I called him four times today and he didn't answer.'

'Elspeth, you're getting into areas that don't concern you. We talked to Radetzky, sure, but that's all. If he doesn't choose to come into his office for a couple of days, that's nothing to do with me. Maybe he's taking a week off for Thanksgiving. I don't know.'

Elspeth took hold of her husband's wrists and lowered his hands off her shoulders. Her face was lined and grim.

'You've had him killed, haven't you?' she said.

Carl grunted, trying to appear amused. 'Killed? You think I've had him killed? Who do you think I am? Al Capone?'

'I think you're worse than Al Capone. I think you're having people killed to help you win the presidential election in 1980. I think you're having a great many people killed.'

He didn't answer her. He went across to the drinks tray, found the brandy, and poured himself a large one, which he topped up with club soda. He paced around the room swallowing it in four or five hefty gulps. Then he set his empty glass down on the desk.

'You haven't answered me, Carl. I want to know the truth.'

'The truth? The truth about what? The truth about the stinking rotten state of this country?'

'The truth about what you're doing, Carl.'

'What you don't know, Elspeth, can't hurt you. I should think, in any case, you know too damned much already.'

'How can I help you if you won't tell me anything?'

He flushed. 'I don't *need* to tell you anything. You have your private detectives following me everywhere, taping my conversations, filming my sex life. You know more about me than I do.'

'Carl, you're arguing again.'

'Do you blame me? I try to be conciliatory, I try to talk to you like a husband, and you never listen. You always keep me at arm's length. You always have your insurance policy. When we first got married, you made sure you kept your little cottage in Wealthwood, just in case. Then you made sure you had plenty of money in your savings account, just in case. Now you've got yourself a pornographic movie of me, just in case. You talk about trust breaking down, Elspeth, but when you talk about it, you just remember all those little insurance policies of yours, and just how much they give the lie to your trust in me, that's all.'

She looked at him scornfully. 'You're full of wind,' she said. 'You have about as much sincerity as a bull-frog.'

'You want insults?' he demanded. 'I can give you insults. Only I hope I've grown up enough not to bother.'

'I don't want insults,' said Elspeth. 'I want truth.'

'Well, you hand over that film, and you can have all the truth you want. One gesture of trust deserves another.'

'Truth first, Carl. Film later.'

He came up close and looked at her with a hard, impatient expression. He was breathing heavily, as if he'd just been running. 'I want that film, Elspeth, and I want it now.'

She turned away superciliously. 'You know my terms.'

'Your *terms*? What are you talking about? We're husband and wife here, Elspeth, trying to patch together a marriage that probably didn't ever have a dog's chance. But at least we're trying. Now, will you give me that goddamned film?'

She shook her head. 'You're talking nonsense, Carl. You're talking as if we were an ordinary couple. But we're not, are we? You're a lecherous, unscrupulous man, with his heart set on the White House, and I'm a woman who recognises that her only chance to make anything out of her life is to go along with this lecherous, unscrupulous man.'

Carl was trembling. He could feel his temper rising

inside him like black mercury rising up a thermometer. He took three deep breaths, and then he said tightly, 'Elspeth, give me the film.'

'No, Carl.'

He paused for a moment, and then he roared, '*Give me the goddamned film!*'

She smiled a contemptuous smile, and that was the worst thing she could have done. Carl seized hold of her hair, and threw her against the settee, wrenching out a whole handful of curlers and dark hair. She shrieked, 'Carl!' and tried to protect herself from him, but he was a big, heavy man, and his jogging had kept him fit. He was angry, too, from years of frustration, years of being patronized, years of sexual disparagement and social embarrassment.

He heaved her up from the settee, and punched her hard in the ribs. He was enough of a politician not to hit her in the face. She doubled up without a sound and dropped to the rug.

Carl, panting, bent down and pulled her to her feet. Her mouth was wide open, desperate for breath, and her face was blue. He waited until she had gasped some air into her lungs, and her colour began to come back.

'Now,' he told her, 'I want you to give me that film.'

Still gulping air, she shook her head.

'Elspeth,' he warned evenly, 'I want you to tell me where the film is.'

'No.'

His mouth tilted into something that could have been a smile. He said, very quietly, 'I'm not giving you five minutes to make your mind up, Elspeth. I'm asking you now.'

All she could do was shake her head.

'You want to be First Lady, don't you? You want to get into the White House as badly as I do. But you're not coming with me unless you learn to do what I tell you, Elspeth. I can't have disobedience. Maybe it's going to hurt my chances, if we split up, but you're going to hurt me more if you act like this, because you're going to make my life dangerous, and I can't have that.'

'Let go of me, Carl.'

He twisted her arm and forced her close to him. 'You tell me where the film is, and I will.'

'There's no chance, Carl. If I give you that film, you'll kill me, too. Just like you did all the others.'

He shoved her violently back against the wall, pressing his full weight against her. Then he seized her breasts in his big hard hands, and screwed them viciously around, twisting her nipples until she screamed out loud. He punched her again in the stomach, and she collapsed on to the floor.

While she lay there, he went back to the drinks tray and poured himself another brandy-and-soda. He felt numbed and unreal and angry. He could have smashed up the whole hotel room. Thrown the damned stupid television out of the window. Torn the pictures off the walls. But he knew that he needed to keep control. He had to keep himself calm. He swallowed his drink, and paced edgily back to where his wife was lying.

She was whining for breath.

'Well? How does it feel on the floor?'

She couldn't answer.

'Now do you want to tell me where the film is?'

Again, she shook her head.

He glanced across at the drinks tray. A bottle of brandy, a bottle of vodka, a soda siphon, a bottle of vermouth, a bottle of club soda, half-empty. 'There was something we used to do in the Army, you know, when someone ratted on us,' he said.

Elspeth lay where she was, saying nothing. He squatted down beside her.

'It hurt like hell,' he told her. 'And if you don't tell me where that film is, I've got a damned good mind to do it to you.'

She shook her head weakly. He looked at her for a while, and then he stood up and went across to the bureau. He came back with the vodka bottle, unscrewing the cap as he came.

He squatted down again. She watched him, but she was too hurt to move. He said, 'You stuck-up bitch. When I think of all the hard years you've given me, it makes me realise I should have hit you the first night we got married. I should have thrashed the hell out of you. Then we would have gotten ourselves straight.'

She turned her eyes away.

'Now, you've got yourself one last chance,' he said quietly. 'Either you hand over that film, or else I'm going to hurt you, Elspeth, really hurt you.'

She didn't stir. Didn't even give any indication that she'd heard him. That was just like her. Even when she was beaten and humbled she was contemptuous.

Carl rolled her over until she was face down on the floor. Then he sat astride her, facing her feet, pressing his whole two hundred pounds on her waist. He lifted her bathrobe at the back, baring her pale bottom, and then he pulled the cheeks apart with one stubby-fingered hand. In the other hand he gripped the vodka bottle, three-quarters full. He began splashing vodka on her thighs and between her legs.

The first time he pushed the bottle, she twisted beneath him and said, *'Aah!'* He waited for her to give in, to give him the film and tell him she was never going to try any stunts like that again. After all, in the Army, he'd seen grown men beg for mercy at the first thrust.

'You give in?' he asked her roughly.

There was no answer.

'You give in?'

He waited some more. Still no answer.

'All right, bitch,' he told her, and he bent his arm to force the vodka bottle harder and harder, twisting it around as he pushed it, and he was grunting and sweating so much that he hardly even heard her shrieking. He took a breath, and then he pushed it again, until almost half of it had disappeared.

'Take it out! Take it out! I give in! Carl! For the love of God! Take it out!'

When it was over, she lay on the floor sobbing, and he stood by the bureau, finishing off his brandy-and-soda. He could see his reflection in the dark glass of the window, with the lights of Century City beyond, and it occurred to him how old and heavy he looked.

Elspeth shaking got to her knees, and shuffled over to

the settee. She lay down on it, white-faced and shocked, and held herself close for security and warmth. He looked across at her, but said nothing.

After a while, she whispered, 'It's in the vault at the Security Pacific Bank, the branch under the Chinese restaurant on Century Plaza. It's under the name of McCarthy.'

'Was that your idea of a joke?' he asked, but she didn't say any more. There was a polite knocking at the door of the hotel suite, and Carl had to go to answer it.

It was the night manager. He said courteously, 'I'm sorry to disturb you, Senator, but a couple of our guests have expressed concern at some of the noise from your suite. Is everything all right?'

Senator Chapman smiled reassuringly. 'Everything's fine,' he said, with his best electioneering clap on the shoulder. 'Everything's real fine.'

SEVENTEEN

The morning of the funeral there was a high layer of cloud. The cemetery was unpleasantly close, like the inside of a linen cupboard, and John stood a little apart from the others, sweating inside his black suit, feeling as if the flesh was melting away from his bones. Perri was there, as she had promised, and stood a few feet behind him, in a plain grey suit and a black hat with veil.

In the blurred, shadowless light, they lowered the casket of William Cullen into the grave, and John sifted a handful of dry dirt on to the polished lid. Then he turned away, hoping that his father was being received somewhere in joy and dignity and grace. Mel came over and put his arm around him, and with Perri staying close, they walked to the cemetery gates.

Detective Morello was waiting beside the white

Lincoln. He shook hands with John and Mel, and John introduced him to Perri.

'I hope you don't think I'm intruding,' said Detective Morello. 'I can come back later if I am.'

'That's all right,' said John. 'I'd be interested to hear what you've got.'

'Well,' said Detective Morello, 'we don't have a great deal. We have some more ballistics results, but they're not exactly conclusive. We ran a check on the Fury that followed you down to San Diego, too, but that's clean of any prints except the owner's. It was stolen, you see. By someone intelligent enough to wear gloves.'

'So you're still some way off an arrest?' asked Mel.

'I'm afraid so. We're making progress, but it's slow.'

John loosened his black tie. It was only eleven o'clock, but the humidity was building up. 'Is that why you came?' he asked Detective Morello. 'Just to tell us that?'

'Well, not exactly. In fact, the reason I came was because of Miss Shaw here. You were seen in her company by some of my men last night. Because of that, I was kind of worried that you might be trying to tie in Father Zaparelli's death yesterday morning with what happened to your father and your fiancée.'

'Is there anything wrong in that?' asked John.

'Not *per se*. But I'm afraid we don't really approve of private citizens trying to undertake detective work. It fouls us up more often than not – sometimes tragically. In the past few years we've had a couple of cases of police stake-outs being blown by some enthusiastic amateur going right in with his Saturday night special blazing, thinking he's Cannon and Kojak and Commissioner McMillan all rolled up into one.'

John glanced at Mel, who simply shrugged.

Detective Morello said, 'I know how you feel about your father, Mr Cullen. I know you're sore and you're mad. I know you want to bring his killer to book. But I'd really appreciate it if you left this Freeway Fruitcake to us, because we're the professionals and we're going to catch him. I'm saying this for your own good. I don't want you to foul up the police department, and most of all I don't want you to get hurt. Neither you, nor Mr Walters here, nor Miss Shaw.'

John opened the Lincoln's doors. 'All right, sir,' he said quietly. 'We won't interfere. You go track down the Freeway Fruitcake, and we'll stay right out of your way.'

Detective Morello looked at John for a moment, not sure whether he ought to believe him or not. But then he said, 'I'm not trying to make you feel that your interest isn't appreciated. We really do appreciate it.'

'Thank you,' said John. 'I appreciate yours.'

'What it simply boils down to is that we can't let you go risking your life,' added Detective Morello. 'It's our job to hunt down killers, and we know what the odds are. But we can't let civilians go taking those risks for us.'

'I understand,' said John.

'It's not that we don't value public help,' said Detective Morello. 'The Los Angeles Police Department depends a great deal on public help.'

'Sure,' nodded John.

'Right, then,' said Detective Morello. He didn't know what else to say. John climbed into his car, closed the door, and rolled down the window. He sat there with an expectant expression, as if waiting for Detective Morello to come up with a resonant and dramatic closing statement.

'Well, that's all,' said Detective Morello.

'That's it?' asked John.

'Just keep in touch if anything happens, if anyone else tries a hit. And let us know if you change hotels.'

'Okay,' said John. 'So long.'

He started the motor, and they drove out along Forest Lawn Drive towards the Ventura Freeway. Mel was sitting on the right-hand side and Perri sat between them. The morning was smoggy as they turned south on to the Golden State Freeway. They didn't talk much as they drove. The sad atmosphere of William Cullen's funeral was still with them, and Detective Morello's warning hadn't done much to cheer them.

They sped along the coast past Oceanside and

Leucadia, and by the time they reached the outskirts of San Diego, it was a few minutes past four. John drove straight to Fairmount Avenue, turned the corner, and pulled up outside Professor Sweetman's house. They got out of the car, and walked across the shrivelled lawn and rang the bell.

Abruptly, the front door of the Sweetman house was opened. A Mexican woman in an apron stood there, looking them up and down with grave suspicion.

'Is Professor Sweetman home?' John asked.

The woman stared at him mistrustfully.

'Professor Sweetman?' he repeated. 'Is Professor Sweetman *a casa?*'

The woman slowly shook her head from side to side.

'Are you sure?' Perri asked her.

The woman nodded.

'If he's not at home, where is he? Where can we find Professor Sweetman?' John asked.

The woman ruminated for a moment, and then said, 'Laboratory. That way. By university.'

They thanked the Mexican woman, and then drove up Fairmount Avenue as far as the university campus. There was hardly anyone around. A couple of students jogging across the grass. A groundsman pushing a lawn-mower. They parked in the main lot, and walked around the block until they found a sign with an arrow that pointed left, and read *Demographic Research Lab.*

'That has to be it,' said John, and they crossed the grass to a small, squat building of concrete and brick. They walked around the front of the building, and found a pair of mahogany doors with windows inset in them. John shaded his eyes and peered inside.

'See anything?' asked Perri.

'There's a small entrance-hall, then another set of doors. Come on, let's go inside.'

They quietly pushed open the double doors and found themselves in a bare, tiled lobby. There were windows in the next pair of doors, too, and from within they could hear the humming of electrical energy and the intermittent clicking sound of computers. John walked softly across the lobby and looked into the next room.

'What's in there?' hissed Perri.

John raised his hand to show that she ought to keep quiet for a moment. Then he whispered, 'There's a whole bank of IBM computers, on three sides of the room. They're all working like crazy. I can see a couple of lab assistants. There's someone else in there, I can't see who it is right now. Some guy in a yellow sport shirt and grey pants.'

'Any sign of Sweetman?' Mel asked.

'No – wait a moment. Here he comes. He's holding a whole armful of print-outs. He's talking to the guy in the sport shirt and explaining something about them.'

For three long minutes, John watched as Professor Sweetman, tall and intense, talked to the short, stockily built man about the print-outs he was holding over his arm. He looked like a head waiter explaining the menu of the day. The stocky man kept nodding, and from the way he was nodding, John guessed that he'd heard it all before. Yeah, professor. Sure, professor.

Abruptly, the stocky man turned around and walked towards the doors, with a brief wave over his shoulder to Professor Sweetman, and a nod to the lab assistants. John said, 'Get back – he's coming out. Get around the corner!'

They slipped through the outer doors and dodged around the corner of the demographics building, keeping as far back out of sight as they could. They heard the front doors of the building open, and the stocky man crossed the lawn to the parking lot. The print-outs he was carrying fluttered brightly in the afternoon wind.

'We ought to stop that guy,' Perri suggested. 'Maybe he knows something.'

'Stop him!' said Mel. 'Are you nuts? How are we going to stop him?'

'I don't know. How does one man go about stopping another man?'

'Perri's right,' John said. 'We've made it this far. Let's take the risk.'

The three of them left the cover of the demographics building and walked quickly towards the parking lot. The short, stocky man was standing by a light green

Cadillac Coupe de Ville, and he was awkwardly reaching into his back pants pocket for his keys. John signalled to Mel to skirt around the back of him, and to Perri to stay close.

When they were only ten or fifteen feet away, the man looked up. He squinted at them across the glare of the hot parking lot, turning from John to Mel and back again.

John said, 'Excuse me, sir.'

The man said nothing. He opened the door of his car, and pushed the print-outs into the front seat, and then stood there staring at them silently.

'Would you mind if we asked you a question?' John asked.

The man had a sour, squashed-looking face. 'If it's money you want, you're out of luck. I didn't get to the bank this week,' he said.

'Do we look like muggers?' Perri asked.

The man shrugged. 'How the fuck should I know?'

'We want to ask you about those computer print-outs,' John said.

'What business is it of yours?'

Mel, coming up close behind the man, said, 'No business at all. But I'm sure you'd like to help with a police investigation.'

'Police investigation? What is this? You're no more police than I am.'

John edged nearer. 'All you have to do is show us the print-outs. Then you can go.'

'I don't have to show you doodly-squat. Now, get out of here, before I call somebody.'

'Mel,' said John, and beckoned him to make a rush for the man, but the man was alerted to what they were doing, and slid quickly into the driver's seat of his car. He slammed the door and locked the power locks just as Mel made a grab for the handle. Then he started the car's motor, gunned it, and swerved away from the parking-space and screeched towards the exit.

Mel was calm and decisive. He pulled the .38 revolver out from his belt, steadied it with both hands, and fired one shot across the parking lot. It hit the Coupe de

Ville's front tyre as it was turning out of the exit, and the green Cadillac mounted the sidewalk outside the demopraphics building and struck a tree. The motor whined for a moment, then died.

They ran towards the car. Inside, the stocky man was sitting dazed and shaken, but unharmed. Mel waved the revolver at him, and he unsteadily unlocked the doors and stepped out. He sat on the kerb with his head between his knees, looking pale, and then he suddenly vomited.

John took the print-outs off the front seat and held them up. They were lists and lists of names, addresses, and dates, followed by coded comments. Altogether, there must have been well over a thousand of them.

Timothy P. Sheldon, Attleboro, Mass. Intersected soonest 77

Margarita Ramonez, Hemet, Ca. Close intersection re-port later e 78

Herman T. Kreisler, Lansing, Mich. Intersected or-dinary 1 77

At the top of the print-out was the heading: Sweetman *Curve Process 35/710/409. CXC. Private & Confidential.*

John pointed it out to Perri. 'You see that? CXC. I don't think it's any coincidence that CXC are the initials of Carl X. Chapman, do you?'

'You think that clinches it? Do we call the police now?' Mel asked.

'I don't know,' John told him. 'On its own, this list doesn't signify anything much. I mean, we're only guessing what it is. And even if it *is* a list of people Chapman's planning to kill, none of them are dead yet, and it's going to be a hell of a job proving that what we've got here is a political death roll.'

'Let's go ask Professor Sweetman,' suggested Perri. 'Maybe you'll find him a little more informative this time.'

Mel prodded the short, stocky man to his feet, and they walked quickly back to the demographics building. This time, they barged straight through the doors and into the computer room.

Professor Sweetman was leaning over a console, tapping out the beginnings of a programme. John said clearly, 'Professor Sweetman,' and the old man raised his head and stared at them all as if he couldn't believe they were real. There was an amber skylight above their heads, and his pinched and elderly face looked oddly unwell in the light filtering down from it.

'Dennis, you came back,' he said, momentarily unable to grasp why the print-out messenger had returned in the company of two men he had thrown out of his house yesterday and a perfectly strange girl. 'Is anything the matter?'

'Better ask these turkeys,' said Dennis. 'I just run the errands and get fucking shot at.'

Professor Sweetman dithered, and then looked around the room. 'You all better come into my office,' he said. 'It's right through here.'

With Mel staying inches behind Dennis, they walked through into a musty-smelling office. There was a clutter of cheap modern furniture and desklamps and scientific periodicals. On the walls were pinned graphs and charts of demographic profiles, and dozens of scribbled notes. It looked more like a stationery cupboard than an office, except for one thing. In a gilt frame on the desk stood a sensitive colour portrait of a middle-aged woman, with a sad, soft face. She looked younger and less emaciated than she was in real life, but John recognised her as Mrs Sweetman.

Professor Sweetman closed the door behind them. 'Now,' he said, 'do you mind explaining what this is all about?'

John held up the print-outs. 'I think it's what they call the end of the line,' he said gently. 'We know who your political client is, and we know what he's using your curve for, and we're pretty sure that you know, too. We're going to take you in to the Los Angeles police, Professor Sweetman, and all these print-outs, too, as evidence.'

Dennis shrugged, and took a crumpled pack of cigarettes out of his shirt. 'Don't ask me,' he said. 'All I did

309

was pick up the stuff every week and take it to Mr Chapman's office. That's all I did. I don't know what the fuck it's for.'

Professor Sweetman sat down at his desk, took off his spectacles, and stared for quite a long time out the window. Eventually, he turned back and looked at them, and gave a small, regretful smile. 'I suppose it was too radical to last,' he said, tiredly. 'You can't expect to change the political pattern of a nation like ours overnight, by fair means or foul.'

'I'd say the means were pretty foul,' said John tersely.

Professor Sweetman nodded. 'You're probably right. I'm not going to confess anything. I shall leave all that to my attorney.'

'But it's *true*?' asked Perri. 'It's actually true that you've been selling this curve for political murders?'

The old man shook his head. 'This isn't the time or the place to admit to things like that. But I will say one thing. When the person you love most of all in the whole world has a chance of survival, a chance for a few more years, then I'm afraid that your sense of morality changes. Mima had a brain tumour that was almost certain to kill her. She was irrational and ill for three years. They told me that the necessary operations would cost over half a million dollars.'

He carefully put his glasses back on. 'Out of the political and commercial applications of the Sweetman Curve, I made nearly three quarters of a million dollars for myself alone, most of that from my political people. Mima has had her operation, and she is recovering. As you saw for yourself, Mr Cullen, she is now quite rational.'

John looked at Mel almost sadly. Now that he knew their hunches and suspicions had all been right, now that he knew their worst fears about the Sweetman Curve were proved, he felt drained and exhausted. He could have dropped into a chair and slept around the clock. Mel didn't know what to say. The enormity of what Professor Sweetman had done was almost too much to take in.

'Dennis, unimpressed by Professor Sweetman's ex-

310

planation, said, 'Do you mind if I leave now? I didn't do anything. This was just a job.'

'Stay here,' ordered John. 'I think it's time we called the police.'

Professor Sweetman got up from his desk and went across to an untidy grey steel filing cabinet. He opened the drawer and took out a bottle of Madeira and a single glass.

'You don't mind if I have one? I think I need it to steady my nerves.'

'Go ahead,' said John. He felt so disgusted with Professor Sweetman that he could scarcely conceal it in his voice. 'Go ahead and drink the whole damned bottle.'

Professor Sweetman poured out a modest half-glass. He took a careful sip, and then looked at his watch.

'I suppose I might tell you something which would mitigate any future prosecution,' he said. 'Something which might stand in my favour.'

'I can't think of *anything* which could stand in your favour, professor,' said John.

Professor Sweetman looked a little hurt. 'No, well, I suppose you can't. But a court might. And I suppose I owe it to myself, and to Mima, if I try. The truth is, we have a very big project lined up for tonight. A special one, which required a most interesting curve. I worked it all out myself, and it was fascinating.'

'A *killing*?' asked Perri.

'Well, the end result is a killing, but –'

'It's a *killing*, and it's *fascinating*?' said Perri, totally shocked.

Professor Sweetman seemed extremely put out by Perri's hostility and shock. 'I don't *plan* the killings, you know. I have nothing to do with their execution. I simply –'

'I don't want your excuses, professor,' John said. 'I just want to hear what you have to say.'

Professor Sweetman sighed, and stood up. He took a chart from the wall, and spread it out on the table. The chart was covered in complicated curves and lines, and marked with dozens of fainter lines labelled 'probability tangents.'

'This is a draft curve worked out for a very talented and complex personality,' Professor Sweetman explained. 'Usually, we're dealing only with very ordinary people, people whose influence is felt on the society in which they live because of their popularity, but not for any other reason. In this case, we're dealing with a man who is politically influential not only because of his personality but because of his talents and the way in which he uses them.

'This is a curve for Anthony Seiden, the movie director, and it shows that his political influence on the movie-going population of the United States will be sufficient over the next three years to sway the voting result in the 1980 Presidential election by 0.02 percent.'

John stared at the chart. 'You're going to kill Anthony Seiden?'

Professor Sweetman nodded. 'It's planned for tonight. It's a very special case, you know, because he's usually inaccessible. He has bodyguards night and day, a bullet-proof limousine, very tight security. I know that as soon as his name came up on the curve, one of Chapman's men tracked him for three weeks, and didn't even catch a glimpse of him.'

'So what makes tonight different?' Mel asked.

'Well, tonight there's a party in Seiden's honour at Palm Springs. It's being given by Adele Corliss – you know, the old movie actress. I don't know exactly what Senator Chapman has planned to do, but he seemed very confident about it. Very confident indeed.'

There was a long, cold silence. Then John said, 'Pass me that phone. If you're damned lucky, we might catch Seiden in time. If you're not, I'll personally stand up in any witness box anywhere and tell them just what a sick, weak bastard you are.'

EIGHTEEN

It was 5:05 by T.F.'s digital watch. Up in Ken Irwin's bedroom in Palm Springs, T.F. sat astride a small gilt chair by the open window, his M-14 resting on the sill, and smoked a cigarette. The bedroom was decorated in golds and greens, with paintings of old San Francisco all around. T.F. had pinned back the drapes a little so that he could see down into the courtyard at the front of the E-shaped house, and so that he could angle his rifle across to the opposite wing of the E, the target area.

There was a downstairs window there, patterned with diamond-shaped leaded lights. At the moment, it was closed, and any attempt to shoot through it would have been too risky. The bullet could be deflected by the angle of the window and by striking the glass, and might even hit one of the lead glazing bars.

At the moment of firing, though, the window was going to be open. Even when it was thrown back wide, it wouldn't offer T.F. more than two-and-a-half to three inches to shoot through, and at a distance of maybe two hundred feet that was a narrow shot. But T.F. was confident he could do it.

He raised his rifle and squinted through the telescopic sight. Dimly, through the closed window, he could see the small side table and the chair where his target would be sitting. He could see the telephone, too – the telephone which was going to ring at 11:01 precisely and summon his target to the killing-ground.

On the bed, his wrists lashed to the brass headboard, Mark the chauffeur coughed and moaned. T.F. turned towards him, his cigarette sloping out of the corner of his mouth, and watched him try to get comfortable. Mark's face was caked with dried blood.

From the back of the house, carried on the warm wind, T.F. could hear the servants setting out buffet tables on the pool deck, and the three-piece Spanish rock band testing out the sound system. There would be sudden blurts of electric guitar, and spasmodic rattles on the bongos. T.F. grinned. He hoped the band could play funeral marches.

There was a rap at the door. T.F. pinched out his cigarette-end, and tossed it out of the window. Then he hauled himself up from the chair, and walked over to the door. He opened it a couple of inches, poking the muzzle of his rifle out first.

It was Adele Corliss. She was dressed in a white lace bathrobe and her face was smeared with cream.

'How is he? Can I take a look at him?' she asked.

T.F. shook his head. 'When it's all over, you can take him in your loving arms and cuddle him like a baby, Ms. Corliss. Right now, just go get yourself ready and act like everything's normal.'

'How can I?' she said, almost hysterically. 'You're holding my chauffeur hostage and you're threatening to kill one of my guests. How can I act normal?'

T.F. tapped the muzzle of the rifle against the door-jamb, a steady *tap-tap-tap*. He said softly, 'You're an actress, aren't you? So act.'

Then he closed the bedroom door and left her standing alone in the corridor.

NINETEEN

At her home in the Hollywood hills, a stark architect-designed chalet with a sharply-sloping roof and a wide balcony that overlooked the reservoir, Hilary Nestor Hunter was stalking about in a temper. The deep blue culottes she was going to wear to the party tonight hadn't yet arrived from the couture house. She smoked furiously, waving her long cigarette-holder in exasperated gestures as she went from room to room, dressed in nothing but a man's denim shirt, see-through French panties with daisies hand-embroidered on them, and high-heeled boots from Chelsea Cobbler of London.

The girls of her entourage sat in the living room, on the Chinese-style settee or the white shag-pile rug, and did what they always did when Hilary was in a tantrum. They kept their mouths closed and their eyes averted, and waited patiently until it was all over.

It was twenty after five, by the antique railroad clock on Hilary's wall. The November sun was already beginning to sink into the brown smog over Los Angeles, and the reservoir had turned to bright but rusty chrome. Hilary came out of her bedroom and snapped to one of the girls, 'Fix me a collins. And get on to that damned fashion house and tell them if they're not here in five minutes I'm going to sue them for everything they've got and everything they haven't got.'

There was a chime at the door, the first few notes of Ravel's *Bolero*. There had been a time when Hilary had been fascinated by the Bolero, and its decadent monotony, and she had danced solo to it at dinner parties, while her guests sat nursing their drinks and wishing they were some place else. Hilary snapped her fingers, and the black-haired girl wrapped herself tighter in her Korean silk robe and went across to the living room to answer it.

There were a few moments of muffled conversation at the door, while Hilary continued to posture and fume, and then the girl came back into the room, followed by a tall hawkish-looking man in a light grey suit. It was Henry Ullerstam.

'Hallo, my pet,' he said to Hilary. 'I finished early at Dutch Oil, so I came on up.'

Hilary's frown faded. She held out her arms in a dramatic gesture of welcome, and said, '*Henry*, it's so beautiful to see you. I thought you weren't coming till nine. Girls, say hello to Henry.'

The girls smiled and gave little waves. Only one or two of them realised who Henry was, but they were all relieved and pleased that he was here, because he'd broken Hilary's sour-tempered mood.

'How long can you stay?' asked Hilary. 'Have a drink, why don't you? Are you coming to the party?'

'I have to leave by seven, I regret,' said Henry. 'There's an OPEC meeting in Iran just now, and I'm going to have to make some policy responses over the weekend. Just boring old business, I'm afraid.'

Hilary sat down on the settee, shooing the girls away. They lingered around for a while, and then they sulkily went through to the bedroom, and closed the door.

'They're an ungracious collection,' Henry said.

'I love them,' smiled Hilary. 'What's the use of having people around who do everything willingly? It's no test of one's power at all.' She patted the cushion beside her, and said, 'Sit down. You're looking so well. You look more like Basil Rathbone every day.'

Henry carefully pulled up the knees of his pants, and sat beside her. Although Hilary was scantily dressed, he was unruffled and unperturbed, and treated her as blandly as if she had been wearing a knitted twin-set. They had, for one night only, been lovers, but at sunrise they had affectionately and tacitly come to the conclusion that Henry's polished athleticism and her need for savagery and sadism were incompatible, and they had never tried again. Instead, they nourished their relationship on the two urges that they did share: the urge for wealth and the urge for power.

'Tonight's the big night, then,' said Henry. 'Is Carl taking his wife?'

'Yes. He was hoping she wouldn't show. Believe me, I'm glad she did. To be pawed by a man is one thing. To be pawed by a human cuttlefish is quite another.'

'Has he made all the necessary arrangements, do you know? I mean, it's going to go off smoothly?'

Hilary shrugged. 'As far as I know. He never tells me the finer details. But he planted a cuckoo in the house about a week ago, and the cuckoo's gotten the hit man inside.'

Henry Ullerstam sat back on the settee and crossed his ankles. One of the girls came through from the kitchen and gave him a martini, which he accepted with an urbane nod of his head.

'They're very pretty, some of your young ladies,' he remarked, as the girl went back to join the others in the bedroom. 'Even if they are sullen.'

Hilary smiled. 'Pretty, sullen, but sapphic, I'm afraid.'

'I always thought lesbians had gruff voices and muscles.'

Hilary laughed. 'I always thought men did.'

Henry speared his olive with his cocktail stick, and popped it into his mouth. 'Poor Carl,' he said in a thoughtful voice. 'I really feel quite sorry for him.'

'Do you want to drink to that?' asked Hilary. 'To pity?'

Henry shook his head. 'I never drink toasts to pity. Or to stupidity. Only to success.'

Hilary called to one of her girls, 'Bring me my robe, will you, Etta? And freshen up this drink.'

The girl went off to do as she was told, and then Hilary leaned confidentially towards Henry, and said, 'Have you spoken to Cault?'

Henry nodded.

'Is he pleased?'

'So far. It's early days yet, of course, and the whole situation could change. But if our friend Professor Sweetman is anything to go by, the future is as predictable as a railroad track.'

'Did Cault say anything?'

'Not much,' said Henry. 'But for somebody to bring him the head of the next president on a chafing-dish, that's what Cault considers to be nirvana.'

'He agreed to everything you wanted?'

Henry beamed. '*More* than everything.'

Hilary's girl came out with her robe, and Hilary unselfconsciously took off her shirt, baring for a moment her small brown-nippled breasts, and then wound herself in Paisley-patterned silk. She sat down again, drawing her legs up under her, and her clear blue eyes looked at Henry Ullerstam with a warmth and an openness that would have galled Carl Chapman, if he could have seen her, to the bottom of his gut.

'Cault's been champing at the bit to do a number on Angelo for two years,' said Henry. 'You can't imagine how frustrated he's been by presidential foreign policy up until now. He told me that he sometimes seriously wonders whose side the last three presidents have been on.'

Hilary tasted her drink. She said, 'Cault's very hard-line CIA, though, isn't he?'

'Well, it's hardly surprising,' said Henry. 'The CIA is a highly competent, highly professional, highly talented organisation. It has its finger on the pulse of everything that happens overseas, and it's capable of responding to coups and take-overs and revolutions in a matter of minutes, not to mention concocting its own. No wonder men like Cault turn into hard-liners, when they have to deal with presidents who don't know Mozambique from Memphis, and who constantly block any action the CIA wants to take, just because the CIA is publicly unpopular, and because the presidents themselves don't understand what the hell is going on.'

Henry stood up. Outside, dusk was drawing in, and there was a faint twittering of birds. A cool draught blew off the surface of the reservoir.

'Cault reckons he has all the resources he needs, and all the contacts he needs, and he believes he can recruit the men,' he went on. 'He's been trying to keep the CIA in control of Angola for years and years, but Nixon didn't want to know, not after Viet Nam, and neither, of course, did anyone else. Oh, they were prepared to contain the spread of Communism within certain limits, and be vaguely supportive, but they weren't going to sanction a damned great bloodbath, which was what Cault and the CIA wanted.'

'Will Carl, when he's elected?' Hilary asked.

'Of course Carl will sanction it,' Henry said smoothly. 'Carl is going to be our little dancing man. If we say "sanction, Carl," then Carl will sanction.'

He paused for a moment, and then he said, 'I couldn't have imagined any politician more suited for all this than Carl. It happens from time to time, that a naive mind has an epic idea, but not very often. Carl's idea of how to apply the Sweetman Curve to politics was truly momentous. To conceive of wiping out enough people to sway the course of the next presidential election – and it really doesn't take very many – well, that wouldn't have entered my mind. An epic idea.'

Henry pulled a wry face. 'He set it all up quite well. A pretty good network of hit men, nationwide. Some of them seem to be less reliable than others, sure. But, mostly, they do their work undetected, and that's all one could really ask of them.'

He looked at Hilary with an expression of satisfied amusement.

'Unfortunately, poor Carl is careless as well as ruthless, and he's sentimental as well as cruel. He believes that he can inflict what he likes on others, and still be loved. He's forgotten, in his heady campaign to be president at any price, that he owes a lot of people a lot of favours, and that a lot of people have a lot of old scores to settle.'

Henry sat down again, and picked up his drink. 'He's got plans to cover his tracks, once he's elected. Some way of disposing of his hired killers, I don't quite know how. But he's forgotten that once he's sitting in that Oval Office, he's going to have to deal with some old enemies like Cault at the CIA, and Stepanski at the FBI, and all those people at the Pentagon who were left with egg on their face when he pulled off that arms deal with the Senegalese. He hasn't been *courting* people. He hasn't made them any *promises*. That's why they've all been so helpful to me. Carl Chapman doesn't know how to *woo*.'

'You can say that again,' remarked Hilary, disgustedly.

Henry grinned. 'He's a true political primitive. He's wily and cunning, and he knows how to survive. But this time, he's out of his league. It's all been so easy that it almost brings tears to my eyes to think about it.'

'Did Cault mention the oil?' she asked him, trying to sound offhand.

'Of course.'

'Well, Don't keep me in suspense.'

'Well, he's worked out a little scheme,' said Henry. 'It's based very largely on a suggestion of my own, but Cault's done a lot to improve on it. I always bow to other people's greater generosity, not to mention their greed.'

He roughly drew an outline of the coast of Angola on the settee.

'After the coup is successfully over,' he said, 'the new Angolan regime is going to announce its intention to seek the financial help of Western countries. One of the ways in which it will do this is to parcel up certain areas of arid and non-agricultural land, and lease them to foreign corporations to put up office blocks and factories. The leases, of course, will be wonderfully cheap.'

He smiled. 'One of these parcels of land will be leased to a corporation called Pan-African Insurance. Oddly enough, Pan-African Insurance is owned by a holding company called Ullerstam Securities (Jersey) Ltd. And even odder, when Pan-African Insurance starts to excavate the foundations of their new Angolan headquarters, they will discover to their amazement that the ground is rich with traces of oil.

'The mineral rights, with a percentage backhander to the new regime, are included in the lease. So Pan-African Insurance will be quite within their rights when they set up oil rigs and pipelines, and start to exploit their find.'

Henry looked serious for a moment. 'I haven't told you this, because I've been waiting for confirmation. But when we first discovered that field, eight years ago, we suspected that it was probably the largest oil well outside of the United States. At a rough guess, I'd say we could ultimately take one hundred million barrels out of Angola, and that's as big as Potrero de Llano No. 4 well, which was one of the greatest gushers of all time. That field stretches right under the sea, and it's just bursting to have itself liberated.'

'Liberated?' asked Hilary, mock-offended.

Henry sipped his martini, and then looked up at her. 'An oil well is like a beautiful woman, my pet. They're both valuable natural resources, and they both deserve to be set free.'

'As long as they're both set free for *your* profit and enjoyment,' retorted Hilary.

Henry looked at her keenly, and then saw that she was needling him.

He said calmly, 'Even money has its price, you know. In fact, it has a higher price than most things, with the possible exception of power.'

Hilary closed her eyes. 'Poor Carl,' she said in a soft sibilant voice. 'Poor, unfortunate Carl.'

The clock on the wall struck five-thirty.

TWENTY

John sat at Professor Sweetman's desk, sweating and tense, as the clock on the office wall crept up to 5:45. He had tried to get through to Anthony Seiden by calling the studio, but Seiden's secretary had gone home, and nobody else was prepared to give him Seiden's home telephone number. He tried to find Adele Corliss's number in Palm Springs, but it was unlisted.

'Why don't you call Detective Morello?' Mel suggested. 'If you tell the cops what's happening, they'll have to check it out, at least.'

John nodded, and dialled the number that Detective Morello had given him, and waited while it rang. Across the room, her face shadowed by the slowly sinking sun, Perri watched him anxiously. Professor Sweetman was silently staring out of the window, while Dennis seemed to have resigned himself to his capture, and was sitting in a chair smoking a small plastic-tipped cigar.

After a long wait, the telephone was answered. A tired voice said, 'Detective Morello's office.'

'Is Detective Morello there?'

There was a pause. Then the voice said: 'I don't think so.'

'Well, my name is John Cullen. It was my father William Cullen who was shot dead on the San Diego Freeway last week.'

'Oh, sure. I remember. Cullen.'

'Listen,' said John, 'it's difficult to explain this, but I have good reason to think there's going to be another shooting tonight. There's a party at a house in Palm Springs for Anthony Seiden, the movie director, and somebody's going to kill him.'

There was another pause. Then the voice said, 'What gives you that idea?'

'I can't go into it now, but, please get someone over to Palm Springs and check out the house. It's urgent.'

'I can call the Palm Springs police.'

'Would you do that? Would you tell them it's serious, and urgent? The party's being held at Adele Corliss's house.'

'Adele Corliss, huh? The lady from *Passionate Pretenders*?'

'That's right.'

'Do you have any idea what the killer might look like?'

John put his hand over the receiver, and called to Professor Sweetman 'Professor? Do you know what the killer looks like? Or anything about him at all?'

Professor Sweetman shook his head. 'They don't tell me anything. I'm sorry.'

John went back to the phone. 'We have no idea, I'm afraid.'

'Okay,' said the voice. 'Thanks for your information anyway. I'll have it checked out.'

John put down the phone. He said, 'You know what a sceptic is?'

'Sure,' said Mel. 'A guy who won't believe he's dead unless they let him check his own pulse.'

'Well, that's what the cop was. I think we're going to have to go to Palm Springs ourselves.'

'What do we do with Sweetman?' asked Mel.

John turned to the tall, elderly man in his white lab coat, and said, 'Professor?'

'I won't run away,' said Aaron Sweetman, in a husky voice. 'I can't leave Mima.'

'And this one?' asked Perri, indicating Dennis.

Dennis shrugged. 'I'll probably run away,' he said.

'That's a risk we're going to have to take,' John said. 'We have your description, we have your car registration, and all I can say is, if you like Mexico, you're welcome to it. The border's only a taxi fare away.'

Mel tucked the .38 back in his belt, under his fawn cotton windbreaker. Then, without another word, the three of them left the office, walked through the whirring humming computer room, and out into the late sunlight.

'How long do you think it's going to take us to make Palm Springs?' asked Perri. 'It's a hell of a drive.'

John checked his watch as they walked quickly across the grass to the parking lot.

'If I take the road through Paloma Valley and Sun City, that's getting on for two hundred miles. It's almost six now – we should get there by eleven. Most of these Palm Springs parties don't start until late, so we may be lucky.'

'Oh God,' said Perri, 'I hope so.'

It was 6:07 as they drove out of San Diego on the Murphy Canyon Road, with the sun sloping across the dusty blacktop, and the air suddenly thick with flying insects. At the wheel, John lifted his sunglasses to rub his eyes and hoped that he had the stamina to make it. Through the window of Professor Sweetman's office, Dennis watched the long white Lincoln swerve out of the parking lot and head north. He crushed out his cigar at once, and went straight to the phone.

A thin voice said, 'Who is this?'

'Dennis O'Fallon. I'm still in San Diego. We've had a hitch.'

'What kind of hitch?'

'Young guy named – what was his name, professor?'

'Cullen,' Professor Sweetman said sadly.

'That's it, a young guy named Cullen, a blonde girl, and a fat guy. They know it all. All about Sweetman, all about the print-outs, all about everything. The professor told them about Seiden, too, and they're hauling ass to get to Palm Springs.'

The thin voice didn't falter, or register any surprise. 'When did they leave?'

'Just a moment ago.'

'By what route?'

'By the look of it, up Murphy Canyon Road to join the Cabrillo Freeway at Miramar. Then I guess they'll take 15E to Riverside, and head east from there.'

There was a silence, and then the thin voice said: 'Okay, you did good to call. Stay there and keep your eyes on Sweetman till we call you back.'

'My car's busted,' said Dennis. 'They shot out my tyre.'

'They're armed?'

'Only the fat guy. A .38 police special.'

Again there was silence, and then the phone went dead. Dennis held the receiver for a moment longer, but nothing else happened, and he set it down.

'Well, professor,' he said, 'it looks like you and me have got a long night ahead of us.'

TWENTY-ONE

At 6:32, Henry Ullerstam kissed Hilary Nestor Hunter's hand, and went down the steps to where his shiny black Rolls-Royce Silver Cloud III was waiting for him. His chauffeur closed the door behind him, and Hilary saw only his crisp white cuff and his glittering gold Cartier watch as he waved goodbye. As the car whispered away down the drive, she found herself longing insanely for 1980, for Angola, for oil wells, and for the riches that Henry was going to heap on her head.

As she stood there in the fading light of the day, a bronze Buick came speeding up the road. It turned into her driveway and stopped outside, and a red-faced young man in white jeans jumped out with a large cardboard box.

'I brought your outfit,' he panted. 'I'm real sorry it's late.'

Hilary smiled distantly. 'That's all right. Don't worry about it.'

The young man blinked. Hilary snapped her fingers to a dark-haired girl and said, 'Give him five dollars for his trouble. Then come help me dress.'

She stalked back into the house. The young man and the dark-haired girl looked at each other in a moment of shared bewilderment, and shrugged.

Anthony Seiden came out of the shower with a dark blue towel wrapped around his middle, and walked through the bedroom into the dressing-room. Dana, in a layered negligée the colour of wild peaches, was sitting in front of her make-up mirror. The bedroom and the dressing-room were both Bel-Air rococo, with a high gilded bed, and cream-painted furniture outlined with gold. On the walls were fussy paintings of Regency ladies on garden swings, amorously ogled by beaux with powdered wigs and quizzing-glasses. Anthony had inherited the decor from the previous owner, the costume epic director Abraham Spiro, and he adored its tastelessness so much that he had decided to keep it intact. Future generations, he used to say, would wander through these rooms and marvel.

'I hope you're not going to argue with Carl Chapman,' Dana said.

'Why should I argue?' Anthony said. 'He can't help being a Fascist bigot, any more than I can help being a warm-hearted liberal.'

'You're going to tell him that?'

Anthony laughed. 'Oh, sure. Right to his face.'

'You can laugh. You told Richard Nixon he was suffering from delusions of grandeur, right to his face.'

'But that was true. Apart from that, I don't think he heard me.'

Dana began to line her eyes. 'Everyone else did, and that was what mattered.'

Anthony appeared from the open door of the dressing-room and looked at her face in the triple mirrors of her make-up table. Full-face, left profile, right profile. Three beautiful blonde Nordic women with six enchanting

325

blue eyes, six long-fingered hands with pearlised nails, six firm breasts, six wide shoulders.

He said, 'Why should you care what I say to Carl Chapman? He's a right-wing extremist of the worst kind, and he's been tied in twice with the killing of Bobby Kennedy.'

'I just think you should let your pictures speak for themselves, that's all.'

Anthony started at her reflection hard. 'Are you trying to tell me something?' he asked.

'Tell you something? What do you mean? What should I want to tell you?'

'Something about yourself, not me. Something about the way you feel. You've changed, Dana, more than I thought.'

'Oh?' she said, her eyes flicking up to meet his in the mirror.

He looked at her hard, and thought for a while. 'I don't attract you any more,' he said simply. 'I sense you're emotionally involved with me, but it isn't sexually, and it may not even be romantically. You may even hate me.'

She gave a quick, uncertain smile. 'You're talking nonsense,' she said.

'Am I?' he asked her. 'I've known you for a long time, Dana. We've been in love. All kinds of love. I know when I turn you on, and when I don't, and I'm not turning you on now. I haven't once excited you from the moment you walked back in through the door.'

She said quietly, 'You're not giving it time.'

'Time?' he said, a little regretfully. 'Why give time to something that isn't even there? Why water a patch of ground that doesn't have a seed in it? Look at me.'

He turned her head towards him with his left hand. She looked up at him, then she turned away again, and there was a faint blush on her cheeks.

'Can you honestly say that you love me?' he wanted to know.

She didn't answer.

'Can you honestly say that you came back because you thought our marriage could work?'

326

'No,' she whispered.

'Then why *did* you come back? If you don't love me, and you're not interested in saving our marriage, why did you bother?'

She said, so quietly that he could scarcely hear her, 'I guess everyone does strange things sometimes.'

'I never knew *you* do anything strange. Not as strange as this, anyway. Everything you ever did was for your own kicks. You wouldn't put yourself out for anyone. So why did you come back here? You're not enjoying a moment of it. It's completely out of character.'

She stared at him, and her face was alight with resentment. 'Out of character? What did you ever know about my character? Or bother to find out about my character? You just dismissed me as a walk-on actress in this wonderful controversial movie called the life of Anthony Seiden. You never gave me credit for any intelligence, any depth, or any taste. Look at this godawful bedroom. You only kept it because you thought I was a stupid starlet, and that this was just the kind of bedroom I'd adore.'

Anthony dropped his gaze. 'If that's true, Dana, even the slightest bit true –'

'Of course it's true. Why do you think I walked out? I was tired of being treated like an idiot with nothing to contribute.'

'Then why did you come back, if you hated it so much?' Anthony snapped.

She placed her hands flat on the dressing-table. She was obviously making an effort to control her temper.

'Because I have something important to do,' she told him. 'For the first time in my whole life, someone's given me something important to do.'

He slowly stood up. He wasn't going to ask her what this 'something important' was. She would make sure she told him in good time, in her own way. They had had this argument, in countless permutations, all through their married life.

He said, 'Okay, I'd better get dressed,' and he went back to the dressing-room. The time on his Baume & Mercier watch was a quarter after seven.

TWENTY-TWO

At 7:58, T.F. got up from his chair by the window of Adele Corliss's house, propped his M-14 against the sill, and paced up and down the room to stretch his legs. Mark was asleep, which T.F. considered was probably the best therapy the chauffeur could get, under the circumstances.

The room was gloomy now. Outside, the desert sky was almost dark. The lanterns that had been strung in the trees were alight, and there was an appetising smell of *hors d'oeuvres* being cooked on the chef's hibachi. T.F. lit a cigarette. He wasn't hungry, and he knew that he wouldn't feel like eating until he'd shot that bullet through those two inches of clear space and knocked out Anthony Seiden forever. A stylish job. Lots of class. And an extra notch in his reputation as a hit man.

T.F. wondered why the world was ordered the way it was. Why you had to kill people to put over your own point of view. It seemed strange, and irrational, and yet he knew that was the way things were. He sometimes dreamed of an existence in which you could do anything you like – kill who you wanted in any way you wanted, and have hundred of girls around you, willing to do anything you told them.

There was a rapid knock at the door. He said quietly, 'Who is it?'

'It's me, Ken.'

T.F. went to the door and unlocked it.

'What's the matter?' he asked. 'I thought you were downstairs keeping your eyes on the servants.'

'I was. But I've just checked with Allen on the phone and he says that Cullen and the fat guy Walters have found out what's going on here. They've alerted the cops

328

and they're driving up here themselves.'

T.F. heard this news in silence. Then he said, 'Cullen, huh?'

'That's right.'

'Is Allen doing anything about it?'

Ken shrugged. 'He wouldn't say. But I think he's going to try to intercept them.'

T.F. sucked on his cigarette sourly. 'Shit. That meddling bastard Cullen. I should have blown his head off the first time I ever saw him.'

It was 8 : 04.

Adele Corliss sat at her dressing-table, with her maid Dolores standing beside her with her towels and her lotions. The brass lamps in her bedroom were turned down to dim, so that her intensely-lit make-up mirror was like an altar, in front of which the high priestess of Palm Springs sat and made her devotions to youth and physical beauty. She was beginning to wonder if her eyes needed another wrinkle treatment. The sun, and the exertion of keeping an indefatigable young lover, were beginning to tell on her. Her superb body was really only meant to be looked at, not manhandled.

Dolores said, 'These bad guys, can't you do nothing?'

Adele gave her a twitchy smile. 'You're not forgetting that Mark's up there, are you? They'll kill him the moment they think we're trying to play games. Did you see that man? The dark one? He's like a rattlesnake.'

Dolores didn't seem impressed. 'Even rattlesnakes got their weak points.'

'Maybe they have,' said Adele, 'but I'm not going to risk Mark's life to prove it.'

'Just somebody else's, somebody more important, maybe.'

'All right, Dolores, what would you do in my position?'

'I tell you what I would do. That dark man sits by the window in Mr Ken's room, looking out most of the time. I saw him when I crossed the front of the house. Now, if you got yourself the shotgun from the library, and you went to the small green bedroom, you could get yourself a shot at that man before he even knew what hit him.'

Adele paused for a moment, and then began to wipe cream from around her eyes with pads of cotton. 'Dolores,' she said, 'you're so absurdly hot-blooded. That man has a rifle, and he's a trained killer. Not one of us in this house can hit a barn from three feet away. What do you think he's going to do if we shoot at him, and miss?'

Dolores kept her muoth shut. Adele looked up at her, and then said, 'You're not thinking of trying it, are you? Because if you do, you're fired. That's if our rattle-snake doesn't get you first.'

Dolores grunted in disappointment. The time by the clock on Adele Corliss's dressing-table was 8:43.

At 9:11, Carl X. Chapman arrived in a chartered Lear-Jet at Palm Springs airport, accompanied by Mrs Elspeth Chapman. An agency correspondent from UPI noted that Mrs Chapman was wearing dark glasses, despite the fact that it was night.

When Carl Chapman was asked what he thought of Anthony Seiden's movies, he said, with a broad smile, 'Every man in these United States is entitled to say his piece, and I'd say that Tony Seiden says his piece with great eloquence and impact. I'm going to this party because Adele Corliss is my friend, and because I respect Tony Seiden's pictures, whether I agree with his politics or not.'

The reporters were unaware as they noted down his words that they were helping to establish Carl X. Chapman's alibi.

At 9:17, the first guests began to arrive at Adele's house, and the music started. The sound of bongos and the amplified warbling of Spanish ballads could be heard for a mile in the stillness of the night. Upstairs, astride his chair, T.F. waited with the patience on which he had always prided himself – the patience of a professional killer whose mind is attuned to the perfect performance of one split-second act.

TWENTY-THREE

With a flackering roar, the Bell helicopter lifted off the concrete pad at Morrow Field, just outside of San Bernardino, and twisted away into the night sky, its spot-lamps sending shafts of white light down to the scrubby soil. In the cockpit, still tucking in the tails of his clean white shirt, sat Umberto. Against his leg rested a Schmeisser MP40 machine gun, black and greasy, and on the floor was a canvas tennis bag crammed with spare clips of ammunition.

At the controls, Val was untidily dressed in jeans and a blue T-shirt with two cartoon turds emblazoned on the front of it. The turds were grinning and shaking hands, under a motto which read 'Get Your Shit Together.' Val wore night-glasses, and a shoulder holster, still unbuckled, with a Colt Python .357 magnum revolver hanging heavily under his arm.

It was 9:44. Over his intercom, Umberto said, 'Head for the Riverside Auto Racetrack. They should have just about reached there by now.'

The world was dark beneath them, spattered with occasional bursts of light. They flew noisily southeast, until they located the Riverside Freeway at Grand Terrace, beaded with moving tail-lights, and then Val angled the Bell towards the Riverside cloverleaf.

'This is like looking for a blade of grass on someone's lawn,' complained Val. 'In the goddamned dark, too.'

'It's not as bad as it could be. They're driving a big white '58 Lincoln Capri. That's almost as good as if they sent up flares.'

Val swooped low down the Box Springs Grade towards the Riverside track, his searchlights briefly lighting up the streams of cars on the highway below. Umberto, tying his white tie, peered conscientiously out of the Bell's bubble cockpit, trying to spot the long white telltale shape of John Cullen's Lincoln.

'Do we blow their heads off?' asked Val.

Umberto nodded. 'That's right. This time, we blow their heads off.'

Val lifted the helicopter over a huge furniture truck, lit up with red and orange lights. He was almost skimming the roofs of the cars now, and Umberto could see pale faces looking up in surprise as they clattered past.

For ten minutes, they flew up and down the highway. They paused a couple of times over white cars, but one was a new Cadillac and the other turned out to be a decrepit Chrysler.

'They go tell us to look for one car in the middle of the night? They're crazy. It could be anywhere,' Val complained.

'Allen timed it pretty close. He reckoned they should have reached this stretch of road between nine-fifty and ten o'clock. That Lincoln's a speedy old car, so T.F. says. They were clearing a hundred-ten when he was chasing them down to San Diego.'

'Well, why don't they show?' complained Val. 'If we stick around here much longer, the Highway Patrol's going to start coming after us.'

Umberto lifted the Schmeisser on to his knee, and inserted a clip. 'Just try a couple more passes. It's only five before ten.'

Val turned the helicopter around, and made another fast tilted run down highway 60, heading east towards the sprinkle of lights that was Beaumont. It was then, miraculously, that Umberto said, 'Hold it, hold it! What's that – just down there ahead of us?'

The helicopter slowed, and circled around the highway. Below them, speeding at over ninety, was the long white profile of John Cullen's Lincoln. Its sides were caked with red dust from the desert, and it looked as if someone, a girl, was sleeping in the rear seat.

Umberto made a circle of his finger and his thumb,

and then indicated to Val to take the helicopter lower One burst from the Schmeisser should finish them off for good. He opened the small port in his perspex door and raised the machine gun to his shoulder.

Mel saw the helicopter first. He thought it was the police, or the Highway Patrol, but when it wheeled around them, its rotors flashing in the reflected light from their headlamps, he could see the private markings and the pilot in his jeans and T-shirt.

'It's after us!' he yelled. 'John – for Christ's sake, it's after us!'

Perri, waking up in the back seat, said, 'What's happening? What's going on?'

'Helicopter,' John said tersely. 'It looks like they want to stop us at any price.'

He put his foot down, and the Lincoln accelerated up to a hundred-fifteen, its engine burbling with power. Moths and insects pattered on the windshield like a shower of summer rain. He overtook a long line of cars and trucks, and then he was chasing nothing but the tunnel of light that his headlamps made out of the darkness.

He glanced to his right. The helicopter was keeping pace, using the white line down the centre of the road to guide it. It was really low now, only twelve or fifteen feet off the road, and a pick-up truck that was coming in the opposite direction flashed its lights and blew its horn in panic.

'We can't shake it off,' John told Mel. 'It's too damned fast. And it's going to catch us wherever we go.'

Mel reached under his windbreaker and took out the .38. He handed it over to John and said, 'See if you can wing the pilot. That'll stop 'em.'

Steering with his left hand, John raised the revolver and aimed it at the perspex bubble of the helicopter's canopy. He fired once, but nothing seemed to happen. The helicopter kept flying along beside them, its rotors kicking up a deafening clatter, and it was even moving closer.

'Again,' said Perri, from the back seat.

333

John rested his wrist against the windowsill, and fired a second shot. The helicopter instantly veered away from them and climbed into the night. They craned their necks to see where it had gone, but it disappeared over their heads, and somewhere behind them.

'Maybe that's scared them off,' said Mel.

John shook his head. 'Don't you believe it. They just want to get out of range. If they took off like that, I couldn't have hit them. Maybe I made a hole in the cockpit, but I doubt if they're hurt worse than that.'

They could still hear the helicopter, even though they couldn't see it. Perri put down her window and looked out, then she said, 'They're in back of us, maybe fifty feet up. I don't think they're going to let us go.'

The highway was deserted now, behind them and in front of them. If the helicopter was going to attack them, now was the time. John slewed from one side of the road to the other, trying to make the Lincoln a difficult target for anyone with a gun.

They heard a noise like a flock of birds whistling. Then, abruptly, three or four holes were punched in the hood of the car, and the rear window cracked.

'It's a machine gun!' shouted Mel.

There was more whistling. Splinters of blacktop and concrete sprayed against the windshield. Then there was a heavy banging sound in the trunk, and John heard an explosion of rubber and air as the spare tyre burst.

His mind worked with strange coolness. A half-mile further along the highway, on the right, he could see a small off-ramp. He didn't know where it went, but anything had to be better than sitting on the highway while Carl Chapman's killers shot them to pieces. He pressed the gas pedal down to the floor, until the Lincoln was slamming through the night at a hundred-twenty.

The half-mile flashed past. As the off ramp rushed up to meet him, he could see that it was a steep downhill grade, but by now it was too late. He swerved on to it without touching the brakes, and the huge car almost flew into the night, its suspension jarring, and he thought for two terrible seconds that he had completely lost control.

334

But then he heard the tyres howling and shuddering, and the sliding sound of grit under the wheels, and the Lincoln held a long, fast, sideways slide. They went down the grade to the side road, losing speed all the way, but still over seventy. All Mel said was, 'Mother of Christ.'

At the foot of the ramp, John stamped on the gas again, and the Lincoln took off up a winding, roughly metalled road, in a cloud of white dust and burning rubber. The car bounced and bucked as they drove over uncambered curves and potholes, and negotiated concrete bridges that spanned one dry culvert after another.

Perri saw the shafts of light from the helicopter, following behind them like the bright legs of a monster on stilts. She said, 'They're still after us! They're catching up! Do you think we ought to get out and make a run for it?'

'We need the car, insisted John. 'And apart from that, they won't find it hard to hunt us if we're on foot.'

As they bounced over another bridge, they heard the whistling of machine gun bullets. Three or four bullets suddenly banged through the roof of the car, and sent up a spray of upholstery, leather and horsehair.

They didn't stand a chance now. On the rough road, they couldn't make more than thirty or forty miles an hour, and the helicopter hovered directly over them, holding them helpless in the bluish-white glare of its lights. Another burst of bullets kicked up dust and chips of rock all around them, and one of the car's side windows shattered into blindness.

John headed for the next culvert as fast as he could make it. Instead of driving over the bridge, though, he steered the Lincoln down the slope into the culvert bed. They were jolted and shaken about as they came down the bank, and the bottom of the culvert was strewn with rocks, but John managed to wrestle the long white car around to the right and under the bridge.

They heard the helicopter clattering around the culvert, and another spray of bullets ricocheted under the bridge. But they were safe here. John killed the engine and they sat in darkness, waiting to see what their pursuers would try next.

'We can't stay here for ever,' Perri said. 'Even if they can't get us now, they're bound to send someone after us.'

John was reloading the .38. 'It's better to stay here than try our chances out there. There just aren't any chances out there.'

Again, they heard the helicopter pass overhead. Then, they saw its lights illuminate the culvert, and heard the sound of it circling. Gradually, it sank into view, its spotlights deliberately pointing their way so that they were dazzled. It settled on the dry culvert bed, and they could just make out the doors opening. The motor was cut out, and the rotors sang their way to a stop.

Two men were walking towards them, one armed with a gun. They stopped a little distance away from the bridge, and one called, 'Cullen? Is that you, Cullen?'

'Don't answer,' Mel hissed.

'If that's Cullen,' said one of the men, 'we want you to get out of the car with your hands up. No tricks, no nothing. Just get out of the car and walk towards us with your hands up.'

'If you don't,' added the other man, 'we'll blow your heads off.'

John said to Mel, 'I've got an idea. I'm gonna do what he says.'

'*What?* He's going to kill us anyway.'

'Just do what he says. You and Perri get out, and walk towards them with your hands up.'

Perri said, 'John –'

He turned and gave her hand a quick squeeze. 'Please, Perri. Just do it.'

'Okay,' said Mel, in a resigned voice.

From the entrance to the bridge, the man called, 'Hurry! We don't have all night!'

Mel opened the door of the car and stepped out into the glaring light from the helicopter. Perri opened the back door, and followed him.

There was a moment's pause, while Mel and Perri stood facing the two gunmen in the dusty brightness.

Then John started up the Lincoln's engine, threw it into reverse, and backed up along the culvert with his foot hard on the floor.

A burst of machine gun fire rattled and pinged against the Lincoln's radiator. But John twisted the steering-wheel, and the car whinnied its way backward up the side of the culvert, its tyres sliding on the loose dirt, its side doors still swinging open. With a last surge of power, he reached the top, and for a few seconds he was safely out of the killers' view.

He shifted the car into drive, and headed for the bridge as fast as he could. He could see the light from the helicopter rising from beyond the bridge, and as he came nearer he glimpsed Mel and Perri, below him, and saw the two killers running back towards the Bell along the rocky, dried-up culvert bed.

John wondered for a terrible moment if he had mis-calculated, and if all he was going to do was kill him-self. But by then it was too late. The Lincoln was almost at the bridge, roaring diagonally across it at fifty miles an hour, and he punched open his door handle and rolled out into the bursting gritty darkness.

The massive white car sailed off the edge of the bridge and landed on top of the helicopter just as Umberto and Val had reached it. There was a screeching, splintering sound, and then a deep, ground-shaking explosion, as the helicopter's ruptured fuel tanks exploded. An orange fireball enveloped the helicopter, and then rolled up-ward into the night sky, leaving twisted skeletons of metal to blaze fiercely on the ground.

John, bruised and grazed, shakily climbed to his feet. Limping, he crossed to the edge of the slope, and found Mel and Perri coming up towards him, equally shocked, but safe.

He held Perri very close, and realised for the first time how much he was beginning to feel for her. Neither of them spoke.

Mel cleared his throat, and said, 'My watch just stopped at ten-ten. How long do you think it's going to take us to get to Palm Springs now?'

John found his lips were dry, and that he was trem-

337

bling. Beside the bridge, the helicopter wreck was still burning.

'Maybe there's a house or something along here some-place. All we can do is try to borrow some transport,' John said.

'Those men ... I know what they were trying to do, but ...' Perri stammered.

John put his arm around her shoulders. The fire was dying down now, and the darkness of the countryside was swarming back.

'I know,' he said quietly. 'But right now, it's Anthony Seiden who counts.'

TWENTY-FOUR

T.F. stiffened. Down below, in the courtyard in front of the hacienda-style house, a black limousine had drawn up, and two thick-set men had emerged. There was a smattering of applause from some of the guests who were slowly making their way into the house, and several of them turned around and clapped with their hands held high.

Out of the car, in a navy-blue tuxedo, came Anthony Seiden, T.F.'s target. Seiden turned, and offered his hand to his wife Dana, who stepped out of the car in a stunning peach-coloured evening dress, cut very low, and a small mink wrap around her shoulders. It could have been T.F.'s imagination, but he could have sworn he saw Dana glance over to the window on the other side of the house – the window where the telephone was.

From the bed, Mark asked, in a blurry voice, 'What's happening? What's going on?'

T.F. said, 'Shut up,' without looking round. He checked the red figures on his digital watch and they read 10:37.

Three minutes later, at 10:40, a private Piper Cherokee landed at Palm Springs airport and taxied around to the terminal. Out of the door stepped Hilary Nestor Hunter, in her new blue culottes and high Russian boots, with her hair brushed severely back from her face. The night flickered with photographers' flashlights as a limousine came across the tarmac to collect her. As she stepped into the car, a woman reporter held a tape recorder microphone close to her face, and asked, 'Ms. Hunter – what's a right-wing militant lady like you doing at a left-wing movie director's party?'

Hilary smiled. 'It's always good to see ourselves as other people see us. It helps us understand them.'

'Understand them, or learn how to get the better of them?' asked the reporter.

Hilary smiled, but didn't answer, and in a moment the limousine was gone.

The motorcycle bellowed through the night at an ear-splitting ninety miles an hour. The highway was almost deserted on this last stretch into Palm Springs, and John had kept the bike's throttle open the whole way. It was ten minutes to eleven, and they still had seven or eight miles to cover.

They roared around a long curve, leaning their weight against the camber of the road, overtaking a slow-moving truck and an estate wagon. John kept his eyes screwed up against the slipstream and the flying insects, and ahead of him, he could see the lights of Palm Springs.

The motorcycle's engine missed a couple of times, and backfired. He prayed it had enough gas. They had found it in the yard of a small house out on the trail near Eden Hot Springs, with the ignition keys still in it, and while Mel had elected to walk back to the highway and try for a lift, John and Perri had silently wheeled the bike away from the house, started it up, and ridden off into the night. John just hoped the owner would forgive him.

'What's the time?' John yelled, as they came towards the outskirts of Palm Springs.

'Five minutes before eleven,' Perri told him, at the

top of her voice. 'Do you know where Adele Corliss's house is?'

'I don't have a clue. We'll just have to ask.'

He throttled the bike back as they entered the town. It was 10:58.

Out on the pool deck, Anthony Seiden was standing with Dana, enjoying his first drink and the congratulations of his friends. The band was playing a slow samba, the tables were heaped with silver plates of fresh salmon and cold beef and lobster, and already the conversation was growing louder and the laughter less restrained.

Anthony looked around for Adele Corliss. She had met him briefly at the door when he arrived, but he had been struck by her quietness and her unwillingness to talk. He saw her standing by the pool talking to her butler Holman; he excused himself from Dana and his friends, and went across.

She looked as much like the ice queen as ever in a white silk '40s-style evening dress with padded shoulders and a deep décolletage decorated with silver sequins. But when he said, 'Hi, Adele,' she turned to him with an awkward, unsettled smile, and he saw none of her usual amused aloofness.

'Adele,' he said gently. 'Is anything wrong?'

She wouldn't look at him. She kept glancing around the guests, as if she expected something unusual to happen.

'Wrong?' she said. 'Why should there be?'

'Adele – you're very twitchy. I've never seen you like this. You look as if you're expecting the IRS to call any moment.'

She couldn't even manage a smile. She looked down at her glass, saw that it was empty, and said, 'Anthony, darling, will you get me another drink please?'

'Adele –'

'Look,' she said, 'that's Carl Chapman over there. By the pool seat. Why don't you go say hello?'

Anthony held her arm. He was surprised how cold she felt. He said, 'Adele, something's really wrong. And you feel freezing.'

Adele turned away. 'Ice queens always do,' she said, in a tight voice.

It was eleven o'clock. The long-case clock in the hallway struck each hour with a brassy, sonorous chime. At his window on the second floor, T.F. released the safety-catch on his M-14, and leaned forward against the window-sill, snuggling the butt-plate against his shoulder. Through the sights, he saw the leaded window, the table, the telephone. His unfinished cigarette smouldered in its ashtray beside him. There'd be plenty of time to finish it when the job was over.

At 11:01, the telephone rang. One of the Mexican servants picked it up, and said. 'The Corliss residence. Who is this, please?'

A thin-sounding voice said, 'This is Fox studios. I have an urgent call for Mr Anthony Seiden. Tell him it's to do with the colour prints on his last rushes.'

'Yes, sir. Hold on, please.'

The man set the receiver down on the table, and went quickly along the hallway and out to the back of the house. On the pool deck, the party was even louder and happier than before, and a few couples were dancing. The servant walked across to Anthony, who had been waylaid by two producers on his way to talk to Carl X. Chapman, and touched his sleeve.

'Mr Seiden? I'm sorry, Sir, there's a telephone call for you. Fox studios, he says.'

'Can't it wait?' asked Anthony. 'Tell them I'll call back.'

'The man says urgent, sir. Something to do with colour prints.'

Anthony sighed. 'Okay. Will you gentlemen excuse me, please? It looks like the work of a movie director is never done.'

Dana, across by the hedge, had been watching him narrowly. As he put down his drink and started to walk towards the house, she broke off her conversation with a young actress and went over to intercept him. She linked arms, and said, 'Anything wrong?'

'It's nothing. Just some damned stupid call from the studio.'

'I'll come with you,' she said.

Together, they went into the house. It was shadowy and cool, and the conversation and music outside could hardly be heard. Their footsteps sounded loud and echoing as they walked along the polished parquet hallway.

'Did you talk to Carl Chapman yet?' Dana asked.

'I was just about to. Peter and Carlo got in first.'

They reached the telephone table. Anthony picked up the receiver and said, 'Hello? This is Anthony Seiden.'

Dana took a cigarette out of her evening purse and lit it. She felt strangely empty and unreal. Now that the moment had actually arrived, everything seemed like a dream, in which the air was as glutinous as transparent syrup, making movement paralysingly slow, and magnifying everything to three times its usual size. She could see her hand reaching for the window-catch, and it seemed to take whole minutes to get there. She could hear Anthony talking on the telephone, and his words came out as endless, incomprehensible blurts of swollen sound.

But then the window was open, and she pushed it with her fingertips so that it swung wide. The sound of the band and the laughter of party guests wafted through the warm night air, and another limousine was just drawing up at the front of the house.

T.F. saw the window open, and Seiden's wife step out of sight. Now he could see Seiden clearly, sitting by the table in his tuxedo, his head bent in conversation. He steadied the M-14, and took a bead on the back of Seiden's skull. One gentle squeeze, and it was going to be brains sundae. It was 11.05 and eight seconds.

Out of the corner of his eyes, he saw the limousine draw up. One of Adele Corliss's servants opened the limousine's door, and three or four women stepped out. They stood beside the car for a moment, and then they began to walk across the courtyard to the front of the house.

T.F. whispered, 'Shit,' under his breath. One by one,

the women passed across his sights, dawdling as they walked, completely unaware that they were intersecting an invisible line that connected T.F.'s gunsights with Anthony Seiden's head. One woman, a tall blonde in dark blue culottes, lingered longer than most in T.F.'s line of fire.

At last, the women had passed, and Seiden was still sitting at the telephone. T.F. held the rifle steady as a rock, and squeezed the trigger.

TWENTY-FIVE

They arrived outside the Corliss house with a roar, and John pulled the motorcycle around on the gravel. The Mexican footman moved towards them with his hand raised, unsure if they were gatecrashers or guests. By the front door of the house, Hilary Nestor Hunter and her three girls turned around in surprise at the noise.

Perri, climbing off the back of the bike, called, '*Hilary!*' in a high voice.

Hilary Nestor Hunter took one step back and that one step was enough. There was a loud crack like a branch breaking, and Hilary's neck burst apart in a crimson spray. She twisted around, and fell to the ground with her face against the gravel.

John threw the motorcycle down, and reached Perri in two strides. He pulled her around behind the parked limousine and shouted, '*Get down! And stay down!*'

The Mexican footman dropped to the ground beside them, with his hands over his ears.

John could feel his pulse speeding up. He took the .38 revolver out of his pocket, and ran with a crouching run to the side of the E-shaped house. Then he sprinted around to the back, through he yuccas and the dragon trees, and suddenly found himself in the middle of a poolside party.

John dodged through the crowd, and into the open door at the back of the house. He paused, trying to get his bearings. The rough-plastered stairs were on his left. He cocked the .38 and climbed up as quickly as he could, into the darkness of the upstairs gallery. Behind him, the party guests were laughing and clapping as a portly movie producer demonstrated the rhumba.

John walked silently and quickly in the direction of the room he thought the shot had come from. He had only seen the black muzzle of a rifle, and a split-second flash. But it had come from one of these upstairs rooms, and he was going to find which room it was if it killed him. And it might.

It was very dark along the upstairs corridor, but he couldn't find the light switches. He walked stealthily, the gun held high in front of him, until the came to the first bedroom door. He pressed his ear to it, held his breath, and listened. He listened for over half a minute, and there was no sound at all.

He crept along to the second door, and listened to that. Outside, he heard screams and shouts, and the music suddenly died away. The partygoers must have discovered what was happening. Someone was shouting, *'Call the police! For Christ's sake, call the police!'*

John heard nothing at the door of the second bedroom. He was about to move on to the third when he heard a metallic rattling noise behind him. He turned, cold with fright, and the man was right there, right behind him, tall and dark, much taller than John had imagined, with a face as hard as a Maine winter.

'Drop the gun,' the man said.

John hesitated for a moment, but then he dropped it. It fell heavily on to the boarded floor.

'Now,' said the man, in a whispery voice, 'you're going to help me get out of here. You're going to walk in front of me down the stairs, and out across the front of the house, and then we're going to get in that limousine and leave. Do you understand?'

'What's to understand?' John said.

The man raised his rifle a little higher. 'Don't talk back. Just do what you're told.'

344

John could feel the sweat sliding down his armpits. 'You killed my father, and you killed the girl I loved. I'm not doing anything for you,' he said hoarsely.

The man smiled. 'It's up to you. If you don't want to be hostage, then I'm sure I can find somebody else: After I'm finished with you.'

He took aim at John's head, only three feet away. John could see the dark barrel, and the man's unblinking eye at the other end of the sights.

'What's it to be?' the man asked, dispassionately. 'Now, or later?'

'I want to know why you did it,' John said. 'I want to know why you killed them.'

The man sniffed. 'I did it because I was told to. That's all. Now, what's it going to be?'

'*Who* told you?'

'What does it matter?'

'It matters to me. I want to know who told you. I want to know who it really was.'

A different, rougher voice said, 'Don't answer that, T.F.'

T.F. turned. Halfway down the corridor, with an automatic in his hand, stood Carl X. Chapman.

'You made a goddamned mess of that, T.F.,' said Chapman. 'You made a mess and they're going to catch you. Now, you know that I can't let them do that.'

T.F. was trained to kill and Carl X. Chapman wasn't.

Before Carl had even raised his hand, T.F. swung the rifle around on his hip and fired. Carl was kicked over backwards by the impact, and blood splashed out of him like someone kicking over a bucket of paint. T.F. lifted his rifle and fired again, and Carl's head was blown into hair and slush and blood.

The flat, fierce sound of the rifle made the corridor ring. With his ears still deafened, John dropped to his knees, reached for his fallen revolver, and pointed it straight at T.F.'s lean and dark silhouette.

T.F. turned back towards him, But the M-14's barrel was pointing the other way, and like a geometrical problem he had to swing it around in an arc before it was pointing at John. In the seconds it took for T.F. to pivot on his hips, John pulled the trigger once, then again, then again.

T.F.'s rifle, his precious M-14, fell from his hands. He collapsed against the side of the corridor, choking and coughing. In the shadowy darkness, John fired again, a blaze of fire and noise, and T.F. slumped to the floor. There was a soft, hissing exhalation of breath, and then he lay still.

John stood up, trembling. The corridor was dense with blue, acrid smoke. He heard people running up the stairs, and somebody shouting.

They sat around the table at their apartment hotel in Hollywood, and made a meal of London broil and Mumm's Cordon Rouge champagne. They didn't talk much, but afterwards they took their champagne glasses and sat by the gas fire and stared at the flames. The heatwave was over, and it was growing colder now.

'I've decided to go to Europe for a while,' Perri said. 'I think I need some time on my own. Somewhere away from all these memories.'

John nodded. He didn't want her to go. Right now, he felt he needed her. But he knew what she felt, and he wasn't going to try to talk her out of it. When she came back – and he knew that she would come back – then maybe they could get together again, without the trauma of the past to haunt them too vividly. One week, he thought. One week in which he had learned how to grieve for his father, grieve for Vicki, and kill a man to revenge them.

'Do you think anything's going to happen? To Sweetman, I mean? Or anyone else who's involved in it?' Mel asked.

John shrugged. 'It depends on the police, I guess – what evidence they find. I've told them everything that we found out. I'm still not sure we did the right things for the right reasons, but at least we did the right things.'

The telephone rang. Perri said, 'I'll answer it,' and got up from the settee.

She said, 'Who is this?' Then, 'Yes. Yes, I see. Hold on a moment.'

She put her hand over the receiver, and said, 'John, it's a woman called Mrs Benduzzi. She's been trying to get in touch with you all week, and she's just found out you're living here. She says could you walk Ricardo Monday morning? And maybe wax the car?'

John looked up. It seemed like the whole week had vanished into nowhere at all, as if it hadn't existed. He looked at Mel, and said, 'Do you hear that? That's reality, come to get us back.'

EPILOGUE

No prosecutions were ever brought in connection with the Sweetman Curve. Professor Aaron Sweetman was interviewed by police and FBI, and his computer records examined, but nothing of an incriminating nature could be found. Kenneth Irwin, unemployed, of Seattle, was at Palm Springs police headquarters for two days before being released for lack of anything but highly circumstantial evidence.

The coronor decided that Senator Carl X. Chapman, the senior senator from the state of Minnesota, had been fatally wounded by a rifle bullet fired by Terence Faust, unemployed, of Venice, Los Angeles, as had Hilary Nestor Hunter; and that Terence Faust, in his turn, had been shot dead by John Cullen. The coroner complimented Mr Cullen for his quick-thinking, but admonished him for carrying an unlicenced weapon.

The FBI, after a three-week investigation, concluded that Terence Faust was a political fanatic and sexual odd-ball with a psychotic grudge against right-wing politicians. He was probably the Freeway Fruitcake, although not all of the freeway killings could indisputably be laid at his door. The FBI dismissed any idea that Faust's actual target was Anthony Seiden, despite Mr Cullen's claims. The only irrefutable evidence of what had happened, they pointed out, was the two bodies of Senator Chapman and Ms Hilary Nestor Hunter. Everything else was supposition.

Vicki Wallace was interred at her home town of Oxnard, California, on the following Wednesday, at a sad and simple ceremony. Hilary Nestor Hunter was buried at Forest Lawn two days after that. Her largest wreath was of white roses, and bore the cryptic message 'Goodbye Angola.' Senator Carl X. Chapman was flown to Minneapolis, and cremated at a quiet private funeral. His widow Elspeth did not weep.

A month later, Dana Seiden left her husband for the second time, and sought a petition for divorce on the grounds of cruelty. A settlement was eventually reached for nine million dollars. Anthony Seiden's new movie was christened *Night Of Revenge*, and received mixed reviews.

Adele Corliss, in a television interview, said that her frightening experience had given her 'new insight into human depravity, but also into human greatness.' She paid for Mark, her chauffeur, to have cosmetic surgery on his nose.

Detective Morello was assigned to the case of the L.A. Strangler, but after having arrested three suspects, all of whom were later released, he was moved onto the Orange Grove Avenue homicide, which was so complex and unsolvable that it was like being sent to Siberia to unravel Balaclava helmets for the rest of his life.

John Cullen and Mel Walters occasionally go fishing together weekends. But most weekdays, John Cullen can still be seen waxing cars, or talking to Yolande in Mrs Benduzzi's garden, or walking dogs around the sloping scented byways of Bel-Air, in his T-shirt and his worn-out jeans. Some days, he gets letters with French or German stamps on them, and he sits on a bench with the dog leash tied to his ankle, and reads them.

Henry Ullerstam, the oil millionaire, has hinted that he is considering backing a new Republican Presidential candidate for 1980, and that his candidate is 'almost sure to win.'

All this happened not very long ago, in the land of the free.